M000159743

Satan's Garden

A Novel

Kit Lyman

This book is a work of fiction. Names, characters, businesses, organizations, places, and incidents either are products of the author's imagination or are used fictitiously. Any resemblance to actual events or locales or persons, living or dead, is entirely coincidental.

Copyright © 2014 Kit Lyman

All rights reserved. No part of this book may be used or reproduced in any manner whatsoever without written permission from the author, except in the case of brief quotations embodied in critical articles or reviews.

First edition: March 2014

Cover Design by Morgan Eastlack
Edited by Laura Sidari

ISBN-13: 978-0-615-98390-5 (pbk)
ISBN-10:   0-615-98390-1 (pbk)
ISBN-13: 978-0-692-02471-3 (e-book)
ISBN-10   0-692-02471-9 (e-book)

For my sisters

CONTENTS

SATAN'S GARDEN

I had always thought that death would be cold. When I reached that edge in time, straddling the line that separated me from this world and another, I prepared for it to come. I waited for the freeze to creep through my body, spoiling the ending of my own sorry story. Instead, all I felt was consuming heat. It was a living thing inside of me, an arsonist that took shelter within my bones and reminded me of the pain one last time. I knew in that moment, I was already halfway to hell.

When I was younger, my dad would tell stories about where we go when we die. Heaven was a little different each time, but he would say it is a place where the birds always sing. I liked knowing that no matter how we die, we still exist somewhere. It made me feel better thinking my favorite cat had four acres of felt towers all to herself and that my great-aunt Hellen was sipping her red drink on a lawn chair somewhere.

"Can we visit heaven sometime, Daddy?" I asked. He was the best at coming up with the stories but never knew quite how to finish them. As always, Mom swooped in and rescued him.

"The thing about heaven is that you have to be old enough to go," she said.

"Like how I have to be tall enough to ride the roller coasters?"

"Kind of, but you won't be able to cheat and wear your soccer cleats to get in," she said, while tickling my rib cage. She had a tendency to do that—using diversion as a way to get out of an uncomfortable situation.

"So how old do I have to be to get in?" It was one of the few times I remembered her at a loss for words. The moment only lasted a few seconds, but she eventually found the perfectly scripted answer.

"Well, it doesn't really work like that, doll. Not everyone is the same age, because people go to heaven at different times. But someone told me a secret once. He said I couldn't tell you until you turned seven, so I don't know if I'm allowed to." I felt the excitement swell inside of me. It was the kind that far exceeded seeing Mickey Mouse for the first time or being told I was getting grilled cheese for lunch. It was the feeling that I was finally old enough to handle the truth.

"But I am almost seven. We did summer birthdays in school so my teacher said I'm pretty much seven. Lenny is seven, and I'm already taller than him. And I can read a whole Berenstain Bears book all by myself. *And*

I stopped sucking my thumb. You told me that if I stop sucking my thumb, then I get a surprise." I hoped that she didn't know Lenny was the smallest kid in class.

"I did say that, didn't I? Well, I think telling you a little early won't hurt anybody." She picked me up and held me like she used to, making me feel like I was still only six years old. I held my breath as she whispered softly in my ear. "Most people don't know when they get to go to heaven. But, when you were born, a man came to see me at the hospital. He said that he wanted to look at you with his own eyes because you are one of the special ones. Sometimes he doesn't know how people will turn out, but he knew that you have all the good things inside of you. He told me you are going to live to be one hundred and six, and you're going to see the whole world."

"Even Florida?" I asked in wonderment.

"Even Florida," she said as she pulled back to look at me with her smiling eyes. That afternoon I started a to-do list of everything I wanted to accomplish in my lifetime. I got as far as "build a birdhouse for the back-yard" before my sister found me holed up in our secret hiding place. She showed me how to catch crayfish with my bare hands that day, and by dinnertime, I had already forgotten about the man and his story. I found my list a couple days later but didn't add anything more to it. Besides, I had a hundred years to figure out how I wanted to spend it.

It was strange how those moments came flooding back when I least expected. I started to remember the little things—the happy things. But then they were replaced by the memories of how it all fell apart. The girl with the to-do list couldn't exist anymore—not inside the person I had become.

It was a scam—the idea that everything happens for a reason. It didn't leave room for the tragedies, the things in this world that didn't make sense.

When the burn started to subside, I could feel myself slowly slip away. In that moment, I realized the man had been wrong about two things. One, he overestimated the good inside of me. And two, I would never live to be a hundred, because I couldn't even make it to sixteen.

As that precious nothingness enveloped me, I sensed her hand in mine, holding me back. I could feel the clamminess of her palm and the coolness of her skin soothing my scorched bones. We were together again, but this time she was asking me to stay. The last thing I remembered as I headed over that edge was to never let her go. I knew she'd always been the one to build me wings for the way down.

Chapter One
September 12, 2000

"Keely, don't be such a scaredy-cat." Those seven words. They were all it took for Dani to get me to do anything. Usually it was just to go lightning bug catching in the middle of the night or drive around on the lawnmower when dad wasn't home. But this time was different. This time she was asking me to break the law.

"Dani, we can't break into their house."

"We aren't breaking in anywhere, we're just gonna walk in."

"Aren't you forgetting that they have three 'Beware of Dog' signs? That's even more than the pound has."

"All they have is a Doberman with cataracts and a Pomeranian with rotten teeth. They just pretend to have scary dogs. And besides, I already have it all planned out so stop worrying." That was Dani's answer to everything. She was the clever one, the girl who could walk as fast as she talked. As always, her hands stirred as she plotted, fidgeting away like they were playing her life's concerto.

She peered down at me over the edge of the bunk, no doubt planning her next scheme on me. I quickly pulled the blankets over my head with hope that she would let me have a few more minutes of sleep. Like an old playground set, the stacked metal began to squeak and shift side-to-side as Dani made her way down to me.

"Keely—we have been talking about this all summer. You even said so yourself that he had this coming," she added, crawling under the covers with me. I habitually curved into the crook of her body, a place I fit so perfectly. I could feel her continuing to scheme, her fluttering fingers brushing lightly against my leg.

If there was anyone who deserved payback, it was Topher Vern. He had been our grandparents' neighbor for as long as I could remember, and he was as big as he was mean. All the kids in Reading knew of Topher, mostly because he was the only sixth grader who was over six feet tall. Mom said it wasn't that impressive considering he had failed two grades, but no one really cared to set the record straight. I asked Mom why mean kids like Topher got to be the big and powerful ones. She replied simply, "Keely, baby, people only get as much power as others give them."

It didn't make me feel any better.

"What are you thinking about?" whispered Dani. I lifted my head from her shoulder, realizing she had been watching me. I looked up into her aquamarine eyes. They perfectly mirrored mine, except for the blotch of gold covering half of my right one. For identical twins, we were made from the same mold but must have had different sculptors. Her blonde waves spilled perfectly down her back while mine rolled up like ragged hay bales. We both stood fifty-five inches tall, but my shoulders hunched slightly below hers. I figured that came from years of cowering from bullies like Topher Vern. I couldn't help but feel that Dani was her sculptor's masterpiece, while I was just an unfinished project.

"I was thinking about that time Topher called me 'chicken wing legs,' so you mushed goose poop into his shoes, and he had to wear them all around camp. I think it was the best week of my life."

"Except for the end," giggled Dani.

"I still feel itchy just thinking about it," I squealed as she cocooned the covers around us. Even though the blanket was just a sheet, it felt impenetrable—as if it protected us from anything the world threw our way. "You do know that it was meant for me," I whispered.

"It was meant for both of us, silly. He knew that I would get scared of the lightning and end up in your sleeping bag." Even though I knew it was a lie, it still made me feel a little less guilty.

"Well, at least we went through it together, oatmeal baths and everything."

"Together," Dani said as she raised two fingers. I raised one finger in response and wove it between her peace sign, making our double cross.

"Three," we said in unison. It was something that we had done since first grade. People would ask us what it meant, but we never told anyone except for Nana.

Our first-grade teacher, Ms. Woodbury, was a cranky old lady who smelled like the inside of a Doctor Dolittle book and didn't care whether or not her students looped their ℓs perfectly. She didn't mind that none of us could actually say "spaghetti" the right way. But what that woman did care about was math. To her, life was something that had to make sense, and everything had to have a definitive answer. I used to think like that too, but Dani taught me that the world was a little more magical than people made it out to be. She transformed plastic grocery bags into our parachutes and cardboard paper towel rolls into pirate telescopes. Dani showed me that it wasn't about having the correct answer—it was about the understanding behind it.

Ms. Woodbury tried all year to get us to admit that one plus one equaled two, but we refused to say it. Dani and I couldn't admit to something we knew wasn't true. To us, we individually counted as one but together created something more than our added parts. I figured we equaled out to a two point seven and Dani thought we were more like a three point four. In the end, we settled on three. I never told her the real reason why I gave us a lower score. I lied and said that it was because we weren't grownups yet. But it was actually because I felt she gave me more than I could ever give her.

"So, are you going to help me today?" Dani asked, our fingers still intertwined. I smiled to myself because I realized she had me right where she wanted.

"Alright, but I'm not in charge of the dogs."

"I told you, it's all figured out. The dogs won't be anywhere near you." She must have remembered my fear of dogs because she lightly touched the deep scar on my thigh. Rapidly, she broke open our blanket shell and cool air rushed into our warm cave. Dani jumped out of bed and began digging for something in the far reaches of the closet. "Scott got all the merchandise for us, and Barry is letting us borrow this beauty right here."

A large container thudded down in front of me, which looked like one of the water coolers Dad would bring out for the Super Bowl. "What is it?" I asked suspiciously.

"Barry says it's an overnight pet feeder. You know, like the kind for when you keep animals alone for a long time? It drops food down when the timer goes off."

"Okay, so we are using that…wait a second, do you have *them* in there?" Her wide smile gave away the answer. "Dani, that is genius! How many did you get?"

"Well, Scott's dad went to this warehouse for pet stores and got three pounds, so a whole lot!"

"Oh my gosh, Topher's going to freak!"

"I know! He's gonna wish he never messed with us after these little critters get out," she laughed as she rubbed her hands devilishly together. I leapt off the bed and into her arms before she could even open them.

"Dani, I can't believe you actually did it. We always talked about it, but I thought we were just going to put stinky tuna fish in his room or something. But this—this is the best prank ever!" It wasn't until I pulled away that I discovered Dani's tears. "Why are you crying? I'm the one who should be doing that," I tried to say lightheartedly.

"I'm just so happy that we can finally get Topher back for all the mean things he's said about us." She reached up and grabbed a batch of my frazzled hair and softly ran her hands through it, the same way as Mom. Those were the moments that made me feel like the younger sister.

It had been that way since preschool, ever since Debbie Groth pushed me off my tricycle and stole it. She was bigger than me, so I just let her have it. But Dani saw the whole thing and wasn't going to let her get away with that. I would never forget how Dani flew across the gym and crashed her trike right into Debbie's. In my eyes, she couldn't have been more of a superhero if she'd been wearing a cape.

We weren't allowed back after that, but I didn't care. Dani said she didn't either, but I knew deep down that she missed doing the sand art with the other girls. I tried to find some extra sand in our old seashell collection for us to play with, but I barely collected enough to make a smiley face. I knew it was mostly for my feelings, but she still acted like it was more than enough.

When kindergarten arrived, I could barely sleep knowing Debbie Groth was going to be in our class. We missed the bus that morning, forcing Mom to drop us off. I knew Dani was up to something. She made us late by pretending to have lost her favorite charm bracelet, even though I had seen her hide it inside her dresser the night before. It wasn't until we walked into class that I finally understood. Dani wanted everyone to see us enter together. She sent those kids a message—we were a team.

No one else messed with us until the summer before sixth grade. It was our second time at vacation bible school, the place we spent three weeks handholding and talking around campfires. Our parents said it was to learn more about Jesus. But I knew it was really because they wanted us to spend more time with Bumpy and Nana in Reading.

That summer, we met Topher Vern. To Topher, Dani was the perfect girl, and I was the misfit. It first started with small things, like whispering, "freak," as I passed by him in the lunch hall and making animal sounds when I spoke up during prayer group. But then he got more kids involved. We would have "worship sessions" where we'd write in our journals for an hour. It wasn't until I reached the middle section of mine that I realized Topher and his friends had marked up a few of the pages. I didn't let myself read any of the comments, but I couldn't help but look at one of the pictures they had created. It was a drawing of two girls, except one of them appeared normal and the other was deformed. They were labeled "girl one" and "thing two."

I cried myself to sleep every night that second week. After all the other kids had gone to bed, I would take out my notebook and stare at the warty, hunched, snarling version of myself. But one night, the tears finally dried up. I could feel the sharp hurt each time I opened the journal, but the pain no longer reached my eyes. It found new nooks and crannies inside of me to burrow away and hide.

Luckily, the third week ended two days early for Dani and me, but not without a price. Topher must have slipped into our cabin during dinnertime and loaded my sleeping bag with poison ivy leaves. Little did he know that Dani kept me company during thunder and lightning storms. And that night, Reading saw the worst storm of the summer.

We cringed at the oozing blisters that covered both of our legs. But it was the burning itch that drove us mad. For me, Nana's black bottle treatments were the worst part. She believed that alcohol could cure anything, especially her migraines that always arrived around one o'clock. However, I couldn't complain too much. I wasn't the one who had it on my private parts. Poor Dani had to get shots and take medicine after it got so bad down there.

"Okay, we have to do it before lunch because Mrs. Vern always leaves for her book club at twelve," Dani said. We all knew that the book club was just an excuse for Reading's housewives to flirt with the police officers at the pastry shop downtown.

"Bumpy is making his soup again, so maybe if we're lucky we can just skip lunch," I said with hopeful eyes.

"Mom will throw a hissy fit if she finds out. Maybe I can get Dad to take her to that candle store so she won't even know we're gone." Her voice settled barely above a whisper, making me think that she was talking more to herself than to me.

"Dad's busy working on that project, remember? Maybe we could get Bumpy to take her and that would fix everything!"

A slow Cheshire Cat smile spread across Dani's face as she added, "You know what, Keely? Today is going to be a great day."

"Why is that?" I couldn't help but mirror her with my own gummy smile.

"Because we're gonna go down in history as the ones who made Topher Vern scream like a little girl."

"Okay, when I get them away from the door, you are going to run inside while I keep them busy," Dani whispered from her crouched position. We both leaned against a tree on the outskirts of the Vern's lawn, watching the two dogs sunbathing on the back porch. Thankfully, the backyard fence wasn't too far away from the back door. I estimated that I could probably get to it in about ten seconds.

Hopefully.

"Alright, so once I get inside, what happens if I can't find the basement?"

"Keel, you'll find the basement. If you get scared down there, just remember you have Mom's saltwater spray," she said as she scanned the lawn with her binoculars. I clasped the thin spray container in my hand, hoping it would give me some amount of courage. Mom always said that saltwater spray would protect us from anything—that if I was ever scared, I could just spray the badness away.

When Dani started opening up the steak packs, I knew it was time. I took a deep breath in, straightened my headband flashlight, tightened my fanny pack, and put the spray bottle in my back pocket. "I think I'm ready," I said with a shaky voice.

"You bet you are! If you can live through the Tower of Terror, then you can do anything." Dani held up her hand for a high-five, which I returned with a weak tap. "Come on, we only have half an hour until she gets back." Dani carried her bag of electronics, while I lugged the feeder towards the bulkhead door that led to the basement.

Once we reached the fence gate, I could feel my heartbeat hammering in my temples. Dani reached into her bag and took out her new remote control car, checking to make sure the battery pack was properly clipped in. She then took out a line of twine and hooked the two bleeding steaks together. "Wait, this is your grand plan? To go...dog fishing?"

"You bet. It's a perfect day to catch some Doberman," she laughed. I looked on as she tied the thread to the back of her car and turned on the remote controller. "The woman at Radio Shack told me this car can go up to sixty miles per hour, and Dad said that a Doberman can only run up to thirty."

"And what if he can run more than thirty?"

"Well, then I have twenty-two days left on my warranty," she said as she directed the car towards the gate opening. The steaks lugged bumpily along behind. I steadied myself behind the remote car, preparing for when Dani flipped the latch. "Okay, moment of truth. Let's see how fast these dogs can really run." As I stood there, rising up onto the balls of my feet in anticipation, I couldn't help but feel like Picabo Street right before she won gold in the 1998 Winter Olympics. If she could get down a mountain in a minute and eighteen seconds, I could make it to that door in under half of that.

The car took off into the backyard. As soon as Dani swung the gate open, both dogs bolted off their stoop in hot pursuit. "Go! Go! Go!" she shrieked. After a slight hesitation, I burst into the yard, my legs feeling as wobbly as a newborn colt's. I could hear Dani laughing wildly behind me, most likely as surprised as I that her crazy plan was working. I didn't dare peel my eyes from the back door, praying that the dogs hadn't seen me.

By the time I crashed through the screen door that sat off of the back porch, I felt like I had run through a sea of quicksand. Once inside, I slumped against the door and blew out a heavy breath. I realized that I hadn't exhaled since I had left Dani's side. I felt a numbing tingle run through my legs, and my blood boiled from the adrenaline.

My legs slowly returned to me as I adjusted to the dimness. I started unsteadily down a tight hallway, crossing my arms so that I didn't knock anything over. The house wasn't how I had imagined it. Its walls were decorated with pictures of Topher smiling in a cheap suit at every age, making him look more like a traveling salesman than a bully. Underneath the frames, upholstered flowers seemed to grow on every bare surface. The space smelled of potpourri and cinnamon, making me feel like I was inside a gingerbread house.

At first, I wondered how such a cold-hearted boy could grow up in such a warm and flowery home. That was until I walked into a side room located off from the kitchen. It was clearly the only room that Mrs. Vern wasn't allowed to touch. There wasn't a flower in sight.

I felt like I had walked onto a stage, as all eyes were on me. Growling animal heads covered every wall space, their expressions frozen in angry snarls. A narrow passage sliced through the dark room between their extended snouts. I couldn't go further than the doorway. All I thought about was how terrible it must be to die angry.

"Keely, what's taking so long? Over." I jumped at the voice coming from my fanny pack, knocking down a suspended owl in the process. Very carefully, I reached into its pocket and drew out the walkie-talkie.

"Uh, just a tiny problem, but I'm almost done!" I turned the volume down to zero, predicting she would want every detail. Even before I turned around, I knew that the owl would never fly again. A crushed wing dangled like a useless flap from its stiff form. I delicately laid its broken body on the hump of a wolf's back and slowly backed out of the room.

It didn't take long to find the basement door. I looked down into the murky abyss below, automatically flicking on the flashlight. It was a known fact that if a basement smelled like old fertilizer and wet copper, it probably only had one working light bulb.

Armed with my saltwater spray, I let out a few squirts for good luck as

I made my way down the stairs. It was the type of basement that had a meat locker in one corner and old dog droppings in the other. The smell alone told me that I had approximately three minutes left of good oxygen before I died from whatever toxin hung in the air. Thick dust caked every surface, with the exception of the towering gun cabinet that appeared freshly cleaned. My headlight did little to help me in the dank dungeon. As I drew closer to one of the walls, I faintly heard Dani yelling into her walkie outside. Pointing my light upwards, I spotted the bulkhead door.

It seemed like three hundred years worth of spider webs stood in my way, their thick and sticky strings blocking the entire stairway. However, they broke apart as easily as cotton candy as I padded through them. I jostled the latch and pushed against the door with my back. Dani stood there in the instant sunlight.

"Keely! Thank God—I was about to come in there and rescue you!" She yanked open the other side, allowing it to heavily thump onto one of Mrs. Vern's rosebushes.

"You do know that I can do things on my own, right?" I asked defensively.

"Let's just get this done and get the heck out of here. I feel like Mrs. Vern will be home any second," she replied, ignoring my question.

"I hope she wore that push up bra. Officer Kingsley never leaves her alone when she wears that thing," I added as I helped Dani haul the bulky feeder down into the basement. When we got halfway to the staircase, Dani stopped dead in her tracks.

"Keely, what the heck is that?" I turned my head, shining the tiny light in the direction she pointed. A deer's lopsided head hung limply in front of us. One of Mr. Vern's latest kills was dangling from a pipe, gutted, with something still dripping from its hollow insides. "Oh my God is that a poor little deer?" she said in a hoarse voice. "Who are these people?" Dani yelled.

"They are monsters, Dani! They murdered all these animals and then put them in this room upstairs—it's Jumanji up there!" We both shuffled as quickly as we could towards the door at the top of the stairs, my pigeon toes not taking it easy on me. "Oh, and I forgot to tell you. I broke one of their owls."

"An owl?"

"Yeah, like that bird in those Tootsie Pop commercials."

"Keely, I know what an owl is for Pete's sake. I was just making sure that that actually came out of your mouth."

"Just be thankful I didn't fall on the ostrich."

When we finally managed to make it up the stairs with the feeder, I led her to the room full of angry animals. "I'm serious. Who are these people?" Dani asked as she walked over to a gray, hairless head with fangs that jutted from its open mouth. "What even is this?"

"I think it's a hippo," I stated dumbly.

"Hippos don't have pointy teeth. They have cute, little square ones."

"I think that's only in the cartoons."

"Whatever it is, I feel bad for it. Where's the owl you fell on?"

"Right here," I said as I held it up by one leg. It looked more mangled than I had remembered.

"Aw, it's cute. We have to take it. We can't leave it, because then they'll know someone was here."

"Oh, really? And you don't think that our container full of crickets will give us away?" Even though she knew I was right, she'd already made up her mind. She probably even had a hiding spot picked out in our secret tree house.

"Who cares? He won't even miss it," she stated. As I looked around, I had a feeling he would know it was gone the second he stepped into the room.

Once we had dragged the heavy cylinder up to the second floor, it didn't take long to find Topher's room. Even though he had two younger brothers, his was the nicest bedroom in the house. It had its very own living room area and a rack of weights that no normal twelve-year-old should have. There were wraparound shelves packed with trophies and ribbons. The only thing that seemed out of place was a shabby bunny doll that lay on his bed. I didn't know why, but it made me hate him a little less.

"Okay, I think that we should put it behind the hamper. Clearly this kid doesn't even use it," she said as she inspected the athletic clothes that littered the floor.

"Yeah, good idea. When did you set the timer for?"

"Eleven tonight. He has a football game tomorrow, so he'll be cuddling with his little dolly by ten for sure," she snickered as she held up the ratty stuffed animal. "Who knew that Topher was such a baby?"

We moved the feeder into position, hiding it beneath a crusty towel. "Do you think he's going to cry?" I whispered.

"Uh, yeah! Didn't you see him flip out when that grasshopper landed on him at camp? He absolutely hates bugs," she chuckled as she readjusted the feeder's opening to point directly towards his bed. I could tell she detected the seed of sympathy that grew inside of me. "Keely, you have to remember we are talking about Topher here."

"I know, it's just that—"

"No, no buts. He sucks. He gave us poison ivy. I even got it *down there*. I think he deserves a lot more than a couple crickets crawling on him."

"You're right. Topher Vern can suck it."

"Suck what?" Dani giggled.

"I don't know. I heard Dad say it to Mr. Howard once. You know how much he hates him for cutting down our mulberry tree. I'm pretty sure the middle finger means the same thing."

"Yeah! Topher Vern, you can suck my middle finger!" Dani yelled. She flipped off the life-sized football photo of him that hung above his weight stack. I joined in with her, whooping and hollering as we ran throughout the house, flipping the bird every time we passed one of his pictures nailed to the wall.

It wasn't until we got down to the living room that we noticed Mrs. Vern had pulled into the driveway. Thankfully, she hadn't yet noticed the hatch door crushing her prized rosebushes.

"Oh my God, go!" Dani shrieked, shoving me from behind as I swept up the limp owl lying at the bottom of the stairs. My headlight bounced every which way as we bolted down to the basement. We rushed towards the stream of light at the far end of the dark room, pushing through fresh cobwebs that had seemingly rewoven in our absence.

We burst into the cool, fall air, throwing the metal door back into its place. I snatched Dani's bag from beneath a nearby bush.

"Did the dogs catch your car?" I panted as we sprinted towards the woods at the back of the house.

"Nope! Looks like Radio Shack got this one right."

"What happened to the steaks?"

"I gave them to the Pomeranian. Nana always said that there's nothing scarier to Mrs. Vern than a fat dog!" Dani hollered. One thing was for sure—if slamming the bulkhead door hadn't given us away, our laughter definitely did. We ran and ran and didn't stop. We had no idea where we were heading, but we didn't care. All that mattered was that we made Topher Vern suck it.

It wasn't until I crashed through the forest's veil of painted leaves that I remembered the owl was still in my hand. In that moment, it came back to life, soaring with us. It made me think that all she ever needed was someone else to help her fly.

"I don't even want to think about where you two have been all day," Mom said from the kitchen. She glared suspiciously at us from underneath her eyebrows as she pulled the twice-baked potatoes out of the oven. Thankfully, Dani was the master of getting us out of anything.

"We just went down to the pond for a little bit. Just skipping rocks and stuff," Dani said with only a slight hesitation.

"Skipping rocks, huh? So you had nothing to do with feeding two pounds of meat to Mrs. Vern's dog or walking all over her roses?"

"Mom, why would anyone want to walk on rosebushes? They have thorns all over them."

"You're right, Dani. Why *would* someone do that? Keely, why don't *you* come in here and explain it to me." Dani instantly grabbed my hands and tried to pull me into the bathroom. "I don't think so, Dani Ray. You aren't going to feed her lines this time," she reprimanded. "Keely, come in here right now."

Panic spread across Dani's face as she turned towards me and prepared me to meet my doom. She rolled down my sleeves to cover the cuts left behind by the pricker bushes and picked all the bedstraw weeds out of my hair. It made me feel like one of those baby chimpanzees at the zoo. "We were just at the pond, we ran into Michelle, and we even got to jump on her water trampoline. Our clothes are dry because…well, because it was stinkin' sunny out," Dani sputtered rapidly in my ear.

We turned around together. Dani placed her hands on her hips and straightened her back, growing a whole foot in that moment. I, on the other hand, discovered a sudden fascination with the tops of my shoes. "Dani, why don't you go upstairs and see if Nana needs help with anything?" Mom commanded. Dani muttered under her breath as she unwillingly left me to walk the long plank to my mother. I had already forgotten if we were supposedly fishing or throwing rocks at the pond.

Once I heard Dani's feet stomp up the stairs, I knew I was all on my own. I stole a quick peek up at my mother and instantly regretted it. Her face mirrored the same expression she got when she fought with Dad—that look always won. Mom's eyes were deep blue, the kind I had only ever seen in marbles. Their shade would change moment to moment. It was as if she had eyes made out of mood rings. "Keely, do you want to know something I haven't told anyone?"

I hesitated. Dani's voice rang through my head, warning me that this was just one of her tricks. "You haven't even told Dad?" I asked into my chest.

"Not even Dad."

"But you tell Dad everything. You even told him that you think he has a receding hairline."

"Well, that's because someone needed to tell him."

"But now he won't stop wearing ball caps, and my teacher said it's rude to wear hats inside."

"Keely, do you want to know or not? Maybe I should go find Dani and tell her instead," she said as she pretended to make her way towards the door.

"No, no! I want to know…you can trust me," I said, giving her my full attention. I walked over to her, realizing all too late that she was already winning. I blamed my foolishness on having a psychiatrist for a mother. Some people thought it was cool to have a mom who always knew what to say, but I thought it was pretty terrible. Up until that point, she had already gotten four confessions out of me. As I stood there, looking up into her lovely face, I promised myself she wasn't going to get a fifth.

"So, you know that one Christmas when the Vern's mailbox got knocked over—the one that you thought looked like a Barbie house?"

"Yeah…Bumpy said the police thought a snowplow hit it."

"Well, it wasn't exactly a snowplow…" she said as her voice drifted off. For once, it was her turn to look away.

"No way! Dani and I were wondering why there was glitter stuck to the back of your car!"

"Yeah, well let's have everyone go on thinking it was from your angel wing costumes I had in the trunk."

"But we didn't even go to the pageant tha—"

"Keely, it doesn't matter. What I am trying to say is that I did something bad and never tried to fix it."

"That thing was ugly anyways," I mumbled, causing my mother to sigh heavily.

"You know, you are more like your sister than you think. Teaching you girls anything is like trying to get Nana to stop drinking her tonic…and I don't mean that as a compliment, Keely," she said as she caught my smile. I loved it when people said I reminded them of Dani. Even when it was for the bad things, like walking around the house in muddy boots or forgetting to put the ice cream carton back in the freezer, it still counted.

"Okay, we didn't go to the pond," I blurted out. Almost the second after the words left my mouth, I felt sweat escape from my hands. I couldn't help but rub my palms on my shirtsleeves, making the scratches on my arms burn. My mother spent every day waiting for confessions, so I knew that I had to give her something more. "We…we were in the woods."

"Keely, you're covered in weeds. Of course you were in the woods. I just want to know what you were doing all afternoon." She was growing impatient. The bulging vein in her forehead told me she wasn't getting what she wanted. I looked around for some sort of clue to save me. Dani had told me that her best excuses came from the things five feet in front of her. All I could focus on was Nana's blotchy lipstick stuck to the side of an empty glass.

"We were making something for Nana. But we didn't have time to finish it."

"What were you making?"

My mind filled with many worthless ideas—the worst being a popcorn maker. "I...I'm not supposed to tell. It's a surprise." I knew she wanted to believe me.

It wasn't that out of the ordinary for Dani and me to make Nana gifts for her birthday. The previous year, we made a clay sculpture of her and Bumpy resting in the hammock—their favorite place. Even though it looked like a lopsided butterfly cocoon, she still said she loved it. Nana set it on a table in the front porch. She told us she wanted it to be the first thing people saw when they walked in. But Dani and I both knew that everyone came in through the back door.

"Well, her birthday is tomorrow. Will you be done with it by then?"

"We think we can finish it by tonight. We're almost done. I was going to ask if we could go out after dinner to finish working on it," I added softly, avoiding her marble eyes.

"I didn't know that you girls were making something extra. I thought the video was going to be her gift this year," she added suspiciously. It had completely slipped my mind that we already had a present. We'd made a family music video to the tune of Nana's favorite song, "Mustang Sally." It took us a whole weekend to finish, and we even rented a brand new mustang. It had been the best weekend of the summer—I didn't know how I could have forgotten.

"Yeah, well we wanted to make her birthday extra special this year, okay?" I said, quickly becoming flustered.

"Did someone say 'birthday' in here? You know that I'm turning forty tomorrow. I hear forty is the big one," Nana chimed as she hobbled into the room. Dani followed closely behind. Her eyes instantly locked on mine, trying to figure out how much trouble I had gotten us into. Little did she know that she would have to get us out of our biggest lie yet. "You aren't beating up on my little girl here are you, Charlotte?" Nana asked. She wrapped her arms around me, just like she would when I had a bad cough. It seemed that Nana must not have heard about catching colds from touching sick people. But I never pointed that out, because I liked her hugs too much. She had that special kind of touch—the type that left warmth behind.

"Keely was just telling me about what you girls were doing all day. She said you both still need more time, right, Dani?"

I thought I saw a flicker of confusion cross Dani's face. But before I could be sure, it vanished. "Yup. Totally. Like at least another two hours," she answered, almost a little too quickly. Dani looked to me for help, but all I could do was stare blankly back.

"So, has Bobby started cooking the steaks yet?" Nana asked, pretending that she didn't know she was saving our butts. I could tell my mom wasn't fully convinced. However, she let it go, at least for a little while.

As if on cue, Bumpy came strolling in, holding a pack of steaks. "I'm just about to fire up the grill...even though two of the steaks have mysteriously gone missing." He said the last part under his breath as he looked from me to Dani. We kept our heads down, hoping that Mom wouldn't catch on. "And I know, Lucille, I'm late and spent too much time on my lures," he quickly added.

Nana often got mad at him for working too long in his workshop, but he had to keep up with the demands from those around Reading. People said he made the most beautiful fishing lures they had ever seen. They said that fish became so hypnotized by the shiny bait that they could simply reach out and grab them straight from the water with their bare hands. Dani once asked Bumpy how he came to be so good at making them. "Just by looking at the beauty around me," he had told her, gazing at Nana the entire time.

"I'll forgive you if you make me another one of these," Nana said as she tapped on her empty glass.

"Lucy, you know what the doctors said," Bumpy responded with a tightened expression.

"Oh come on, it's my birthday. Has it killed me yet?"

It always hurt Bumpy's feelings when Nana talked about death. I knew that he wanted to hold on to her for as long as he could, and she didn't really think much about her tomorrows. "It isn't your birthday yet, love. Tomorrow you can bribe me all you want," he said with his sideways smile. Nana's eyes shifted towards the cabinet near the ceiling and then back to Bumpy. She couldn't help but catch his smile. They were "contagious for one another," as Mom would say. It was my favorite thing about them.

Nevertheless, if there was one thing that Nana loved almost as much as Bumpy, it was her alcoholic drinks. Bumpy only let her have one every other day, which drove her slightly nuts. He used to have a hard time controlling her drinking. However, when they started getting older, he found a new method to get his way. He would hide her bottles in the highest kitchen cabinet, the one she could no longer reach. Nana would try to sneak out and buy more. But Bumpy had every storeowner in Reading right in his back pocket in return for his beautiful fishing lures.

People thought my nana was an alcoholic, but I knew better. Some kids in my class talked about their parents being scary when they drank and how they would sleep all day. However, Nana never got angry when she sipped her tonic. Instead, she would giggle a lot and tell the best stories. Her favorite one was about the time she first met Bumpy and how she had hated his guts. It was my favorite, too, because it wasn't like all the other fairy tales. Dani liked the happily ever after stories, but I thought they were all lame. I hoped that I would find a boy just like my bumpy someday. I'd wished for it on my past two birthdays. I didn't know why, but I had a feeling that my tenth year would be the lucky one. Dani and I had just started sixth grade, and a new boy, Max, sat right in front of us in almost every class.

I thought I could hate him.

I looked at Bumpy and tried to imagine what he looked like when he was younger. Even though he had brown spots and a lot of hair springing from his ears, I knew he must have been the kind of boy who all the popular girls flirted with. He must have smiled a lot, too. His smiles had left behind wrinkles that made him look happy, even when he wasn't. Bumpy used to be over six feet tall, before he grew a big hump on his back that kept pushing him down. Dad said it was some kind of medical condition, but Bumpy told me it was from having to bend down to kiss his wife for the past fifty years. I liked his answer better.

Even with his hump, he was still able to reach that highest cabinet. It had almost been two years since Nana fell off a chair and hurt her hip while trying to get to her bottles. Bumpy had taken her to the hospital, and they ended up discovering she was more hurt than we had thought. They found something in her throat and ran a bunch of tests on her. That was the year I found out there was something worse than skinned knees and mean kids like Topher. It was something called "cancer."

She had to take medicine for almost a year, which made all her hair fall out. I didn't get to see Nana much during that time; Dad kept saying she had to go away to fight some bad guys. I didn't like it when he treated me as if I was a little kid, because I knew she wasn't somewhere riding on a horse and hitting people with a sword. She was lying in a hospital bed, probably wanting to tell Dani and me more stories.

I would never forget the first time I saw her in the hospital. It was during Christmas time, and Mom said she had to stay in a "sick bay." For some reason, it made me feel better knowing she at least wasn't in a "dying bay." When we walked into her room, all I could think about was how smooth her head looked and how I wanted to touch it. I knew my reaction wasn't normal, because Dani could barely look at her. She was holding back tears the entire time. It was one of the few things that I couldn't figure out about Dani and me as twins—how was it that she was the strong one, but I was the one who never cried?

In the beginning, the doctors didn't think she would make it. But Bumpy never gave up on her. He said all along that she was going to get through it, even though Nana didn't think so. He ended up winning their biggest disagreement.

When Nana started getting better, there was one thing that she was sure of—if it hadn't been for her gin and tonics, she probably would have been dead. Bumpy was so happy she didn't die that he was willing to agree to just about anything. He never really liked Nana's drinking habit, but he couldn't deny that they would have never found the cancer if she hadn't been trying to reach that cabinet.

Although I knew she no longer had cancer, I could tell that she still felt some kind of pain. My mom worried about her, but Nana would just say that she had been falling apart for years. She liked to tell us that she hit her peak at age thirty, and it was just downhill from there, whatever that meant. But Bumpy always told her she looked beautiful, even though she didn't have much hair left. For some reason, even after she stopped taking her medicine, only half of it decided to grow back.

"Keely, would you please go get your father and tell him that we are getting ready for dinner?" my mother asked, breaking me out of my trance.

"I'll go with her," Dani said as she grabbed my hand.

"No, you're going to stay right here, miss. I'm going to need some help with this salad." She used her psychiatrist voice, so we knew there was no use fighting. I figured we would have to plot our next move after dinner. I went in search of Dad, knowing he was probably holed up in his favorite spot on the front porch. He also knew that no one ever came in that way and he could have the most privacy there.

Exactly as I had expected, I found him there, huddled over his computer with a pen between his teeth. He didn't use it to write things down. Instead, he simply kept it with him to make him feel more imaginative. I didn't know much about his job, only that he worked in one of the really tall buildings in New York City. He tried to explain his work to Dani and me once. The only thing I got out of it was that he decided what went up on the big posters placed along the highway.

"You still working on that project, Daddy?" I asked him from the hallway. I liked to pretend that I knew what he was working on. In my mind, I imagined him writing poems and finding pictures to go with them.

"Oh hey, doll, I didn't see you there," he said without looking up from his computer. He was wearing his Giants hat that day, his favorite one. Stains covered the faded letters.

"Mom said that dinner is almost ready."

"Uh huh, sounds good," he said, showing no sign of moving. He tried to avoid work during family time, but since it was the middle of the week, he didn't have much of a choice. Because Reading was only a four-hour drive from New Jersey, Mom wanted to go up for Nana's exact birthday that year to make it extra special for her. I got the feeling that she didn't think Nana was going to have many more birthdays. Dani and I loved that we got to skip school for it, but our teachers didn't like her taking us out so early in the year. I told Mom that we were only learning about photosynthesis and what a democrat was, two things Dad had already taught us. It made her feel better.

"Hey, Dad?"

"Yup."

"Can I ask you a question?" I waited for him to look up, knowing then I would have his full attention. He didn't do well with focusing on too many things at once, something that drove my mother crazy. The question sank in after a few seconds. He took the pen out of his mouth as he closed his computer. If there was one thing that my dad loved, it was trying to answer my questions about the world.

"Of course you can," he said as he crossed his legs in the same way my principal did. I walked over and sat on his lap, making him unfold them because I didn't like thinking of my dad as Mr. Dugardi. My principal was known as The Trunchbull of the middle school, but my dad was the nicest guy I knew.

I ran my hand over his cheek, something I had done since I was little. It was sandpaper beneath my fingers. I searched for the small scar hidden under his chin, drawing a circle around its edges with my pinkie. Whenever I sat on his lap, I liked to make up stories about the heroic battles and dangerous adventures that had led to the secret mark.

"What were you like as a kid?" I asked abruptly. I could tell it wasn't the question he'd been expecting.

"Me as a kid, well, I was a pretty good kid. Didn't get into too much trouble."

"Were you popular? Did a lot of kids like you?"

"Kids liked me. I don't know if I would say I was popular, though." I thought about his answer and decided that I didn't believe him. Everyone liked Cole Millen—even the mean, old lady on our street who yelled at people for leaving their trash cans out for too long. People liked him because he always knew how to make things better. I never had to tell him when something was wrong—he would just know.

"Did you ever think you were different, you know, not like everyone else?" He curled me up in his arms and gently tucked me under his chin. His fingers swirled over my back, as if creating pictures for his next project. I placed my ear against his chest, making his voice echo in my head.

"I was a little different, but I didn't let too many people know that. I was kind of quiet and didn't really come out of my shell until high school."

"Why didn't you let people know you were different?"

"Probably because I was scared. I cared too much about what other people thought."

"What made you different?"

"Well, I was probably the only twelve-year-old who thought train sets were super cool. I enjoyed building them from scratch and trying out different tracks. I liked how every piece had a place and that you had to discover how it all came together. But you know what? I never told anyone that I did that. I didn't have any brothers or sisters to share it with, and your grandpa wasn't really around much." Dad rarely talked about my other grandparents. His father was a truck driver who was always on the road, and his mother died the year he turned thirteen. "But you know what, Keely? I didn't know it then, but it is better to be different. You don't want to be like everyone else, even if it's easier."

"But is it okay to want to be more like someone else sometimes?"

"I think you are perfect just being you," he finished.

I lifted my head from his chest and leaned up to kiss his sandpaper face. "You know what, Dad? I think train sets are pretty cool, too."

"Keely, what the heck are we supposed to make in the woods? A plate of bark?"

"I don't know. I'm sorry, I couldn't think of anything else! She's going to find out about Topher's anyways when those crickets get out," I stated.

We were heading to our secret tree house, and I hoped that we could figure out what to make before dark. Mom had let us go after dinner, but I could tell it was only to prove that we were lying when we returned empty-handed.

"Why didn't you just say we were hanging out in the woods and, I don't know, playing a card game? Why did you have to say we were making something for Nana?"

"I wasn't thinking, okay? It just came out."

"Well, there is nothing we can do now. We are just gonna have to find something," she replied with a heavy sigh. She stomped angrily ahead, and I stayed three steps behind.

Eventually, she looked over her shoulder and said, "Maybe there is something that we can use in the tree house. Or maybe we can give her that stupid owl."

"Do you really think she would believe we shot that thing out of the sky and filled it with paper?" I asked doubtfully.

"She might. She did believe that we made her those bracelets we bought at The Bon Ton."

"Dani, those bracelets had two beads on them. This is a wild animal that has actual eyeballs in it. There is no way that she will believe that."

"Well then, do you have any better ideas, smarty pants? You were the one who got us into this." I didn't respond, because I knew she was right. She could get us out of anything. But when my turn came, I would screw it up for the both of us. She could easily concoct that we were down at the pond jumping on some trampoline, but all I could think about was how I wouldn't have let my underwear get wet.

We walked quietly the rest of the way to our tree house, the short trip feeling endless. The woods stood just down the street from Nana and Bumpy's house. We had to cut through the middle school yard to reach it, through the playground with ten whole sets of swings and the world's fastest merry-go-round.

We had discovered the tree house by accident a couple years before, after our favorite kite broke loose and flew into the woods. The kite was lost forever, but what we found instead was so much better. In the middle of a forest opening, the small structure sat attached to a crooked tree. Seven nailed planks led up into the secret hideout. The tree's large branches wove around and through the ancient wood frame. We returned every time we visited Nana and Bumpy. It soon became our secret place, a hideaway for our favorite treasures. We never found out who owned it before us. Dani thought Peter Pan used to live there, but I was sure that Huck Finn built it so he had a place to go when he skipped school.

When we reached the parting in the woods, I knew that something was different. Maybe it was a missing board or that the scattered leaves layering the ground appeared staged. However, Dani didn't seem to notice anything unusual, so I continued to follow as she climbed the ladder that led up into our tree, high above the cloudy sky.

The hideout looked small from the ground, but inside it felt like an entire home. Little by little, we had filled it with our riches, transforming it into our own private vault. Dani added the rows of stuffed animals, but my possessions were much smaller. I kept little wooden boxes filled with special knick-knacks. My lucky pennies filled one box, and I had a story for each. The one from 1934 was my favorite. It was the penny Dani had fished out of a mall fountain for me. I was having a bad day, and she had said it would change my luck. Mom tried to get us out of there without anyone seeing us, but we ended up on the local news. Security caught Dani on camera right as she dove in.

"Do you see anything that looks like we could have made it?" Dani asked.

I scanned the toys lining the wall, knowing that Mom would never believe we sewed a stuffed animal. "We could use one of my boxes and fill it with some cool leaves."

"Does Nana even like leaves?"

"Probably. She likes everything that we give her."

"Okay, we'll just pretend she told us fall is her favorite season. So, what box do you want to use?" I looked carefully through my pile, trying to decide which collection I was willing to give up. I picked up one of the more raggedy boxes and gently ran my hands over it. Despite its slightly crooked sides, it still meant something to me. Inside, it held my Popsicle stick collection. I carefully removed the colorfully-stained sticks and added them to my movie ticket box.

"This is totally something we could've made. But we're going to tell her the glue job was all you," Dani said when I handed her the empty box. "Okay, let's go find some leaves. Mom wants us back before dark, and I want to get home so we can spy on Topher." As Dani made her way down the ladder, I looked for a good spot for our owl.

Scanning down the row of stuffed animals, I found a single empty space left. I placed her with a wing leaning against a brown teddy bear, figuring she would also want to be in the stuffed animal heaven. *At least it was better than living with all of those angry animals at the Vern's house.*

As I tucked the owl into her new home, I noticed only two of Dani's stuffed pigs seated beside it, even though I could have sworn there used to be three. I remembered when Dani told me the story about the three little pigs and the big bad wolf.

"You're losing it, Keely," I mumbled to myself. Pushing the missing pig to the back of my mind, I followed after Dani. By the time I had jumped the last two planks onto the ground, Dani wasn't anywhere in sight. I figured she went to the nearby field. There was a large maple tree at its far end, which would have been a leaf jackpot for Nana's present. I headed to look in the opposite direction.

After about fifteen minutes, I had found the twenty best leaves in the whole forest. I made sure to only pick the brightest ones, some in shiny reds and others in glowing yellows. Most of the trees hadn't changed colors yet, making the search feel like a treasure hunt. Before long, darkness had spread over the corners of the forest. I headed back to our tree to show Dani my stash, carrying the pile of leaves carefully in my shirt.

I had almost made it to the forest opening when I noticed the silence; it stopped me in my tracks. The crickets weren't chirping and the birds wouldn't sing—not even a tree rustled. I felt the ground slowly release its chains on me and began to run, letting my leaves fall behind me. It wasn't until I came around the row of cedars that I saw him. He stood at the center of the opening, towering over Dani as she scooted backwards towards the base of our tree. He stepped past her large pile of leaves, approaching her with a single step. I felt my throat close, as if the man had shoved his fist straight into my stomach.

He had his back to me. I could tell he was taller than Bumpy, even without his hump. The man wore all black, from his dusty ball cap down to his heavy boots. I couldn't see his face, but I could see the sideburns that stuck out like wiry sheep's wool. He stood with his hands straight at his sides like a mall mannequin, making me question if he was even human.

He said something to her in hushed whispers, his sheep's wool rapidly shaking with the movement of his words. Dani stared back at him with wide eyes; I had never seen that kind of fear. My legs gave way under my heavy body.

I couldn't bring myself to look away from her, digging at the tears that blurred my vision. I kept looking at her hands, silently pleading with her to play her concerto. *Please, Dani. Come on, move your fingers.* My throat suddenly gave way, releasing the harsh whistle trapped in my tight windpipe. Her eyes instantly locked on mine.

In that moment, our lives flashed before my eyes. We raced our bikes down our road in Ridgewood, heading to our favorite candy store on

Franklin Ave. A couple years passed and we entered high school. She sat right in front of me in social studies. We joined the soccer team together. She was the one who scored the goals, and I was the first one she ran to hug. Around eighteen, we scraped a pole with Mom's car because we were too busy singing along to a Christina Aguilera song. Dani of course got us down to only a week of grounding. Next, we were high school graduates and leaving for college. I got into a university only thirty minutes from hers, and we visited each other every weekend. She was a star on her college soccer team, and I made it to every home game. I sat in the front row, holding a sign with slanted letters. She looked up at me as I waved from the stands. However, she didn't wave back. She mouthed something to me, but I couldn't make out the words. I tried to focus on her mouth, but I couldn't bring myself to look away from her eyes.

Suddenly, the soccer field disappeared. I was no longer sitting in a stadium holding on to a paper sign. Instead, my cold fingers dug into the ground, trapping dirt beneath my fingernails. We were back in the woods, and I was staring at Dani, still just ten years old.

Her eyes jerked back to the man as he reached into his coat pocket. I couldn't see what he held within his dark leather coat. However, it brought Dani to her feet against the crooked tree. His hands fell back to his sides, revealing it to me—a giant needle, the kind that doctors stuck you with to keep sickness away. His giant thumb pressed on its back, releasing a small spurt of clear liquid.

Dani looked back at me, mouthing the same word she had in the stadium.

Run.

The world froze. We were prisoners of that single moment, paralyzed by the knowledge that everything was about to change. I blinked the blinding tears out of my eyes and realized—the man was staring at me. The shadow of his hat covered his face, but I could feel his dark eyes fixed on mine.

In the blink of an eye, the world rapidly advanced again. Dani pushed off from the tree, heading straight at the man. She had my warped box in her hand, pulling it high above her head before smashing it over his back. The glue broke apart in all the places it was supposed to hold it together. A scream exploded from her mouth, sending a burning sensation down into my toes. I watched helplessly as he whipped around and grabbed Dani's hair. He threw her against the ground, among the scattered and broken Popsicle pieces.

She continued to yell as he filled her mouth with dirt and leaves and bugs. Through a muffled voice, she kept telling me to run. But all I could do was stand there as he put that needle in her back. I watched as her kicking feet slowly went still, as if she was his wind-up toy whose crank had stopped turning. Her eyes remained slightly open, but they no longer focused on mine.

But his did.

And so I ran.

I ran, and I didn't look back. I left her there, facedown in the moss with mud dribbling down the side of her cheek. All I wanted to do was go with her—I didn't care where we went. But my legs kept taking me farther away. My heartbeat pounded in my head, feeling like someone was trapped inside, banging to be let out.

It wasn't until I reached Nana and Bumpy's backyard that my unsteady limbs gave out. Only then did I start screaming. The horrible sound ripped through my chest as I buried my forehead into the damp grass. I heard my mother crash through the back screen door, collapsing near my head. She kept asking me over and over what was wrong—kept asking where Dani was. But I couldn't stop screaming long enough to answer her. Someone else had taken over, and I was left only a spectator. She pulled me into her arms, rocking me like I was four instead of ten.

Only snapshots remained from those early moments when three became one. Dad jumped straight off the deck, causing his Giants hat to tumble to the ground. Nana and Bumpy held each other in the shaded doorway, their wrinkles curved in all the wrong directions. My mom covered me with her sweater when she discovered my pants were wet with urine. She somehow knew, even before the words left my mouth, that Dani was gone.

The screaming stopped, and the noises around me began to fade away. My mother shook my shoulders as Dad yelled my name. But I was being pulled somewhere else. As the darkness closed in around me, I said, barely making a sound, "He took her."

The last thing I remembered was looking up into my mother's mood ring eyes, watching as they went from their most perfect blue to their darkest black.

Chapter Two
September 13, 2000

I awoke to the sound of dripping. It must have been coming from the bathroom across the hall. Keely sometimes forgot to turn the handle all the way to the right after she brushed her teeth. I figured Dad would turn it off—he had always been a light sleeper. I rolled onto my side, but my bunk didn't make its usual creak. My hand reached for my pillow, but it wasn't nearby. I thought it must have fallen off the bed in the middle of the night. I placed my head back down and burrowed my face into the mattress. The sheet felt different against my skin, like it had been washed too many times. There was a strange smell to it, similar to the old dresses Nana kept in her attic.

I opened my eyes, but all I saw was black. I blinked but nothing changed. My eyes searched for our Aladdin nightlight—in its corner was only darkness. Even with all the signs telling me otherwise, I wouldn't let go of the thought that I was safely tucked away in Nana and Bumpy's house. I could even sense the comforting sound of Keely breathing softly below me.

I wanted to call out to her. My jaw ached as I puckered my lips, a crusty film cracking apart as I ripped them open. I felt the jagged residue with my papery tongue, telling myself it was only toothpaste—the Arm & Hammer kind with baking soda in it. Or maybe it was old gum that I had forgotten to spit out before bed. But I knew it was all a lie.

It was blood.

My eyes adjusted to the darkness, and things slowly took shape. I could make out boxes placed atop one another. They reminded me of the empty crates Mom kept stacked against our barn—the ones she had planned to turn into "artistic shelves" for our bedroom. I tried focusing my eyes. But black, vertical lines blocked my every angle. I reached my hand over the side of the mattress, hoping it would only swipe the open air. Instead, it hit ground. The dirt was thick and cold to the touch, like a sandbox after days of rain. A chill stung my body, deep into my toes. My feet felt exposed to the heavy air.

I never went to bed without my socks.

Then it started coming back to me.

It came back in pieces, the lens in my mind clicking in and out of focus. I remembered the moving van. I was curled up, my forehead pressing against my scratched-up knees. The hard cage stopped my legs when I stretched to fix the ache in my back. It was made of metal—the kind used for bad dogs. There were other cages around me, but all were empty. I remembered the distant sirens, fading away in the other direction. When I tried to lift my head, I found only the strength to move my eyes. Beneath their heavy lids, I saw a familiar pink. It took me only a second to realize that it was one of my stuffed animals—the pig I named Elmer, covered in dirt.

I remembered the trail of muddy boots through the endless forest. I had never seen so many trees, all upside down with their leaves swallowed by the black sky as he carried me. Even in the darkness, I could tell his boots were at least three sizes too big. My limp arms dangled numbly in front of me, as if they belonged to a puppet.

I flashed to the tree house, looking up into the man's terrible face. His nose curved to the side, looking as if half of it used to belong to someone else. There were deep holes covering his cheeks, the kind that looked painted-on. But his eyes were what scared me the most. They were gray, steely beads that never blinked.

Then all I could see was Keely's terrified face. She was begging me to tell her what to do next. I looked back into the eyes that mirrored mine, frozen in that moment when we both realized what was about to happen.

My feet lightly brushed the dirt floor as I pulled myself up to sit. The thin mattress rested only a couple inches off the ground. My head began to ache in my temples when I finally forced myself to stand. I shuffled forward with my hands extended out into the damp air. My eyes could barely make out the tips of my fingers. After eight steps, my palms hit something hard. I knew, deep down in the pit of my stomach, even before my hands wrapped around them, they were metal bars.

I stood there, gripping the thin poles until they grew warm beneath my palms. It was then that I stopped lying to myself. It wasn't a bad dream. I wasn't imagining the blood in my mouth or the cold dirt between my toes. It was real.

I collapsed to my knees, my hot hands raking over the cold ground for anything hard. Dirt flew into my face, but I didn't care. I discovered the thin metal tray when I reached the back corner of my jail. A dried layer of grubby food clung to it, digging its way beneath my fingernails.

After I had returned to the bars, my fingers found the cage's pegged hinge. I began to hit the plate into it over and over. The room filled with its clanging, but I couldn't stop. With every strike, I told myself I would escape.

"It's not going to work," a voice shot through the dark. I ignored it and kept going, my knuckles stinging as they repeatedly came down on the peg's hard edge. "I promise, it's not going to do anything," the voice called again.

"Who's there?" I shouted back, holding the tray above my head.

"Over here," the girl's voice rang, that time, softer. "Follow along the bars until you feel my hand."

"Do you know a girl named Keely? Do you know if she is here?"

"I don't know anyone named Keely. You came alone."

"Do you know where I am? Why am I here?" I asked, my voice cracking.

"What's your name?"

I hesitated. Keely and I had always made up different names when strangers asked us. We thought it would protect us from the bad ones. "People call me Dani."

"Short for Danielle?"

"No. Just Dani."

"Dani, why don't you follow the bars and come find my hand," she repeated. I hesitated. I didn't trust her. But in the darkness, all I had was her voice.

I felt my way along the bars with my right hand, counting in my head each time my fingers flicked one. The tinplate remained in my left hand, which I held out in front of me. I was just about to thirteen when the tray clanged out. I hesitated, knowing that the girl would be just on the other side.

"It's okay, Dani. You don't have to be scared of me," she said. She was close-by, maybe only eight more bars down. My fingers continued counting the bars as I shuffled to the left towards her voice. As I drew closer, the scent of apple cinnamon filled my nose.

The smell grew stronger until I felt the brush of her hand. She wove her warm fingers through mine, hers only slightly longer. We stood like that for a while, connected silently through the bars—my shaking hand within her steady one.

In that moment, I knew—even before I said it out loud—she was a prisoner just like me. Except, she wasn't breathing heavily or slamming tinplates into metal hinges until her knuckles bled. The calmness in her voice told me she hadn't just arrived. "Why isn't it going to work?"

I felt her hand tighten as she paused. "Because Kayla tried everything to get out of there," she responded softly.

My heart stopped. I could hear waves crashing inside my ears. My cell was small, about twelve steps long and sixteen bars wide. I would have known if someone else was there with me. "But…then where's Kayla?" I heard myself ask.

"She went away." Something changed in her voice. I dropped the tinplate and reached my empty hand through the bars. This time, the girl didn't take it.

"My mom said that when people go away, they don't go too far. She said that if you close your eyes, you can see them standing right next to you," I said.

"Have you ever had someone go away?"

"Yeah. My great-aunt left me when I was five, but I didn't know her very well. The only things I remember are that she smelled like cigarettes and that she liked to eat a lot of cherries," I remarked.

"Spring used to be my favorite season. Me and my dad would go to Brooklyn to pick the cherries fresh off the trees." I didn't have to see her face to know that she was upset. Her voice said it all.

"Is that where you're from?"

"I grew up in Bronxville, but we used to go to Brooklyn a lot. It's what I'm named after."

"Brooklyn?"

"Yeah, but I like to be called Brook."

"Brook…how long have you been here?" She fell silent again.

I felt two fingers softly brush my left hand.

"Dani, I'm going to tell you something that I wish someone had told me in the beginning."

"Okay," I whispered. I tried to pretend that we were sitting in a dark closet, and she was about to tell me the secret to never getting caught in hide-and-go-seek.

"You've been kidnapped. You aren't going to see your family, and you aren't going home. He brought each of us here for a reason. I don't know what that is yet, but I do know he wants us for something. I want you to know that I will figure it out, and we're going to get out of here."

My black world somehow grew even darker as I felt myself fall backwards. An invisible force pulled my body towards the floor, and the waves in my ears washed over me. A final thought remained—I believed her. I just didn't know which part.

I woke up to three voices. Brook's was the only one I recognized. The other two were boys'.

"Did you really have to tell her the second she got here?" one of the boys hissed.

"She deserved to know. I didn't want to lie to her."

"The girl can figure it out on her own."

"No. The more she knows now the better it's going to be for her."

"Maybe she's right, Chet," the other boy said from nearby.

"It doesn't matter what we tell her. It's not going to change a damn thing," Chet said.

"No one helped me when I got here and look what good it did me," Brook said. The other two fell silent. The pause made me feel uncomfortable. I slowly opened my eyes, surprised to see a dim light showering the room. My head ached under its hazy glow. One side of my face lay stuck to the ground. A clump of dried mud neighbored an overturned plastic cup.

We were in some sort of basement but not the kind found in normal houses. There weren't any large water heaters or pipes that covered the ceiling. I couldn't find a single window, and it stank of dampness. Long lines of fluorescent lights divided the room, like the ones in my school classrooms. I could see other cells across from mine, but my eyes couldn't focus long enough to make out the details. There were six cells in all, a thin dirt pathway separating the two rows.

Pain shot through my neck as I tried to lift my head. I groaned, causing a girl to appear only moments later. She crouched on the other side of the metal bars that divided our two cells. Brook looked exactly as I had pictured her in my mind, except for her scattered freckles. Tiny, brown dots covered her cheeks and nose, looking as if someone had flicked a paintbrush over her face. She had long, jet-black hair, the kind that I had only ever seen on an American Girl doll. Her eyes were bright, blue crystals under the light that reminded me of my mom's.

Brook nervously peered at me through the bars. She cradled her right hand in her left arm as she hunched forward—her floppy fingers covered by a silky, white glove. Her matching white uniform contrasted with the dark, brown grit covering the floor.

"I'm sorry. I didn't mean for you to get upset," she said.

"It's okay," I replied, propping myself up. I attempted to brush the clumps of dirt from my face. Then I wiped my dusty hands on my shirt— the "My Little Pony" one Mom had given me for my tenth birthday.

"Are you mad at me?" she asked, squinting slightly as if waiting for an incoming blow.

"No...I want to figure it out, too." Slowly, a massive smile spread across her face. Scattered braces covered her teeth, their wires crooked between missing brackets. She looked as if she couldn't have been much older than I.

"Are you feeling okay? I think you hit your head," she asked worriedly.

"Um, my head does kind of hurt," I replied, feeling the large bump beside my left ear. "Do you have any more water?"

"I used all my water last night trying to wake you up. But you have a tank that's full over there," she said, pointing over my shoulder. I turned in that direction and took a closer look around me. My cell formed a perfect square, covered by metal bars on three sides. Stacked stones formed the fourth, reminding me of the castles in Nana's storybooks. The edge of my mattress rested against the solid wall. As Brook had said, a water tank filled one of the far corners. It was a cylinder, with a plastic pole stuck in the bottom. It reminded me of a giant version of the one Keely and I had for our hamster before he escaped from his cage. The water was cloudy, as if it had come from a mud puddle instead of a faucet.

There was a small dresser underneath the water tank. It was plastic, too, and had three drawers in it. I walked over and opened the top one. Underwear filled it to the brim, all stiff, clean, and white. Shirts of the same cotton filled the second one. I didn't have to open the third drawer to guess what was inside—sterile, white pajamas identical to Brook's.

"You will get used to it, Dani," I heard Brook say behind me. I couldn't look over at her. I didn't want to get used to it. The tears burned my eyes, and I hated myself for crying. Somehow, the thought that I may never wear green again upset me the most.

Once the tears had started, I worried they would never stop. I plopped down on top of the thin mattress and curled myself into a tight ball, keeping my head tucked between my kneecaps as I forced myself to count to fourteen. Mom had taught me that—to count when I was upset. She said that fourteen was the perfect number. "Ten is too short but anything past fifteen is just unlucky," she would say. "But by the time you reach fourteen, you forget why you started counting in the first place." That day was the first time I couldn't stop at fourteen. It wasn't until I reached two hundred that I felt my breathing begin to slow and my hands steady. I opened my eyes slowly, hoping the tears had fully dried up.

I could feel their eyes on me, but I kept mine focused on the tops of my knees instead of returning their gaze. From the corner of my eye, I could see Elmer's pink tail peeking out from under the bunched-up blanket. I stopped myself from reaching for him. He didn't deserve to be there. If he had belonged to any other kid, he could have been sitting on top of a big, fluffy pillow instead of jammed under a scratchy sheet.

"Psst. Hey, Dani," a voice drilled into the side of my head. It came from the boy whose name I didn't know. It wasn't until he called my name a second time that I finally looked up. He stood alone in the cell across from Brook's, swinging back and forth through the bars. His head was so small that it could slip between the spaces without getting stuck.

"Dani, do you know how to play Twenty Questions?" he asked. He was smiling, but not the real kind that made your eyes squint. However, I could see through the fake grin that there was a kindness to him.

"Yes. I like to play it when we're in the car," I responded. He didn't ask me about who "we" were, which I was glad about.

"Did you know that the number one thing people pick is a panda bear?" He didn't wait for me to reply. "I always wondered why people picked animals. Wouldn't you think that they would be the *last* things people would pick? Like, why wouldn't they choose something harder like bacteria or pastel paints? I mean, if I was ever going to pick an animal, I would at least go with an alpaca or just some really weird bug." His dark eyebrows came closer together as he talked. Just like Bumpy, he had the kind of face that didn't look angry no matter how hard he tried. It made me instantly like him.

"I think it's because we secretly want them to guess it right," I said quietly. His eyebrows shot back to their original position as he returned a smile that reached his eyes.

"But wouldn't that mean you lose?"

"As you can see, Kai isn't competitive at all," Brook said with a roll of her eyes.

"Says the girl who wouldn't talk to me for two days after I beat her at Jenga…three times in a row." Brook crossed her arms and glared at him, his smile growing wider. Even though she appeared angry, I knew that she didn't mean it. They acted just like Keely and me when we got on each other's nerves. We never could stay mad at each other for more than a couple hours. I could tell that Brook and Kai were the same way.

But everything else I couldn't understand. Why were we just standing there talking about Twenty Questions, joking about who was the most competitive? How could Kai just hang on the bars like he didn't care that they were there? When had that become normal for them? Maybe they were just pretending that everything was okay. My mom did that with her patients, the ones going through hard times. She would have them talk about what they had for lunch or if they had any fun plans for the weekend. They would talk about all the things that didn't matter so they wouldn't have to think about all the things that did.

I looked to the cell past Brook's and saw a girl lying in her bed reading a book. Her fire engine red hair spilled loosely over the edge. Unlike the rest of us, her mattress sat on a tall, white bedframe high above the ground. It was like the one that I was supposed to get when I turned thirteen. She had a lot more things in her cell than I did. There were two shelves, one completely filled with books. A thick, green throw rug covered the dirt floor, and a matching pearly desk and chair sat on top of it. Drawings covered her entire wall, all in only the brightest of colors. There must have been hundreds, which made me think: *that must have taken her years.*

I looked around at the remaining divisions of the large, rectangular room. The boy they called Chet stood in the cell across from the fire-haired girl. I noticed his cage was bare compared to hers, a flimsy floor mat the only thing that differed his cell from mine. Even leaning against the wall, I could tell he was taller than Topher—except he must have weighed half as much. His pasty uniform loosely hung from his wiry frame. He looked like the kids Mom said had a "fast metabolism." His skin appeared a faded tan, as if he had spent hours in a tub full of bleach. He glanced over at me occasionally but coldly looked away when our eyes would meet.

Finally, I noticed the cell across from mine. The light didn't quite reach the distant corners of the far wall, and shadows covered the sunken mattress. He sat with his back against the stone and tucked his knees tightly to his chest, the same as me. A blue Power Ranger sat slightly off to his left, but he didn't reach for it. He too was wearing a pristine, white jumpsuit. I looked more closely. His puffy eyes gave away his secret—he was new, as well.

"He hasn't said anything since he got here," Brook whispered to me. She leaned farther through our shared barred wall.

"How long has he been here?" I questioned, without taking my eyes from him.

"Two days. He doesn't really eat, and I don't think he's slept yet."

"Wait, what do we eat?" I asked, then looking to her. Until that moment, I didn't realize I was hungry. She looked up at a handwritten chart that hung above her mattress. Next to it was another diagram, which I recognized as a calendar. The boxes and dates were drawn in marker, the top half covered in X's.

"Oh, today we are getting alfredo pasta!" she said a little too excitedly.

"Well, how do we get it?" I asked, hoping it wouldn't involve the man with the over-sized boots.

"It comes down through those things," she said as she pointed to a clear pipe near her bed that stretched from floor to ceiling. "It just shoots right down, and when you are done with it, you just shoot it right back up!" she said lightheartedly, as if trying to make me feel better about it. But nothing could make me feel good about my food coming from a tube. That was only cool if you lived in Willy Wonka's factory, and we definitely weren't there.

I didn't know how I hadn't noticed them before. The tall, plastic cylinders entered each cell, exiting through large holes in the stone just beneath the ceiling. Each had a little window near the floor, between a red and green button on either side. They looked like the long tubes at the hospital where my mom worked, except bigger. Mom once showed me how they worked using a small cylinder with secret notes inside. I remembered how, seconds later, it was sucked up and disappeared into the piping. I hadn't thought of the container-sucking tube until then.

"Don't worry, it isn't hard to use. I can show you how," she said, as if she hoped I wouldn't start crying again. I nodded my okay.

"Brook, can I ask you somethin'?"

"Of course you can." I walked over to her to whisper in her ear so the others wouldn't hear me.

"Brook, where am I supposed to...ya know, go to the bathroom?" Her face dropped at my question.

"Well, there is a nice bathroom that we use when we get let out, but sometimes we have to use the pit if we can't hold it."

"The pit?" I asked. Instead of answering, she swung to her feet and walked over to a rock next to her mattress. She shoved the large stone a little ways to the left, uncovering a dark hole in the ground.

"It goes down a long ways so you don't have to worry about the smell," she said as she kicked some dirt over the edge to prove it to me. "But I would still keep the rock over your pit just in case."

I looked around my cell. Sure enough, I found a rock in the same place as Brook's. I sat back down on my mattress as my head became heavy again. *My mattress*. It started to sink in that it would be where I would sleep—where I would live.

"I took some extras from the real bathroom so I have more than enough to share," she said, passing a roll of toilet paper through the bars. When I didn't get up to grab it, she placed it carefully on top of the dirt.

"Brook, when you said 'when we get let out,' does that mean that *he* is going to come down here?" I asked in a shaky voice.

"Yes. You are going to see him again." She waited for a few seconds, giving me time to let it sink in. "There is one thing you need to remember. You can't forget it, okay?"

"Okay." My voice sounded small.

"He wears a gold chain. It has a cross on it, and you need to make sure to look for it. When he is wearing his cross, you don't have to be scared—he isn't going to hurt you."

"Brook, can you seriously stop? Just *stop* for Chrissake!" Chet said from his corner. He paced back and forth, digging his hands through his overgrown, brown hair.

"What happens when he takes it off?" I whispered, ignoring him. Brook bit down on her bottom lip.

"You just do what he wants, and you don't ask questions." It was the girl with the fire hair who answered. Until then, I hadn't realized that she was standing up and facing me. She had bright, green eyes, like a woman I had seen on the cover of a *National Geographic* magazine. Her skin was the color of Snow White's, making it difficult to know where her jumpsuit began and her body ended. She reminded me of the marble angel Keely and I saw every summer at vacation bible school.

No one, not even Brook, said anything for a while. I got the feeling that the green-eyed angel didn't speak very often. Bumpy told me that I should listen when someone quiet had something to say—that it usually was important. I believed him because that was exactly how I felt about Keely.

Brook had started to speak when a loud hiss came from my large pipe. Seconds later, something shot through it. The red button lit up when a box landed at the bottom.

"Oh, good! Your alfredo is finally here!" Brook said a little too cheerfully. "Here, I will show you how to work it." She motioned me towards the package, and I knelt down in front of the pipe's window. "Okay, so you first have to press the red button to open it up. It won't open unless you hit that, because it has to let the air out." I did as she told. A warm breeze escaped from the tube's sides a moment later. It smelled like a mixture of garlic and the inside of a Barbie box.

Once the air stopped, Brook gave me the okay to lift up the window. A plastic container sat inside. It was divided into two parts and was about the same size as Nana's sewing box. There was a note taped to its top, enclosed in a small envelope. On the front, in thin, red lines, it read: **From Dias.**

I couldn't bring myself to see what was inside. I ripped it off and handed it to Brook, watching closely as she opened it. She removed the small slip of paper, acting as if she already knew what was on it.

"What does it say?" I asked uneasily. Nervously, I held the container close to me. I could feel the warmth inside. It was the first time since waking up there that I felt anything but cold.

"Pandora," she read, holding the paper up towards the light. It was written in permanent marker, the black, thick lines bleeding through to the other side. "It is what he is going to call you," she added offhandedly. My face started to feel warm, but it wasn't because of the food. It was because I was angry. I was angry that he thought he could just write it on a piece of paper and make me into anything he wanted.

"My name is Dani." I didn't say it because I was confused. I said it so that everyone would know I wouldn't be anything but Dani Millen.

"I know. We all have one—a name that he calls us. But no matter what, we will always know you as Dani. I promise." I nodded my head and tried to give her a little smile.

As much as I didn't want to eat his food, my stomach gurgled the moment I first smelled it. I placed the container down on my bed and opened its top. Inside was a plastic fork and spoon—the type that bent easily and usually broke off against hard ice cream. There was also a linen napkin, the frilly kind that reminded me of fancy restaurants. I wanted to throw it in the dirt the second I saw it.

Its sauce didn't taste as good as Dad's, because it had fake cheese on top. But it was at least better than the food from school. The garlic smell filled the stuffy basement as the food shot down to the others. Brook and Kai sat cross-legged, facing each other as they ate. I listened as they talked about a book they both had read, confusing me with how Brad wasn't good enough for Patrick and how Sam and Charlie were soul mates, they just didn't know it yet. Chet and the other girl—the redhead they called Clara—didn't act like Brook and Kai, though. They sat on opposite ends of their cells, and neither spoke as they ate their dinners alone.

The boy across from me quietly watched me eat. He took the container out of his tube but didn't open it. Instead, he simply let it lay in front of him. His eyes gave away his hunger, as he followed my hand every time I brought the noodles to my mouth. He had moved a little bit into the light, revealing his small face that hid beneath a thick mop of blonde waves. There was a swirl in the front that made his hair stick up on end. It must have driven his mother crazy that she could never make it lay flat.

Even though I was in a room with five other people, I felt completely alone. It was the first meal I had ever had without Keely. I felt badly for thinking it, but more than anything, I wished that she could have been there with me.

I started drawing lines in the dirt with my fingertip, tallying up the number of meals I had eaten in my life. Before long, I began running out of room, which made me regret that I had even started counting in the first place. It didn't make me feel better seeing all those tallies surrounding me. They reminded me that from then on, I had to count for something entirely different. After a short while, I rubbed away all the marks in the ground, turning it back into a plain dirt floor. Then, with the end of my plastic fork, I drew a single line.

I let the rest of my food go cold. Brook showed me how to send it back up the tube after she had finished hers. I reassembled the container into its original form. Brook double-checked that I had done it correctly, making sure nothing would leak out on its way back up. She wouldn't tell me why that was important. I placed the container inside the window and hit the green button, watching it disappear into the plastic pipe.

After dinner, I lay down on my lumpy mattress. The fluorescent lights seemed dimmer than before, and I tried to focus on their soft hum instead of how badly I needed to go to the bathroom. I glanced at the rock covering my pit but forced the idea out of my head.

When I thought that I couldn't hold it any longer, a long, achy creak came from the other side of the room. I shot up in bed and watched a blinding light slowly crawl into Chet and Kai's cells. The brightness led to a doorway I hadn't noticed before. I prayed it had only opened by accident, crossing my fingers so tightly behind my back that they began to tingle.

Then he stepped into the doorway. The tall man filled the entire space, blocking out the light with his large, black shadow.

I flew back to the far end of my mattress and pulled the covers tightly over my head. I tucked the blanket under my body, just like Keely and I did to keep the monsters away. Mom had said that the boogieman couldn't get us under the covers. But this time it didn't work. The blanket wasn't a shield; it was just a flimsy rag. I closed my eyes tightly, trying to bring the lie back to life. Over and over, I repeated, "It's just me and Keely here in this room. It's just me and Keely here in this room. It's just me and Keely here in this room."

At first I thought it had worked. I listened closely, but all I heard was silence outside of my fabric shell.

Ting. Ting. Ting. It didn't sound like the droplets from before. *Ting. Ting. Tingtingtingting.* I recognized the sound. It reminded me of how I used to stop the park merry-go-round with my hand when it spun too quickly— the ting, ting, ting as my hand tapped from one pole to the next. The only difference was this sound was louder. It echoed outside of my sheet, like someone using a hard stick instead of a hand to stop the ride.

Then it all came together. Someone was outside my cell, dragging metal across the bars that caged me in.

"Pandora, there is no need to be afraid." The false softness of his voice reminded me of how grown-ups talked to little kids. I didn't move, hoping he would just go away. But then the tapping stopped. I heard the door creak and the sudden crash of the cell as it closed.

Even though I couldn't hear his footsteps on the dirt floor, I knew he was in there with me. It was the same way that I knew when the school bus was only five minutes away or how I could sense when it was just about to rain.

I tightened my grip on the blanket, but it didn't matter. The sheet quickly slipped through my fingers as he whipped it off me. I started screaming, shrinking myself into a tight ball.

"Please! Please let me come in! I can help her!" Brook shouted over my screams.

He wrenched my shoulders, pulling me towards him. With his giant hand, he grasped and lifted my jaw, forcing me to look into the stone eyes from my blurry nightmares.

"*Enough*," he said in a hiss, the voice for children completely gone.

My mouth froze open, but the next scream remained lodged inside my throat. His fingers began to slowly loosen.

"Good. That's a good girl, Pandora," he said, as if I was his brand new puppy who had just sat for the first time. "You will learn to not fear me. I am not going to hurt you." My eyes drifted to the gold cross hanging from his neck, reminding me of Brook's advice. *He won't hurt you if he is wearing his cross.* It should have made me feel better, but it didn't. Maybe it was the long metal pole that hung from his belt or the fact that his fingers still dug into my skin as he inspected my face. Either way, I knew that it would be best if I did as he said.

"Now that we have that settled, follow me." He released his grasp and took the metal rod off his belt. I tried to do as he told, but my feet stuck to the floor, like dried superglue. I looked over at Brook. Her arms were extended out through the bars, reaching for me. There were tears in her eyes; somehow, that made me feel better. It reminded me that I wasn't alone.

I felt myself rise and walk towards him. My legs felt like they belonged to someone else, moving before my mind told them to leave the mattress. I walked through the open entrance of my cell, so focused on the pole in his hand that I didn't see the raised metal edge. Stubbing my bare foot, I fell face-first into the cell across from mine. However, instead of hitting the metal bars as I had prepared for, I fell into open arms. They didn't feel strong like my dad's, but they were still able to hold me.

It was the boy with the golden hair. He had his head pressed against the bars, reaching his arms as far as he could into the open space. Even after I found my balance, he didn't let me go. He helped me up through the bars, his arms wrapped securely around my back. It only lasted for a moment, but it felt like a hug.

"Let's go, Pandora." He sounded irritated, like my fourth-grade teacher, Ms. Botts, when I tried to stay on the swings an extra minute past recess.

The boy shot back from me, as if he had touched a steaming pan. "Thank you," I whispered into the shadows. He didn't reply, but I knew he heard me.

As I walked past Brook's cell, she reached out and grabbed my hand. She silently slipped something inside, squeezing my hand twice before letting go. I felt the metal string between my fingers before shoving it into my pocket. The bad man looked back at me as we walked through the door's opening and into the bright light.

The hallway looked nothing like the dirt jail. I felt like I was in a hospital. Spotless, white walls formed the narrow passage. I looked at my reflection in the shiny, blank tiles covering the floors. They seemed to go on forever down the long hallway, under the fluorescent ceiling squares. There were five doors on each side of the hall, all leading to places that I couldn't imagine. The doors were polished metal, newer than the kind that made up my cell. Each had a slotted handle, the type that hotels had for plastic keycards.

But the door at the opposite end of the hallway was different. It was blood red. As we drew closer, I noticed dark, metal pegs extending up either side. A white keypad with black numbers sat above a coal-colored lever. I hoped with everything in my bones that he wasn't taking me there. Instead, we stopped two doors down from the dirty jail. He inserted a white keycard, opening one of the metal doors on the right and pointing inside.

"Come along," he said, returning to his nice voice. A smile appeared, his teeth sharp and crooked but all a clean white. It was a smile that reminded me of the creepy clowns in a carnival fun house—the kind that only crazy people wore. It made the black holes spread like a hundred evil eyes over his cheeks.

I had only ever seen one crazy person before. He was one of my mom's patients, but they had to take him away to a special hospital after he tried to hurt someone. I remembered the first time I saw him. It was in the waiting room of my mom's office. Keely and I were out sick from school that day, and Mom had run in to grab some files before taking us home. He was sitting next to the magazine pile, and we were in the back corner by the fake tree.

I usually didn't stare at people, especially at my mom's office. She told me it was rude, that most people couldn't help that they were sick. I liked to believe that they just wanted to get better. But there was something about that man that made me believe he wasn't there to fix the badness inside. A pretty woman sat across from him, but she didn't notice his stare. He held a magazine in his lap, but I could tell he wasn't looking at the pages. Instead, he was focused on her. I didn't really know what it all meant, the way he licked his lips each time she re-crossed her legs or the way he rubbed his thigh underneath the magazine. But what I did know was that he had something evil stuck inside of him, and he wanted to use it on that pretty lady.

"Pandora. Come," he said firmly, snapping me out of my buried memories. I heard a buzzing sound as he spoke, a white spark coming from his metal pole. There were two points extending from the end of it, making me think of the sticks I used for roasting marshmallows. The longer I stood there, the more I could tell he was trying too hard to keep his fake smile. He may not have been looking at me the same way that man looked at the lady, but I knew he too had the badness trapped inside of him.

I walked forward like he had asked, hoping he wouldn't make his stick buzz again. Staying close to the wall, I kept my eyes on him the entire way.

It was a small room, just big enough to fit a shower in one corner and a toilet in the other. There was a sink against the far wall, but it didn't have a mirror like a normal bathroom. The room had a mild bleach scent that stung my eyes and nose. Its white walls and flooring matched the sterile hallway, and fluorescent lights flooded it as well. A clear, plastic box stood against the wall beside the shower. I could see the white clothes that filled its insides.

"In five minutes, the water will come on. It will stay on for ten minutes. You have twenty minutes, and then I will be back." Before I could say anything, he had already shut the door. I waited for the tap of his boots to fade off down the hallway before I ran to the door. There was a part of me that thought the door would be unlocked. I stared at the unlit green dot above the empty card slot, pleading for it to light up. Despite pushing its handle up and down over and over again, it wouldn't move. Somehow, I felt more trapped in there than in my dingy jail cell.

I slid down the door to rest on the ground. The tile felt cool beneath me, and something poked into my bottom. I felt for it inside my back pocket, pulling out the long metal chain. It was a necklace—the one Brook had slipped into my hand. It wasn't covered in shiny rocks or fancy diamonds. The silver chain appeared old and worn, ending in a silvery pendant. I traced the thin, long metal lines inside the oval charm, wondering at first if it was a spider web. But as I looked more closely, I noticed the upside down trunk. It was a tree—a cherry tree to be exact. The branches looked like they could have gone on forever if they hadn't been captured inside the thin ring. I scanned over the charm, almost missing the writing carved into three of the branches. The words blended with the weaving lines of the bark. But slowly the cursive took shape, and the words became clear. It read: **We'll Stand Together**.

I sat there for a while—just reading those three, separate words.

We'll.

Stand.

Together.

I heard the shower come on, but I didn't move during its ten-minute cycle. I wasn't ready to take my clothes off, knowing that meant I would have to put the white ones on.

I pulled the necklace over my head and let myself feel its weight on my neck.

It felt nice, the warm steam rising from the shower. Swirls of damp clouds surrounded me, and just for a little while, I imagined I was up in the sky, in a place far, far away. There weren't any metal bars or door handles that wouldn't turn. The floors weren't made of dirt, and there wasn't any white in sight. I felt my breathing start to slow as I let myself be in that place. And I thought, maybe if I got to go there, even for just twenty minutes a day, I could be okay.

The water stopped, reminding me that I only had five minutes left. I tried to keep it out, but the fear crept its way back in. Moving to the far corner of the bathroom, I wedged myself between the toilet and the wall. I waited for him to come back, promising myself that he would still be wearing his golden cross.

He knocked before he came in. As he opened the door, I kept my head lowered so I didn't have to face the steely eyes I felt glaring into my skull.

"Get up," he said, his voice emotionless. I heard his boots tap towards me as I tried to sink further into the tiny space. "I will not ask again." The buzzing began, growing louder in the background. I felt my body push itself out of my hiding place, my head drooping forward as I rose.

"Good. Now I want you to listen closely. This is the only time I am going to do this. I'm going to run it again. When that water comes on, you are going to take off those piss-smelling clothes, get in that shower, and put on your clean ones. If you do not, then I will come in here and wash you myself." His hand opened and closed around his gold chain as he spoke. I couldn't get rid of the feeling that he was about to pull it off his neck at any moment.

The thought of him washing me made my stomach sick. I used to love when Nana washed Keely and me in the bathtub when we were younger. She used a soft sponge that looked like a rock straight from the ocean. But I knew that it wouldn't be like that. He wouldn't be anything like Nana. It would hurt, and there wouldn't be stories of mermaids or treasure boxes from the bottom of the sea.

I nodded my head to show him I understood. He walked out without saying a word, but I didn't run to the door after he left. I simply stood there, looking down at the large, darkened circle below the zipper of my jeans. There was something unsettling about discovering that wet spot. It was like the time I woke up with my pajamas on inside out, even though I wouldn't have gone to bed with the sewn on Minnie Mouse poking into my skin. It scared me—the thought of losing control of myself. I tried to pass the mark off as some old stain, even though I could feel the sogginess of my underwear and my pants stuck to my leg.

Suddenly, my clothes felt as if they were too small for my body, tightening around me. I began ripping them off until I reached my dirty underwear. There was something uncomfortable about being naked in a room I didn't know. It reminded me of elementary school physicals, standing in line with the other girls in only my Little Mermaid undies. Somehow, that one tiny piece of cotton made it a little bit easier.

The water felt steaming hot when it shot on, and there weren't any handles to adjust the temperature. I forced myself under the showerhead, knowing I didn't have much time. I covered my mouth to hold in the sound. My body never adjusted to the pain, as the pelting water prickled my body and stung the colder area around my neck that held Brook's necklace.

There was a shelf next to the shower full of shampoos and soaps in big plastic jars. They all smelled of apple cinnamon, the same scent that I had noticed on Brook. But it didn't seem to matter how hard I scrubbed or how much soap I used, I couldn't get the apple smell to stick to my skin. I couldn't wash off the stench of dirt and musty blanket.

In the middle of cleaning the dirt from my feet, the water suddenly shut off. Not a single, extra drop fell from the showerhead. I grabbed a scratchy, white towel from a cubby on the wall, my wet underwear quickly soaking it all the way through. I slipped off my panties, holding the towel tightly around me and grabbing a fresh pair from the bin. They were too big on me and sagged down like a diaper, making me feel like the kid from *The Jungle Book*.

The white clothes smelled like the inside of a medicine cabinet. They were stiff and rough against my skin. The socks were long and bunched up inside the brand-new shoes set out for me. They were at least two sizes too big. I wondered if they were meant for someone else or if I was supposed to grow into them.

He didn't knock when he entered the second time. He gave me another too-wide smile that didn't reach his cold eyes. "The white suits you, little one," he said, acting as if I had chosen the clothes myself. "Now come along," he finished as he motioned for me to follow him.

The man led me into a room two doors closer to the blood-red door. Inside was a short, rectangular metal table. Two matching steel chairs appeared on each side, one large and the other small. The only color in the room was from a large poster placed on the wall, the kind that usually hung in a counselor's office. It had a quote in bright letters about attitude with a picture of two baby elephants that seemingly had nothing to do with the words.

He had me sit in the small seat across from him. My wet hair dripped down the back of my shirt and made me feel cold all over. I looked at my wavy reflection in the shiny table, hearing the slow movement of him breathing in and out. He leaned towards me with his hands folded in front of him, close enough to reach out and grab me. I tried to push myself further into my tiny chair.

"Have you ever heard the story about the girl named Pandora?" I kept my head down, slowly shaking no. "Well, she was a young woman who was curious, like you. One day, she was given a gift—a box—that she was told not to open. She wasn't told what would happen to her if she disobeyed, only that she wasn't allowed to look inside. You see, it was a test for her, to see if she was strong enough to overcome her curiosity. Now, what do you think happened next in the story?"

"She opened it," I mumbled.

"Yes. She opened it. And what do you think it was that she found?" I shrugged my shoulders. I didn't care about Pandora or her stupid box of hidden things. I didn't like how he acted as if the girl and I were the same person, as if he knew anything about me. "Inside she found all the bad things in the world. Disease, sickness, hate, envy, evil—all the things that would plague mankind 'til the end of time. She released all that badness out into the world simply because she was just a little too curious."

My ankles started to itch underneath my socks, making me think of the cinnamon soap still between my toes. I wanted to reach down to scratch them, but I forced myself to stay still. Out of the corner of my eye, I saw his fingers occasionally flick back and forth over his hands. His nails were manicured, with fingers red and raw, as if they had been cleaned too many times.

"There is a part of the story that I left out. Would you like me to tell you?" I kept my lips tightly shut. I *was* curious, and I hated that I needed to know the answer—even more than how I hated the way he acted like he knew me. He began to laugh. It was a terrible sound that stayed in the back of his throat, reminding me of grinding meat.

"It's a funny thing, curiosity. Most people spend their whole lives trying to figure out only what is in front of them, and they miss all the things just out of reach. They never wonder about what they don't understand. Like how can one cancerous cell become strong enough to kill an entire body? Or how does a tiny, green sprout grow into a tree that is two hundred feet tall? You see, if it weren't for curious people, we wouldn't have these questions. We wouldn't have any chance at the answers." He opened his hands as if the answers would be inside. Instead, all I found were seven circular, red scars trapped inside his palms.

"I admire curiosity, even if it leads to bad things like our dear Pandora," he said. It made me wonder if he was still talking about the girl from the story. "Now, you still haven't asked for the end of the story, my little Pandora." *My little Pandora*, like I was a toy he kept on the shelf until he chose to play with it again.

I wanted to scream. I wanted to yell my name over and over so that he would stop calling me Pandora. I wanted to dig my nails into his round scars until they started to bleed again. But most of all, I wanted to prove that I would never belong to him.

I looked up at him for the first time since he had brought me into the room. He appeared surprised when I stared him straight in the eyes. I gave him my most defiant look, the one I had given to only one other person. His name was Connor, and he was a grade older than Keely and me. He was known as the biggest bully in the entire middle school, and I knew the exact moment he set his sights on Keely. We were in the lunchroom on the second day of sixth grade. As she walked by him, she accidently knocked a milk carton off her tray; Connor noticed. He always chose the kids he'd bully in the first week, and I wasn't going to let Keely be one of them. Right when he started towards her, I stepped in front of him. He was taller than I was and could have easily pushed me out of the way. But he didn't. In that moment, I could tell he was scared of me. He thought about saying something, but in the end, he turned around and went back to his seat. Instead, he ended up choosing a small redheaded boy and never looked at Keely again.

"My, my, you aren't like the others now are you?" he said with a crooked smile. I wiped the look off my face and brought my eyes back down to my lap. I didn't want him to think I was different. I didn't want to be his favorite toy. I wanted to be the one that he left alone and put at the bottom of the toy chest.

"The part of the story that I left out was that not everything escaped from the box when Pandora opened it. She forced it shut as she saw all of the bad things getting out, leaving just one thing stuck inside. Do you know what it was?"

You, I thought silently to myself.

"It was hope," he continued without waiting for my answer. "The spirit of hope was the only thing left inside Pandora's box."

"Was it able to get out?" I was surprised by my voice, the words spilling out before I could stop them.

The bad man went completely silent. I forced myself to look up at him again, instantly regretting it. One hundred of his evil, empty eyes stared back at me.

I didn't need him to tell me the answer, because I already knew it. Hope was still trapped at the bottom of Pandora's box the same way I was trapped inside his. And I didn't know if I was ever going to find my way out.

By the time he brought me back to the room of cells, the lights on the ceiling were dimmed again. The others were in bed, but I knew that they weren't asleep. The dank air was too still—even sleeping people weren't that quiet.

I walked ahead of him this time, counting down the seconds it took for me to be back in my cage and away from him. He pulled out a big ring of keys, like the ones my school janitor had for all of the classrooms. But these keys looked bigger, older—the kind that had a puzzle piece on the end of the thick metal. They all looked the same to me, except for different colored flags of tape attached to their loops. The key for my cell was the purple one—Keely's favorite color. I promised myself it was a good sign.

The moment the door opened, I ran to my mattress. "I changed your sheet because of your little *accident*," he said, making me feel like that little puppy again. With that, he disappeared back into the brightness of the hallway.

After he was finally gone, I let myself cry. I released the badness that had been building inside. I let my breath move hard and fast, as if I had finally resurfaced from the bottom of a dark ocean.

"Dani, are you okay?" Brook had returned to her spot near our bars. This time, she had a stuffed elephant wedged in the crook of her arm. "Did he take you to the attitude room? What did he say to you?"

I didn't want to talk about it and continued to cry in long, loud sobs. She didn't say anything else, but I was sure she would ask me again the next day. I would have to go through it all over again—more meals shooting from plastic pipes and showers too hot for cold bodies. Maybe I would cry less. Maybe I would find a way to be okay. But that night...I was alright with not letting it be okay. I could be angry and feel badly for myself. But the next day, or maybe the day after, I would find a way out.

As Brook started to head back to her mattress, I remembered I was still wearing her chain.

"Brook, here's your necklace back," I said, while starting to take it off.

"No, you keep it for now. You need it more than I do," she said with a sad smile.

"Is it from your Dad?"

"Yeah, he got it for me after my mom died."

"It's really pretty." I didn't know what else to say. I wasn't good at talking about people after they had died.

"It's from a song, you know. We'll stand together? An old guy named Ricky Jenks wrote it, but maybe only people around my town would know that. He started writing love songs ever since he got cancer, and my dad thought he had the most beautiful voice."

"How did it go?" I asked quietly.

"*There will come a day when things get lost and taken away. But we'll stand together, and we'll carry on,*" she sang softly. Even though I didn't know the song, it still sounded pretty the way she sang it. For a moment, she looked happy. But then I saw the exact instant when she started missing him. Her face looked like a landslide as the smile quickly fell off. She forced it back on when she saw that I had noticed.

When she lay down in bed, her soft hum filled the emptiness of the room. I listened to her as the lights continued to gradually dim back to black. Even though I didn't know the words, I tried to fill them in with my own. In the slow parts, I heard my dad's voice, telling me that I was his shining star—the one that made all the others make sense. I heard my mom in the high parts, telling me I was the reason all of her hairs were turning gray. Mom sang it in her I-hate-it-but-I-love-it voice. And during the quiet moments, the times when Brook paused before letting the next verse come, I thought of Keely. She didn't need to say anything for me to know that she was a part of me, and I was a part of her. We would always be three even when we were apart. No person was going to change that.

"Dani." I had been concentrating so closely on the song inside my head that I didn't realize the little boy was talking to me. He sat near the edge of his cage, the one closest to mine. I opened my mouth to say his name before realizing that I didn't know it. "Mika. My name is Mika," he said, reading the exact thought inside my head. He had a kind voice, the type that belonged in an animated movie instead of a dark place.

"You just got here too?" I asked, already knowing the answer.

"Yeah, just a little bit before you. I think two days."

After a long pause, I blurted, "Do you think we'll ever get out of here?" It wasn't the question I had planned on asking him.

"Yes," he said, slow and hard. I could hear the anger in his voice.

For the first time since I was taken, I smiled.

I fell asleep with Brook's song in my head. *There will come a day when things get lost and taken away. But we'll stand together, and we'll carry on.* The words slid into my mind like a fortune slipped through the crack of a Chinese cookie. I just hoped that nothing would break it open and steal it away.

That night I dreamed of boxes. They all had a keyhole like the one in my cell door. I had their keys in my hand, all of them marked with white tape. I opened one after another, leaving each top hanging open. After every box I opened, I would hear another child start to scream. They became louder and louder with each one, but I couldn't stop. I kept unlocking the boxes and looking at the bottom, searching for what Pandora had trapped inside. But hope was nowhere to be found.

Chapter Three
September 12, 2001

I never used to care about the details. It hadn't occurred to me that it took exactly three hundred and seventy-two steps to get from the bus to my locker and an extra seventy-eight to reach my homeroom on the second floor. I never noticed that the picture Dani drew for me three years ago was actually a drawing of an elephant, not a rhino. I didn't see that two of the sticky glow-in-the-dark stars had fallen off our bedroom ceiling, something Dani would have noticed because it completely screwed up the Little Dipper. The details just didn't seem to matter until they did. Like the fact that it took 1,440 minutes for September 12 to be over or the fact that my dad's office was located on the eighty-ninth floor of his building.

They said that all it took was nineteen people and four airplanes. American Airlines Flight 11 left Logan airport in Boston at 7:59 a.m. with ninety-two people on board, taking only forty-seven minutes to crash straight into the North Tower of the World Trade Center. Everyone thought it must have been a mistake, a glitch in the flight plan. It wasn't until seventeen minutes later when a second plane crashed into its sister tower that everyone knew.

We were at Allaire State Park's Historical Village in East Jersey— Dani's favorite place to visit—when it all happened. I was in the carpenter's shop watching a man make his own hammer out of wood when I heard a woman begin to scream outside. The sound instantly stiffened my spine. My hands dug deeper into my pockets, a reaction I had yet to grow used to. The lady was shouting something over and over, but I couldn't make out the words. She stood in the middle of the village's dirt road, her puppet arms dangling limply as an older man propped her up. All I wanted to do was get away, but I followed my mom towards the open doorway.

It was the first time I had heard the words "terrorist attacks." I didn't really understand what it all meant. What I did know was that a plane had crashed right into my daddy's building. Before my mother could stop me, I began to run. I could hear her yelling my name as she chased after me, but I was already too far ahead of her.

It wasn't until I reached the Village's entrance that I saw his blue hat floating atop the crowds of people. I pushed my way through the mob, doing whatever I could to get past them. It was next to the roasted peanut stand that I finally reached him. I ran and wrapped my arms around his middle, knocking the picnic basket out of his hand.

"Why hello, doll. You missed me already?" he said as he locked his arms around my back. I didn't know what to say, so I just squeezed him tighter. Mom eventually found us, she too unable to find the words to tell him. She hugged him with me sandwiched in the middle, a place that I had come to know far too well in the last year.

For the first time since that night, I felt Dani there with us. She was there, telling me in her know-it-all voice, "See, I told you it would all work out." I didn't know what to feel in that moment, because the only reason he was still there was because she wasn't. If it wasn't for the anniversary of Dani's disappearance, we wouldn't have been there in the first place, pretending she had never gone missing.

I remembered watching the footage on a small television in the general store—the three of us huddled around its thirteen-inch screen along with a group of crying strangers. The burning rubble and thundering explosions felt out of place among the shelves of bonnets and glossy clay souvenirs. I watched my dad more than I watched the screen, taking in every flinch and shallow breath. He couldn't seem to let go of my mother, who kept her face buried in his chest.

It wasn't until the next day, the one-year mark of Dani's kidnapping, that I fully realized the impact of what had happened. Like me, he had become the one left behind. He lost sixty-seven coworkers that day—people who were a part of his life all suddenly vanished.

I used to think that the greatest talent of any magician was his ability to make something disappear right in front of my eyes. I was too caught up in the poof of smoke and slip of his hands to even think about what it all meant. What I had come to realize was that the real miracle wasn't in his ability to take it away but rather in his ability to bring it back.

I would have given anything for the ability to bring her back.

Two days after Dani went missing, I went back to our tree house. It was different than I had remembered. Yellow tape surrounded the entire forest opening, and trails of crushed leaves led to nowhere. Another wooden plank had broken off of the ladder nailed to our tree, most likely due to a grown-up trespassing on our private place. It took me a little longer to make my way up without Dani there to give me a boost, but I eventually entered our special space. The room felt different, our favorite things disturbed. I found my feather collection scattered atop Dani's stuffed animals and a part of my pog collection mixed in with my dice box. The police must have taken some things. All I could think about was how upset Dani was going to be when she found out someone had removed her favorite elephant—the one she called "Blue." I knew that I shouldn't have told them that Elmer had gone missing. Maybe then I wouldn't have lost our special hideout, too.

Once I climbed down from the tree house, it didn't take long for me to find Dani's pile of leaves. There were a couple stray ones that had been kicked from the mound, but most of her collection was still preserved. I rested on the same root she had sat on, leaning against the cool, rough tree trunk. A piece of bark pushed into my back, and I let the pain creep into my body.

I stared at the pile of leaves for a long time. I thought about what each leaf meant to Dani and tried to imagine her reason for picking each one. The longer I looked, the more the beautiful reds and yellows began to fade. They eventually turned into all the others—just another pile of rusty, dead leaves.

It only took four hours for me to become a missing person. I wasn't thinking about my parents when I went to the tree house or that they would go through the pain all over again when they realized I was gone, too. After it all, I heard that my mom had searched the streets of Reading, yelling my name over and over. I was gone for almost nine hours before they found me at four in the morning. It felt like nine minutes to me—nine endless minutes trying to figure out why he hadn't taken me.

The last place they looked was the tree house. They must have thought that a normal kid wouldn't go back to the place where it all happened. At first, I didn't hear the yelling or notice the lights crisscrossing through the forest. It wasn't until I heard my father's voice that I finally looked up.

"I see her! Oh my God, I see her! Over here—I see her!" The blinding beams hit me all at once, as if I was a runaway prisoner spotted in a jail courtyard. My dad reached me first, his flashlight creating shadows that made his eyes look swollen and raw. He pulled me into his arms, and it wasn't until I felt his warmth that I realized I was ice cold. All I had on was a pair of khaki shorts and my favorite Snoopy T-shirt, the one that read, "Happiness is Peanuts." I must have been shaking, as I felt someone throw a blanket around me, my dad still holding me inside his arms.

When Mom reached me, she threw her arms around both of us, the same way she later did that fateful morning at Allaire. Only that time, she wasn't screaming.

"Keely, what were you thinking? Why did you leave us? Don't you know how much we need you?" The questions kept pouring from the voice muffled against my back.

"He never came. I thought he was going to, but he didn't. He didn't come back for me," I heard myself say.

"Keely, no baby," Dad said. "Don't say that. Oh God, please don't say that." We kept on like that for a while, my parents taking turns telling me how much they needed me to stay. I didn't say anything back—I just let them carry me out of the woods and away from the darkness.

We stayed in Reading for two more weeks, hoping for any kind of news. It was a lot of waiting and dead ends. The police told us that there was a kidnapping that happened a few days before Dani's, about sixty miles north of Reading, but they didn't think the two were connected.

In the beginning, we all thought we were going to find her. The police kept telling us that they had a "good feeling" about their chances and that they found a full boot print in the woods. It was in a size a lot bigger than a normal shoe—a size thirteen. Apparently, that made it easier to find someone. But all I could think about was how there must have been more than a hundred boots in the shoe store at the mall. How were they supposed to find that one, exact boot?

They sent out an alert named after a girl called Amber. When I asked my dad why they picked her name, he said it was because she was famous for being the best at hide-and-go-seek—that she was the best at finding people. It wasn't until I snuck on his computer late one night that I learned the real reason. Amber Hagerman was a nine-year-old girl who was kidnapped in Texas five years before Dani and was found dead in a ditch a couple days later. I should have known he was lying to me because things don't get named after people unless they are dead.

Dani's picture appeared on printed posters all over New England, even showing up on the news for a few days. The picture had been taken the previous summer while we were at the State Fair. I sat next to her in the photo, but they cut me out completely, all except for my hand. People may not have noticed, but our fingers were tangled together into our double cross.

The hardest part was that none of it helped. All it brought were strangers who stared a little longer and phone calls to our house from people my parents only ever heard from in a yearly Christmas card.

It wasn't that the posters or news bulletins weren't working. I had been approached six times in those first three weeks as "the little girl from the poster." Grown-ups always seemed to notice when something bad happened, so it wasn't because people weren't paying attention. Rather, she must have been in a place where no one could see her.

At first, the police were convinced she had been kidnapped for something they called "ransom." It basically meant that the man had taken her just so that he could sell her back to us. Everyone said it was what made the most sense; they could find no other reason. They said it didn't seem planned or thought-out—that a man just followed two kids into the woods and decided to take one of them. But all I could think was, *why would someone just walk around with a needle in his pocket?*

It didn't make sense to me. We were just a normal family. My mother had shown up in a medical magazine once, but the world had otherwise never known our names. We weren't famous and didn't have a whole bunch of money. But my parents didn't ask questions or wonder why. They just went straight to the bank and were ready to hand over everything we had for Dani.

"How much money do you need to buy someone back?" I remembered asking Nana.

"I'm not sure, Keely," she said softly. "I don't know how someone could put a price on a girl like Dani—as if she was just a carton of milk or a sweater in a store window. I just don't know how someone can put a price on that." I could tell she wanted to give me a good answer and make me believe that it would all be okay. But I knew that she didn't even believe it herself.

When my parents returned from the bank, I met them at the door with a slip of paper. Inside, I had written "$139.55" with a purple colored pencil—the kind of purple that people often confused for black. I had seen a lot of people give money by writing the number down on a flimsy piece of paper. So I knew it would count. Back home, I had a jar that sat on my desk, which held my entire savings. The money was supposed to be for a Game Boy Color. However, it was one of those moments when I realized none of that stuff mattered.

"I hope this makes it enough," I said when I handed the self-made check to my mother. "It took me a year to get all that. With your money and my money, we can get her back, right?" She then knelt down in front of me, her eyes in line with mine. It was the first time since that night that she looked me straight in the eye without turning away. She reached up to run her fingers through one of my clumps of curls, something that only reminded me more that Dani wasn't there to do it.

"Do you remember that time when you asked how the tooth fairy doesn't run out of money?"

"Yeah," I said.

"And do you remember what I told you?"

"You said that she sells our teeth to dentists for a whole lot of money so that they can make fake teeth for old people to wear. You said that it makes her sad to give away our teeth, but that's the only way she can make enough money to make us happy."

"And what else did I tell you?"

"That no matter what, she isn't going to let me down."

"I want you to remember that. No matter what it takes, no matter how much we have to give, we aren't going to let Dani down. Do you believe me?" I did believe her—that she would give the man anything he asked for. But I worried that we didn't have the things he wanted.

My parents didn't want me to hear about the details. They didn't want me to know that after five days had passed without any contact, the police gave her a one in ten chance of being found. Even though I was only ten, I knew that the ten percent chance they gave Dani also meant more dead than alive.

Once the third week hit, the police told us that we should just return home to Ridgewood. They said they would call us if anything came up, as if Dani was some old sweatshirt that I had left at the YMCA. I didn't understand how we were supposed to just pick back up. It wasn't like I could just rip her pages out and start fresh. Her ink had bled through every single page of my life, and everything reminded me of that.

The day we decided to go back home, Bumpy asked me if I wanted to go on a ride with him. He didn't say where we were going and simply told me to dress warm. The only coat I could find was the one Dani had brought. She was always the one who prepared and planned for everything; I never thought about those kinds of things. Our visit to Reading was supposed to be a quick trip, two to three days at most, during some of the warmest September days Massachusetts had ever seen.

Bumpy already had the truck warming up by the time I met him outside. He and Nana were lifting a cooler onto the tailgate. When they turned to look at me, I knew immediately that they thought I was Dani. Although it only lasted a brief second, I couldn't tell what hurt more: the look of relief when they thought the nightmare was over or the pain in their faces when they realized it was only me.

It must have been the coat, as green had always been Dani's color. My dad used to say that it was easier having color-coded twins. Dani and I used to joke about switching without him knowing. However, we never ended up doing it, probably because I felt like I wasn't good enough to wear her color. That was the first time that I had ever worn Dani's green, and I couldn't help but feel like an imposter.

We drove along for a while, simply listening to the oldies station on the radio. Some guy by the name of John Lennon sang for part of the way, asking us to dream about a world he thought would be great. I took my normal seat in the middle, my legs on either side of the large stick shift that rose out of the floor. I liked listening to the clanking sound it made when Bumpy moved it back and forth as he drove. It reminded me of the noises my dad made when he fell asleep in his recliner chair.

I figured out where he was taking me before we got to the water. The big, yellow sign for "Joe's Fish Fry" on North Ave always gave away that we were getting close to the lake. He turned off the main road onto an old dirt path, the type that made my seat bounce up and down and sent the mirror ornaments swaying back and forth. It led to a small house, the kind that you'd almost miss if you didn't look hard enough. It used to belong to Bumpy's best friend—the man we called Uncle Paulie. He had gone to heaven the year before and left the whole place to Nana and Bumpy. Uncle Paulie didn't have any kids, but he used to have a wife. She died long ago, and Bumpy never told me how. All he said was that Uncle Paulie never stopped being sad. I couldn't help but wonder if that was how everyone felt after someone went to heaven.

It was the first time that he had taken me there that year. Even though Bumpy had a boat docked at the yacht club up the road, he would say that there was nothing quite like fishing right off the riverside. He would sit with Dani and me along the bank, teaching us about the fish types and the perfect speed for reeling in the fishing line.

As we drove down the dusty road, I could almost hear Dani singing "Down by the Bay" beside me. It had always been her favorite rhyme. She would always start it when we went around the last bend, the one right before you could see the water. I closed my eyes so I wouldn't see the lake, my mind replaying her voice in my head.

"Down by the bay," Bumpy sang in his deep voice.

"Down by the bay," I repeated back, my eyes still closed tight.

"Where the watermelons grow," he continued to sing.

"Where the watermelons..." My voice faded as the words disappeared into the back of my throat. Bumpy pretended not to notice and just went on as if I was still singing along with him.

"Back to my home...I shall not go...for if I do...my mother will say...did you ever see a goat pooping on a boat?" My chapped lips cracked at the corners as I tried to hold back the smile, and I felt the giggle grow in my belly. Once I began laughing, I couldn't stop. The harder I tried to hold it in, the louder the noise grew. Bumpy didn't tell me to cut it out or ask what was wrong—he just laughed right along with me.

By the time we reached the riverside, our sides hurt as much as our insides had been over those long three weeks. I couldn't catch a breath, and my laughter began to sound something like a cat wheezing up a hairball. Before long, I found myself cradled in my bumpy's lap, his hunched back curving overtop of me, making me feel like I was curled inside a hollowed-out tree. It felt safe, and for a moment, I tried to forget why he was holding me that way. I kept my ear against his chest, listening to the quiet thumps hiccupping inside. They sounded tired, like they were trying too hard to keep going. But every time I thought the beats were going to stop thumping back, they hiccupped once more. I took comfort in that.

"I turned twelve the same year we entered the big war," Bumpy started. "I grew up in a tiny town down in the South, the kind of place that people only stopped at if they meant to. We didn't have many passerbys or people from too far outside town. There wasn't much else to do other than swim in the ponds when it got too hot or head down to Reinmans when the latest action comic came out." Bumpy spoke in a sad kind of way. The only time he ever talked like that was when he was about to tell me something very serious.

"There was a boy who lived next door to me. Augustus was his full name, but he only ever responded to Gus. He was two years younger than me, but he was still my closest friend growing up. We would skip school here and there, and we liked to sneak out late at night to catch the creepy-crawlies to use for fishing. He was always ready for somethin', always looking to take over the world in a small kind of way—in a very Gus kind of way." His arms wrapped tighter around me as he spoke. They felt shaky, but I couldn't tell if it was from having to hold me in his lap or from his story.

"We had this one place that only we went to. It was an abandoned house, but not the kind with scary ghosts or rotted-out staircases. From the outside, you would've thought it was just 'nother gutted, run-down, old house. But on the inside, it was like a family had just gotten up and left the day before. There were even cups left out on the kitchen counter. The dressers still had clothes in them, and there were beard trimmings left in the sink. No one really liked to talk much about the old Hillings house. All people ever said was, 'they kept to themselves,' and, 'they just decided to up and leave one day and never come back,'" I didn't say anything as he spoke. I closed my eyes and just let his words wash over me.

"Me and Gus knew there was more to the story, but no one really knew what actually happened. People in town had their assumptions. There was talk about the mother running off with another man and the father running after her—that he was just too heartbroken to come back. Others said their youngest child caught the devil's flu and that they went off to get him cured at a mental hospital. Either way, they never returned. For twelve years the house just sat there. No one went in, and no one bought it. After a while, Gus and me just sort of claimed it as our own. We didn't go there to wreck things or anything like that. It was more like a place that we could make up stories and pretend we were somebody else for the day.

"It was a Saturday night. The crickets were louder than normal. They sounded annoyed...upset at each other. We were Officer Gus and Detective Bobby that night, responding to a house call. We had played the part before, but that time we were walking into a suspected bank robber's house. Based off an imaginary tip we got, we were trying to find the hidden stash of money that was supposedly inside. We went from room to room and checked every tucked away drawer and loose floorboard. Gus had a knack for seeing the small things—the things that most people would overlook. He probably knew every square inch of that house, but he always pretended like he was seeing it for the first time. I remember Gus made sure to put everything back the way it was so that the 'bank robber' wouldn't know we were there when he came home.

"By the time we got through the last room in the house, it was my idea to check the attic. We hadn't been up there before, but I convinced Gus that the stash of money just had to be up there. The attic had one of those staircases that came down from the ceiling. I went up first because I was in charge of the flashlight. I thought we were going to find all sorts of treasures, but there were just two boxes up there. We tried to guess what was in them before we looked. I hoped they were filled with board games, but Gus thought they would be filled with old wigs like his Aunt Wendy had in her attic."

"What was inside of them?" My question startled him, as if he had forgotten I was there with him. He stared out the window, not looking at anything in particular.

"They were filled with dolls—the kind with the glass faces that don't have any eyebrows...just those big, buggy eyes and bright red lips. There must have been over a hundred dolls between the two boxes. We noticed that none of them were smiling. We dug through that entire pile, and every single one of them had the same sad kind of expression painted on, as if the dolls were just about to start crying. Do you know what else was odd?"

He didn't look away from the window, but he must have known that I shook my head no.

"The Hillings never had any daughters. Why would a family have boxes full of dolls if there were never any girls to play with them?" It made me think of the one time I went to buy a kitten from a pet store, but all I could think about was that the puppies needed it more. They lined the wall in their steel homes, trying to fit their tongues through the small squares, hoping that there would be a finger on the other side. I remembered thinking, *how could there be so many puppies but not enough kids to love them?*

"I was so busy worrying about why the dolls weren't smiling that I didn't even notice the smoke. It was coming up through the floorboards, and soon the entire attic was filled with it. I knocked out a window to let some out, but that seemed to only make it worse. I didn't realize until I got to the staircase that the entire second floor was covered in fire. I had no idea where it came from. We had only been in the house for all of thirty minutes.

"I remember how scared Gus was. He didn't know what to do, so I had to pretend that I did. The heat was so hot that it made me feel like my skin was peeling off my face." His hand settled on a patch of discolored skin at the base of his neck, something I hadn't noticed before. At first, it only looked like the dark spots that old people collected with age. But as I looked closer, I realized it wasn't that at all. I began to see the spidery web that spread down along his collarbone and disappeared under his coat. It was exactly how Nana's red peppers looked when they had cooked for too long.

"Even though we'd been in the house so many times before, the smoke made it impossible for us to see anything. I kept telling Gus to follow me, like I knew where I was going. When we reached the staircase, I could feel him holding on to the back of my shirt. I told him to hang on tight and then began to run. I prayed on every step that the staircase would hold us and that my throat wouldn't close up before we made it outside. I could feel the fire all around me, but I kept on running. I didn't even stop when I made it off the porch. All I kept thinking was that I wanted to get as far away as I could." He paused for a second, moving his hand over his mouth the way grown-ups did when they were about to say something they didn't want to, as if trying to trap the words inside. "I thought Gus was right behind me—I could even feel his grip still bunching up the back of my shirt." I didn't need him to tell me that Gus wasn't there. It was written in the lines of his face as he began to cry.

I lifted my head and sat up. Automatically, I wrapped my arms around his neck and reached up to kiss the shimmering scar that he always hid beneath his collared shirts. When I pulled away to look up at him, there was something in his face that I hadn't seen before.

"Gus was your Dani," I said, my voice cracking at her name. He nodded his head slowly, his tears raining down on me as I pushed my face into his chest.

"He was my very best friend. I should have made sure he was right behind me. I should have made sure that he made it out. I didn't realize until it was too late. The fire must have reached the oil tank because one second the house was there, and then the next, it was just...gone."

"Why did it happen?" I whispered. He paused before he answered—he knew I wasn't really talking about Gus and the fire anymore.

"Sometimes you don't know why. Sometimes you are just left with the how. I don't know why two boys woke up one morning and thought, 'I'm gonna burn down that old Hillings house today, just for the heck of it.' I just know it took two cans of gasoline and one match. And I don't know why someone would follow two kids into the woods and just take one of them. I don't know why bad things happen, Keely. All I know is that it's up to us to find a way out of the smoke."

"But how do we do that?"

"That's what I wanted to talk to you about because I don't want you to end up like me. You have to find a way to forgive yourself. You have to promise me, Keely. You need to promise me that you won't think you left Dani in a burning building. You didn't let her down, and you can't blame yourself for what happened to her."

"Okay, Bumpy. I promise," I said into his shirt. But I didn't mean it. I knew it was what he wanted to hear, but things didn't work that way. I couldn't just forget that it had happened. I couldn't simply turn it off, like ripping the batteries out of an old, beeping smoke detector. I knew, just by looking at him as he thought of Gus, that I was going be exactly like Bumpy, forever stuck in that smoky attic with the sad-faced dolls, wondering why they never smiled.

When we returned home to Ridgewood, the first thing I did was move Dani's bed. Hers was still pushed up against mine, its green comforter mixing with my purple one. It made me think about all the nights I had fallen asleep listening to her bedtime stories. I told myself the change was only to make it easier to walk around the room. But deep down, I knew the real reason—I couldn't fall asleep feeling all that emptiness beside me.

I remembered wrapping myself in one of her sweaters left behind on the floor, finding a spaghetti sauce stain still on its sleeve. I pushed my face into the fabric, hoping it still held a piece of Dani. But all I could smell was the woody mustiness from the floorboards. It wasn't like Nana and Bumpy's clothes where the scent could have filled an entire room. Instead, it smelled like any other worn sweater, one that could have belonged to anybody. Maybe it took a long time to get one of those lasting smells— years and years of living sticking to skin. It made me think, *I just hope that Dani can live long enough to get a smell like that.*

Mom and Dad didn't make me go back to school right away. They said that I could take as long as I wanted to because they didn't want to push me into anything too soon. They seemed to know that I needed a little more time. Or, they may have known that I didn't have any friends to go back to.

One of them always seemed to guard the front entrance. At first, I thought they were just worried I would run off again. But their distant looks out the front window told me it was something else; they were waiting for someone with news to come to our doorstep. I imagined it being like the movies. No one would call or send a letter when it was bad news. They would simply come to the front step, knock once, and take off their hat as the door opened.

In my mind, those who brought bad news always wore hats.

For my parents, it was watching the front door. But for me, it was writing her letters that got me through those first couple weeks back in Ridgewood. I wrote down the things I would normally tell her: like how the greedy squirrel that stole all the sunflower seeds from our birdhouse was fatter than ever; and that Mrs. Bradbury still hadn't yelled at us for leaving our trash can out all week; and how our neighbors had just put up an invisible fence for their dumb dog so it wouldn't be able to chase our cat, Killa, anymore. They were things that only we would have cared about. One day, I also tried to tell her about the serious stuff, about how sorry I was that I ran away. I ended up ripping it to pieces and burning it in the backyard where no one could see. I didn't burn it because I wasn't sorry— I was. I burned it because it sounded too much like a goodbye.

Mom and Dad tried to act normal to make me think they were okay, but I knew they were only pretending. Dad spent a lot of time cutting the bushes around the house. Before long, there wasn't much left of them besides brown, leafless stubs. Mom spent a lot of time crying. She would do it in private when she thought no one was listening. There was a corner of our basement—next to the big water tank—that she often went. She would wait for the large tank to start humming before letting herself cry. If it wasn't for the register vent in my room, I wouldn't have heard her. At first, I tried to block out the sound. However, as time went on, I found myself lying on the floor with my ear against the grate and listening quietly. In a way, it felt like she was crying for the both of us.

No matter how much it hurt, no matter how much I wanted to, I couldn't bring myself to cry. It had been a problem since I was young. I'd always had a hard time letting things out. Mom told me that when I was a baby, I had a tendency to hold my breath whenever I got upset. Sometimes, I held it so long that I turned blue and passed out. Once, it was so bad that they had to take me to the hospital. The doctors told my parents that there wasn't anything they could do for me, that I would eventually outgrow it. Mom tried many things to break me out of my spells, one of the worst being her ice-cold spray bottle. However, the only thing she found to work was tickling the bottoms of my feet.

I wished that was all it took to make me breathe normally again.

Dani used to say, "Keely, one of these days you're just gonna pop like a balloon!" I wished that could have been true—that I could find a breaking point. Instead, my balloon had become a rubber ball, too hard for even the sharpest point to pop.

I knew the day would come when we couldn't hide away any longer. My parents would have to return to work. I would have to go back to learning about presidents and guessing the number of dumb jellybeans it took to fill a sauce jar. We would be forced to return to our old lives, whether we liked it or not.

My first day back at school, I learned that there was something worse than being the kid sent home for having lice—it was being the girl whose sister had been kidnapped. I was the kid they all talked about, the girl who split a hallway the moment she appeared. No one looked me directly in the eyes, but I could hear the whispers all around me.

"That's the girl from the news."

"No stupid, that's the sister. She's the one who was there when it happened."

"I heard that she had to go to one of those mental hospitals after her sister was taken."

"Yeah, someone told me that she didn't talk for weeks, and she already forgot how to say some things."

"Well, you know what I heard? The girl—the one that went missing—someone told me that she ran away, and they are just pretending she got kidnapped."

"Wait, you said her name was Dani Millen? Dani Millen had a twin sister?"

"I guess so. Maybe they're the kind that don't look alike."

"Well, what happens when one of 'em dies? Like, does that mean the other one isn't a twin anymore?"

"Yeah, totally. It basically means that she's just, I don't know, one person because there's only one of her left."

"It must suck to be her."

"Yeah, I would probably, like, kill myself if I was her."

"Seriously. Hey, do you know if there is coleslaw instead of tater tots today? I'm trying really hard to lose five pounds," Amy said. Amy Taber was the girl who started wearing thongs in the fourth grade and had highlights that made her hair look like a skunk's tail. She was also the only girl who could talk about me dying and then ask what was for lunch in the same sentence.

I tried to block it all out. A part of me wanted to scream at the top of my lungs, telling them that they were wrong. I wanted them to know that I would never, ever stop being Dani Millen's twin. Instead, I just kept my head down and walked by them. Dani would have said something. She would've told them, "Your butts aren't hats so pull your heads out of 'em." She would have gotten them to shut up, making them all go back to pretending I didn't exist.

I was far from popular, but that didn't used to matter. I never had to make any friends, because I had Dani. She was in every single one of my classes. There was a group of girls we sat with during lunch, and a bunch of them even came over to our house a couple times. But they were never "our friends"—they were "Dani's friends." She knew all of their inside jokes and kept track of what boy each of them had a crush on. It wasn't like Dani didn't try to explain it to me, because she did. I just didn't really care to keep up.

Before, I didn't need to be friends with them. Girls like that had to have ten people around them at all times, even if they didn't like them. It was that dancing circle mentality, where you only felt safe if you were standing shoulder to shoulder with someone, pretending to act like you were having the time of your life. I didn't mind standing outside that circle, and Dani didn't mind joining me. She picked me over them every time. Deep down, I knew it drove them crazy.

As I stood at the front of the lunchroom that very first day back, I wished I had cared more. I wished that I knew if it was Dave or Kenneth that Sarah wanted to hold hands with. I wished I remembered if it was Mr.

Keller they called Charizard or if that was Mr. Fetter. And most of all, I wished I hadn't made Dani pick me over them just to prove that I could.

My eyes anxiously searched for an open seat as I walked towards our usual table. It was circular, so I could easily see that there weren't any seats left. Two new blonde girls sat where Dani and I had before, the ones whose heads bobbed when they talked and who popped their gum loudly in Geography class. In that instant, I was so mad at myself for feeling like I needed them. I hated that I wanted to be inside that circle because for the first time, I felt like the only one outside of it.

I knew they saw me standing there, but none of them looked up. They all hunched closer to their lunches, looking as if they were about to play a game of Heads Up, Seven Up. The girl named Hannah appeared to have taken over the "group." Without Dani there, everyone looked to her. They waited for her to tell them the coast was clear—that I had walked away. I stood there a little longer than I should have, hoping their necks would hurt from having to keep their heads down. I wanted them to feel some kind of pain for what they had done—for replacing Dani so quickly. It wasn't about them ditching me, because I had figured they wouldn't have included me without Dani there. We were a package deal. It was about the way Hannah smiled, as if she was glad that Dani wasn't there anymore. I gave the top of her head one last, hard stare before making the long walk to the empty table at the back.

It was like every school was required to have one. No matter how packed the lunchroom, there would always be that one table in the back, completely open. It was positioned slightly away from the other tables and conveniently located right next to the emergency exit. It was as if someone wanted to give the lonely kids an escape route, one last mad dash away from the embarrassment of eating alone. I didn't run, though. I forced myself to take one of the nine, empty seats and dump my bagged lunch onto the table.

Mom packed our lunches only on special days. Usually, we had to buy the cafeteria food because she didn't have enough time most mornings. She must have thought that day was an important one—special in the worst sort of way.

I looked for it immediately, the note that she would hide under my yogurt's lid. I normally didn't read it during lunch, because I didn't want Dani to see. It was a secret only Mom and I knew about, something she only did for me. She must've known that I needed the notes the most or else she would have written them for Dani, too. They were usually short and included only the nicest adjectives. They made me feel like they were describing someone else.

You get lovelier by the day. You are a superhero, so let your cape fly. You are funny and make people happy. You are the best kind of friend.

Her notes always ended in "Love Mom," as if I wasn't going to know who wrote them. They were written in her perfect, non-loopy handwriting, the kind that I could actually read. Even though I didn't believe everything they said, I still loved them. They made me think that for even just a moment, I could turn into that person who hid within her handwritten words.

That time, her note was different. It was longer, and her writing looked slanted and rushed. I found it shoved between my banana and bag of graham crackers instead of its usual hiding place. I opened the crinkled, folded piece of paper and read:

I want you to listen closely. If anyone says anything mean to you or talks badly about Dani, I want you to tell them to fuck off. I know I told you never to say that because it's a very, very bad word, but I'm going to let you use it just this once. I love you. Love Mom.

P.S. Don't tell Dad

I almost spit out my Capri Sun when I read it. I had heard my mom say that word only a couple of times before. Even though I didn't understand exactly what it meant, I knew rappers liked to yell it and that it was rude to say to someone's face; I remembered she had told me to never use it. As I read the note a second, third, and fourth time, I could feel that laugh—like the one I had felt in Bumpy's truck—bubbling up inside of me. There wasn't anything funny about the note, but there was something about seeing that bad word in my mom's crooked handwriting.

It wasn't until I looked up from the table that I realized everyone was staring at me. I could see it written all over their faces. *Why is that loser in the corner, Dani Millen's weirdo sister, laughing to herself?* I focused on shoving the food back into the paper bag, stopping myself from bolting out of the cafeteria.

Instead of hiding out in the bathroom, I took the stairs that led to the basement. I had seen a janitor go down there before and figured it would be the last place people would look for me. Luckily, the basement door was unlocked, probably because grown-ups didn't expect any normal middle schooler to go down there. Most kids were too afraid to go into that basement—even if they were dared to. Boys in the grade above me told all the girls that there were ghosts down there, but Dani said *they* were the real scaredy-cats.

It wasn't as scary as I thought it would be. There was a friendly hum to the old light bulbs lining the ceiling of the long hallway. Unlike what the seventh graders had said, there weren't any cobwebs or creepy-crawlies covering the walls.

A dusty closet stood off from the basement's hallway, filled with beat-up brooms and blackened soap buckets. Dried-up, crusty mops lined the wall and reminded me of Dani's paintbrushes, the ones that I always forgot to wash after we watercolored. The room had a strange stench, like Nana and Bumpy's old tent that we had packed up too soon after a rainstorm.

Even though the dust made my nose itch, that closet became my hideaway. I would go there when everything became too much, when I needed to get away from all of the whispers and stares.

During those first couple weeks back at school, there were many times that I came close to using my mom's F-word. I kept her note buried in my front pocket, like a private permission slip to say it. But I never found the guts. Instead, I would go to my closet. I would disappear from the world a couple times a day to sit in silence among the forgotten mops and brooms. No one came looking for me or wondered where I was—it was the only good thing that came out of being the sister of the kidnapped girl. Teachers let me come and go, as their pity earned me an unlimited hall pass.

A janitor eventually found me there on a Tuesday afternoon. He was an older man with a limp, the kind where he had to drag his heavy leg behind him when he walked. We just stared at each other when he first opened the door, caught in a game of "who's going to blink first." He didn't say anything to me and simply reached up to grab the bleach from the top shelf before quickly turning to leave. I could have sworn, just before the door gently closed, I saw him wink.

After that day, I would hear his quiet shuffling outside my closet. He never came in again, but neither did anyone else. Most afternoons, I could hear his *slide-thump* back and forth, up and down the hallway. He ensured no one else discovered my secret place.

During those few times a day, I turned myself off so that I wouldn't have to feel anything. Mom said that it wasn't good to block out the rest of the world, that the people who shut off their feelings too often could sometimes forget how to turn them back on. But it was the only way I could escape the pain. I hated that the only time I felt okay was when I was inside my closet, shutting Dani out. It made me feel guilty thinking that she was somewhere out there, and I was just sitting around in a dusty storage room. I should have been out looking for her, but I didn't know where to start.

It wasn't until three months after Dani went missing that I finally found my way out of that closet. My class took a "field trip" to the county library—the big building on the other side of the middle school parking lot—a week before Christmas break. We all had to get permission slips from our parents, just because Principal Dugardi told us to. My History teacher, Mr. Kretz, didn't like him, either, and would always say, "If Mr. Douchegardi says we have to, we better do it." It made my whole class laugh every time, and I just pretended that I knew why it was so funny. It was probably a joke that only the kids with cable understood. Either way, it made me like Mr. Kretz the most out of all the teachers.

I had been to the county library a bunch of times before but only when Dani and I wanted to rent a movie without Mom and Dad knowing. It was the only library that had *White Fang*, which we rented the most. I guessed that Mom didn't like us watching it because there was a dead body in it, but we made sure to close our eyes during that part. We would wait until they went to bed before sneaking out to the barn and watching it on the TV Dad used in his workshop. We made a fort with our blankets, popping them up like a tent around the screen, just in case our parents happened to wake up and see the light in the barn window. As I walked through the front doors of the library, I thought about cuddling up with her and hearing her say, "You know what I think? I think that all White Fang needs is a very best friend." Dani made sure to hold my hand every time when she said it.

The lady at the library's front desk was named Kansas, like the state. The mean people said she was called that because she was about the same size as the whole state of Kansas, but I didn't think of her that way. I liked her because she had a kind smile and called me "sweetheart" whenever she talked to me. Also, she couldn't tell Dani and me apart. Each time we rented a movie, she would ask me which one I was. I usually waited for Dani to tell her. Kansas liked to joke that her glasses were making her see double, and she would usually ask us if we were playing a trick on her. It became our own private joke. Dani and I would laugh and say, "Nope! We are twins, silly!" It made me feel happy every time.

I made sure to look up at her right when I walked in, but it was the first time that Kansas looked away and didn't smile. She glanced around at everyone else, pretending that she never saw me in the first place. I didn't have to guess why she acted like I wasn't there.

At first, I thought we were there to find something to read for our next book report. Instead, Mr. Kretz took us upstairs to a room I hadn't been to before. It was the biggest room I had ever seen. There were rows and rows of tall bookcases, stretching all the way up into the high ceiling, filled by drawers instead of shelves. Tall ladders lined each row. They were the sliding kind, attached to wheels, like in Belle's favorite bookstore in *Beauty & The Beast*.

An old lady greeted us at the door. She had hot-pink blush on her cheeks, piled onto pale, leathery skin. She had teased her hair a bit too much, making it look like a pile of pulled-out feathers. I could tell by the way she looked at me, over her wiry reading glasses, that she was the type of librarian who shushed kids for being too loud. Her name was Agnes, which made me think that she had been an old lady her whole life. There was a pin stuck to her sweater that said in bright, red letters: **World's Best Librarian**. I got the feeling that she had probably bought it for herself.

"Welcome, welcome, welcome," she said, talking like we were her honored guests. "Welcome to the Newsroom, children! All that lies before you is the pride of Bergen County and, might I add, something I myself have been working on for the past ten years." She made it sound like she had built the entire room all by herself.

"We call it the Newsroom," she went on, "because in here we have stored every newspaper dating back to the 1920s. Each of the newspapers is cataloged by the month and year, and we have even taken it one step further. All the librarians here, me especially, have gone through the newspapers and inputted the keywords of every article title into our system. That way, you don't have to go searching for the needle in the haystack! We finished everything through 1929, so that means we only have eight more years to go!"

You could tell that she was prepared for a loud applause, her back even slightly bent as if ready to take a bow. Most of my class stared back with bored, blank looks, ready to walk back to school for lunch. But I was hanging on her every word. I felt like I had just opened a puzzle box, and all I had to do was figure out how the pieces went together.

We were supposed to split up into pairs and practice using the catalog system by looking up the assigned keywords. My classmates all clung to their friends at the word "partner," leaving only me and a kid named Levi standing by ourselves. Levi didn't talk much; in fact, everyone said he used to be completely mute prior to sixth grade. Like me, he was an outcast. But kids stayed away from Levi for a different reason than me. His nickname was "Leaky Levi" because he had a hard time making it to the bathroom. People said it was because he was born so early that his bladder never grew in right. But I didn't think that Levi peed his pants because of his bladder. Rather, it was because everything about the world scared him, and that was how he let his fears out. It made me think that no matter how much time someone had to grow and prepare for the harshness of the world, some people like Levi would never be ready.

It was in that moment—standing alone next to Levi—that I decided I didn't want to be one of those people. I didn't want to hide anymore, and I wanted to go get her back. Standing in front of the rows and rows of bookcases, I began to feel like I had a place to start.

Mr. Kretz handed us an index card that read: **Earthquake**. Long lines had already formed behind the two main computers. The same kids who wanted nothing to do with the old lady and her newspaper room pushed the hardest to get to the front. That was the thing about sixth grade—everyone wanted to be the first in line, even if it was for something they hated. I moved to the back of the longest one and waited patiently. I didn't want anyone standing behind me when it was my turn. Levi held on to the index card, which he kept folding and unfolding into a tiny square.

When it was finally our turn, I was surprised to see Levi rush to take the seat at the computer. He seemed excited about using the keyboard, making a few happy grunts now and then whenever he pressed enter. The search results popped up, and there must have been hundreds of newspapers that came up on the screen. It was a long line of text, continuing down and down until finally reaching the bottom. We both looked at the screen, unsure about what to do next.

"Wowie! Look at that! You guys had a whole bunch of results pop up, now didn't ya?" It was Miss Dingleberry, our math teacher. She talked to us like we were preschoolers. Everything she said sounded like it had way too many *e*'s than it needed, and she had a habit of clapping her hands rapidly whenever we did anything right. It wasn't how she treated all the kids—just the ones like Levi and me.

She wasn't actually supposed to be on the field trip, but she had a free period right before lunch and invited herself along as a "chaperone." It wasn't a secret that she had a big crush on Mr. Kretz. There were rumors that she would hide in his bushes and watch him at night through his living room window. Kids said she stole his coffee mugs and licked the rim where his mouth had been. Even though I didn't care for how she treated me like a four-year-old, I still felt badly for her. She was a little bit older than the other teachers at school and wasn't nearly as pretty. Mom said that it was a shame she hadn't found someone to marry her yet. I overheard her tell Dad one time that it wasn't right for a woman to go through life with a last name that had anything to do with poop stuck to hair.

"You did a super duper job with that, Levi! Can I get a high-five, big guy?" He slapped her hand excitedly, smiling ear to ear. I pretended that I didn't hear her ask me to give her one, too.

"So, how do we find where the newspaper is?" I asked.

"I'm not sure, sweetie. Let me go bring Steve over here." *Steve*, never Mr. Kretz. She only called him by his first name, as if they were best friends. However, I noticed that Mr. Kretz never called Miss Dingleberry by her first name. She was only ever "Ms. D" to him.

"What can I do to help over here?" Mr. Kretz said as he bent down to look at our computer screen. Miss Dingleberry made sure to stand right behind him so that he would back into her when he stood up.

"We want to know how to find the newspapers," I said, knowing Levi wasn't going to answer him.

"So, look here on the left. You see those two numbers? The first one tells you what row it's in. And then the second number—the one right before the article title—that is the bin you're going to find it in. Stick to the smaller bin numbers because those are closer to the ground. We don't want you getting hurt on the ladders. If you really want to see something, I'm sure Agnes can grab it for you guys" he said with a warm smile, his teeth a milky white. He looked just like Eric from *The Little Mermaid*, except Mr. Kretz wore glasses and made sure to button his shirts all the way up to his neck.

"Or, I'm sure a strong man like *you* can grab it for them. We wouldn't want the librarian to hurt herself," Miss Dingleberry said as she put a hand on Mr. Kretz's lower back.

"Oh, I am sure Agnes has mastered those ladders by now, Ms. D," he said while making sure to brush her hand off of him and move just out of her reach. I wondered if Miss Dingleberry noticed that he even called the old librarian by her first name. If Dani had been standing next to me, she would have leaned over and whispered into my ear, "Burn, Ms. D, burn." She would have made sure to drag out the *ur's*, making the words sound longer. It was her favorite thing to say when something embarrassing happened. She started using that phrase ever since she heard Dad say it while they were watching a hockey game.

We ended up choosing an earthquake that happened in the year 1998 in California. The computer said it was located in 48, 4, and the article was in the *Del Rio News Herald.* I raced off through the rows of bookcases, my heart starting to pound inside my chest. Levi struggled to keep up with me, probably wondering why I was in such a rush to find a newspaper. The fact was that I needed to know that the system worked. When I reached bin 48, 4, my hands began to shake as I reached down to open the drawer. It was located near the floor, just like Mr. Kretz said it would be. The drawers were much longer than they looked. Inside, there must have been over a hundred different newspapers, all neatly folded on top of one another. I quickly flicked through the pile as Levi stood over me and looked on. It didn't take long for me to find the newspaper we were searching for.

The earthquake had barely made the front page. It probably was because Texas cared more about Irma Almeda winning Miss Congeniality in Miss Texas that year than about California. The first page contained a quick description of the event, with the rest of the article found at the very back of the paper. Two people were injured during the event, and there was a church that had been damaged in San Juan Bautista. Stores lost a lot of money from items falling off the shelves. Nine different counties were affected. I wrote everything down word for word in my notebook, even though I knew I would never use any of that information again. I didn't know why I cared so much about those details when they meant nothing to me. But for some reason, writing those words down, despite having nothing to do with Dani's kidnapping, made me feel closer to her.

We were supposed to find newspapers on three different earthquakes, but the field trip was cut short when two boys from my class thought it would be funny to adjust some of the pictures in a bunch of newspapers. Sue, the class tattletale, ratted them out to Agnes. We were the first and last sixth grade class of Benjamin Franklin Middle School to take a field trip to the Newsroom. Mr. Kretz probably apologized a dozen times, but Agnes still said sixth grade classes weren't going to be allowed back there.

For the rest of that day, I couldn't stop thinking about the Newsroom. Instead of going down to my closet during lunch, I went to go see the nurse, Ms. Crawley. She normally wasn't very nice to students and was known for making kids cry. Somehow, though, she seemed to like me. I figured she just felt badly for me. Nevertheless, I went to her when I needed help. We normally weren't allowed to make phone calls to our parents during the school day, but she let me use her office phone to call my mom. She picked up on the first ring. Ever since Dani went missing, Mom never let her cell phone ring more than twice.

"Hello, this is Dr. Millen. How may I help you?" she answered with her psychiatrist voice, likely not recognizing the number.

"Mom, it's me." There was a long pause on the other end. I waited for her response but then realized that she must have thought I was Dani. "Keely, it's Keely," I added a little too forcefully.

"Oh, Keely! Honey, is everything okay?" Her voice was shaky, and I could tell she was holding back tears.

"I was wondering if you could pick me up at seven-thirty instead of right after school today. I am just going to be at the library. We have a class project that is due, and I want to get a head start on it." She didn't answer right away. I had a feeling she wanted to say no. "I'll be with friends, so I will be okay." Whenever I said that I was doing something with "friends," she seemed to agree to anything.

"Well, I guess that would be okay. But you need to promise me that you won't leave the library. I want you to stay inside until I get there."

"I will stay there the whole time, I promise! Thanks so much, Mom. I'll see you at seven-thirty!" I hung up before she had a chance to change her mind.

I couldn't sit still the rest of the school day. Everything felt different, like I finally knew what I had to do without Dani telling me. For the first time, it didn't matter what the other kids were saying behind my back.

When the last bell finally rang, I ran straight over to the library. I headed right to the room on the second floor, finding Agnes still standing guard at the front desk. Right when she saw me coming, she shook her hand, telling me to stay away.

"No, no, I remember you. You're from the class this morning. You young kids aren't allowed up here anymore unless you have an adult with you." She must have been too busy reading the old newspapers to look at the new ones. I could tell she didn't know who I was. I couldn't use the pity card on her.

"But that sign says it's open to the public," I said, pointing to the paper taped to the door. She quickly ripped it off a moment later.

"Well, I guess not anymore," she said as she crushed the piece of paper into a tight ball. She stood in the doorway, blocking my way. Her feather hair stuck up more than it had that morning, and her blush appeared slightly smudged. She had black blotches under her eyes, like the kind my mom would get after she had cried for a long time.

"Please, please let me in. I promise to put everything back where it is supposed to go. You won't even know that I'm here." I felt like it was something Dani would say, as if the answer came too quickly. I could tell Agnes wanted to believe me, but she still wasn't quite sure. She looked me up and down, probably trying to decide if I was the type of kid who liked to draw devil horns on the pictures of people's faces. That day, I was wearing a glittery butterfly shirt and slightly outgrown pants, the ends not quite reaching my shoelaces. I had two pink barrettes in my hair, something my mom had forced me to wear that morning. *People always feel bad for kids wearing barrettes and high-water pants*, I thought, hoping it would be enough.

She let me in, making me promise to put away every newspaper and keep them near their drawers. I was willing to agree to just about anything to get inside that room. I kept myself from walking too quickly to the computers, knowing she was the kind of librarian who also yelled at kids for running through the aisles. As I passed by the front desk, I saw a layer of scattered newspapers, their pictures covered in drawn-on mustaches.

When I reached the two computers, I noticed their screens were blank, except for a box at the top of each that held a blinking cursor inside. I slowly slipped into the chair, never taking my eyes off that flashing line. I sat there, feeling as if the answers would simply appear on the screen, telling me where Dani was. Instead, the line continued to flicker back at me, waiting for the words to flow from my fingers. The keyboard was bulky, the kind that I had to hit each individual key, one finger at a time. I reached my hands up to the keyboard and typed: kidnapping.

I pressed enter and the screen came alive with letters. The list scrolled down as before. But that time, it kept going. The air caught inside my chest, the chance for finding Dani feeling further and further away. I tried hitting the escape key, but it wouldn't stop. Line after line kept appearing.

"You having trouble lookin' for something?" The girl's voice shot me straight out of my chair. She took a step back, likely thinking I was crazy, the same as everybody else. I had seen her around school but couldn't remember her name. Like me, other kids talked about her and not in a good way. Everyone said she had put a whole pack of Listerine strips into Mr. Higgs's coffee cup. Other kids made fun of her black shirts with the mythical creatures on them—all two sizes too big. However, she never seemed to care what the other people thought. I stared at her wizard shirt, the one I had seen her wear at least a couple times a week. The bearded man in his purple robe stood there and looked back at me, reminding me of something off a Magic card. "Um, hellooo. Earth to blondie."

I looked back up at the girl's face, expecting to find a nasty look. Instead, she was smiling at me, the slanted kind, as if we had just shared an inside joke. "No, I'm fine. I just typed in the wrong thing and was trying to go back."

"It didn't look like you were fine. I thought you were going to chuck that thing right across the room. Then Saggy Aggy would be over here ripping your head off."

I knew that the kids would have a name to call the old librarian.

I tried to block her view of the screen as she started towards me. She stepped in close to study me, her face only inches from mine. I had to look up a bit to meet her stare. I noticed her hazel eyes, the kind that changed from brown to green in the light. Her hair was parted down the middle, giving away the natural brown color that hid underneath its dyed, reddish tint.

Before I could say a word, she slipped past me and sat down at the computer. "So, what you need to do is be more specific about what you want to know," she stated. A group of new blinking boxes seemed to magically appear as her fingers raced across the keyboard. "These spaces here," she said, pointing the mouse arrow at the two boxes near the bottom of the screen, "are for putting in the years you want to search. What years did you want to look up…things?" I then realized she knew who I was. She tried too hard to avoid the "k" word.

"I don't know. I think from when I was born until now," I said, moving next to her.

"Okay. And what year were you born?"

"1989." She typed the years into the boxes and pressed enter. The running list started again but was shorter that time.

"Alright. Since the ones at the top of the list are the newest, I would start there."

"K, thanks," I said, waiting for her to give me back my seat.

She hesitated for a moment before getting up, still scrolling down the search results. "No problem. I'll catch ya later." She turned and walked away without another word. I stared at her back as it disappeared behind one of the bookcases.

I scribbled down the first twenty entries into my history notebook, figuring I didn't take notes in that class anyways. The 2000 newspapers filled bookcases 141-143, which I found at the far end of the massive room. Agnes must have just gotten to them, as the pages were neatly tucked into drawer after drawer. I could have sworn I saw a flash of red-orange out of the corner of my eye as I pulled out my list of papers.

The first group was all from small towns in Iowa. I soon learned that people really cared about their goats out there. They called him the "Goat Napper," the man who kidnapped around eighty goats in just over two weeks. It looked like it took the police a month to catch him. Supposedly, one of the farmers shot him in the leg after he ran off with two baby goats. The newspaper said that one of the goats got shot in the process and ended up dying. In the report, it said the police found the man holding the dead goat to his chest, and he didn't stop crying until hours later.

The kidnapper's name was Ryan Thomas. He had some kind of "social disorder" that I couldn't pronounce. He refused to tell the cops where he was hiding the other goats, but they ended up finding them a few days later in an abandoned warehouse just outside Latimer, Iowa. A man who lived nearby called the police when they woke him up in the middle of the night—he said they sounded like a bunch of screaming children. The cops from the interview said Ryan Thomas took the goats because "he was sick in the head and wanted to do weird things with them." But I didn't think that was it at all. The picture showed a skinny kid who couldn't quite look directly at the camera. Just by looking at his picture, I knew he was trying to protect them.

It made me think that maybe not all kidnappers wanted to hurt someone. Maybe the reason people did bad things was because they thought it would do a little bit of good.

From the other newspapers I read, I realized that Ryan Thomas was probably the only nice kidnapper out there. Most of the stories didn't make sense to me. There were no signs to show it was coming, no way that anyone could have prepared. They were mostly young kids; the oldest I found was only thirteen. One girl was twelve and rode her bike to the gas station up the road from her house so she could get a Nutty Buddy bar. She was found four days later, floating facedown in the same river that cut through her backyard. Another girl was taken right from her front yard in broad daylight. Her mother went inside to answer the phone, which ended up being a wrong number. When she went back outside, her daughter was gone. All that was left behind was the girl's favorite blue blanket, the one that she carried everywhere with her.

When I finished paging through the last newspaper on my list, my fingers were all black from running my hands along the chalky ink. I leaned my back against the giant bookcase and looked down at my notebook. All I had written was: **82 goats (81 alive 1 dead), 12 kids (11 dead 1 still missing)**.

I closed my eyes and saw Dani's picture in my head, the one that was used all over the news. I never used to think about what happened to the kids on those "Missing Person" posters. They didn't used to look like real people to me. Before, the posters were just pieces of paper with a face, something to be ripped off a telephone pole or covered up with a new one the next week. But then I knew their names. I knew how old they were and how they might have looked in five years—if they were still alive by then. I knew about their favorite foods and how some still had a couple baby teeth left to lose. And I hated that I never used to care.

When I forced myself to look down at the two lines I had written in my notebook, I saw them differently. Before I could stop myself, I crossed out the twelve and put a "13." I changed the number missing to "2." After "still missing," I added: "**gonna be found**." If Dani was going to become a number on a page like all the rest, she was going to be one of the good ones.

I stared down at those three words, reading them over and over inside my head. They soon became a chant in my mind, shaking the corners of my skull like the stomps of football fans at a home game. I was so focused on my notebook that at first, I didn't notice the newspaper spread out beside me. It was opened up to the third page, and there were two orange Post-its attached to it with an arrow drawn on each. The arrows pointed to an article along the side. It wasn't as long as the other reports, but it was the only one with a picture above it.

A young boy looked out at me, his eyes slightly hidden behind the curled tip of a baseball cap. He was in a full baseball uniform, posing as if a photographer was saying, "That's it, champ, just imagine yourself on all the baseball cards!" He stood with his feet slightly apart, holding a bat that rested on his right shoulder. The boy had a wide smile, showing off the slight gap between his two front teeth.

At first, I didn't want to read the lines that followed. I wanted to think of him still playing in those baseball games, his mother sitting nervously in the stands and his dad leaning on the fence, reminding him to keep his eye on the ball. No matter how hard I tried to resist, my eyes eventually drifted to the Post-it notes. The first one pointed to the second paragraph, which read:

Mikael Dyer, a 10-year-old boy from the small town of Sharon, NH, was last seen on Mill Road Sunday afternoon. He was returning from a friend's house located on Spring Hill Road and was reported walking with his chocolate lab. The distance between the two houses is less than a mile, and his mother informed authorities it's a walk he was used to making. "He likes to go over to his friend's house to play ball. I make sure Hershey is with him, but we just never thought something like this [would happen]," Caroline Dyer said. She had no further comment.

I imagined the mother's voice cracking as she spoke, cutting the interview short. The article talked about how special he was, just like the stories of the other missing children. His tenth birthday was at the beginning of August, just eight days before Dani and I turned ten. He was last seen wearing his blue Little League shirt, the one that had "Champs!" on the front. The police ended up finding the chocolate lab five miles outside town—the parents thought she was trying to follow after the boy.

The second Post-it note was underneath one of the sentences near the bottom, the one that read:

Authorities searched the entire stretch of road between the Hillsburg residence and the Dyer home, only finding one area that showed signs of struggle. There were disturbances in the soil alongside the shoulder of Mill Road, but the police were unable to pull any concrete evidence. They have a partial boot print, which they projected would fall between size 9-11 in a US men's shoe.

A sinking feeling grew in my chest, and my stomach turned. I didn't know why reading it made me feel hopeful—like I was somehow close to a breakthrough. But those boots just weren't big enough for the man who took Dani. His were a size "13."

"It was just a couple days before, you know?" I jumped at the sound, her voice catching me off guard. I'd been completely unaware of the girl, who then crouched at the end of the aisle. She faced me, sitting with her feet underneath her. She looked nervous, something I hadn't seen in her face before. "I didn't mean to butt in—I just thought I could help. I come here sometimes, to look at stuff, so I know my way around. I'm Hillary by the way. I know, it sounds like I'm some kind of Girl Scout, but I can promise you that I'm definitely not one of those chicks. I have never gone camping in my life, and I think those thin mint cookies taste like chalk."

She talked for quite a while, telling me about how she wished the library had a vending machine and how she spent more time looking up old murders than actually doing her homework. The girl didn't mention anything about Dani, but I knew that she wanted to talk about her. I sat there quietly for a long while, waiting for her to run out of things to say. There was something about her that made me like her, and I found myself smiling at some of the things she said.

"So, what do you think?" she asked, looking at me anxiously. It took me a moment to realize she was talking about the newspaper article again. I looked back down at the boy in the baseball uniform, my throat starting to tighten.

"I don't know...I don't know why these things happen," I said softly. We sat quietly, each waiting for the other to start the topic we had been avoiding over those last fifteen minutes.

"Don't you think it's weird that they happened so close together?" she asked, breaking the quiet. I nodded my head in response. "I think there just has to be something here. Like, there was a boot print with yours, right?" She called it "yours," as if I had been the one shot with a needle and dragged through the dirt. But I knew she didn't mean it that way. She was one of the few who wanted to figure it out.

After that day, I started to think that I may have had one friend. Hillary and I would meet in the Newsroom every day after school, poring through newspaper after newspaper for kidnappings. It became our obsession. We looked at each case and tried to make sense of the details. My notebook became filled with kidnapping descriptions and facts, mixed in with the notes about dead presidents. I had one page in the back filled only with numbers: 8, 9, 8, 11, 14, 10, 6. There wasn't a title or description for the list. To the average person, it would have looked like a log sheet tracking nothing at all. But to me, each number represented a kid I had read about in the newspapers. I knew each one, just by the number. Eleven was Harry, the redheaded boy from Troy. Six was a little girl from a small fishing town that had a population of only four hundred people. Fourteen was the angry boy who had a scar slicing through his upper lip, making it look like his face had been sewn together.

I often found myself staring at the lists of numbers during class, wondering if anyone else still thought about them, too. Some of the numbers were circled in red, and I tried to look at those a little longer than the others. There was one page almost entirely filled with red circles. Some days, I had to avoid that page.

My parents didn't ask what I did at the library; they were just happy that I had a friend to hang out with. Hillary Atwood was the first friend I ever made on my own. Even though she was in the grade above me, I started sitting at her table during lunch. The grades split the two sides of the cafeteria, and the sixth graders usually didn't go anywhere near the older kids' section—not even the cool kids.

It came out of nowhere. One day, while sitting at my usual table in the back corner, I looked up and saw Hillary walking towards me.

"What are you doing sitting by yourself at the loser table?" she asked obliviously.

"Um, I don't know if you go to this school or not, but I'm pretty much the biggest loser here."

"Well, that's just stupid. Here, get up, let's go," she replied.

"Where are we going?" I asked, trying to quickly shove all of my food back into my paper bag. It was one of the good days when Mom had packed me a lunch.

"Over to my side. Sixth graders are dumb anyways." I didn't remind her that I was one of those sixth graders. I followed closely behind her, noticing the scared looks that waved over each table as we passed by. My classmates kept their eyes glued to their feet, Amy Taber the only one to say something as we walked past.

"Doesn't she know that wizards are totally lame?" Amy said, pretending as if she didn't know we could hear her.

Hillary didn't slow down or even bother to look in Amy's direction. But she smoothly replied over her shoulder, just loud enough so that everyone would hear, "Amy, why don't you tell your mom to stop being such a slut and sleeping with my dad. It's really starting to make me want to vomit." Everybody went completely silent, but Hillary just kept on walking as I tried to keep up.

It wasn't a secret that Mr. Atwood slept around, despite still being married to Mrs. Atwood. Hillary pretended that she didn't care and made jokes about it, but I could tell that deep down, it bothered her. The Atwoods were the richest people in town, and that probably made Hillary's dad think he could get away with just about anything. He owned over two hundred Taco Bells, but my mom said that was nothing to brag about. They lived in a big house on the outskirts of town—the one I used to call "Belle's mansion" when I was younger. I heard they owned all the land that surrounded it for miles.

"Okay, just make sure that you don't say anything about Tommy's hair. He is really sensitive about it right now." I nodded my head, even though I had no idea who Tommy was. Hillary and her friends sat at a table in the center of the seventh grade side of the lunchroom. Three boys spread out around the table that seated nine. They were the same group I had always seen riding their skateboards off of church steps around town. Each of them wore tight pants that made their legs look extra skinny. There were holes in each of their shirts—the kind sold that way.

I immediately knew which one was Tommy. He had a head of curly, orange hair with a large chunk missing from the front. The shorter hairs stuck straight up from his scalp, uneven, like they had been burned off. For some reason, that made me instantly like him. When he saw us approaching, he pushed his curls overtop the spiky patch, only to have them stubbornly spring back to where they belonged. He kept his head down and didn't look up at me when I sat down next to him. The other two were named Fletch and Buzz, but I had a feeling those weren't their real names. They both had jet-black hair that fell over their eyes like the anime characters on Saturday morning cartoons. Fletch had a lip ring that he liked to nibble at, surprisingly the only piercing I saw on his body. Buzz was the fidgety one. He constantly kept a pen in his hand, twirling it between his fingers and drumming it on the table. Hillary later told me that he had "severe ADD," and he used the pen as a way to help him concentrate on something for an extended period of time.

Hillary didn't introduce me to the group that first day; they acted like they didn't need an introduction. We talked about the normal school stuff, like how Miss Dingleberry still stalked Mr. Kretz and how seventh grade was the worst because you had to dissect a dead baby pig. I had only ever dissected owl pellets, so I just pretended to know what they were talking about.

I found out the truth behind Tommy's hair but not because I asked for it. He had supposedly had a bad run-in with his sister's hair straightener. Tommy tried to play it off as a "reverse Mohawk," but Buzz and Fletch kept on him about his mom not allowing him shave his head.

It wasn't until the end of lunch that anyone said something about Dani.

"So, you hang out with Hillary after school, right? To figure out what happened to your sister?" Buzz asked casually. He drummed away with his pen to the beat of the sentence.

"Um, yeah. I guess," I said looking down at my feet. It was the first time someone had brought up Dani without the cover of whispers and hallway corners.

"Ah, don't worry, we aren't going to tell anyone. We think it's cool what you are doing." Fletch threw his arm around my shoulders, the same way Dani used to.

After that day, I was no longer the loner sitting in the corner of the cafeteria. For the first time, I had a real, honest-to-God group of friends. They weren't like the cousins whose parents forced them to come to your birthday parties or the posers looking for what they could get out of the deal. They wanted me at that big table in the middle of the lunchroom. They included me in their inside jokes and taught me the best one-liners to get back at Amy with. Tommy traded me his favorite granola bars for my chocolate puddings. Buzz and Fletch took turns walking me to my classes, even biology on the opposite end of the school. The judging whispers grew quiet, and I stopped noticing the stares of the other kids.

I probably should have felt pitied, but instead, I felt protected. Other than Dani, no one had ever watched over me. We looked out for each other. However, there were times that I wondered if they were starting to fill that huge, empty hole that she had left behind. As much as it hurt, I hated the thought of anyone else filling that space. Those were the days that I went to the library alone, losing myself in the stacks of newspapers. It reminded me that I could never forget that she was coming back—that somewhere, hidden in the details, I would find her.

It wasn't until after Easter Break that Fletch, Buzz, and Tommy started showing up at the library, too. I never asked them to come—they just joined in one day. Agnes pretended to be concerned about having us all there at once, but I knew that she secretly loved seeing us use her Newsroom. She always made a point of updating us on the number of hours she had spent that day organizing her papers. Mr. Kretz told my class that there was a new website on the Internet that let you read newspapers right off a computer screen. I wondered what would one day happen to Agnes and her "Pride of Bergen County."

Is that what happens to the things we care about, that someday they just stop mattering? I was afraid it would happen for Dani. People had stopped asking about her, as if she had never existed. Teachers didn't look at me with pity anymore. The police stopped calling to check in on us. Other students started thinking of me as "just Keely" instead of "the girl with the missing sister." I hated the thought of it all becoming *normal*—life without Dani.

By the time summer arrived, I had nearly filled ten notebooks with six years of kidnappings. I would spend hours going back through them, trying to find anything to connect them. The majority of facts seemed to come out of the endings, even though none of them finished with a happily-ever-after. And those were the parts that stayed with me the most. They made me feel like I was back in the woods, looking into the tall man's empty, black eyes.

Three weeks after school ended, we had our first breakthrough. I was in the middle of reading about a runaway teenager when Fletch and Hillary came running over to my table. Usually, we each worked on our own and met up at the end of the day to talk about our findings. But that day was different.

"I think we have something," Fletch said, his lip ring threatening to split open his bottom lip under his wide smile.

"It's just too much of a coincidence. It has to be something," Hillary said excitedly. My heart began to race, but I prepared myself for another dead end. They each had several newspapers with them.

"Okay, so Fletch was the one who found the first connection. There were two kidnappings that happened back in 1991—just a day apart from one another. The first one happened on September 5 up in North Windham, Maine. A boy was at the local park with his family when he was taken. Take a guess how old he was," Hillary said as she placed a newspaper in front of me.

"Ten?" I asked, already knowing the answer.

"Bingo. He was only gone a couple minutes before his parents went to check on him. He had gone to the drinking fountain by himself, which was only a hundred yards away from where his parents were. The fountain was behind a building, so they never actually saw what happened. It was as if he vanished out of thin air," she said, letting her words hang eerily between us.

"Were there any clues about what happened?" I asked hopefully.

"Not really. The police found evidence of him being dragged into the woods directly behind the building. The only thing they found at the crime scene was a boot print in the dirt."

"It was a size ten," Fletch chimed in.

"But then it can't be the same guy. The one found in our woods was a different size," I said, overcome by defeat.

"We don't know that for sure. Here," Hillary said, placing the other newspaper in front of me, "just take a look at this." I looked down at an article about a nine-year-old girl from Tamworth, New Hampshire. She had turned ten just five days after she was kidnapped. Her name was Kayla Bensley. There wasn't a picture of her in the newspaper, but I could tell that she smiled a lot just from what people said about her. I scanned the article for the small piece of information I was looking for. It was towards the end, almost like an afterthought. A small "13" was hidden among the quotes from the parents and the reporter's recap.

"So I know what you are thinking because that's exactly what we thought. It had to be a coincidence—two ten-year-old kids that were taken a day apart, just by chance. But Hillary and I kept looking to see if there were any other kidnappings that happened close together. We found two back in 1993, but the second one ended up being nothing—I guess the father took the girl out of town when he wasn't supposed to. But then we found this." Fletch put two newspapers in front of me, placing them side by side. Both articles had a picture of a child, one boy and one girl. The boy had curly hair that covered his eyes, and he grinned a closed-mouth smile. As for the girl, even though the newspaper was in black and white, I could still tell that she had red hair.

"The girl was taken on October 10, 1994, from a town called Greene up in Maine, and the boy was kidnapped just two days later from Hardwick, Vermont. They were both ten years old when they were taken," Hillary said.

"Did they find any boot prints?"

"Just at one crime scene. It was an eleven. But the paper said that the police found it in the mud, so perfect that it could've been planted."

"It was like he wanted them to see it, Keely," Fletch said.

"But...why?"

"It's like the most basic trick in the book. I've seen it all the time in the murder mysteries I have looked through. By giving them a clear piece of evidence, it will make the cops focus all their time on that one single thing. He was giving them a distraction," Hillary said.

I looked at the pile of newspapers lying in front of me, trying to make sense out of it all. "So, do you think all of these were done by...him?" I asked, looking at Hillary. The man's blacked out face appeared in my mind, always too dark for me to fully see his face. He wore all black, and his hat stooped overtop his eyes.

"He could be getting help. But for some reason, I don't think so. Even though they're all different sizes, there was only one set of boot prints found at the crime scenes. I mean, come on, Keel, they've just gotta be connected...six different kidnappings, only a couple days separating each pair, boot prints found at almost every crime scene, all the kids having just turned ten..."

"Yeah, but why so spread apart? This one happened in 1994," I said, my finger covering the face of the boy with shaggy hair. "Why wait six years to do it again?"

"Maybe we're missing something then?" Fletch said.

"I mean, okay, there are some weird similarities between them all. I'm not denying that. But what if we're wrong, and they don't end up being connected at all?" I asked.

"Keely...I think the bigger question is, what if they do?" It wasn't what Hillary said that gave me a goose bump trail up my body. It was the glow that filled her eyes when she said it.

A little over two months passed without another lead. We went all the way back to 1978 but couldn't find any other kidnapping pairs. Hillary was sure that the answer had to be hidden in the newspapers, but I could see that even she was starting to second-guess herself as we kept coming up empty.

One night—three days before the anniversary of Dani's kidnapping—I had a dream. In it was a girl from the newspapers. She appeared in black and white, except her hair glowed a brilliant red, like I had imagined. In the back corner of my mind, she stared at me with her newspaper print eyes. Suddenly, her head tilted back as her eyes shot upwards. I wanted to see what held her gaze but could not unlock my eyes from her. It was like a vise held me, its metal arms wrapped tightly around my neck. The moment I felt myself breaking free to catch a glimpse, I woke up.

The room was pitch black except for the last few glow-in-the-dark stars clinging to the ceiling. Two more had fallen off since Dani had been taken. No one would have guessed they used to form a constellation— connected to one another in the familiar pattern we spent summers gazing up at in the night sky. Instead, they then appeared as lonely dots scattered across the cracked plaster.

I bolted up in bed, an idea bursting through my hazy mind. My head spun from sitting up too quickly, as I hurriedly switched on my bedside light. I pulled out the plastic bin of journals from underneath my bed. The notebook was closest to the top—the red one labeled "1998." Somehow, the missing stars showed me where I was supposed to go.

I turned about fifteen pages in, skimming my finger to the middle of the page. Her name was Brooklyn Parker, age ten, and she was last seen walking home from the park in Bronxville, New York. She had been wearing a red dress, one her mother had picked out. The article was dated April 30, 1998. It talked about how much her father missed her, that he would give anything to have his little girl back. At the bottom of the page, in parentheses, I had written:

(August 19, 1997)

Until then, I hadn't realized she had been put in the wrong year. There wasn't an article from when it first happened—missing girls must not have been that unusual around New York City. That, and people were probably more interested in reading about the Boston Red Sox trading Mike Stanley to the New York Yankees or that man who blew up Oklahoma City being given the death penalty. The girl's father had managed to get a spot in the newspaper because the reporter seemed to have a thing against cops not doing their job. According to Mr. Parker, the police were only pretending to be looking for his little girl.

My hands didn't immediately reach for the 1997 journal that I knew would be on the floor next to me. I was afraid that I was wrong and that I had only imagined the missing stars in the constellation. The 1997 journal wasn't as worn as the others, probably because it was one of the bad years. There weren't any kids in that one who had returned. I slowly flipped to the second half of the journal, looking for the section labeled "August." There were only two kids listed, one from a small town in South Dakota, and the other from East Granby, Connecticut. The South Dakota kidnapping was of a twenty-four-year-old woman whose body was never found. The East Granby one was of a young boy, exactly ten years old. Police didn't know precisely where he was taken, but they eventually found one of his shoes in the woods behind his house. His mom said that he would often walk through them as a shortcut when he came home from the skate park. She told him to always take the long way around through the neighborhood, but the boy was known for doing things his own way. Stubborn, just like his father.

Not too far from the single shoe, the police found a full boot print. They said it looked bigger than an average man's—a size 13 in U.S. men's shoes. My eyes scanned the page for what I was looking for, my heart stopping in my chest when I found it. In the far margin of the sheet, the squished and somewhat smeared scribble read: August 15.

Just four days before the girl from Bronxville.

I stayed up the rest of that night digging through the notebooks and trying to put the stars back together. The connections weren't obvious, but maybe that was the point. *Maybe that was what he wanted all along.* I flipped to the pages summarizing the eight kidnappings we had found—including Dani's. I snuck downstairs to my dad's study, grabbing his laptop and the road map he kept tucked between two books on his shelf. It was the one we had used on our cross-country family vacation, Mom directing as Dad drove our old station wagon with the wooden siding. I unfolded it and spread it across my bed, its wide ends spilling over the sides. It forced me to push Dani's bed back next to mine, our green and blue comforters blending to form my table.

It was a sign I didn't fail to notice.

The map was a blown-up version of North America, but the United States was the only part that really held any detail. Tiny, winding lines filled the page, with larger webs giving away the major cities across the labeled states.

I started with Reading, a dot marked with my green gel pen. I searched for the place named "Sharon" but couldn't find it anywhere on the map. Thankfully, it came up on my dad's computer when I searched it in MapQuest. It was about an hour and a half away from where Dani was taken. I put a second green dot right below the town labeled "Peterborough."

For that next hour, I went down the list and labeled all the locations for the other kidnappings. Reading was the only spot that I didn't have to look up on my dad's computer. The other places were all small towns. The locations for the 1991 kidnappings were only an hour and seventeen minutes apart. I marked them both with navy dots. I labeled the next two from 1994 with the light blue marker, their dots slightly farther apart than the dark blue ones. They were a little higher up, one dot on the Maine border and the other in the northern part of Vermont. The final two were farthest from the other dots. One was all the way down in New York City, and the second—the one for the boy from East Granby—was a little higher up but still not as high as the one I had in Reading. I marked those two with a yellow marker.

After I finished, I stared at those eight dots, trying to see the pattern in the scattered points. The more I tried to piece it together, the harder it was to remember what I had seen in the first place. I kept going back to the notebooks, trying to find anything that I had missed. *The kidnappings happened three years apart. Boot sizes 10, 11, and 13 were found. Each time there was one boy and one girl. All the kids were ten years old.*

And then it hit me.

I quickly folded the map back up and threw it into my backpack, along with the two notebooks. The sun hadn't come up yet, so I grabbed a flashlight from the bin next to our back door and made my way to the barn. I knew my parents wouldn't be up for another two hours, but I still left a note on my bed in case they went in looking for me. It read: Gone to Belle's Mansion.

Luckily, my bike's tires hadn't lost too much air over that last year, and I had enough to get me to Hillary's house. I duct-taped the flashlight to my handlebars but made sure to keep it off until I was halfway down our road.

The Atwoods lived on the other side of town, but it felt like an eternity away. By the time I reached her house, the sun peeked above the manicured lawn. I stopped my bike at the start of Hillary's long driveway, the large, swooping willows bowing over either side. *It's the type of driveway that deserves an iron gate at the far end*, I thought as I started down the pathway.

As I neared the house, a string of lights automatically sprang to life. I instantly felt on edge, the rest of the house remaining hauntingly dark and the air still and quiet. I leaned my bike up against a nearby tree, as the kick-stand was still broken from the time Dani dared me to ride it down a flight of stairs.

The pebbled drive crunched underneath my shoes as I walked to the main door. I didn't know what to do when I reached the front step—whether to ring the doorbell or knock with the large metal ring that hung from a golden lion's mouth. Instead, I gently hit my knuckles against the thick wood, part of me hoping no one would hear.

It didn't take long for a light to come on in the entryway. A tiny woman opened the door just a crack, wearing a frilly black and white uniform and her hair in a perfect bun. I didn't think people still had maids, let alone required them to wear ruffles like in the olden days.

"Can I help you, Miss?" she asked with a slight accent.

"Yeah, do you know if Hillary is home?" I said awkwardly.

"Ms. Hillary is still sleeping. May I pass along a message for her?"

"Um, I was wondering if I could come in and see her. It's kind of an emergency."

"One moment, please," she stated after a brief pause. "I will alert her. And your name is?"

"Keely. Tell her it's Keely." She shut the door as she turned on her heel, leaving me standing there uncomfortably on the front step. A few minutes passed in the cold quiet. I started to think that maybe she wasn't coming back. As I began to turn back towards my bike, the door suddenly jerked open, sending the metal knocker pounding against the door.

"Keely! What are you doing here? Is everything okay?" Hillary asked anxiously. Her eyes squinted from sleep; pillow marks still indented the side of her face.

"I'm so sorry for coming here so early, I just couldn't wait." Her eyes drifted to my backpack, causing her to instantly awaken.

"Come with me!" she said as she yanked me inside. The small maid stood stiffly by the door and glared suspiciously out of the corner of her eye. I tried to keep up with Hillary, my arm on the verge of popping out of its socket as she pulled me through the wraparound staircase that led to the second floor.

"Don't feel weird about Joana. She is always super uptight about letting guests into the house," she said when we were safely out of earshot from the snooty maid.

"Are you guys like some kind of royalty that I don't know about? I thought maids were only for like presidents and people who lived in the 1950s," I said breathlessly as we bounded up the stairs.

"I don't know—it's my dad's thing. I guess he just likes to say that we have a maid or something, and it's not like my mom's gonna clean anything around here. That, and my brother is the biggest slob on this planet."

Hillary didn't talk much about her brother. All I knew was that he was supposed to be in ninth grade but was held back a year, probably because he skipped school half the time. He was the first middle schooler I had ever heard of trying a cigarette before sixth grade. When people talked about him, they never called him by his real name. They called him the "Viper." According to every mother and father in Ridgewood, Vander Atwood was "bad news." Grown-ups left it at that.

There were approximately twelve separate rooms on the second floor, and Hillary's room was at the very end of the hall. It was nearly as large as my entire living room. At first, I wondered if we had wandered into the wrong room. A giant canopy bed with pink lace filled the center. It reminded me of the story of "The Princess and the Pea" that Mom read to Dani and me when we were little. A life-like Barbie mansion filled one of the corners, partially covered with a pink, ruffled sheet. If it weren't for the sci-fi posters covering the floral wallpaper or the action figures stacked in front of the rows of dolls, I would have thought Hillary had a sister.

"They used to be my thing," she said, noticing me eying the dollhouse. "I don't play with them anymore, in case you were wondering."

"Oh, no it doesn't matter to me. I just didn't take you for a Barbie kind of girl, that's all."

"Well, I'm a lot different than I used to be. I'm not into that 'be a girl like everyone else' kind of thing. I used to care what people thought, but now I just don't give a shit." If there was one thing I had come to learn about Hillary over those first nine months, it was that if someone told her to jump, she would sit down and not move for hours. She didn't like that people automatically assumed she wanted a girl toy in her Happy Meal at McDonalds. She refused to wear dresses simply because she could. It was that determination to be different that I envied most.

"Okay, so spill!" she shouted, bringing me back to my mission. "You had to have found something if you woke me up at the butt crack of dawn." I pulled the map out of my backpack, unfolding it in front of my chest. Her eyes roved over the colored points, a confused look crossing her face.

"I honestly don't know why it came to me, but I found the missing connection," I said as I reached into my bag for the two notebooks. I opened them to the marked-off pages, setting them side by side on the pink bedspread. "There were two kidnappings in August 1997," I said with excitement bursting in my voice. I pointed out each of the circled dates.

For the first time since I had met her, Hillary was speechless. When she lifted her gaze to mine, she looked at me through moist eyes. It was then that I realized she was truly in it—that she hadn't forgotten about Dani like the rest of the world. She and I were in it together.

I explained the pattern of dots to her, highlighting the links between the kidnappings in the constellation we had formed together over those long months. My finger traced from one dot to another as I spoke; a tingle shot through my fingertip each time it ran over a colored mark.

"Keely...you did it. I can't believe you found it, but you really did it." She threw her arms around me, catching me by surprise. I stiffened for a brief moment. Her hands gripped on to my shirt as she held me tightly. I felt my arms reach up to hug her back, a reaction I had almost forgotten since Dani went missing.

"There's something else," I muffled into her shoulder.

"There's more?"

"If these *are* all connected, I think there's a way for us to find where he's taking them." I pulled the wrinkled map from between us and spread it across the bed.

"Spit it out, already," Hillary eagerly said as I paused over the map.

"I kept replaying the facts in my head, trying to look at it in a different way each time. First, I checked to see how far away each place was from the other. It didn't make sense. The two that took place the most days apart were actually the closest to each other. And for the one that happened up in Maine and the other in Vermont, the towns were three and a half hours away from each other, but there were just two days separating the kidnappings."

"I don't think I'm following."

"You see, it's not about the distance between the towns at all. It's how long it took him to *get* somewhere. For the two blue dots, those kidnappings only happened a day apart. But then the light blue and green ones were both two days apart. So it took him a longer time to get to those places."

"But how are we supposed to know where he is coming from?" I couldn't help but smile, because it was the exact question I wanted her to ask.

"Don't you see? It's the yellow dots all the way down here. Those happened four days apart, which means it took him the longest time to get there."

"Okay. I still don't think I get it," she said, slightly frustrated. I took out a red marker from my backpack and drew a circle around the empty space between the dark blue and green dots. I waited for her to catch on to what I was saying. But for once, she was doing the following while I was doing the leading.

"Here!" I said, driving the tip of the red marker into the center of the circle. "It means that he must have taken them to someplace in here. Just think about it. He has to come from somewhere, right? And he can't be driving around with a kid in his car, because the police set up roadblocks after kidnappings, just like they did for Dani. So he had to have a place to take them after he did it—before he went out and got the next kid."

"But why there?"

"Because the green and dark blue dots were the kidnappings that happened the closest together, so he would have had to come from somewhere in between them."

"You really think he would bring them all back to the same place?"

"It's the only thing that makes sense. Come on, Hillary—he had a needle! He knew exactly what he was doing, and he knew exactly where we would be." The room went silent—I had never talked about the actual kidnapping before. Hillary's eyes were downcast, and she fidgeted with a stray string at the bottom of her oversized nightshirt. "All I'm saying is that he had to have done this before. He knew exactly what he was doing. If these were all done by him, then he probably knows that it works. He knows what he has to do to get away with it."

"Do you think they are all still out there?" She spoke very quietly, almost like she wasn't sure she wanted to ask it. I had never seen Hillary look anything other than tough. But in that moment, I could see the little girl who used to play with Barbie dolls under the safety of her ruffled canopy.

"I ask myself that a lot. I wonder if she is…still here. And the only answer that I come up with—the only one that I can live with—is that she's got to be. I think that I would know it, or feel it in some way, if she was gone." It was one of the many times that I felt like crying but knew the tears wouldn't come. No matter how heavily they swelled inside, they wouldn't teeter past the brims of my pooling eyes.

"So, what are we going to do next?" she asked.

"The only thing we can do. We go find her and bring her home."

I planned to show the map to my family on the anniversary of Dani's kidnapping. It was as if it was supposed to be the "gift" I brought to the "party." Mom asked me what I did the morning I ran off to Hillary's house, and I lied to her, even though I could feel the weight of the notebooks in my backpack. Instead of showing her what I had found, I just walked past her and up the staircase. All I said was that I was finishing a summer project with a friend.

I told myself that it was because we needed something to help us get through that second Wednesday of September. I wanted to give my family some hope in the moment they needed it the most. More than anything, I wanted to be the person to give it to them.

It was supposed to happen when we got back from Allaire—right after Nana and Bumpy got to our house, when we were all sitting around the living room. I pictured what I would say, and I even drew out four separate maps in preparation. Each map was labeled with the person it belonged to, with Mom and Nana's written in my most careful handwriting.

But then September 11 happened. Nana and Bumpy stayed in Reading, mostly because they didn't like leaving their house when something really bad happened. We ended up spending the night in Farmingdale, Mom and I at a loss for what we could do to make Dad feel better. He didn't say much of anything after the planes crashed, not even when we asked him a question. He would just gently shake his head "yes" or "no." When we got to the hotel, he skipped dinner and went right to bed—he didn't even brush his teeth. Mom took me out to a Denny's up the road, and we ordered a dozen pancakes and more strawberry topping than two people could eat. There was something about ordering breakfast at night that made me feel better inside, as if I was breaking the rules and wouldn't get in trouble for it.

"You know, I didn't have to face anything tough like this when I was your age. The first time something really difficult happened to me was back when I was twenty-three. It took me, well, I'd say it took me years to bounce back from it. I just hope you know how proud I am of you, for being so very brave and strong this past year," Mom said halfway through our fourth pancake.

"What happened to you?" I asked, ignoring the warmth that grew in my cheeks with her compliment.

"You know those two pictures I have on my dresser—the ones with the lady in the yellow sundress?" I nodded my head, my mouth still full with food. "That was Frannie. She was my closest friend in college, and she died of cancer just a year after we graduated. It was fast, like she was healthy one second and then gone the next. I didn't know how to handle it, and I was angry for a long time."

"Is that why you talk to other people who have problems? To figure out why it is that people get sad?"

"I used to think that. But then I realized, maybe if I focus on other people's problems, I don't have to think so much about my own." I didn't really know what to say back. She was talking to me like I was older, as if I was one of the women who came over to our house for book club every other Sunday, the ones who smelled of flowery perfumes and liked to talk about complicated things.

"Mom, do you think Dad is going to be okay?" I asked quietly. She bit down on her lip, giving away that she was trying not to cry.

"Well, sweetheart, Dad is going to be okay because he still has us. We still have each other."

"And Dani, too," I said, more like a statement than a question. There was a moment after I said it that she looked like she was about to correct me. Instead, she just forced a smile and nodded her head in agreement.

We didn't really talk for the rest of dinner. I thought about telling her about the maps, telling her that I knew where we could find Dani. But each time I was about to, she would sigh heavily and look distantly out the window, staring off into the nothingness.

When we arrived back at the hotel room, Dad was asleep in the far bed with his back to us. I crawled into bed behind him and rested my palm on his back. I didn't wrap my arms around him like I usually did, but I still wanted him to know I was there. Mom followed behind me, sandwiching me into the warmth between them.

I had lightless dreams that night, pitch-blackness pierced by loud explosions going off in the corners of my mind. I awoke from one of the loud bangs, finding the room still dark in the deadened night. Mom was still folded up around me, but Dad's spot lay empty. I reached my hand across the sheet, his indented spot cool to the touch. Trying not to wake my mother, I rolled to the other side of the bed and swung my legs over the edge.

Light came from the crack beneath the bathroom door, but I didn't hear any noise on the other side. I tiptoed to the door, placing my ear against it before lightly pushing it open. It groaned in response, but my dad continued to stare ahead of him. He lay fully clothed in the empty tub, his knees bent in towards his chest. There was a bottle half-filled with golden liquid resting next to him, reminding me of the ones Bumpy hid in the top cabinet. I moved slowly towards him, not quite sure if he wanted to be left alone. I pushed the bottle towards the toilet and sat down in its spot. My arms automatically reached up to rest on the edge of the tub, my chin following to sit on top of them.

I didn't know how long we stayed like that—his eyes fixed on the white, tiled wall and I resting next to him. My eyes roamed over his face. There were puffy bags underneath his glassy eyes. He kept his hands folded atop his belly, moving up and down with the rise and fall of his chest. I realized he wasn't going to be the one to break the silence. I went back out to the main room and grabbed the bulging folder from my duffel bag. Mom was still fast asleep as I went back in the bathroom and shut the creaking door behind me.

I opened the folder onto the floor and took out sheet after sheet, lining them up along the tub's edge.

"You and Mom probably have been wondering why I've been spending so much time at the library. And I know I should have told you the real reason I was there, but the truth is that I didn't know if I was even going to find anything. I didn't want to tell you guys unless it actually worked." He continued to stare blankly ahead. I placed my hand on his shoulder and gave it a light squeeze, hoping to break the spell. "Dad, I think I know where Dani is."

At first he remained motionless, still lost in his trance. Then, ever so slowly, he turned his head to face mine. He gradually came back to me, a hint of recognition shining through his bloodshot and misty eyes.

"I know it sounds crazy, but I really think I know where he took her." I handed him each photocopied newspaper clipping one at a time, starting with the ones from 1991. I covered each kidnapping, walking him through the details. With each paper, life began to fill his eyes once again. Little by little, he found his way out of his dark place.

"Each happened within days of the other, and that's how I was able to figure out the pattern." I ended by handing him a tracing of the map, pointing out what each colored dot stood for. He hung on my every word, but I noticed that his eyes kept drifting to the red circle I had drawn near the top of the page. "This is where I think he is taking them," I said, putting my finger inside its center. I waited for him to say something, anything. His eyes scanned over the sheets in front of him, as he occasionally shook his head. When he finally looked up at me, I knew he was starting to believe it, too.

"When you were much younger, probably too young for you to remember, Dani got really sick. We didn't know what was wrong with her—some doctors thought it was a bacterial infection; others thought it was just a bad virus. Either way, she ended up in the hospital for four days, and none of us were allowed to go near her because they worried she was contagious. For those four days, you didn't sleep, you barely ate, and for the life of us, we couldn't get you to stop crying. Your mother and I didn't know what to do, because you had always been the calmer baby, the one who rarely cried or fussed. It wasn't until Dani came home that you stopped screaming. It was like magic. We put her in the crib next to you. You turned your head, looked at her, and just went to sleep."

His voice didn't break, but he cried as he spoke, trails of tears soaking his cheeks. I didn't remember the story, but it still made my heart grow heavier, as if at any moment I would turn back into that screaming baby.

The tub groaned as he lifted himself out and quickly pulled me into his arms. I pushed my face deep into his shirt, breathing in his familiar safe, musky scent.

"Keely, I don't know how I didn't see it. You haven't changed one bit. You were screaming then, and you are screaming now, only this time we just weren't listening." I lifted my head to see his face. What I found was something I didn't expect. He looked at peace.

"I just really want her back, Daddy."

"I know you do, baby. And if there's anyone who can bring her back to us, it's you."

Chapter Four
September 12, 2001

I had always been good at uncovering the answers. When the street artist who played outside Penn Station changed to sad songs, I knew it was because his black lab no longer sat beside him. There was one time when Ms. Potts, our next-door neighbor, bought two hundred containers of Hollywood Beauty Queen Cream. She said it was because of the sixty percent discount from the company going under, but I knew it was really because her husband had moved in with a younger lady. And I knew that Bumpy wore collared shirts, buttoned to the top, to hide the mysterious scars at the bottom of his neck.

My mother used to tell me that I could figure out anything—I just had to look hard enough and ask the right questions. And like everything else she told me, I had believed her.

That was until everything changed. Like how we couldn't choose the food that shot down to us from the ceiling. Or how we only had ten minutes to shower when we needed at least twenty to get the basement smell off our skin. My ability to understand the things around me seemed to escape the moment I was trapped in that basement. But I knew that the only way out of there was getting that back.

It happened on October 1, the exact day Brook had predicted. She said it didn't happen every year—only when you turned sixteen. It meant that it was Clara and Chet's year, which explained why Clara spent all day drawing suns in packs of clouds and Chet lay silently in bed the few times he was in his cell. Chet disappeared two weeks before it happened, just like Brook said he would. I'd only been there five days and was still hiding under my blankets when Dias—the name he insisted we call him—took him away. I didn't know that would be the last time I'd ever see Chet.

It wasn't until he came for Clara that Brook told me the clues she had put together. She said that it always happened the same way—we came in pairs and left in them, too. Brook explained that we each had a "partner"—hers was Kai and mine was Mika. And before us, there was Kayla and Brent.

Kayla was the one who first noticed the patterns—like how he took us all at ten years old and how each pair of kidnappings happened within days of the other. She and Brent seemed to have been the first. They were alone in the basement for three years before Clara and Chet arrived. It was another three before Brook came, just a few days apart from Kai. And like Clara and Chet, Kayla disappeared on October 1, two weeks after Brent went away for good. They had just turned sixteen. Brook had only been there seven weeks.

"Where do you think they go?" I asked, not knowing if I wanted to hear the answer.

"I think he takes them to the room with the red door," she said, her face wiped clean of emotion.

"How do you know?"

"Kayla told me a couple days before she disappeared that he had taken Brent there. Brent told her bad things happened."

"Have you ever gone there?" I asked hesitantly.

"No."

"What was Kayla like?" I said, trying to force the red room out of my mind.

"I didn't know her for very long, but I really liked her. Kayla was pretty quiet but in a nice sort of way. She didn't have to say much to make you feel connected to her. I think that's why Brent didn't change as much as Chet did."

"What do you mean?"

"Chet never used to be that way, you know, angry and annoyed at everything. He used to smile. Even being down here, he found reasons to let himself be happy. But somewhere along the way, things changed. Kayla noticed Brent change over time, too. At first it was small things, like the way that he talked or how he looked at her. Then they got bigger. She told me that there was something bugging him, that she thought he was hiding something from her."

"Did she ever find out what it was?"

"No, she didn't. And I have tried talking to Clara about Chet, but she just wanted to go on pretending that nothing was wrong."

"I guess she just thought it was easier that way?"

"Yeah, I guess so," she said, more to herself than to me. "I remember Kayla telling me the last morning I saw her that she thought something wasn't right. She kept saying that something was coming—something was coming to get her. Of course Clara thinks that Kayla imagined things, but I think there's a part of her that knows Kayla wasn't just making it up."

"Do you think Clara feels it, too?"

"Yeah," was all she said.

October 1 became the date that everyone feared after Kayla and Brent disappeared. Clara was even quieter than usual that morning. When he came to get her, I didn't hide under my covers. I stood right up close to the front of my cell, my hands wrapped tightly around the bars as I watched him.

He came in the moment the lights came back on, his electric poker faithfully at his side. Clara came dutifully out of her cell when he asked, clenching one of her drawings at her side. It was one of her sun-in-the-clouds paintings, except I could only see the clouds through its crinkles. The sun must have been caught in her hand. She had tears in her eyes when she stepped out of her cage, and I noticed her take a moment to look at each of us. She didn't have to say anything for us to know she was saying goodbye.

"Why? Why are you doing this to us?" The words forced their way out of my mouth. They came out high-pitched and weak, and I regretted not sounding braver. He turned to me, his cold eyes on mine. He began slowly walking towards my cell, his face empty and his hand wrapped tightly around Clara's as she followed. I wanted to move away from the bars when he arrived, his huge body casting a shadow over me. But I kept my feet firmly planted.

"'Why,' you ask? 'Why' is the hardest question for a curious person. 'Why' never has a full enough answer to satisfy, for it is the one that drives curiosity into madness. Be careful with that, Pandora," he said with a smile in his voice. My eyes moved to his chest as he leaned in closer with each slow word. It wasn't until then that I noticed.

His gold cross was no longer there.

"People like you don't stay here forever. One day you will go back down to the dark, the same place that you came from," I said as I looked up at him, hoping he could feel all of the hate growing inside of me. There was a brief moment that he looked almost saddened by what I had said, looking to Clara at his side. His hand reached up for the cross that was no longer there, as if its presence could have been enough to make him feel good again. It wasn't long before the last sign of sadness was replaced by rage.

"So be it," he said chillingly, lifting his electric stick just enough to draw my eyes to it. He turned and left, dragging Clara along with him. The door shut with a deafening slam, its metallic crash ringing in my ears long after he had left.

I fell to my knees, kicking the dirt up around me. "He's going to kill her, isn't he?" I said softly.

"I think so," Brook replied.

"We don't know that. We don't know for sure where he takes them," Kai said from across the way.

"Well, he's not going in there to play patty-cake with them. And he sure doesn't just send 'em back home. He does something with them," Brook countered.

We all fell silent, trying to take comfort in the quiet. We didn't hear any screams or banging, but we never heard much of anything through those thick walls. I tried to tell myself that they were fine, that they would return later in the day. But when the fluorescent lights dimmed and he brought me for my shower, the overpowering smell of bleach in the hallway burned my nose. The stink stayed with me long after the lights went out, reminding me of death.

It scared me how quickly the memories of my old life began to fade—how I stopped remembering what it felt like. I started to forget what Dad's eggs tasted like on a Saturday morning and the things Keely and I talked about as the world grew hazy in the glow of our nightlight. The good moments were painted over by a new, dark layer, and it became harder to see what it looked like before.

Every day felt the same. The lights would gradually turn on every morning and then fade each night, as if a strange sun had been trapped in there with us. Cereal would shoot down as the lights grew brighter, alternating between Raisin Bran and Corn Flakes. I used to be picky about my cereal, but little things like having extra sugar or marshmallows mattered a whole lot less down there. The cereal would come in a small box with an even smaller carton of milk, the kind that came with lunches at school. He didn't bother giving us a bowl or spoon. I learned that if I closed my eyes and drank the milk right after throwing a handful of the cereal into my mouth, I could almost fool myself into believing I was eating at my family's breakfast table. It was a trick that Kai had taught me.

"Why is it that they call it a 'breakfast table?' I mean, it *is* the same exact table you eat lunch and dinner at. That never made any sense to me," he said the morning he first showed me his ritual.

"It's the same thing as when people say 'baby names.' It isn't like they're going to be babies forever, so why do people say that?" Brook chimed in, washing her cereal down with her milk the same way.

"That's why you get grown-ups with these little kids' names like Gigi and Franny," Kai joked.

"Or Wendy!" Brook laughed.

"Yeah, but I can't really rag on the Wendys, because they already have a hard life. You either have Peter Pan trying to tell you to never grow up, or you have your dad naming fast food restaurants after you."

"Well, that's not technically right. Her real name is actually Melinda Lou, but they started calling her Wenda because she had a speech impediment when she was younger and couldn't say her own name."

"I honestly don't know what is worse. The fact that someone actually named his kid Melinda Lou or the fact that you even know all of that."

"What? My dad and I used to look up random facts together. He always dreamed of going on *Jeopardy!* one day." They would often go back and forth for a while like that, trying to one-up each other. I didn't like to interrupt them. Instead, I would listen quietly and laugh to myself. I liked sitting back and hearing about their past lives. I didn't know how they remembered so many of the details, but it gave me hope that I could get to that point, too.

Mika wouldn't interrupt them either, but he rarely talked anyways. The most I heard him speak was in "the playroom." Brook and Kai chose the name, not because they thought it was a fun place, but because it was filled with toys. Brook said the playroom was just a trick, to make us feel more at home so that we would accept our new lives. However, I couldn't help but feel that there was more to it than that.

The playroom was hidden away behind one of the metal doors off of the white hallway. It was slightly larger than the attitude room. White carpet covered the floor and all of the walls were blank. It was neat and tidy, as if out of a movie scene. Organized rows of toys were arranged on small bookshelves against the wall. In the middle of the room, there was a circular, plastic table with two children's chairs across from each other.

There were board games in perfectly squared stacks, but all of their hard pieces had been replaced with paper figurines. It made it hard to play *Life*, each of us trying to shove a load of paper kids into flimsy paper cars. Mika and I usually stuck to *Monopoly*, but even with that game, we had to draw slips of paper with numbers on them because it didn't come with dice. It made me feel like a toddler, as if we couldn't be trusted with anything small or sharp.

One of the bookcases was filled with various stuffed animals and action figurines, all of their faces pointing forward. Unlike the other toys, they all were a little worn, as if they used to be loved by someone. They looked like they had been there a long time. I wondered what had happened to the kids they once belonged to. I wondered if Elmer would end up there one day, too.

Dias always kept two blank sheets of paper on the table, along with different colored finger paints. He told us that we had to leave behind all of our drawings, but they would be given back to us later. It reminded me of the drawings that covered Clara's cell walls before it became an empty room with just a mattress on the floor. I wondered what he could want with a bunch of overly happy suns and bright rainbows.

Even though the room felt fake and staged, it was a place I could go and briefly feel like myself. It was the only room we went to where I didn't feel like we were being watched. He would take us there for an hour every three or four days, just with our partners. I figured Mika didn't mind talking in there, because he thought I would be the only one listening.

The first time Mika and I went to the playroom, we didn't really know what to do with ourselves. We felt strange moving the perfectly arranged toys. So instead, we just talked the first couple weeks. It took a little while for him to open up in the beginning, but I soon figured out that he liked anything to do with baseball. He was in Little League before he was taken, and he made sure I knew it wasn't as wimpy as it sounded. He had just been made starting pitcher because he could throw a fastball sixty-two miles per hour. It didn't mean much to me, but I could tell that was a big thing for a ten-year-old. He told me how his dad had started teaching him the curveball that year and how close he was to getting it.

I started to get the hang of when to change the subject with him, looking for the moment he would hide his brown eyes under his blonde waves. That was when I would tell him stories about Keely and I. He would laugh every now and then, which made me feel like I was doing something right.

"What was the most trouble you ever got in?" he asked.

"Definitely the time we drove the lawn mower into town. We got it all the way to the grocery store before Dad found us. If it wasn't for the nosy lady who told on us, we would have gotten our candy and been back before he'd even known we'd been gone."

"And he didn't hear you turn it on?"

"Well, he would have if we hadn't pushed it down the road first. We turned it on when we got far enough away that we figured he wouldn't hear us." I couldn't help but smile at the memory, especially when I thought about the look on Keely's face when I told her what I wanted us to do. She gave me a hard time about it, as always, but I knew that she would eventually give in to me. She never let me do anything without her.

"It sounds like you guys were really close."

"Yeah, we are," I corrected him.

"I'm sorry, I didn't mean to say it like that. It came out wrong," he said as his face grew red. He pulled nervously on the cowlick at the front of his hair, it flipping back into its original position the moment he let go.

"That's okay, Mika," I said softly. "I know you didn't mean it like that."

"She was with you when it happened, wasn't she?" he asked hesitantly, focusing on the blank piece of paper in front of him.

"Why'd you ask that?" His question caught me off guard.

"Because it sounded like you did—do everything together. I just figured she would have been there, too."

"Yeah…she was." I tried shutting the memory out of my mind as it immediately crept back in.

"What happened?" I pictured her face, confused and scared. I remembered telling her to run, wanting to make sure she would get away. I knew how easily she'd trip over her feet when she ran. I was so focused on her that I hadn't imagined him coming there for me.

"We were in the woods. I was waiting for her by our tree house. He came out of nowhere—one second I was alone, and then he was right in front of me. He said my name and then asked where Keely was. I kept thinking that he was there for her and that I needed to warn her. But now that I think about it, I realize he didn't want my sister. He was there for me."

"Why do you think?"

"I don't know what I think. It's just a feeling I got—how he kept his eyes on me even after he saw her. But I can't know anything for sure. Like, why are we stuck down in this basement, and why are we sitting here whispering in the most un-fun playroom that ever existed? I just don't know."

"Do you think he took us for a reason, like Brook said?"

"He has to have some kind of reason. I mean, Mika, he knew exactly where I was going to be, and no one but me and Keely knows where our tree house is."

"Well, he could have just followed you."

"He knew my name. He knew my sister's name. He had a needle with him. It was more than just following us into the woods. I felt like he…knew us."

"He had a needle when he took me, too," he said, looking defeated.

"Did you have anyone with you?"

"No, just my dog, Hershey. She's a real sweet girl, so all she did was bark when he grabbed me. It happened right on my road. I was only six minutes from home."

"He took you in the middle of the day?"

"Yeah. There aren't many people who drive down that way. The houses are pretty spread out, so it wasn't like I could scream or anything. Everything happened kind of fast. He pulled his van up next to me and stopped to ask what kind of dog Hershey was. I told him she was a chocolate lab, but he said he didn't believe me. So, he parked the van and walked over to where we were standing, like he wanted to get a better look. I didn't think anything of it—I just figured he was some lonely guy who didn't have many people to talk to."

"How long did he talk to you for?"

"Not long, maybe like five minutes before I saw him take the needle out of his pocket."

"Did he say anything weird to you? Did anything give you the feeling like he knew who you were?" Mika thought silently to himself, his eyebrows scrunching together.

"He asked me if I was a Dyer boy because he said I looked like my brother, Gabe."

"Did he use Gabe's name?"

"Yeah, he said exactly, 'You a Dyer boy? Because you look an awful lot like the great Gabe Dyer.' And then I said I was, that Gabe was my older brother."

"Isn't it weird that he knew your brother's name?"

"Not really. Everyone knows Gabe. He's a senior this year, and he's really good at football. He got a big scholarship for Penn State next year, so he's kind of a hero around my town."

"Had you ever seen him before?"

"No. Never."

"Did he ask you anything else?"

"Like what?"

"I don't know, did he call you by your first name? Did he ask you anything else about your brother?"

"He never said my name, or at least I don't remember him saying it. I don't really remember anything else he said after I saw him take out the needle," Mika said timidly.

"What did he say before he took out the needle?"

"He was talking about Gabe, about how he was a heck of a football player. He asked me what it was like being his brother."

"And what did you say?"

"I said it was cool."

"And that's when he took out the needle?"

"No," he said, thinking to himself again. "Then he asked me if I was going to be a big ball player like my brother. I told him that I wasn't very good at football, that I was too skinny, so I was trying to get good at baseball instead. He asked me if I was any good, and I told him I had a good fastball but wasn't that great at hitting. He told me that if I ever wanted to be a real baseball player, I had to get the hitting down. *Then* he took out the needle." We sat there quietly for a while. In my mind, I tried to find clues hidden behind their seemingly ordinary conversation.

Soon afterwards, we went back to talking about Mika's favorite baseball stars and his tips for hitting a home run. But I couldn't shake the shiver that told me Dias hadn't randomly chosen us. It bothered me that he knew our names, our siblings' names. It made me wonder what else he knew and how long he had been watching us. Regardless of why he chose Mika, part of me was happy he did. There was something comforting about our time together in the playroom. There was something comforting about him. That hour together always seemed to be the fastest.

After our time in the playroom, he would take us down the hall to the room next to the red door. Each time he had a leather-bound notebook, which he carried closed at his side. First, he would take Mika. Then, he came for me. The room was large, its walls covered by whitewashed shelves packed with books. There were rows of perfectly aligned desks, reminding me of school classrooms. A large TV with an attached VCR sat atop the large table at the front of the room. Its bright, blue screen greeted us each time we entered.

Brook called it "the greenhouse," after the pink-tinted fluorescent lights that lined the ceiling and felt like grow lights. The floors and walls resembled the long hallway, all a spotless white. A long, black mirror extended across the back wall on the side closest to the red room. It reminded me of interview rooms in the police shows that Dad liked to watch.

He started taking us there in our second week. There were old textbooks stacked on the two desks at the head of the room. Inside the front cover of each, I found a faded sticker reading, "The Waring School." Underneath, there were kids' names doodled into a two-column chart, but I didn't recognize any of them. All of the names had a date next to them, chronicling back to 1981. The last ones listed in the four textbooks on the table were "Patrick," "Evie," "Leon," and "Jamie"—a slanted "1987" scribbled to the right of each. I searched through the textbooks, noticing the many highlighter marks and notes added in along the sides of the pages. Nothing had to do with why we were there. The only things left behind were answers to test questions that had long since been taken.

Dias would leave directions for us each time, instructing which chapters to read and questions to answer. There weren't any tests, but we couldn't leave the room until we had completed his assignments. He would also play videotapes—home schooling lessons and news reports.

I didn't know why he brought us to the greenhouse. There were times we learned about normal sixth-grade things like English, science, and math. But other times, we studied things that didn't make sense. All of the news reports, history lessons, and even pop culture facts were old—all from the 1980s. It made me wonder what exactly he was preparing us for.

Everything became colder after Clara and Chet went away. I didn't know if it was a sign of bad things to come or if winter had just shown up early. But I didn't complain when he moved the space heaters down to us. He only turned them on at night, which meant that I didn't start feeling the warmth until hours later. They sat in Clara and Chet's emptied out cells. There was no longer evidence of them ever being there—even the dirt had been freshly raked into a flat, even layer.

Other than that, little had changed. Dias had returned the cross to his neck. Food continued to shoot down the tubes three times a day. We pretended to entertain ourselves with block towers in the playroom and answered *Jeopardy!* questions from 1984 in the greenhouse. It was only at the end of the day, after the lights had begun to dim, that I felt I could escape from the prison. It was then that Brook and I would push our mattresses together at the edge of our shared bars. She would slip her ungloved hand through the cage to rest on my bed, and I would put my hand on top of hers. In the moments when the room faded to black, I imagined I was cuddled up next to Keely again. I could almost see our glow-in-the dark stars lighting up the basement sky.

It wasn't until after Dias took away the heaters that Brook and I began putting together more of the pieces. We started to spend our time at night going over what we had come up with. There were the similarities, like how each time he took a boy and a girl—both at age ten, always just a few days apart. But then there were things that didn't make sense, like how we all looked so different and came from various places. Sometimes, I felt like Brook held back some of what she knew, but I figured there was probably a good reason for that. She had a reason for everything, like how she made us move our mattresses back against the wall in the morning to prevent him from finding out about our secrets.

"When you first got here, what did he say to you in the attitude room?" I asked her one night, our faces turned towards each other in spite of the pitch-black room.

"He told me a story about a woman called Athena. He named me after her and told me all of the ways I was like her. He said that she was really smart and liked to think things through, but there was a side of her that was too competitive. And he talked about her mother. He said that Athena didn't have a mom, just like me."

"What do you think he meant by it?"

"I've thought about it a lot, and I still don't know if it means anything. He acted like the story was important, like I needed to know it but not understand it."

"Do you think he is trying to teach us something?"

"Not teach us—warn us. I just don't know why."

"But why call us by all these weird names?"

"I found a book in the greenhouse about Greek mythology. It is a children's book full of tales about gods and goddesses. They aren't like normal kid stories, though. There aren't any happy endings in these ones. They're mostly about people doing the wrong thing and what happens to them because of it."

"Was the story about Pandora in it?"

"Yeah, all of ours are in it. Kayla was named after Artemis, a goddess who protected young girls and innocent animals. But the stories showed how she cared a little too much about justice and that sometimes got her into trouble. And Clara was Persephone. She told me how he said Persephone was beautiful and adored but trusted in people too easily. The book said Hades, the God of the Underworld, kidnapped her and made her spend half of every year underground with him."

"Underground, like where we are?"

"No, farther down, where dead people go."

"But dead people can also go to heaven, so does that mean since it is under the ground…it's hell?"

"It sounded like a terrible place. But the book said even the good people went there."

"Kind of like down here," I uttered.

"There was something I noticed, though," she said, briefly pausing. "What Dias told the boys in the attitude room was different from what he said to us girls. Like, he told Chet that Hermes wasn't trustworthy and was a liar. And then with Kai, he said Ares was a war god who liked making people bleed. He was told that Ares was always causing trouble, and it wasn't until he was captured by these two brothers that the wars finally stopped."

"But what did the books say?"

"It didn't make them out to be so terrible. They had good parts, too, just like the goddesses did. But Dias only told the boys the bad things."

"Did you find out anything else?"

"Yes. All the ones he picked for us were gods and goddesses. Well, all except for you. Pandora is the only one who was human."

"Why do you think he did that?"

"I don't know," she said softly. "Did Mika ever tell you what Dias said to him?"

"Only a little. He named him Prometheus, a traitor who went against the gods. He took something from them—fire, I think it was—so they chained him to the side of a mountain."

"But did Mika say anything about why he got called that? Did Dias say why they were similar?" she asked.

"I don't think so. That was all he told me."

"What do *you* think it all means?"

I thought to myself for a moment before answering. "Doesn't it feel like he is giving us roles to play? Why give us names and tell us these stories? It makes me feel like he wants us to play some kind of part in his own stupid story."

Brook became very quiet, even her breath seeming to slow. "I think that, too. But if that's true, what part does that give him?"

"Did the book say anything about who Dias was?"

"No," she said gloomily. "It didn't say a thing."

"So what should we do?"

"If we ever want to get out of here, we're just going to have to play along," she said as she rubbed the hand she always kept covered.

It began when we stopped needing our blankets at night. Kai started to change, even though he promised Brook that he wouldn't. Dias would take him away from the basement more often. Brook said that Kai rarely went with her to the playroom or the greenhouse anymore. There were days that went by where we wouldn't see or hear from him. When Kai was returned to his cell, he didn't smile or laugh like he used to. Brook would even try their favorite inside joke about finding a new way to "Shawshank" out of there, the one that used to make him crack up every time. But he said it wasn't funny anymore. He said that we were never getting out of there.

At first, it would only take a couple days to get the old Kai back. He would apologize for being in a bad mood or say that he just wanted to talk about something else whenever Brook asked about his time away. But each time, it took longer for him to come back to us.

I worried about the time when he would eventually disappear for good.

It seemed like the more Brook and Kai drifted apart, the closer Mika and I became. He was there for me in a way that no one else could be, not even Brook. We discovered that when it came down to it, we were all each other had.

"Since we are partners, that means we have to stick together," I said to him one day in the playroom. We were playing Slap Jack, but neither of us cared to slam our hands down when a jack turned up. Instead, we just kept turning the cards over one by one.

"You're my catcher. And I will always be your pitcher," he said. Sometimes it was hard to keep up with his baseball talk, but I figured that meant I was pretty important. Mika liked to make sense of things through analogies, which sometimes made me feel like we were talking in riddles.

"So, I'm just in charge of catching all the balls for you?" I asked.

"No way. You are the most important person on the field. You're the one who makes all the calls and tells me what to do. I'm just the one who tries to get it right."

"So being the catcher is a good thing?"

"Catchers save the game most times. They tell the pitcher when someone is trying to steal a base, and they can do this thing called 'framing' where even if a pitch is just outside of the strike zone, the catcher can frame it just right so the ump will call it a strike. It helps the pitchers look good."

"But how do they talk to each other?"

"Through hand signals. Really good players use more than one each time, like the first signal they give is what kind of pitch it should be. If the catcher holds up one finger, like this," he said, pointing his index finger down towards the table, "then it's a fastball. Two fingers is a curveball, and three is a slider. And if he gives four fingers or wiggles them around, it's a changeup."

"What's a changeup?"

"Some people call it an off-speed pitch. Basically, it's made to look like a fastball, but it doesn't come to the plate as fast."

"Like a trick play?"

"Sort of. I guess you could call it that."

"How do catchers know where to catch the ball?"

"They can tell the pitcher where they want the ball to go. If they throw a second hand signal, that's going to tell the pitcher where the catcher wants it. If it's an odd number, it should be outside, farther away from the hitter. And if it's an even number, it should be inside, closer to the hitter. There are other things for how high or low the ball should be, but I'm not good enough to use those yet."

"So, what's our hand signal going to be?"

"Whatever you want it to be. You're the catcher." I immediately thought of the handshake Keely and I had. Before, I'd never had one with anybody else.

"How about this one?" I said, raising four of my fingers.

"The changeup. I like it. You have to make sure you wiggle them though, like this," he said, moving four of his fingers over the table. "And the most important thing to remember is you can't let the hitter see your signal. It has to be where no one will notice it." I nodded my head excitedly, feeling almost giddy about our special sign. We giggled together as we flashed our secret hand signal at one another under the table.

"That's going to be our reminder, okay? The changeup. It means that I'm your partner and you are mine, no matter what."

"No matter what," he repeated back.

"You promise?"

"You give me that changeup signal, and I promise I'll give you the right pitch."

Even though I still didn't fully understand everything he had said about pitchers and catchers, I knew that Mika cared about me just like he did his baseball. It made me feel grateful for him. I was happy that he was my pitcher down there in the dark.

I didn't find the mythology book until Brook's calendar hit July. Before, I had tried looking for it when Dias brought Mika and I to the greenhouse. However, it wasn't until the summer that the lessons became long enough for me to have time to search for it.

The book was shoved on a far bookshelf, the one closest to the mirrored wall. I kept my back to its dark reflection, just in case Dias was watching me from the other side. Brook had said it was a children's book, but angry monsters covered the front instead of the flying horses and angels that I had expected. On the second page, I found a small inscription in the bottom right corner. It read:

To Catherine, Love Poppy

It made me sad to think that some other kid's special storybook was stuck down in that awful basement. I found Pandora's story towards the back of the book, and it was only a page and a half long. The book said she was created because a Titan named Prometheus stole fire from the gods and gave it to the humans. Prometheus angered them, but his loyalty to helping humans made him a hero on Earth. Zeus, the father of the gods, gave Pandora a box filled with terrible things because he knew she was going to open it. He wanted her to release all those bad things into the world. And just like Dias had said, she did—leaving only hope behind.

I looked for something more behind the story. I wanted to know why Pandora cared so much about the box. But the book only blamed it on her curiosity. I didn't believe that. I knew Pandora must have had another reason to open her box. In the picture next to her story, she looked out at me like she had a secret she wanted to whisper into my ear. It made me think that maybe she already knew what she would find inside.

I placed the book back on the shelf and returned to my desk next to Mika. He looked at me expectantly, but I simply sat down and went back to filling out questions about molecules and their atoms. I couldn't help but look over at him from time to time. I thought about how Pandora and Prometheus were connected. She couldn't have existed without him, and there was some truth to that for Mika and me. He seemed more like Prometheus than Dias had said. Just like the Titan, I felt he would stand by me until the end.

Brook was good at keeping track of things. She always knew the day of the week and whether we were having cold chicken patties or hardened lasagna for dinner. I used to be like that, too. When it was just Keely and me, the world made sense. I could see things coming from a mile away.

But in that basement, I could predict everything and nothing. The days blended together, a mixture of useless textbooks, old videos, too bright lights, too short showers, plastic tasting food, and white jumpsuits. I never knew when it all could change again.

I told Brook not to tell me when that day in September came around again, but my untrustworthy eyes kept drifting to the red X's on her makeshift calendar. When that day arrived, I thought about my family. I imagined Mom and Dad taking Keely some place special, like our favorite ice cream joint or maybe even Marine World to make it easier on her.

I knew I was supposed to want them to continue on without me. It wasn't fair for them to only hold on to hope, as if it was the last thing they had left amongst all the terribleness. But for that one day, I prayed that it was hard on them, too. Maybe then it would help them find me, pulling me out of the place where all the dead were sent.

Chapter Five
September 12, 2002

Twelve was the age girls were supposed to start caring about makeup. People said it marked the beginning of adolescence, when you began worrying about bad breath and if you had the coolest posters taped to your bedroom wall. Seventh grade signaled the start of shaving your legs, plucking your unibrow, and wearing low ankle socks. These were the things twelve–year–old girls were supposed to care about.

I worried about surviving. Not in the traditional ways like finding enough food to eat or a thick enough coat to outlast the Jersey winters. No, I worried about the things that couldn't be fixed with macaroni and cheese or a tablespoon of pink liquid that tasted nothing like bubblegum. I feared that the growing hole in my belly would eventually consume my insides—that the tightening cramp in my chest would ultimately suffocate me.

I worried that I couldn't endure a life without Dani.

I thought it was all going to be over. After I'd shown Dad my map, we would just go to the police and get Dani back. But it turned out that the police were strong supporters of coincidence. Mom and Dad both believed my map, Nana and Bumpy thought it was possible, but the Reading police department thought we were all out of our minds. It didn't matter how many times we tried to explain it to them, going over every newspaper article and pointing out each similarity. Nothing seemed to make them care. They said they appreciated my "project" and that they would take it all into consideration. But they made it clear they had a lot of other stuff on their plate.

"Dani is still a priority, though, right? I mean, it's not like this is a closed case. My baby girl is still out there, and I expect that you are still looking for her!" my dad said, slapping his open hand onto the Chief of Police's weathered desk.

"Mr. Millen, all of our cases are a priority. We still have bulletins out for Dani, and we have followed up on every lead," the Chief said. He was a large man, the type whose buttons appeared on the verge of popping under the pressure of his belly. His face had a purplish complexion, almost like he had a piece of food permanently lodged in his throat.

"Yeah, but none of them have led anywhere! I want to know that there is an active team out there *right now* looking for her."

"Listen. We only have so much manpower to work with and have already dedicated almost eight months to your girl's investigation. We know about the Sharon boy and have worked extensively with their department as well. But as I said before, our investigation is only as good as the evidence we have to work with."

"But you have something right here! You have eight different kidnappings with similar patterns. You have an approximate location—I just don't understand why you aren't going to do something about this." I stood in the back of the Chief's office with my mother, both of us focused on our shoes as we let Dad do the talking. It was hard for my mom not to take charge, but we both knew that she would just get emotional and do more bad than good.

"What you have here is a hunch. It's a very interesting hunch, and your daughter here sure is *quite* the little researcher," he said with an exaggerated wink in my direction. "But this isn't substantial enough for us to go off of. If we followed every hunch that came across my desk, then we wouldn't get anywhere, now would we?" He leaned back in his chair, his neck bulging underneath his even fatter chin.

"All I am asking is for someone to look into this. Just give it a chance. That is all I'm asking for." My dad raked his hands over his bald spot as if it still had hair, a sign of his growing irritation.

"Fine. If it will make you happy, I could have one of our volunteers…interns or whatever you call them, look into this. You said that I could keep these copies, Little Miss?" It took me a moment to realize he was talking to me. I nodded my head as I kept it focused on the floor.

Once we realized that we weren't getting any help from the police, Dad and I went out to look ourselves. Mom wanted to come along too, but she had to go back home because one of her patients did something illegal and was in big trouble.

We spent four straight days driving, seeing about every neighborhood and road from Hanover to Portsmouth. When we reached the coast, we headed north to Portland and then traveled west again. We tried to map out our routes in the beginning. But before long, we were just driving and choosing our turns as they came. We drove through run-down towns I never knew existed. Each time we passed a large, tucked-away house, I couldn't help but imagine Dani hidden away inside. I didn't know what we hoped would come from our directionless road trip. It was as if we expected to drive past and just know, without a shadow of a doubt, that Dani was there.

In the beginning, it almost felt like an adventure. Dad and I were "private investigators," out looking to round up the bad guy. It started to feel like I was getting my old Dad back, the one who had existed before Dani went missing and the planes started crashing. He told jokes again and tickled my sides, while I pretended that I hated it. We even made walrus faces with our French fries like we used to. He didn't look quite as sad—he looked almost happy—and for the first time in a long while, I thought maybe we were all going to be okay.

On the morning of the fifth day, I woke up still filled with hopefulness, like it was going to be *the* day. But Dad was different—something had changed in him. I found him outside our motel room door, crouched against the weathered plastic siding and looking out at the ocean. We were staying in Cape Elizabeth, a place we had promised ourselves that we would never visit again. I think Dani and I were six when we vacationed there; we ended up leaving early after we were robbed twice in the same day. We had woken up to find someone had broken into our car the night before. Later that day, a man ripped my mom's purse right off her shoulder while we were walking down the boardwalk. From that point on, we always called Cape Elizabeth "That Evil Place."

I guessed it only made sense that evil had brought us back there.

I went to sit down next to him, just close enough that our shoulders could touch. With each minute of silence that passed, I knew with greater certainty that our road trip was over—that we would be heading home without Dani.

"Keely, can I ask you something?"

"Yes, Daddy," I said in a shaky voice.

"It is something I never planned on asking you—I guess I didn't think things would turn out this way." He paused, as if trying to gain the courage to continue. Whenever I didn't want to ask a question, I slowly counted down from ten in my head, forcing the question out just before zero. He must have started at a much higher number, the silence continuing for a long while as we sat and listened to the crying seagulls.

"Keely, if we fail—if Dani never comes back—will you be able to move on without her?" It wasn't the question I planned on answering. I knew he was going to ask me to do something hard, like come up with a new way of looking for her or try to find more people to help us. But I never thought he would ask me to give up. "I mean, what are we even doing? We are driving around looking for a place we don't know exists and a person we won't even recognize. This is just hopeless. Just so goddamn hopeless."

I started to stand when he stopped me. He grabbed my hand and kept me there beside him. "Please stay. I'm sorry. I'm sorry I said all that—I didn't mean it. It's all too soon, and I should have known that."

"Too soon for what?" I stuttered, my head pounding.

"To start thinking of a world without her in it."

"Then how 'bout we never start?" He briefly stopped before nodding back, trying to add a convincing smile. Just like that, he had fallen back into the land of nonbelievers, the growing group of those losing hope that she could still be out there.

We continued our trip to nowhere for one more day before turning around and heading home. There were no more knock-knock jokes or walrus fry faces. All that seemed to be left was an uncomfortable silence, an endless quiet that left no room for "maybe's" or "what if's."

"In the very beginning things hurt—they are rubbed raw…they blister and bleed. But as time passes, they callus over. They harden, and the pain no longer hurts quite so much. Losing someone is like that. Eventually you take some comfort in the roughness, and you begin to heal."

I couldn't fully explain how I had ended up in the basement of that church, getting a lesson from a makeshift "grief counselor" on how to handle death. Ever since the September 11 attacks, talking about feelings became my town's latest obsession. Ms. Tabitha, an older lady who normally worked at the homeless shelter in Bergen County, had started doing weekly counseling sessions for "Children of 9/11" every Sunday. I avoided the grief group when it first began, but it wasn't long before my mom forced me to go, too.

"It would be good for you to talk to people who have gone through similar things," she had said.

"But Mom, I'm not one of them. I'm not a child of nine eleven, so we haven't gone through the same things. They know someone who died. I don't."

"You were still affected, Keely. We all were."

"We all know that this isn't about what happened last month or wanting me to talk about my feelings. This is about getting me to forget her and act like she isn't coming back!" I didn't realize until I heard my ears ringing that I had been screaming.

"She might not, Keely! She. Might. Not. And I need you to understand that. You think it doesn't kill me to say that? Or that I don't think about her and wonder if she is okay? I miss her every damn day, but me missing her and wishing this would all be over doesn't change the fact that she isn't here. I mean, for God's sake, Keely, you have barely eaten or said much of anything since you and your father returned from your trip. Your friend with the weird shirts has come by almost every single day this week asking where you are, and I have to keep telling her that you are busy—"

"Her name is Hillary, Mom! She is a person and has a name!"

"Well, I'm sorry, okay? I'm sorry that you don't talk to me anymore or tell me what is going on in your life. I'm sorry that you are shutting us all out and for trying to ignore it. I'm sorry. I'm just so sorry." Whenever I made my mom cry, I always ended up feeling sick to my stomach. Her face would scrunch up when she tried to keep herself from crying. When the tears eventually came, they would only pour more heavily. Whenever I saw that face, I would agree to almost anything.

So I went. I promised my mother I would go, but not because I had a change of heart. I went so that she would stop looking at me as if I too was going to disappear.

"Keely, how do you feel about that?" Ms. Tabitha had a habit of doing that—narrowing in on the kids she knew weren't paying attention. For a moment, I looked around at the eight sets of eyes focused on me. That was the thing about support groups. Most people liked to listen to everyone else's stories but dreaded the moment when it became their turn.

"Feel about what?"

"About losing someone. About how the loss doesn't go away but gets easier with time." She stared intensely at me through cloudy eyes. It made me wonder if she had spent too many hours looking at the sunny side of things. Her bulky, knickknack necklace jingled as she settled back into her chair, crossing her arms across her mobile percussion set.

I kept my eyes downcast, my hands tightly clasped in my lap. I normally just avoided her questions, occasionally adding an, "I guess," in there so that she would move on to bug the next kid. Then I could go back to being nonexistent. But that time, I knew I wouldn't get away so easily.

"I think that for some people it can get better," I started. "But what about the people with those scabs that never heal—the ones that just keep getting ripped off? What happens to them?"

She jingled as she stirred uncomfortably in her chair. I could tell my question had caught her off guard. She was expecting another one of my two word answers. I hoped that asking something she couldn't answer might get her to leave me alone. She was used to kids saying the usual things like they were sad and missed the people who were gone. But she didn't know how to help the kids who refused to let go. I wasn't like the girl next to me who had lost her father and wondered who was going to take her to Six Flags the next summer. Or, like the boy across the circle, wondering if he would have to call his dad's girlfriend "Mom." Dani wasn't just an empty spot that I needed to find a way to fill. Her disappearance left a bleeding wound that would never seal up and would just keep gushing forever.

"Yeah, and like what happens if you don't have any Neosporin and then it leaves a big, ugly scar," said Carrie, who sat diagonal from me. She was one of the younger ones, like me. I remembered that Carrie had said her mother worked in one of the towers. Carrie had been staying at her grandparents' but didn't seem to fully understand that her mom wasn't coming back.

"Well, Carrie, that could happen. Have you ever had a cut that turned into a scar?" Ms. Tabitha asked, looking somewhat relieved that she had escaped my question.

"Yeah, right here," she said as she lifted up her shirt and pointed to a light circle next to her belly button. "My brother, Nick, was shooting his BB gun in the backyard, and I got in his way. It was an accident," she added quickly.

"And when you were first hit with the BB gun, how did it feel?"

"It stung a lot. It took my breath away, and my stomach hurt for like three days straight after it happened."

"And how does it feel right now?"

"It doesn't hurt at all," she said, completely clueless.

"And even though it doesn't hurt now, you still remember what it felt like and that it happened, right?"

"I guess so." Carrie began to look nervous, finally catching on that they weren't really talking about BB guns and upset stomachs. I could tell that Ms. Tabitha was thinking about how far she wanted to take it.

"That's good, Carrie. That's a good thing, my dear," Ms. Tabitha added before she moved on to her next victim in the circle. "Ray, was there anything that you wanted to talk about today?"

Carrie must not have been ready for her wake-up call.

I couldn't help but shake my head and smile quietly to myself. Again, I felt a set of eyes on me, staring back as mine met his. He sat three kids down from me in the circle. His name was Max, but I only knew that because he was in half of my classes that year. Even though his desk sat in front of mine in each, we hadn't spoken a word to one another. He had moved to Ridgewood from Florida the year before, and it seemed like he did a better job fitting in with the "popular crowd" than a girl who had lived there her whole life.

It was the first time that I had really looked at him, other than staring at the freckles dotting the back of his neck during class. He was taller than the other seventh graders. His jet-black hair swooped perfectly across his forehead but never long enough to cover his steel-blue eyes. It was clear his mother believed in sunscreen, his skin fair but not too pale. His lips turned up at the corners and sometimes could have been mistaken for a smile. He was studying me like a viewer at an art gallery, deciding how to feel about the latest exhibit.

I stared directly back, challenging him to get a good look before he wrote me off like the others did.

"I know there are still ten minutes left in the session, but I'm going to let you kids go early, just this once. Make sure you do not leave the building until you see your *guardian* out front," she said awkwardly. "We have made some real progress today, and I am proud of you all for *opening* and *feeling*," she said, seeming to direct it at everyone except me. She made sure to end every session that way, as if she needed a tagline like one of those talk show hosts.

As usual, I was the first one to escape. I made sure to never bring notebooks or backpacks like the other kids. There was nothing Ms. Tabitha said that made me want to take notes. I took the basement stairs two at a time, running away from all that opening and feeling crap and the stuffy air that smelled like expired milk. It didn't take long to reach the front doors of the small church. However, I was surprised when I didn't see my mom's car sitting in the first parking spot. She usually remained there during the sessions, as if standing guard outside.

Instead of waiting near the entrance with the other kids, I walked out into the cool, October air and sat down on the ancient bench outside. It was the one with rusted-out nails and two missing planks, looking barely able to hold the weight of a single person.

Perfect.

As I sat down, I thought about how it probably wouldn't make sense to most people that I didn't want to make friends with the grief group kids. My mom likely hoped that we would all come together and heal each other's pain. But it didn't make sense to me that much good could come out of all that badness.

"Hey, Keely." I shielded my eyes as I looked up into the blinding afternoon sun, trying to see the face inside the brightness. It was the boy with the curved-up lips, only that time, he was actually smiling at me. He had perfectly straight teeth, the kind that never needed any braces in the first place. I should have known he would be one of those kids.

"Hey…Max." His name felt strange on my tongue.

"So, interesting session in there, huh?"

"Yeah…super thrilling, as always," I said, turning to face the end of the street and hoping that Mom would round the corner in time to save me. Without asking for permission, he took the open seat next to me, causing the remaining three planks to groan underneath our weight. Unfortunately, the bench was sturdier than I had thought.

"Thought we were goners for a second," he went on.

"Yup," I uncomfortably replied, scooting farther down the bench and continuing to look for an escape route.

"I was on a wooden teeter-totter once that split right in two. Luckily, I was the one closest to the ground when it happened," he said, again flashing his perfect teeth. I gave a sideways glance, breaking the staring contest with my shoelaces. A set of dimples appeared, proving then that he was really smiling.

"So, I don't really remember. What made you come to this group thing anyways?" I asked, folding my arms across my chest and turning to look at him head-on. His face immediately dropped as he looked away uncomfortably, just as I had hoped. However, to my surprise, he then raised his head again to meet my glare. His eyes were fire and water in the sunlight, their sea-blue rims crashing into golden centers.

"I say it's because of my uncle, but that's not really true. I mean, yeah, I don't have an uncle anymore, but he died a long time ago. I guess I met him when I was a baby, but I don't remember anything about him."

"Let me get this straight. You come to a grief group when you don't even have anyone to grieve?"

"Yeah…I guess. You make it sound more weird than it is."

"Um, how else am I supposed to make it sound? Are you coming here to what, get a kick out of us?"

"No, that's not it at all. I'm not making fun of you guys or anything."

"Then what are you doing here?"

"I don't know. I guess I just want to know what it feels like."

"What *what* feels like?"

"What it feels like when something bad happens. When someone dies, when your house burns down, when you get in a car crash, when someone disappears one day and never comes back…I just want to understand what it feels like. So, I thought if I listened to other people who *do* know, maybe I would too."

"Well it feels like crap, okay? And I don't know why someone would ever want to know what that feels like." We fell into an awkward silence, both just wanting the conversation to be over. By some stroke of luck, my mother pulled into the parking lot only a minute later. I pushed off the bench in an instant and walked to her car without a backward glance.

"See ya at school," I thought I heard from behind me as I bolted into the passenger's seat.

"Who is that? A new friend?" my mother asked a bit too excitedly.

"No, just some kid I go to school with. We aren't friends."

"Well, he looks like a nice boy. Maybe you can become friends once you get to know each other," she said, reversing out of her parking spot.

"Maybe," I said as I turned to face the window, hoping to put an end to the topic. As we drove away from the church, I found myself glancing back at the boy still on the rickety bench outside. He was leaning forward, his elbows resting on his knees and head slightly lowered. His fire and ice eyes peered out from beneath his hair, piercing my own. I wanted to believe he felt sorry for me—that he was thankful he was at least better off than me. That way, it would have been a little easier to just go on hating him. But I knew that wasn't it. I felt his sadness cutting through me, pulling a small part of me back out into the autumn air.

I tried my best to avoid him the following day at school. He was in three of my six classes, but at least those were in the second half of the day. I knew the hardest part was going to be getting through lunch, as I had to walk past his table to get to mine; I was back to sitting alone at the "loser table." Eighth grade lunch had changed to B period, taking Hillary and the boys with it.

Maybe it was for the best, I thought. Things had gotten strange between Hillary and me, ever since Dad and I returned to Ridgewood. I found myself pulling away from her and the boys. All they wanted to talk about was The Search—what we had found and what I planned to do next. They kept telling me that it would all work out. Being around them just reminded me that I had failed. I was out of ideas, and so were they. At first, they wouldn't let me push them away. But I could tell that little by little, they were slowly starting to give up.

The lunchroom seemed busier than usual that day, something I was thankful for. I took the long way around to get to my table, weaving in and out of the crowded circles bordering the lunchroom. As I passed the final group, I noticed someone sitting at my usual spot. I stopped short as he turned to face me, causing my milk to tumble off my tray and burst open on the tile floor. His black hair whizzed past me as he leaned forward, quickly plugging the carton's spurting corner with his pinkie.

"Here, you can have mine," Max started. "I haven't even opened it yet." He passed me his chocolate milk, downing the remnants of my broken one with a single gulp. "Five second rule," he added, crushing the carton between his hands and flashing a smile.

My eyes scanned for a quick exit, the room then completely filled with seventh graders. Reluctantly, I sat down across from him, pretending to focus on my turkey sub and hoping he would just go away.

"I wanted to ask what you meant yesterday, about what happens when the scab keeps getting ripped off." I rolled my eyes, taking a large bite out of my sandwich.

"Look, I don't know where this 'I want to feel like crap' thing came from, but you're gonna have to go learn from somebody else," I shot back. I was surprised by how easily the words rolled from my mind to my tongue. It was something *she* would have said.

"I'm not looking for you to teach me anything. I didn't mean to say it like that yesterday, and I'm really not trying to get you to talk about Dani. I guess I just want to talk to *you* is all." Hearing her name out loud sent a shock down my spine. I paused, unsure about how I felt. I squinted at him from across the table, trying to see behind his soft expression.

"Okay," I said with a heavy sigh. "You can talk to me, but you aren't allowed to talk about her or what happened to her. Deal?"

"Deal!" His dimples appeared like the lines on a smiley face.

"And you aren't allowed to talk to me about *that group*... or the things we talk about there."

"Okay," he said, his smile widening. "But what about when we are there? Am I allowed to talk to you then?"

"No," I continued, making up the rules as I went. "Unless it has something to do with Ms. Tabitha smelling like stray cats or how annoying Ray is when he grinds his teeth real loud."

"What if it's about how Jenna picks her nose when she thinks no one is looking?"

"Wait, oh my gosh, I totally saw her eat a booger once!"

"Well, at least it's better than when she flicks it somewhere. She sits behind me in first and second period. I'm scared one will get stuck to my back one of these days. That's why I like having classes with you."

"So I can block you from Booger Flicker?" I laughed. Unfortunately, alphabetical order had stuck Jenna Milmer with us until graduation.

"Well, that and I like it when you bounce your foot on the back of my seat. It's like I have my very own massage chair."

"Oh, I didn't even know I did that."

"It's usually when we are taking tests. Or when a teacher asks you something." It was weird, sitting there learning about myself from Max Lerman. I wondered what else he had noticed about me.

"It's probably just when I'm nervous, then. I hate tests, and Mrs. Kalon always says my name like she's mad at me. I also suck at science, so I never know any of the answers."

"You know, I'm really good at science. If I sit low enough, you could look off my answer sheet." My body went still. It was something Dani had let me do. Whenever I needed an answer, I would tap my pencil on the desk the same number of times as the question. She would tap hers back— one for A, two for B, three for C, and four for D. If she had been in seventh grade with me, she would have had to add a fifth for E. The teachers never questioned when we got the same grades. They must have figured it was a twin thing.

"Or not," he continued reluctantly, studying my face. "We don't have to do it if that isn't your thing."

"Oh it's not that, it's just...I can't see that well far away," I lied, remembering my rule that we wouldn't talk about Dani.

"Well, I can always help you study...that is if you want me to," he added shyly.

"Yeah. Maybe we could do that."

"Okay," he ended, his dimples returning. We both went back to eating our lunches, as if finished with negotiations. Occasionally, I glanced up at him, watching as he licked his pudding cup clean before finishing off mine as well.

I questioned how long it would last, figuring he would eventually go back to his old friends and forget about ever trying to be mine. But he returned the next day and then the day after that, accompanied by his turkey sandwich, chocolate milk, and chocolate pudding. I told him that someday all that chocolate would give him a heart attack. He simply replied that Lermans had chocolate-proof hearts. That was how he talked about his family—as if they were one big group instead of individual people.

He even acted like my friend outside of the lunchroom. When he passed papers down the row in class, he would flash me one of his quick smiles. He walked with me to my classes, even the ones we didn't share. It surprised me that people didn't really question how Max Lerman and Keely Millen could be friends. The other kids, even the popular ones, seemed to leave us alone. I guessed that they must have found it easier to just move on to the newest victim.

For the most part, Max seemed to stick to my rules. He didn't talk about Dani or ask about the hurt that still stung my insides. We didn't talk much about the past but instead focused more on the present. He told me he was trying to get good at skateboarding but that it was really hard since he was accident-prone, just like me. I talked about how I had gotten a high schooler to buy me the new Ludacris CD without my parents knowing, the one that had all the swearing left in it. My favorite song was "Roll Out," and even though I didn't really know what the song was about, Max and I learned every word by heart. We agreed that it sounded like Ludacris had a lot of money and really liked cars.

Max broke the rules for the first time during support group. It was during one of the "Open Floor" sessions where people could ask whatever they wanted.

"How do you know someone is really gone?" he began.

"What do you mean, Max?" Ms. Tabitha asked, her face mirroring the surprise of the other members at his newfound group participation.

"Like, how do you know if someone is still in this world and hasn't gone off to heaven?" I could tell he was resisting the urge to look over at me.

"Well, Max, some people go straight on to heaven when they pass," Ms. Tabitha began. She spoke slowly, her bracelets clattering annoyingly as she twirled her hands to the flow of the words. "But some may take a bit longer, stuck here with those of us not yet ready to let them go. Sometimes, we hope so deeply that they stay that we end up hurting them."

"How is that hurting them?" I blurted, the words unexpectedly spilling out. She turned towards me, clasping her hands in her lap.

"I have the belief that holding on can make the pain last longer. Those we love sometimes wait for us to heal before passing on to their happier place."

"Is that what ghosts are?" Jenna asked dumbly, squishing a fresh booger she had "secretly picked" between her thumb and pointer finger.

"I don't really like calling them ghosts. I'd rather say they are 'energy.' When you are by yourself, do you ever feel that someone is there with you? I believe that is the energy of the spirit."

"But what if you don't feel anything? What does that mean?" Max said, as if continuing on for me.

"You may not be ready yet to feel the energy. Acceptance is the first step. It helps you realize the person is really gone and can't come back," Her foggy eyes briefly drifted in my direction before scanning across the remaining circle. "That is why we have funerals—they allow the living and the dead to take the first steps towards healing." It was the first time she used the "D" word, but the lost faces made me wonder if anyone else had noticed.

"But what happens if you stop feeling them?" Sam asked. His voice cracked under the weight of holding back tears. He was the smallest boy, despite being one of the older ones. He seemed to further shrink as he folded his body in on itself, fitting it inside the narrow boundaries of his aluminum chair. His mother and father had both been working in the city that awful day, leaving him with only an aunt and uncle to care for him.

"That means they have continued on, that you have let them find peace. But that doesn't mean they have left you. No, they stay with you forever in a different way—in your memories, and right here, where you will always keep them," she said, placing her clanging hand over her heart.

It had always been clear to me that Ms. Tabitha was a bit loony. Her weird speech only confirmed that. But no matter how hard I tried to shut her out of my head, her words had tunneled deep inside of me, reaching all the parts I had tried to keep buried away. My body automatically rose out of the cheap, fold-up chair, overwhelmed by the sudden need to escape. My Jell-O legs somehow carried me out of the building and to the safety of my mom's car. She jumped as I burst through the passenger's door, my breathing labored and heavy.

"Keely, what's wrong? Is everything alright?" she asked worriedly. I rested my forehead on the dash. She reached across the divider, drawing circles into the curve of my back with her gentle fingertips. It reminded me of bedtime stories and lullabies, Dani and I curled up in her lap.

"Mom, what if she's stuck forever? What if I never let her go on to the happy place?" I said desperately into the dashboard.

"Keely, honey, what are you talking about? Stuck where forever?"

"Mom, what if she has been gone this whole time, and she has been stuck there waiting for me to feel her again? What if she has been hurting because of me?" I felt it coming, that moment when it was all going to find its way out. Instead of a release, it felt like an unceasing torture as it billowed to the surface. The tears felt like acid against my eyes, each inhale like fire licking my insides. It was the first time I had cried since that night, and once I started, I didn't know if I was ever going to stop. In the distance, I heard my mom trying to soothe me, telling me I was going to be okay.

I allowed myself to say the words. *Dani is gone. Dani. Is. Gone.* The words shook the very insides of my skull, threatening to rip apart the back corner of my mind where they had taken refuge. I sat there, trying to feel the energy that Ms. Tabitha had talked about. Over and over in my head, I repeated the words, hoping to let Dani come back one last time. I waited for the moment to arrive—the time to say goodbye, to give her her wings. But all that I felt back was nothing.

I didn't remember how I had gotten up to my room. I couldn't recall leaving the car or the number of times my mom told me it would be okay. I didn't remember changing from my jeans into panda pajama pants. My eyes ached beneath heavy lids, and the fan blew stale air against my cheeks. I wiped away the crusty residue at the corners of my eyes, erasing any reminder that I had been crying.

I pushed away the covers and threw aside the stuffed animals that had found their way back into my bed. They were the ones Dani liked to sleep with, something my parents had failed to recognize. I heard their muffled voices coming from their room down the hall. I moved towards the noise like a moth to a light bulb, hoping to make out their words.

"She was absolutely hysterical, Cole. I couldn't get her to stop crying for close to three hours," my mother said.

"Well, what the hell happened?"

"I called the center when we got home so I could talk to the counselor, and apparently, the woman had said all of this bullshit about energy and needing to let go. Honest to God, I didn't understand a word she was saying. If it had been face-to-face, I'm not kidding, I would have strangled her."

"What did she say to Keely exactly, though?"

"She claimed that she never spoke to Keely directly, but she basically said that Keely has to come to terms with the fact that her sister is gone."

"She used *those exact words?*" my dad yelled.

"I don't know, Cole. I wasn't in the room with them. From what I could get Keely to tell me, it sounded like this woman led our daughter to believe that she was hurting Dani by not admitting that she was dead." They both suddenly fell silent. I pushed my ear up against my door. "I just don't know what to do."

"Well, why the hell not! You're the expert, aren't you?" His voice sounded harsh, pain mixing with anger.

"How dare you say that to me. Don't you think that if I had all the fucking answers then I would just fix this! You think I don't wish I knew how to make this right, how to get our lives back?" she barked at him. I startled at a loud crash, followed by the clattering of shattered pieces against the floor. Their voices lowered, as if in response, to barely above a whisper. I stepped into the hall, moving quietly towards their room to make out the rest of their conversation.

"I'm sorry, sweetheart. I didn't mean to say it like that."

"Then how *did* you mean to say it," my mom hissed.

"I just want it all to be over—this entire nightmare to be over."

"Well, it's not going to be, okay? I hate to be the bad guy here, but someone in this house has to say it. It's not going to get better unless we start focusing on what we do have, just down that hall. She is so fragile, Cole. If we aren't careful, we are going to lose her, too." My mom's voice became softer, almost soothing as she went on. "I'm just so afraid that she is going to close up—that she is just going to shut us all out, and we are going to have no way to bring her back, either."

"I know, baby. I'm worried about her, too. I'll do whatever you need so we can put this family back together."

I remained rooted to my spot just outside their doorway, unable to escape as the words invaded me. After a few seconds, I broke away, running back to the safety of my bed. I yanked the covers over my head, trying to keep out the sounds and the thoughts and the feelings. But they had already worked their way inside, filling my ever-expanding capsule with all of the terribleness I couldn't keep out.

There's something that happens to wishful people when wishing no longer makes sense. It's like the time Dani and I got our boots stuck in the mud near our tree house—every step became harder than the last, our feet sinking deeper beneath the swampy muck. The old path that felt so simple and easy—*get her back*—couldn't exist anymore. Reality had snuck her ugly way in and taken it away. The morning after I fell apart, I found my parents sitting awkwardly at the breakfast table, pretending as if they hadn't spent the last twenty minutes waiting for me to come down. They had forced smiles plastered on their faces, looking like cheesy TV stars about to sing some stupid song.

They talked quickly and kept interrupting each other, while I pretended like I didn't find it weird, for their sake. I shook my head yes or no to their many questions but focused most of my attention on picking the marshmallows out of my cereal. I didn't even look up when they started talking about going to Marine World for Christmas, a place I had wanted to go my whole life.

"Keely," my mom said, likely noticing I was only half paying attention.

"Hm," I muffled back into my soggy cereal.

"Keely, your mother is trying to talk to you," Dad reprimanded. "Would you mind leaving that alone and giving her your full attention?" Whenever my dad talked like that, I knew that it was easier to listen than go on ignoring him.

"Keely, sweetie, I was thinking that if I picked you up right after school, would you be willing to meet someone with me?" I didn't know how to answer my mom. Dad had been picking me up from school for the past three months, ever since I stopped staying after at the library. I wasn't sure what difference it would make.

"I guess."

"Okay, great. You can tell your friends that I am sorry you aren't able to hang out with them today." I didn't bother replying. Surely, she must have known that it had been weeks since I had hung out with anyone outside of school. Hillary and the boys had left me alone for good. Max was an in-school-only type of friend, and I didn't know what to think after the Ms. Tabitha episode. Mom must have thought that pretending would just make all the loneliness go away.

That day at school, I faked a stomachache so that I could eat my lunch in Nurse Crawley's office. I didn't want to sit through an hour and ten minutes of Max's questions. She allowed me to stay there all the way until the last period, leaving me with only one class to get through with Max before I was free.

I felt his eyes on me the moment I walked into the classroom. But I was surprised when he didn't try talking to me as I took my seat behind him. He sat rigidly in his chair, appearing to focus on the old pencil drawings in the center of his desk. Then, ever so slowly, he reached his arm back without turning towards me. A piece of folded notebook paper slid softly in front of me.

I didn't open it right away and pushed it to the top corner of my desk. Even though I tried to focus on Ms. Smith's social studies lesson, my eyes kept drifting back to the crinkled square. When I was ready and Ms. Smith seemed fully wrapped up in her description of the Native Americans, I quietly unfolded the note and placed it on my lap.

Written in sloppy chicken scratch, it said:

> Are you going to stay mad at me forever?
> No Never Absolutely not
> (circle one)

I tried to stop the smile from coming, but it spread through my body and into my cheeks. Max had a way of making me feel good inside—like I was special enough to be his friend. I used to think he was just curious like everyone else, trying to get me to talk about the kidnapping. But the longer we stayed friends, I started to think that maybe he liked me for *being Keely* and none of that other stuff.

"I gave you a lot of hard choices to pick from, huh," Max asked, as if cued by the bell sounding the end of class. He had turned around, addressing the note in my lap. His sweaty hands gave away his nervousness, as they left a fleeting imprint on the back of his chair.

"Yeah, I'm having a really hard time deciding," I said teasingly, returning the note to my desk. I flicked my pencil between my fingers, pretending to be lost in thought. I let the lead tip hover over each answer. The other students wandered out of the classroom, eventually leaving us alone with a lingering silence. Max shoved his hands into his pockets, as if trying to smother the nervousness that had spread to his fingers. When I thought he couldn't take it any longer, I quickly circled "Never" and slid the note towards him. He rapidly snatched it off the desk, folding it back along its creases and stuffing it into his back pocket. As he turned to leave, he glanced back and flashed me one of his easy smiles.

"Good answer. That was the one I was hoping you would pick."

"I did eeny, meeny, miny, moe, so I guess it wasn't really up to me."

"That makes it even better. It means that luck is on our side," he said with another playful, sideways smirk. I grabbed my books from my desk and met him at the door.

"Well, it's a little late." I immediately regretted the harshness in my voice and offered a slight grin in hopes of making up for it.

"I really am sorry about yesterday. I didn't mean to make you upset." He briefly touched my hand, the warmth rapidly spreading from my fingers into my cheeks.

"It's okay. Mom says it was Ms. Tabitha's fault. I don't think she is going to let me go to those things anymore."

"Wait, but then who am I going to talk to about Ray? I give him only a couple more weeks before he grinds his teeth clear off. You need to be there with me to see it!"

"I just don't think I belong there is all," I said. He squinted slightly, studying my face.

"Yeah, I probably should stop going, too. Gotta move on to my next support group," he said, his half-smile returning.

"What is it going to be this time?"

"I don't know. Maybe I'll join an easier one, like something for people who miss their pets."

"Have you ever lost a pet?"

"I had a hamster named Chicken Nugget once. But he more of *escaped* than anything else."

"Max, you need to start going through bad things if you want to get in on these support groups," I joked. Someway, the support groups didn't seem so awful when I imagined us gathered to talk about misplaced toads and cherished goldfish.

"This is what I have been trying to tell you! I'm really trying my best to fit in here."

It still didn't make sense to me—why he wanted to understand the loss and pain so much. I realized I didn't know a whole lot about him, other than regular kid stuff. For some reason, it didn't really bother me. I didn't need to know his secrets, the same way he didn't need to know mine. He could just keep going on being Max, the boy who stole my food at lunch and could make me forget all about Ms. Tabitha's judging, cloudy stare. Somehow, having Max made missing Dani hurt just a little bit less.

"So, are we good?"

"Yeah, I think so."

"Okay, great, because chocolate pudding was on the line, and I was getting real worried there." He winked at me as he said it, managing to be the only seventh grader who looked as cool as a teenager when he did it.

We walked silently the rest of the way to my locker. He placed my newspaper-covered textbooks onto the top shelf, repeating the same routine that we had created over those last few months.

"I'll see ya around, Keely Millen," he said.

"See ya, Max," I responded, as if we were reciting lines to our own private play. As always, we then went our separate ways. He headed towards the buses, and I went to be picked up at the front circle. A growing piece of me wished that we could change the ending to our final scene.

Until I saw my mom pull up to the school, I had forgotten that she was picking me up that day instead of my dad. She greeted me with the same plastered-on smile as she had that morning.

"Hey, sweet pea. How was school?"

"It was fine," I stated shortly, wondering how she hadn't gotten the memo that kids stopped telling their parents about what they did in school once they hit fifth grade. "So, where are you taking me," I asked suspiciously.

"We are going to visit my friend, Debbie. I don't think you have ever met her before, but she is a good friend of mine."

"But why do you want me to meet her?" I questioned. The last "friend" Mom introduced me to, an old teacher she knew from college, had onion breath and kept asking me what time it was.

"Because she wants to meet you, and I think you will enjoy chatting with her."

We didn't talk the rest of the drive. Instead, we sat listening to the classic rock station, the one that played Christmas music starting in November. I was surprised when she continued on past the long line of matching office buildings just outside of town. She didn't slow down until we pulled in front of a small brick house.

Gardens covered the front yard, partially blocking the view of the blue door and wooden porch swing. Even though it was already mid-December, flowers of every color rose out of the soggy slush covering the browned lawn. They seemed to point straight towards the sky, each in perfect bloom. I wanted to reach out and touch them as we passed through the front iron gate. However, my mother took ahold of my hand and pulled me towards the front step.

She quickly knocked three times on Debbie's door. It surprised me when a tall woman with long dreadlocks greeted us. I had pictured all Debbies as little girls with curly, red hair and freckles on their noses. However, this Debbie had the most beautiful caramel skin that accented her wide, white smile. She wore thick glasses, the kind that magnified her almond-colored eyes.

"Oh, Charlotte, it is so good to see you after all these years," Debbie said as she leaned down and wrapped my mother in a warm hug. "And you must be Kelly. It is very nice to meet you, Kelly. Welcome," she said, extending her hand to me.

"It's Keely," I said uncomfortably as I placed my hand in hers.

"Oh, my apologies, Ms. Keely. I am sometimes hard of hearing on the phone," she said, which told me that maybe she and my mom weren't as close as I had originally thought.

She took us down the dim, narrow foyer that led to her large kitchen. It looked like one of the old-fashioned diners I had seen in the movies. Black and white tiling covered the floor, and antique appliances with large dials lined the wall. There was a plate full of peanut butter cookies placed on the small kitchen table at its center, making the entire room smell like the inside of Pat's Place, a cookie shop downtown.

I noticed only two chairs placed at the table. As if on cue, my mother said, "There are just a few errands I have to run, but if it's okay, I can come back in say...half hour to forty-five?" I looked up at her confusedly, but she continued to focus on Debbie.

"Sure thing, we are all set here. But you can't be angry when we eat all of these cookies here while you're gone," Debbie answered.

"Oh, that is fine by me," Mom said with a smile that didn't quite reach her eyes. "I have high cholesterol, so it's probably best if I get out while I still can." My mom pulled me into her chest and kissed the top of my head. I could hear her throat tighten, as if she held back tears. Before I could say anything, she was already halfway down the hallway. "And thanks again, Deb. I can't tell you...I just...well, I just really appreciate it," she added, before I heard the heavy blue door close behind her.

Debbie stared at the empty place where my mom had been standing, looking lost in thought. It wasn't until I pulled back one of the kitchen chairs and took a seat that she snapped out of it.

"So, I'm guessing I'm here to talk about Dani," I said flatly.

"Actually, you're here so we can talk about me. That is, if that's okay with you?" she said as she took the seat across from me.

"Oh," I said dumbly.

"I thought we could get to know one another. Since I have heard so much about you, it is only fair that you get to learn a bit about me."

"What have you heard about me?"

"Well, for one, I know that you are very smart. And I don't mean just in school. I can see you have an understanding of the world around you."

"What do you mean?" I asked skeptically.

"I can tell you have an awareness of what happens around you. You can see the finer details, the pieces that exist beneath the surface. It's a very special ability."

"It doesn't really sound like it," I mumbled, taking a large bite out of my cookie.

"I never said that it couldn't be burdening at times. Tragedies are hard for everyone to bear. However, I think that it can be even more difficult for those who try to understand why these things happen."

"So you're saying it's better to shut everything out then," I stated.

"No, I don't think that. Coping is a hard thing to learn, but it's not about shutting things out. It's about learning how not to."

"How am I supposed to do that?" I asked, her soothing voice blending with the gentle hum of the radiator.

"Unfortunately, I can't answer that. We all must discover our own ways to cope."

"It sounds like this happened to you before, too," I mindlessly replied. I immediately regretted my response as the hurt spread across her face.

"I haven't experienced what you have. But I have gone through that kind of pain, yes." She stared intently, studying me with her magnifying-glass eyes. I nervously tried to shift my attention to brushing the scattered cookie crumbs into a pile.

Suddenly, the room echoed with her laughter. I jumped at the sound, my nails digging deeper into the chair's wooden arms.

"I apologize. I didn't mean to frighten you," she said as she quickly calmed herself. "I laugh only because you proved my point exactly just now. You could see beyond my answer. And when you saw my discomfort, what did you do? You moved your attention elsewhere." I waited for her to continue. "How about this—today, you can't ask me about what happened. But I'll let you ask me anything else."

"Anything?" I asked hesitantly.

"Whatever your heart desires," she said warmly.

"Okay. How do you get your flowers to stay so pretty?" She raised her eyebrows curiously in response.

"You know, not many people ask me about my flowers."

"But why not? I've never seen flowers like those in the wintertime."

"It's probably because they know the flowers are fake, and they most likely find it odd. Most times in life, people don't like talking about odd things."

"You mean the flowers aren't real? They are plastic?"

"Well, the stems are plastic, but all of the petals are a special silk. It makes them more lifelike." I imagined the winter snowflakes gently kissing their perfectly formed petals.

Then I understood.

"Do you have fake flowers because that way they never die?" She smiled softly to herself, as if enjoying a private joke.

"You are very smart, Keely. Just like your mother told me." I wanted to continue hearing about the silk flowers, but I had a feeling that they had to do with the things she wouldn't share. So instead, I asked how long it had taken for her hair to grow out. She said she hadn't cut it in twenty-four years, which was more than double the time I had been alive. We also talked about how she met my mom, about fifteen years before when they worked together. Debbie said she was my mom's attending physician, which meant that she had been her boss. She was a psychiatrist, too, which made me start to worry that our meeting might have been a trick after all.

"Even though that is what I do for a living, I'm not seeing you as a psychiatrist right now, Keely. I'm simply seeing you as a friend." I hoped she hadn't noticed me stiffen in my seat.

"But you're my mom's friend," I cautiously replied.

"Yes, your mom and I are friends," she continued. "But that doesn't mean that you and I can't be friends as well. Would you like that, if we could be friends?" Even though she was older and a little weird because she planted flowers that didn't grow, I had to admit that I liked being around her.

"Yeah. I think that would be nice." For the rest of our time together, we ate cookies and talked about the places she had traveled to: Africa, Europe, South America, and a small city in Asia. She said her favorite was St. Louis, but not the one in America. It was in Senegal, where she used to watch the pirogues navigate their way through the wharf. I hoped that someday I would see them, too.

By the time Mom returned, I had decided that I liked Debbie. I liked her outdated kitchen; I liked her twenty-four-year-old hair; I liked that her cookies tasted more like peanut butter than dough; and I liked how her glasses let me see the shine in her eyes as she talked about the things she loved.

"Will you come back and visit me again, Keely?" she asked as Mom and I walked out her front door.

"Yeah...yeah, I think I will," I said, heading towards our car. I made sure to look back and wave as we pulled away, which she returned as we rounded the corner.

I had expected Mom to attack me with questions on our drive home. However, that day, she looked nervous. She gripped the steering wheel and focused intently on the road.

"Why haven't I ever met Debbie before, Mom?" I asked.

"She has always been a busy lady, sweet pea."

"She doesn't seem that busy. Why doesn't she ever come to your book club parties?"

"I guess things just get complicated over the years and people lose touch. Debbie and I lost touch is all."

"But why?"

"I think that is something Debbie will have to tell you herself, in her own time." She changed the conversation after that to planning for dinner, as I only half paid attention. Part of me kept drifting back to the house with the blue door, wondering about the pain hidden amongst the flowers that never stopped blooming.

For those next eight months, I went over to Debbie's house after school every Monday and Friday. I pretended like I was only doing it to make Mom and Dad happy. But the truth was, it was my escape. Whenever I sat in that old kitchen of hers—eating her peanut butter cookies and listening to the humming radiator—I felt like I was slowly finding my own way to cope.

She never pushed me to talk about Dani or the kidnapping. However, little by little, I found myself telling her things—like watching our pile of golden leaves turn brown and rot and how I blamed myself for running away and leaving her there in the dirt. She made sure to stay quiet when I talked about things like that but always had something nice to say when I finished. During our time together, it became a little easier to endure the bad things that I remembered. It was okay to be angry or sad. And piece by piece, we chipped away at the awful things that lived inside of me.

"You know what's one of the worst things about Dani not being around anymore? When she would get really excited about something, she would grab my elbow just like this," I said, cupping my elbow with my palm. "And I would let her drag me wherever she wanted me to go. That was how we were—she led and I followed. And you know what else? Since she's been gone, there have been times when my whole arm has gone completely numb for no reason at all. It tingles all over, sometimes lasting for a couple hours. It makes me feel like one of these days, it's just going to fall off and die."

"When do you get those feelings?" she asked, concern blanketing her face.

"Usually when I'm alone or when I start thinking about her."

"And do you think of her often?"

"Kind of. I try to think about her at least once a day."

"Why do you feel the need to do that?"

"Because…she is Dani, and I am Keely. She's my twin. If I think about her, she can still exist somewhere. It's only fair."

"What do you mean by that?" she went on.

"Because she was taken. And I wasn't."

"Do you think it's fair to yourself or to your friends at school, like Max and Hillary? Where is their place in all of this?"

"I don't know," I said, dropping my head towards my lap, my cookie forgotten in front of me.

"I think that it's time I tell you then—that question you asked me all those months ago." She took a deep breath before she began, making me also feel nervous. "Nine years ago, I lost my son, Timothy. He was my only child and all I had in this world. He didn't have a father, because I went to one of those banks that could put a baby inside of me. And for many years, it was fine being just the two of us. Then, something started happening to Timothy. He started getting easily upset and at times became violent. Being someone who normally treated problems like this, I blamed myself for not knowing how to help my own son. I took him to a therapist, but in the end, she couldn't help him either." She hesitated at that part, like she was clearing a bitter taste from her mouth.

"Timothy ended up taking his own life, and I was the one who found him. For a while after he was gone, I felt I had to suffer a certain amount because of what had happened to him. I kept reliving that day over and over and retraced the weeks leading up to it. I felt I owed it to him to keep those things alive, to find where I went wrong and piece together the signs that I had missed. Eventually, I had to accept that doing that wasn't going to bring him back. It didn't matter how many times I reviewed our last breakfast together or that I blamed myself for taking a bath instead of a shower that morning. None of those things could change the fact that he was sick. I learned that I needed to forgive him, to forgive myself."

"What did you do?"

"It wasn't easy. It took a little while for me to get there, but I found a way to accept happiness back in my life, even if Timothy was no longer in it. That was when I started planting the flowers. I wanted flowers that would never lose their color or wilt when the sunshine went away. I planted flowers that would continue living even in the coldness of winter. That way, each spring, I wouldn't have to start over." I sat there for a while, thinking silently. I thought about how unfair life had been. I thought about the pain and wished things could have worked out the right way. And I thought about Debbie's forgiveness. It was the kind that Bumpy had searched for but never found.

"But how am I supposed to do that? I don't know how I can do that," I said, my voice sounding small and childlike in my ears.

"How you're supposed to forgive yourself?" I slightly nodded. She reached across the table to put my clasped hands inside hers, gently rubbing her thumb along my palms. "Keely, you are such a strong girl. I look at you and see this great, bright light coming from you. But for some reason, you keep trying to put it out. I know how much Dani means to you and how much you miss her—I really do. But I also know that Dani doesn't seem like the type of person who would want you to live like this. She would want you to continue on, don't you think?"

"Probably," I said into my chest.

"Sweetie, look at me." I eventually lifted my head to face her great, big eyes. A tear appeared at the edge of her eyelashes, a shimmering crystal behind her lenses. "You deserve a good life. You *deserve* a good life. *You* deserve a good life." She repeated it over and over, as she gripped my hands tighter.

"Doesn't Dani deserve a good life, too? Don't we both deserve a good life together?" Her lips tightened, and I already knew the words she held back. They were the same ones Ms. Tabitha kept inside when Carrie asked about her mother. I wondered if Debbie thought I was strong enough to handle it.

"Of course she deserves a great life, Keely. But sometimes, we have to live our lives as a way of honoring those who don't get that same chance— the way I do for my son and the same way you will for Dani."

"So you're saying I should give up." I didn't know whether I meant it as a question or a statement.

"No, I'm saying that you need to let go—in your own time. I'm not saying right this moment. But eventually, you're going to have to let her go."

"Isn't that the same thing? Letting go is still giving up. It'll make me like everyone else who has already forgotten her. It's going to mean that she's dead." That last word sucked the air out of my lungs, suffocating me before it slowly found its way back in.

"I don't like to believe that any of us ever truly die. I think we exist in other ways."

"What does that even mean?"

"Well, some people call it Faith—believing in God and that there is a heaven. But as for Dani, she can exist through you. You have her eyes, her lovely smile, and her giving heart. You, Keely, have been given this chance at life. I think it's up to you to do something with it."

"Because he didn't take me, that is what you're saying. You think I should just celebrate how lucky I am for not being the one he kidnapped." It was the first time I had ever raised my voice at Debbie.

"No, that is not what I am saying. I mean that we have to give Dani back to the world in different ways."

"So, what, I just pretend to be her and that will make it all okay? Like, I just go ahead and steal the life she was going to have?" I twisted my hands out of hers and abruptly pushed out of my chair.

"No one is telling you to be anyone but yourself, Keely," she said, managing to keep her same soothing voice. "I'm just saying that you owe it to both yourself *and* Dani to make the most of what you are given."

"Well, I'm not gonna do it! If Dani's not getting the chance to live, then I shouldn't either!" I bolted from the table and ran out through the front door. It was a warm summer day, which made Debbie's flowers gleam beneath the sunlight. I slapped at their silky blossoms as I ran, their rigid stems quickly righting themselves after I passed. As I had expected, Debbie didn't follow after me. After a couple of minutes, I slowed my run to a fast walk.

By the time I had passed the same stone house twice, I realized I was walking in circles. I didn't know how much time had passed or whether my mom had started looking for me yet. I could feel my heartbeat returning to its slow thump, the hot anger cooling inside my body. Before long, all I had left was the familiar cramp gripping my chest.

I eventually found my way back to Debbie's house. She was there, sitting in her sea of flowers, calmly waiting for me. Thankfully, my mom's car was not yet parked beside the large elm trees lining the street. I hung my head and scuffed my shoes as I made my way up the drive.

"I'm sorry I yelled at you," I said, kicking a pebble with the tip of my shoe.

"You don't have to apologize to me. Getting angry is okay."

"Do you get angry like that?"

"Sure I do. The things I get angry at have just changed over the years." She clipped at a couple of her flowers, removing some of the frayed petals as if they were real. "It's not about forgetting Dani or pretending she never existed. It is about knowing when it's time to let go."

"So you agree with Ms. Tabitha—that it hurts people when you don't let go." A sour look appeared on her face, the same one that surfaced each time we talked about Ms. Tabitha and my old group sessions.

"I think that woman doesn't know her right hand from her left foot," she said under her breath, just loud enough for me to hear. "I don't think you have been hurting Dani by not letting go. I think you have been hurting yourself."

The rest of that afternoon, I quietly rocked on Debbie's porch swing while she tended to her artificial garden. Her words played over and over in my head. When my mom finally arrived, we said goodbye but without the usual, "See you next time." I didn't know if there would be a next time.

"How did it go?" Mom asked like always. That time, I didn't answer right away, trying to put words to the uncomfortable feelings inside. Meanwhile, Mom adjusted her car mirrors, waiting patiently for me to reply.

We were just about home when I turned to her and asked, "Mom, did you know Timothy?" Her hands tensed on the steering wheel.

"I knew Timothy for only a short period of time."

"Did you know him during the bad parts?"

"Yes. He used to be one of my patients," was all she said. I understood then why I had never met Debbie before.

"Mom?"

"Yes," she responded, lost in thought.

"I want to give Dani a funeral. She never got one before. And if anyone deserves a special funeral, it's Dani." Mom stared ahead at the road for a long time before she finally looked back at me. Her eyes were misty, but I couldn't tell if it was sadness or relief behind their topaz blue.

"Okay," was all she managed to get out. She reached over and took my hand, holding it for the rest of the ride. She squeezed it gently from time to time, as if to remind me that she was still there.

"Mom, when did you realize it—that you were never going to see Dani again?" I tried to hold the question back, unsure if I wanted to hear the answer.

"It was six months ago. I was with a patient, a woman who had just lost her baby. The baby was only a couple days old when she died, but it was long enough for her mother to love her. The mother said something that stayed with me. She told me, 'Death doesn't have to kill the living.' It was then that I realized I was holding on because I thought it made it easier. But in reality, I was stuck. I will never stop loving Dani, and there won't be a day that goes by that I won't think of her. But I can't be stuck anymore."

Let her go. Those three words sounded so easy, as if releasing Dani was as simple as cutting a balloon's string and watching the sky swallow it whole. Instead, her memory was an anchor, pulling me into the darkness below. It reminded me that I was still just ten years old, stuck alone in the forest.

I wanted it to be small. Bumpy and Nana obviously were there, as well as Mom and Dad. Hillary came also. She cried when she saw me standing on her doorstep and made me promise that I would never desert her again— that I was stuck with her from then on. She asked if the boys could come, too. I agreed, so long as they pulled the hair out of their eyes and put on nice ties. Debbie attended, her flowing, black dress and dark straw sunhat rustling against the autumn breeze. My mom started to cry when Debbie reached out to hug her, and I could feel the mixture of sadness and for-giveness as they held one another.

Max showed up even though I said he didn't have to. I was thankful he was there, standing with me as we said goodbye.

It wasn't in a church, and sad music didn't play in the background. It was held in our backyard in the one spot that never blocked out the sun-light. Bumpy brought a large stone from Reading. In perfectly carved cur-sive, it read: *Dani, Lost but Never Forgotten.* The bottom held only our birthday. I could only look at it briefly, knowing I would otherwise lose the nerve to go through with it.

Everyone stood around the rock, each sharing memories of Dani. They talked about her spirit, how she never backed down from what she believed in, how she took care of others—how she took care of me. It didn't matter that half the people there didn't know her like I did, because she managed to make them love her anyways. That was the person she was, the part that I loved the most.

I was the very last one to speak. When that time came, when all the eyes turned towards me, I looked down at the small letter in my hand and questioned if it was enough.

How could it ever be enough for Dani?

Even though it had been my idea in the first place, when my turn came to say goodbye, I couldn't bring myself to do it. I crumpled against Bumpy, who hovered overtop of me, shielding me from the sunlight.

I handed the letter to my mother, who had always been brave like Da-ni—strong enough to handle anything.

"Dani," she began to read, just her name taking the breath right out of my mother's voice. "Dani. I don't know why the world gave me a sister like you only to take her away. I don't know why this happened to us or who I am supposed to be without you here. I don't know how to be three with anyone but you, and I don't think I ever want to be. But this I do know. I know that I will never look at another glow-in-the-dark star with-out thinking of you. I will never forget how you used to tickle my back right when we were about to fall asleep, and I will never watch *White Fang* with anyone else. I know that I will only miss you more each day and that I have to be brave now because you would want me to. I am going to try and be bigger like you always said I could be. I'm going to do it because maybe then I can be the person who doesn't run away but the one who stays. I want to be that person for you because that was the person you were for me."

When all the words were used up and the tears turned dry, we each walked away from that rock feeling a little bit weaker, a little emptier. I didn't think I would ever go back to it, because it would take a larger piece of me the next time. But I made sure to do one last thing before I left for good. I made sure to plant flowers all around her rock, all of them in the most beautiful shades of green. They were the ones that would never wither up or die, just like Debbie's for Timothy. It was what Dani deserved, something that stayed perfect forever.

Chapter Six
September 12, 2002

When we were eight, Keely and I put together a time capsule. Some people imagined the future or what they wanted to become when they made them. But back in 1998, Keely and I didn't really think about whom we were going to marry or the fancy houses we might live in. We didn't have to create a better future, because we knew, no matter what changed or stayed the same, we would always have each other.

We didn't put the normal stuff in it, like newspaper clippings or a brand new dollar bill. Instead, we filled it with letters to each other. We used an old container that once held Dad's dusty maps and buried the capsule in our backyard. We found a nice spot next to the barn, just far enough away from the chipmunks' nest so that they couldn't get at it.

As I sat in my cell, I thought about how it had been seven hundred and thirty days since our future had changed. I worried that Keely hadn't paid attention to where we hid the capsule—that she would never have a chance to dig it up. I wondered what she had written to me and tried to imagine her slanted writing curling in front of my eyes. But more than anything, I wished that I hadn't spent half my letter telling her how Chuckie was my favorite Rugrat and that the *last* thing I wanted to do that summer was take swim lessons.

I hoped I would get another chance to tell her how I felt.

There were a lot of times in the basement that I had only my thoughts to keep me company. Sometimes, I felt suffocated by them in that small space. Little by little, they became too big for me, just like the doors for their frames at Nana and Bumpy's house in the summertime. No matter how hard I tried to push, I eventually realized they just weren't going to fit together any longer.

That was the hardest thing—coming to terms with it. I had to accept the fact that I had forgotten how it felt to breathe in real air or drink water without a plastic aftertaste. I realized I had no power to help Kai in his fight against the demons that Dias threw at him. Kai would scream out in his sleep, begging that he wouldn't have to go to the bad place. It seemed that the harder things grew for Kai, the worse they became for Brook, too. It became worse for all of us.

No matter the reasons that Dias brought us there, we were tied to each other because we went through it together. It made me think of the time when a high school boy from my hometown died just a couple months before I was taken. He was a senior, and even though not many people knew him or really even liked him, his car accident seemed to bring everyone together. It didn't matter what group he hung out with at school or the kind of grades he made. Everyone was impacted. That was the thing about tragedies—the worst misfortunes seemed to have the greatest ability to make people care about one another.

The only difference from those tragedies was that ours was neverending. He controlled everything, even down to our haircuts. Just like Chet before him, Kai no longer had his hair trimmed every couple months. It started growing longer, jutting out in weird angles. It made his face look smaller. The longer it grew, the more Kai seemed to shrink inside of himself.

We all thought that Kai would be strong enough. That was his personality—the stubborn kind. At first, he tried to defy him. He would rip out large chunks of hair, especially the parts that fell over his eyes. But every time he did that, he would return to his cage with bruises covering his face. Dias started taking him for longer periods of time. We knew he was trying to break him.

Brook tried talking to Kai, but she soon saw that things would never go back to the way they were before. Instead, they would only get worse.

"I feel like he is pitting us against each other," she said to me when it was just the two of us in our cells. She tried to avoid talking about Kai in front of Mika. She worried the same thing would one day happen to him.

"In what way?"

"In every way. I feel like Kai blames me for all the stuff that Dias does to him."

"But Kai knows that isn't true."

"Does he? I mean, he won't even look at me anymore. He doesn't really talk to me. And if he does, it isn't the way he used to. It's almost like he's…angry."

"Has he started letting Kai go with you to the greenhouse or playroom again?"

"Kai comes with me to the greenhouse, but it's not like how it used to be. We work alone now, and Dias usually sits in there with us. Kai is only there on the test days. Dias started giving us these long exams, like the big state ones. I used to take them once a year back in school. But most times they are on things that Kai wouldn't even know. I do better on them, but only because I get to read the textbooks and watch the videos beforehand.

Kai doesn't get to do that."

"Who cares about his tests? It's not like they mean anything."

"But they mean something to Kai. I think that if he doesn't do well on them...he is punished."

"Punished how?"

"He doesn't tell me a whole lot and keeps mostly to himself. But I got him to talk about it a little when he was allowed back in the playroom a couple days ago. He said he gets locked up in this room with no lights, and it is either too hot or too cold. Sometimes he gets fed, and sometimes he doesn't. He also told me that sometimes he gets taken outside and is chained to a pole."

"He gets to go outside?" I said, unable to keep the envy out of my voice.

"Trust me, it isn't a good thing. It only happens at night, especially when it gets really cold. He doesn't get any kind of jacket, either."

"But he could die!" I yelled, horrorstruck.

"I know, but I doubt Dias lets it get to that point. When Kai told me about it, I got this feeling that Dias was trying to see how far he could take it."

"How far he could take what?"

"Kai's breaking point. He's trying to see how far he can push him."

"What else is he doing to him?" I asked hesitantly.

"He has Kai watch these really awful videos. Kai doesn't tell me exactly what is on them, but he said they make him sick to his stomach."

"Why does he have to watch them?"

"He doesn't know. He doesn't really have a choice. The videos are left on for hours. Even when he closes his eyes, he can still hear the loud, awful sounds. Other times, Dias leaves on music with the same song playing over and over. Kai said it is the kind of rock music with lots of screaming in it."

"How come we can't hear it?"

"I don't know. I feel like he might be taking Kai someplace that we don't know about. Kai mentioned something about a shed once and how he hated when he had to go there."

"A shed, like in the woods?"

"He didn't say. He refused to talk to me about it. He said it was better if I didn't know what happened when he went there."

"And he thinks it's your fault that all these things are happening to him?"

"I don't know what he thinks," she said with her head bowed. "It's not just the tests though. It's other stuff, too. Dias has been having us play these games. They're not like the games in the playroom. All of them are wooden and look handmade. Some are puzzles and others are reaction games, like being the first one to hit a button when the light turns green. But the thing is, even when I try to lose, I still end up winning somehow. It's like the whole thing is rigged so that Kai loses every time."

"Did you ask Kai about it? You should tell him that it's just another one of Dias's tricks."

"I did. I just don't think he believes me," she said, almost as if she blamed herself. "You know what else is weird? Whenever Dias is in the room with us—when both Kai and I are together—he goes out of his way to be nice to me. He ignores Kai most of the time but compliments me over even the littlest things. But when Kai isn't there and it's just us, he barely even looks at me."

"I don't get it. He told you not to be competitive but then he makes sure you win every time?"

"I don't think it's about some stupid story anymore. In the end, it doesn't matter what I do or don't do. I'm still going to walk right into his trap."

"And what kind of trap do you think it is?"

"I'm not sure. All I know is that he is using Kai for something. And I'd be willing to bet that eventually he is going to use it against me."

He started taking Mika and me to a new room—the other one close to the red room. It was smaller than the greenhouse, and there weren't any desks or shelves. There were two beanbags on the tile floor and another mirrored wall at the back. A movie projector hung from the ceiling and shined videos on the front, white wall. But they weren't like the ones that we had to watch in the greenhouse. All the videos included a tall woman with pale skin and short hair. She stood in a white room, so bright that you couldn't see any of the walls around her. She talked in a voice that reminded me of those ladies who sold beauty products on infomercials.

Dias would keep us in there for different amounts of time, however long it took for each video to finish. Mika and I would sit in the beanbags and watch silently. We did so only because we knew he was staring at us from behind the reflective glass. The moment we would turn to talk to each other, his booming voice would come over a loudspeaker. It would command, "Watch."

At first I didn't think it was going to be that hard. We could just sit there and wait for it to be over. But I soon realized they were instructional videos, and throughout them, the lady required us to do tasks. Some of them were easy, like sitting across from a partner and looking into his eyes without speaking for sixty seconds. Others took more time and forced us to work on projects together. One told us to build a tower that was three levels high out of two pieces of paper. We weren't allowed to use any kind of glue or tape, just the two sheets of paper. Another required us to take turns blindfolding one another and getting the other person across the room using only verbal instructions.

If the video called for any supplies, they would always be laid out next to the beanbags when we entered the room. It took ten trips to the room to finish all of the videos. Then they started all over again. It became easier the second and third and fourth times through, which meant that we didn't have to spend as long in there. We had to do all of the tasks together, and we weren't allowed to leave the room until we completed them.

Even though we weren't being graded like in school, it still felt like it was going to count for something.

"Why do you think he makes us do all those things in the activity room?" I asked Brook one day. Kai had been missing again, that time for almost eleven days.

"It's just another one of his games. He likes feeling that he can get us to do all these dumb things, just like all those 'classes' in the greenhouse."

"So, you don't think it's for something…I don't know, to prepare us?"

"For what, the longest staring competition?" she snapped. It didn't hurt my feelings, because I knew she was just worried about Kai. On the days that Kai disappeared, Brook was constantly on edge. "I'm sorry, I didn't mean to get mad at you. Honestly, I just think he likes feeling like he can control us. Just like the timed showers, just like everything. He says jump and so we jump. He says eat this, and we have no choice but to eat it. I just don't know where it ends."

"Do you think that we should stop doing what he says?"

"That's not going to make him leave us alone."

"But what if we use that against him?" Mika piped up, startling Brook and me.

"Use what against him?" I asked, turning towards him.

"We do what he wants, right? We play along and make him think that whatever he's doing is working. And then when it really counts, we use it against him," he said, his eyes focused on me.

"I don't think I understand," Brook said, her eyebrows drawing together.

"It's like this one thing my coach taught me in baseball. I'm not the best hitter. I have a hard time reading what kind of pitch I'm going to get, so he told me that if I wanted to fool the pitcher, I had to pretend I had a weak leading arm. I would drop my shoulder for the first couple balls, that way, he would think I was slow on my release. The pitcher would then get too confident and give me a fastball, which was the exact pitch I wanted all along. Fastballs come in hard and straight, and I have an easier time knowing where they are going to go. Even though I had to fake something in the beginning, it gave me that one open shot in the end. It didn't work every time, but when it did, I made sure to make it count."

"I wish it was that easy," Brook said dully.

"All I'm saying is that maybe if we make him think we have that weak leading arm, we can be ready when he gives us the fastball." I couldn't help but smile when I looked over at Mika. He looked so excited, as if he had finally figured it all out.

"But what if down here, you really do have a weak leading arm. What if you aren't actually fooling anyone at all?" Brook challenged.

"I don't know what you mean," he said through a frown.

"Whatever is happening to Kai, it's going to happen to you, too. Just like it did to Chet and just like Brent before him. I don't think pretending is an option." It was the first time I had heard her say anything like that to anyone.

"Maybe I wasn't talking about me or Kai. Maybe I was talking about you and Dani." He stated it with confidence, making me wonder if he had seen something Brook and I had missed. Even though he was quieter than the rest of us, it didn't mean that he had nothing to add. "I don't know why, but I get the feeling that you guys are going to be the ones swinging."

"So what does that make you?" I asked, not really sure if I even understood my own question. Whenever Mika got into moods like that, where he spoke in metaphors, he seemed to jump several steps ahead of me. I always tried to keep up.

He looked from me to Brook, both of us staring back at him as if he held all the answers.

"I think I'm the fastball."

The days I hated the most were the ones he brought me into the attitude room. It would just be us; Mika didn't come. I wouldn't speak unless I had to and mostly kept my eyes focused on my lap.

"How are you feeling, Pandora?" he would usually start the conversation with. I would often shrug my shoulders dumbly, trying to divert the question without having to say anything. We would continue like that for a while. He would ask me questions, and I would do my best not to answer them. I didn't really understand the purpose of our sessions. Most of them lasted all of ten minutes, and he did most of the talking.

At first, I was afraid whenever I had to be alone with him. Even when he wore his cross, I didn't feel safe. There was something about him that didn't seem completely right, despite how well he appeared to keep himself together. It felt like there was a missing piece or a rip at the seam.

I felt myself growing bolder each time we went to the attitude room. I caught myself saying things that I had held back before. I went from desperate to angry all in the same breath and worried it would get me into trouble one of those days.

"I want you to do me a favor. I want you to look down at your stomach and tell me what you see," he asked me during one of the sessions.

"My stomach," I mumbled, failing to keep the sarcasm out of my voice.

"Yes, you can see your stomach," he said, ignoring my tone. "You see the clothes you are wearing; you see how your chest rises up and down when you breathe. You are able to see everything that is around you. But you are missing the very thing that's right in front of you. Do you know what that is?"

"The things I miss are nowhere near me. They are someplace far away, and it's all your fault." I had a tendency of doing that, bringing up my family and the life he had taken from me. Most times, it didn't make sense in the conversation, but I still found a way to work it in each time.

"It's your nose, Pandora," he said with a growing grimace, as always ignoring my tirade. "Your nose is always there, and you're always able to see it. But your brain tunes it out. It ignores that it's even there." I tried to focus on the spaces between the floor tiles, pretending to look uninterested. "I'll tell you why because I know you wish to ask me. It's because your brain cancels out what isn't useful to it. Your mind doesn't register the things that it no longer needs."

"It's too bad it doesn't work for everything," I mumbled again, that time muffled under my breath.

"I know you used to go by Dani and that you used to live on Beechwood Road in New Jersey. You would go up to Reading for the summers so you could spend more time with your grandparents, and your grandfather would often talk about when he would take you and your sister to go fishing at your Uncle Paulie's place. Except he wasn't your real uncle, was he?"

I sat completely still, telling myself that anyone could have known the list of useless information that he had rattled off. Someone could have just looked it up or asked a passerby. But the longer he spoke, the harder it became to pretend that he didn't know anything more than the average stranger.

"You would go to that bible camp down by the lake—the campground right off North Ave. It's pretty down there, especially right around the beginning of August. You never understood a lot of the God talk when you went there, did you? You wondered about the possibility of it all. You asked questions about believing without seeing, and it showed me that you were someone who wanted to look past the parts right in front of her."

I looked up at him and searched his face, trying to bring back any memory of him from the summer camp. I would have remembered his face, especially his deep-set eyes and crooked, half-pieced nose.

"You never saw me, if that is what you are wondering. I made sure of that."

"Why are you doing this to us? Why me?"

"It's always about the *why*, isn't it? The *what* and the *how* just never seem to be enough, do they?"

"I promise if you let me go, I won't tell anyone. You say you know me and about my life. You must also know that I was happy. Please. *Please.* I was happy." I hated the times I would beg. It would happen in those fleeting instants when a small part of him felt human—those brief times that made a tiny piece of me feel that maybe, if I just found the right words, he would let me go. But each time reminded me why I hated myself in those moments. I was a fool. No matter what any of us said, he wasn't going to let us go.

"Oh, Pandora. You shouldn't make promises that you cannot keep," he tsked at me. He made me feel like a small child whenever he did that, shaking his long sausage finger at me. "All of these things that you once knew, those meaningless things about where you grew up and what you did over distant summers, they are all just a bunch of noses. Those things are no longer useful to you, and in time, your mind will learn to no longer register them." I wanted to tell him that it would never happen. I wanted to tell him those things would always be a part of me, no matter how hard he tried to make me forget about them. But then I remembered what Brook said about pretending and Mika said about faking the slow swing.

As much as it hurt me to do it, I nodded my head slowly with him, letting him believe he was right. Just as with everything he asked us to do, I didn't do it because he wanted me to. I did it because I hoped that Mika had called it—that there would come a time when I could use all of it against him.

When that date in September returned, I couldn't push the time capsule out of my mind. I couldn't stop thinking about that letter being the last thing I gave to Keely, and I couldn't stop wondering if it would be enough.

So, I decided to write her a new one. There weren't any rules for time capsules about having a do-over. As long as we both were living, I wanted those words to exist somewhere. I ripped a blank page out of one of the books from the greenhouse, folding it into a small square and tucking it inside of my sock. It sat there for several days, being switched from one sock into the next. I didn't want to rush writing it. I wanted to only put down the best words. I wanted the best for Keely.

For at least a little bit, the feeling of the bulge in my sock—the rough scuff of the paper against my bare skin—made me feel like I had a piece of her with me. It didn't say anything more than the copyright information from the dated textbook, but then I thought, *maybe that was the point.* I felt closer to her, knowing it didn't say anything at all. It didn't have any words of goodbye or all of the small, subtle details that only I knew about her.

It didn't say anything, because it wasn't time for our last letter.

I buried it deep into the ground of my cell, in the patch of dirt hidden beneath my large water tank. I made sure to smooth the dirt over the hidden hole, my dirty fingers the only sign betraying my secret.

There it would sit, for how long, I didn't know. All I knew was that I wasn't ready to write it just yet. Not yet.

Not yet.

Chapter Seven
September 12, 2003

I'd heard about the five stages of grief. I'd been told I would pass through each one, making my way naturally from one emotion to the next. But I had discovered that was a load of shit. As far as I could tell, there were only two phases to losing someone. The separation between each felt something like a teeter-totter; right when I had become comfortable with the first, I was launched straight into the next. And I couldn't know for certain if my feet would ever find the ground.

I called the first part of losing Dani the "Snow Globe." I was stuck in a place where only I existed. Right when I thought things were starting to settle, everything would be shaken up again. My world revolved around waiting for the chaos to come, watching it swirl around me to make me relive it over and over again. In some ways, I took comfort in it—knowing it was only a matter of time before the turbulence returned. That first stage was about surviving inside my own misery. For me, the Snow Globe stage lasted exactly two years, one month, and eighteen days.

The second phase was the "Ball of Clay." I had to remake myself; I had to create a new Keely because the old one couldn't exist without Dani. In order to escape the "Snow Globe Keely," I needed to become something different, something more durable.

It started by removing Dani's things—her bed, mountain of stuffed animals, all of her green. We couldn't bring ourselves to throw anything away, so Mom packed up her things and set them in the attic. It made me feel better knowing that I wouldn't see her Mickey Mouse T-shirt on some other middle schooler or have to imagine her teddy bear sitting on some other kid's bed.

We cleared out the whole room so that we could start from scratch. Mom and Dad said I could paint my room whatever color I wanted. I ended up choosing a bluish-gray, wanting to leave behind Dani's green and my purple. I didn't care that it made the room look smaller or wasn't the typical "teenage girl color." It felt like the right color for *me*, the new "Ball of Clay Keely."

After the room had been emptied and the walls painted, it hit me—for the first time, I had my own room. And I had absolutely no idea what do to with it. Dani had set up everything for us before. The only decorations I added to my new room were two posters that had been forgotten in the furthest corner of the closet. One was of Jonathan Taylor Thomas that I had ripped out of a magazine, and the other was a movie poster for *The Man in the Iron Mask*. I taped them up on opposite walls, managing to make the room seem even emptier. Mom suggested that I tape up some of my old drawings, but even I knew that only a five-year-old could get away with that. Instead, I hoped I could just get Hillary to help me with it later.

The one thing I couldn't change was the collection of plastic stars glued to the ceiling. I didn't fix the crooked ones or replace those that had fallen off. I knew that little by little, they would grow dimmer and more would drop to the ground. But I wanted to let them do it in their own time.

I thought that eighth grade would be like all of the other years. I expected snickers behind my back and shifty eyes in the hallways. But it ended up being something I wasn't prepared for. Eighth grade marked the year that I learned what it meant to be popular.

I used to think that popularity took a lot of work. I imagined carefully picking out cool clothes and sucking up to the kids with rich parents. It seemed I lacked all of the things that should have been essential to becoming popular. I was the last kid picked in gym class and large groups made me uncomfortable. It took me forever to get jokes, and I didn't have the knack for talking over people. Even after more kids started sitting with us at lunch, I figured it couldn't have had anything to do with me. They wanted to hang out with Max, and I was just the tag-a-long.

But one single night changed it all. It was the last Saturday of September 2002, and the news was all over town that the boy's varsity soccer team had just won the biggest game of the season against Ramapo. Ridgewood wasn't just a football town; we also took our soccer very seriously. We used to go as a family and watch the games under the lights, but I hadn't been since Dani went missing. It was more her thing than mine, and I didn't know the rules well enough to get into it.

Hillary had invited me over to her house for the night. We planned to stay up late watching *The Lord of the Rings* movie, and the house was supposed to be all ours. Hillary's parents were away for the weekend, something I made sure to leave out when I asked Mom and Dad if I could go.

We ordered pizza and camped out in her bedroom. She talked all about high school, while I didn't say much at all. I liked hearing her talk about homecoming and how she had two lockers, one for school and the other for gym class. Hillary told me about the cute boy she had a crush on, the best singer in the drama club. He was a sophomore, like her brother, but he already had lead parts in all the plays. I found myself giggling and getting excited for her, thinking maybe I could do the whole girl thing after all.

It wasn't until around ten o'clock that I got the text. Dad said the phone was only to be used for emergencies, but Max still messaged me from time to time. He was my only exception.

"Hill, Max is asking me if people are over there yet," I said as I read the text off of my flip phone.

"Over where, here? Does he know you're at my house?"

"I think so. I told him yesterday that I was going to be hanging out with you tonight." Hillary angrily jumped up and reached for her phone, punching in two numbers and bringing it up to her ear. I knew who she was calling even before she said his name.

"Vander. What the hell is going on?" I couldn't hear what he was saying over the loud music blasting through her phone. "You do know that Mom and Dad are going to kill us if they find out. It's going to be way worse than last time." My palms started to sweat as I listened to her talk to her brother. I still hadn't met him, mostly because he was never home. It seemed like they didn't have the best sibling relationship. "Three hundred people! Are you crazy? I don't care if they beat Ramapo! Why can't they do it somewhere else?" She stood tapping her foot and biting her lip the rest of the call.

"Unbelievable," she yelled, slamming her phone shut and tossing it onto her bed. "Well, it looks like the sleepover just got a whole lot bigger."

"What did he say?"

"Apparently, almost half the school is on their way over here right this moment."

"Wait, is there going to be…" I let my question hang in the air uncomfortably.

"Alcohol? Um, yes. And if the Underground comes, you can bet that won't be the only thing."

"What's the Underground?"

"Never mind. Come help me hide all of my parents' things before these stupid people get here." We rushed through the downstairs, grabbing vases off of mantels and throwing all of the expensive jewelry into a giant bed sheet. We hauled everything upstairs and locked it up in the bedroom across from Hillary's. Before we could reach the crystal glasses, we heard the cars pull up to the front of the house.

When the group came through the door, it sounded like someone had set off fireworks throughout the downstairs. We rushed back to Hillary's room, propping our stacks of large paintings against her wall.

"Okay, so you stay here, and I'm going to go find my brother. Are you fine in here for just a little bit?" I nodded my head in response. She replaced her pajama pants with a pair of jeans and dashed out of the room. I sat down on her bed and listened to the loud music vibrating the carpeted floor, trying to make out people's voices over the blare of the speakers. Now and then, I heard people chant our school's cheer, the one about killing the competition like a bunch of dead raccoons. Parents didn't like that one all that much, but there wasn't much that rhymed with the Ridgewood Maroons.

The noise became louder as time went on, and from what I could hear, it sounded like people were having a great time. There was a part of me that wanted to go down and join them but another part liked being upstairs, hidden and tucked away from everyone.

"Oh my God, he's here!" Hillary yelled as she burst through the door. She rushed to her desk mirror, running her hands frantically through her hair, trying to make the stray strands lay flat.

"Who's here?" I asked, slightly alarmed.

"Cute drama boy! Here, help me!" she said as she handed me her hair gel. I squeezed out a small glob and tentatively scrunched it into her hair, trying to do as she did. Until then, I hadn't realized that at some point she had dyed her hair back to its natural color. Hillary then emptied a purse out onto her desk, creating a large pile of powders and cylinders. It was the first time I had ever seen Hillary appear self-conscious, as if high school had transformed her into a typical girl.

"Are you going to go back down there?" I asked nervously.

"Uh, duh! Big Boobs Tracy Francis is down there talking to him, and I can't let him make that mistake," she said, applying her red lipstick.

"Then what am I going to do?"

"You're going to come downstairs with me, dummy. I'm not going to let you sit up here by yourself."

"But I have nothing to wear and...I don't think I'm old enough for the party."

"People aren't going to care how old you are. They will all be drunk anyways. Your friend, Max, has come to a couple of these, so you won't be the only eighth grader." Max told me that he drank beer a couple times with his cousin before, but he never told me anything about going to high school parties.

"Hillary, have you ever been...drunk before?"

"I've taken a shot once or twice, but I don't drink much. I usually just go so I can laugh at everyone acting like idiots. Here, sit," she said as she grabbed my shoulders and pushed me into the chair facing the mirror. For the next thirty minutes, she wrapped my hay-bale hair into curlers and drew around my eyes with her colored pencil. She used her black liquid wand to make my eyelashes stick up and dabbed my cheeks with the pink powder, making me feel more like a doll than a pretty girl.

She forced me into jeans that sat low on my hips, adding a shirt that barely made it past my belly button. The top of it left a V for boobs, but since I didn't really have those, it loosely hung around my neck like an empty hammock.

"Here, put this on." She tossed me a bra, different from the flat, cotton rectangle that I usually wore. It looked like it already came with a set of boobs. "Guys hate it because they think it's cheating, but they won't know unless they grab it."

I must have looked shocked.

"Don't worry, Keely," Hillary laughed. "No one is going to grab you, I promise."

"Have you ever been, you know, touched there?" I asked while uncomfortably eyeing her chest, noticing that hers were much bigger than mine.

"Just once. I kissed a boy named Davy in one of the baseball dugouts, but he was just a little too touchy for me. I let him hold one for a few seconds and then I made him stop. I told him it wasn't a dang water balloon so he better not squeeze so hard for the next girl."

Eventually, after getting me to put on the boob bra, she grabbed my shoulders and turned me towards the mirror.

"Well hot damn, Keely's a little babe!" she said, looking quite pleased with herself.

"Oh, I am not," I said shyly as I tucked a curl behind my ear.

"No, no. Leave that right where it is. That way it won't get messed up," she said, putting the curl back where it was supposed to be.

"You know, you look really pretty, too," I said, looking at her flowy shirt that didn't have a wizard anywhere in sight. The gel made her hair curl gently around her face, reminding me of the woman on the cover of the bottle.

"You're sweet. Hopefully it is enough to beat out Big Boobs Tracy," she joked as she headed out the door, me tagging anxiously behind. Whatever I thought I was walking into, nothing prepared me for what met us when we reached the stairway. The noise hit me like a physical wall, as did the stink of something fruity and a weird smelling smoke. People lined the walls, everyone holding a bright red cup and swaying to the bass of the music. The overflowing crowd made the large entryway appear cramped, as people spilled out into the many side rooms.

Hillary held my hand as she pushed us through the swarm of people. I kept my head down, trying to avoid tripping in the wedge shoes Hillary had let me borrow. The air appeared foggy, and sweaty arms rubbed against me.

"I last saw him on the back porch," she said to me over the noise. We wound our way around the rest of the crowd, slipping out through the back end of the house. It looked like he was still where she had left him. Even though I didn't know what he looked like, Big Boobs Tracy quickly gave his location away. She hung on his arm like an umbrella on a hook, her lacy bra sticking out from under her shirt.

"So, what now?" I said to Hillary as we looked over at them. As far as I could tell, he wasn't enjoying her breasts as much as she thought he was.

"Okay, so you know how I said I don't ever drink. I think, just this one time, I may need something." I instantly became nervous at the thought of drinking alcohol, making me reach up and run my fingers anxiously through one of my dangling curls. Hillary grabbed my finger mid-pull, re-twirling the curl around her thumb to fix the damage. "You don't have to drink anything if you don't want to, I promise."

She once again took my hand as we made our way back through the horde towards the kitchen. People were packed around the counters, pouring clear liquid into little glasses. They gulped down the tiny drinks and followed them with limes, looking at first like they didn't enjoy them. But the cheers that came afterwards said otherwise.

The air stung my nose, smelling like Nana's gin and tonics. A group was gathered around the kitchen island. Bottles holding different colored liquids filled its center. A set of people stood at far ends of each other, tossing Ping-Pong balls into plastic cups.

"Where did they get all this stuff?" I said into Hillary's ear.

"My brother's friend has a cousin who owns a bunch of liquor stores. We don't know his name, we just know that he's the one who gets the stuff." As if on cue, the music suddenly stopped and a guy leapt up onto the island, straddling the collection of bottles beneath him.

"People of Ridgewood, my mighty Maroons! We drink tonight, not only because we kicked the shit out of those Ramapo pussies, but also because we have a new faithful among us." He then took a swig straight from the bottle he was holding, which appeared a little under half-full. He wore a loose flannel shirt over tight pants. They could have been confused for skater jeans if it wasn't for the muscular legs that filled them. His back was towards me, so I could see out into the mob in front of him. One thing was clear—they all adored him. "Now, we all know how we treat our new faithfuls, am I right?" he yelled to the crowd, making them cheer even louder. He took another swig from his bottle, that time spitting it out like a fountain onto the crowd. They acted like he had thrown a wad of hundred dollar bills on top of them.

I was so focused on the herd of people that I hadn't even noticed Max being pulled up onto the island, the yelling guy's arm wrapping around his shoulder. "We have here, Maximilian Thomas Lerman, a boy who will soon become a man. He will learn to kill a bear with his bare hands and then eat its meat raw just because he can. I want you to welcome him the only way we know how!"

All of a sudden, the whole pack started yelling, over and over, "Dirty six! Dirty six!" Max was pulled down off the counter and pushed into a tall chair that faced the crowd. Six guys, all wearing flannel, each held out one of the small glasses to him. All were filled with a golden-brown liquid, and I didn't even want to ask Hillary what was in them. I couldn't see Max's face, but I imagined him nervously biting the corner of his mouth.

As the crowd kept chanting those two words, Max swallowed each glass one by one. When he finished the last glass, everyone cheered his name and raised red cups in salute. The guy leading the group jumped down off the counter, putting him face to face in front of us.

"Seriously, Vander? Did you really have to spit the vodka everywhere?"

"Come on, H, they liked it!" he said with a sideways smile.

"You could have vomited on them and they would have still liked it," she said bitterly under her breath.

"What can I say—the people know what they want!" Vander Atwood wasn't like the eighth grade boys. He had a small amount of dark stubble that covered his square jaw. I found myself mesmerized by the half-moon that easily appeared over his left cheek each time he smiled. He ran his hand quickly through the messy waves in his thick, dark hair, and one eyebrow appeared permanently arched. I tried to look away before he changed his focus from Hillary.

"Well, the *people* want you to clean this up before Mom and Dad get home tomorrow."

"What, isn't little sis having a good time? You look all jazzed up, so you must be down here for other things than to just bitch me out. Wow, I think that's even a little perfume I smell," he said, leaning into her.

"Why don't you go annoy someone else," she said as she grabbed the bottle from his hand. Until then, he hadn't noticed me standing there. When his dark brown eyes settled on mine, I felt my heart switch places with my stomach.

"Maybe I will," he said, the smirk returning as he nudged past Hillary. "I'm Vander. My little sister isn't very good at introducing me to people." I was about to take his hand when Hillary moved in between us.

"She is my friend, Vander. You know what I told you about my friends." Hillary looked like she wasn't going to back down. He threw his hands up in defeat as he turned to walk away.

"Alright, I give up! I was just trying to be nice, you little brat." As he turned the corner to leave the kitchen, I could have sworn he threw me a quick wink as he glanced back.

"He seriously drives me nuts. Just so unbelievably annoying," she said to herself as she poured some of the clear liquid into two of the small glasses. I stood rooted in my spot, still focused on the doorway that he had disappeared through. "Keely, earth to Keely."

"Huh?" I asked, a bit dazed.

"Whoa, what's up with you? I asked if you wanted one. You don't have to. I just thought I should ask." She was holding out one of the glasses to me, her fingers magnified in the see-through glass. It was filled to the top with the vodka. I hadn't planned on drinking anything when I first came down the stairs, especially after seeing a girl covered in vomit and sleeping on a sofa couch. But there was something about that moment, standing there listening to everyone raise their glasses to Vander and cheer on Max like a hero for drinking the line of small glasses. In that moment, all I cared about was holding on to the feeling I had gotten from her brother's bow-shaped dimple.

"Here goes nothing," I said as I grabbed the glass from her hand and swung my head back. Numbness instantly spread through my mouth, and the burning inside my throat made me wince. I imagined gasoline tasting the same.

"What are you, crazy? You're supposed to take that with some juice or Coke or something!" she said as she yanked one of the soda bottles off the counter. I grabbed it from her hand and drank as fast as I could, hoping the awful taste would eventually leave my mouth.

"Oh my God, I can't believe you people drink this stuff! Why is everyone smiling and cheering after they drink this?" I said as I resurfaced from my desperate gulps of Coke. My eyes began to water, and my body felt hot all over, like a heating blanket hid underneath my skin.

"You're not supposed to do it straight up like that, silly. That's the quick stuff. See, you're supposed to drink it like this," she said, drinking her glass of liquid and then gulping a cup of orange juice shortly after. Her face scrunched up as she did it, but she didn't seem to hate it as much as I did. "The quicker you drink something else, the better it's going to be for you."

She tried to teach me what the high school kids did—how they called it a "shot" and drank a "chaser" afterwards. Somehow, she got me to take two more. Both times were about as bad as the first. The "chaser" made the horrible taste not last as long, but it didn't take it away completely.

The fogginess set in after the third one, my head starting to feel lighter. The warmth spread everywhere, even to the tips of my ears that hid underneath my fraying curls. And then the giggles arrived. I found myself laughing for no reason at all. Hillary and I continued to stand there and let it wash all over us.

"What do you think I should say to get Lucas away from Big Tits Tracy?" Hillary asked, her eyes looking glassy.

"Tell him they aren't real and that she's wearing one of these," I said, cupping the fake mounds bulging off my chest.

"You let those stay put, my little Keely. We have to keep those things under wraps. Think of them as the secret weapon that we never want to use," she said as she brought my hands back down to my sides. "And I wish I could say that they are fake, but there is no way a bra can make boobs do *that*! I'm going to have to find something to lure him away from her, like a Josh Groban CD!"

"Or we could say that we have tickets to the *Pirates of Penzance*!"

"Or *Cats*! Drama people love *Cats*!" We both couldn't stop laughing, neither of us really caring if it was funny or not.

"You could ask him if you could be his Tiger Lily and then he can be your Peter Pan," I said, in between giggles.

"No way, Tiger Lily is too easy. Wendy is totally the one who plays hard to get. Tits Tracy is a Tiger Lily or maybe even a Tinker Bell."

"You two okay over here?" We were so focused on our own horrible jokes that we didn't even see Hillary's very own Peter Pan standing there in the kitchen with us. He held a water bottle, and by the way he drank it so easily, I knew it couldn't have been the awful tasting vodka. Big Boobs wasn't anywhere in sight.

"Yup. We're good," Hillary said, suddenly becoming hushed and nervous. It was the first time I had seen her become quiet around a boy. I could see why she liked him; he had a comforting voice and eyes that looked an even brighter shade of green against his tanned skin.

"Ha, okay. If you say so," he said, about to walk away. I nudged Hillary forward, causing her to bump into his back.

"Do you like *Cats*?" she blurted out as he turned towards us.

"Like the kind that old, single ladies collect?

"No. I mean, like, the musical."

"Not really. Their costumes are probably as creepy as those Furby things everyone was so obsessed with," he laughed. Instead of continuing to walk away like I thought he would, he turned to fully face Hillary, adding with a smile, "But I do like *Me and My Girl*."

I slowly backed away because even *I* was capable of knowing he was flirting with her, despite never experiencing it myself. I made my way around the kitchen island and headed towards the doorway Vander had disappeared through. It led into one of the many sitting rooms in the Atwood house. Suddenly, a pair of arms wrapped around me from behind and lifted me off the ground.

"Keely, is that really you?" Max slurred into my curls, eventually returning me to the floor and slinging his arm securely around my shoulders. His breath felt hot against my cheek. I felt myself lean into him and rest my head on his chest as I hugged him back, surprised by my own forwardness.

"Hey, Max. How are you feeling?"

"I feel *fan*-freaking-tastic," he said. He lifted his hands into the air, stumbling slightly backwards. His arm felt heavier when it dropped back onto my shoulders, sending us swaying. Right when I thought we were in danger of taking a trip to the floor, I felt his weight lift off of me, and someone took my place.

"How's our little faithful doing?" Vander asked Max with his eyes directed towards me.

"Doin' great man. Just great," Max said, his eyelids half-closed. Vander patted Max's chest with his free hand, still holding my gaze.

"You both know each other?" he asked me.

"Oh yeah, me and Keely are real close. She's all about not feeling, and I'm all about the feelings," Max said, his words blending together. I smiled, my mind feeling slightly foggy and my body light.

"That's great, buddy," he stated. "Wanna help me take him upstairs?" Vander asked me.

"Sure." I grabbed Max's other arm and wrapped it around my neck. We walked him to the second floor, Vander leading the way. He took us to a room off to the left on the opposite end of the hall from Hillary's. Its walls were white and bare, all except for the banner with a giant "U" painted in black. A king-sized bed on a simple wooden frame sat centered against the far wall. The room was spotless.

"This is your room?" I asked, my voice sounding strange.

"How'd you guess?"

"Well, maybe a lucky guess, but I think the key from your back pocket gave it away." The words didn't feel like they were mine.

"Ha, I should have been less obvious, made you work for it a little bit more." I didn't exactly understand what he meant by it. We moved Max onto the bed, and he fell asleep the moment we laid him down. Vander placed Max's head so that it faced off the side of the bed. He put a garbage bin on the floor nearby, and I helped Vander remove Max's shoes.

I made sure to place a blanket overtop him before we left, my hand lingering on his shoulder as I watched him sleep. When I removed my hand, he reached out and pulled it back in, saying, "Keel ya' looked super pretty tonight." His words continued to drift together, but it didn't take away from how they crashed inside of me.

"Thanks, Max," I said, smiling even though he couldn't see it.

"I mean it Keel ya' jus' so pretty." Mid-sentence, his hand loosened inside of mine. I placed his palm next to his face, making him look like a younger version of himself. Without knowing why, I leaned down and kissed his cheek, causing his lips to curl upwards in his sleep.

"Do you always make sure to tuck him in before he goes to bed?" Vander asked, his eyes looking inky in the dim light.

"I think this is the first time I've tucked in anyone, actually."

"It's a shame. You're good at it," he said, leaning against the doorframe with his body silhouetted by the light. My body began to buzz. I wasn't sure if it was the alcohol or Vander's smooth voice. Or, maybe it was the smell of cologne that only men wore as he walked towards me.

He stood over me as I leaned against the large bedframe for support. Ever so gently, he ran his fingers down the sides of my face, starting at the top of my forehead and stopping at my chin, trapping my breath inside my chest.

"Max is right. You are very pretty." His voice sounded like silk, and my skin warmed along the trails made by his fingers.

"Thank you," was all I managed as I stood paralyzed in place. I tried to remember all the bad things people had said about Vander Atwood. But all I could focus on was the slant of his mouth as he moved in closer.

"My sister said that I'm not allowed to talk to her friends," he said. His broad shoulders expanded against the slit of light from the doorway.

"Why?"

"She said I'm only bad news, and she doesn't want them around that."

"You don't seem like bad news to me," I said, my voice catching in my throat. My hand clenched on to the wooden poster behind me.

"Oh, trust me, I am bad news." Before I had a chance to answer, he slipped his hand through my hair and pulled me in, catching my open mouth with his. My body instantly tightened, his rough chin awakening my skin. I didn't know what to do with my arms, so I crossed them in front of my stomach to keep them from shaking. His hand drifted slowly down my back, each muscle slightly tightening beneath his sturdy grasp. His lips were warm and smooth, catching mine and silently telling me their secrets. I felt my mouth soften beneath his as his tongue briefly touched mine.

"I like your lips," he whispered coarsely. I looked up to find his other hand grabbing the post above me, his face still close to mine.

"I like yours, too," I said back. He smiled at my answer, leaning closer in and again dragging his lips across mine, that time briefly catching my lower one with his teeth. I kept my eyes closed, trying to settle the dizziness in my head.

"Lets go back down before my sister catches me and my bad news. This can be our little secret, okay?" he said, dragging me out of the fog and back into the dark room with its distant sounds of heavy bass.

"Okay," I said in a voice that felt more innocent than flirty. He wrapped his fingers around my waist and led me back down to the party. When we made it to the bottom of the stairs, I spotted Hillary standing at the edge of the room with Lucas, her eyes scanning the crowd. Vander's hand slipped from my back, and he turned to slyly wink before veering off into the mass of people. I tried to hold back the smile as I made my way towards Hillary. My small body easily slipped through the spaces between the stumbling teenagers. When I eventually reached Hillary's side, she immediately threw her arms around me.

"Where have you been? I've been looking for you everywhere. I was afraid something bad happened to you!" she said, her words slightly slurred.

"I was just helping out Max. He was pretty tired from all the alcohol."

"Ha—he is going to be way worse than tired tomorrow," Lucas said, returning his arm around Hillary when she released me. She staggered slightly when he pulled her towards him.

"Have you had any more to drink?" I asked Hillary, ignoring Lucas's comment. I could tell the answer from her flushed face.

"Like one or two."

"Try like three or four," Lucas said as he nudged her side with his hip. I noticed he was still drinking from the water bottle.

"Okay, like three. But I feel fine, I swear." She wore a lopsided smile, Lucas likely the only reason she was still standing.

"I'm going to have three then so that we're even," I said as I pulled her along with me to the kitchen, leaving Lucas behind. People had cleared out into the main living room, leaving the area mostly to us. I filled three of the small glasses and readied my cup of Coke next to it. Hillary tried to drink along with me, but I didn't let her. I didn't know much about drinking, but I knew from seeing Bumpy with Nana that it wasn't good to drink too much.

I drank them quickly, almost enjoying the burning down my throat that time. I waited for the numbness to creep back through my body.

Suddenly, Hillary started to cry, throwing her arms around me a second time. Except, that time, it kicked the breath right out of me.

"I love you, Keely Millen," she said. "And I'm so happy that you're here." Her words hit deep inside, further than alcohol could ever go. "Here" meant more than just in that physical moment. For the first time, I felt like maybe there were worse things than being left behind. Maybe surviving wasn't the worst that could have happened to me.

"I love you too, Hill. And I'm happy that it's you I'm here with." The tears wouldn't come, even with the warm liquid oozing through my body.

"Good, I'm glad that's settled," she said, wiping away her tears and trying to force her tough face on again. "I can't believe I am crying—I'm never the crier." I gave her another hug and tried not to laugh at the crushed look on her face.

"It's okay. I like criers. Dani was always a crier, and they are the best kind." Just like that, another wave of tears passed over Hillary again. I laughed, she cried, and we didn't really care who was watching.

At that moment, Nelly came on over the speakers in the other room, forcing us out of it. "Hot in Herre" was playing, and by the looks of it, people were taking the song pretty seriously.

We pushed through the topless boys and shirtless girls, making our way to the long dining room table at the far end of the room. We took our stage above the mob below us, and just let it all go. It felt like it was just the two of us there, and all the others had disappeared.

It made me feel like I was a young kid again, back at Graydon Park. They had concerts there at night, closed off to only those who had a ticket. Dani and I would sneak into the field behind the stage, the place where the music carried farthest. We never knew any of the songs or even the bands that played. But we danced until the stars came out. It didn't matter who was watching us. All that mattered was that in that space, we were completely and utterly free.

That next morning, I felt like I had forty twelve-inch nails in my skull. I woke up in Hillary's bed but had no recollection of how I got there. One minute I was standing on the table, singing along to a Nelly Furtado song, and the next, I was lying in bed, spooning a smelly trashcan next to Hillary.

I tried to sit up but instantly regretted it. Instead, I rolled onto my side, placing the rancid plastic bin on the floor next to the bed. I managed to turn my useless body back towards Hillary, sending up an empty prayer that the misery would soon be over.

The pounding in my head worsened the longer I tried to think about the previous night. I remembered Hillary and how she cried into my hair. And I remembered the kiss—my very first kiss.

A groan came from Hillary's side of the bed, which made me somewhat glad that I wasn't the only one dying a slow death.

"Hillary," I said, my voice sounding like I had aged eighty years.

"Hm," was all she managed to let out.

"I think something might be wrong with me. I feel terrible, and I can't remember anything."

"Ditto." We lay there—silent for a long while—both living in our own private balls of pain.

"Knock, knock," we heard someone say at the door. Neither of us looked up, but we heard the door creak open. The next thing I knew, Vander was standing at my side of the bed, looking down at me with his crescent dimple smiling. "Rise and shine, beauty queens," he said with a laugh.

"You have zero seconds to get out of my room," Hillary said.

"Is that really how you want to treat someone who has water and French fries?" he said as he held up his pass to remain in the room, even for a short time longer.

"What is happening? Why are you being nice right now?"

"What are you talking about? I'm always nice."

"Are you kidding me? You are never nice," she said with a snort, throwing her face back into the pillow.

"You should talk, smartass. Look who isn't being the nice one. You still haven't even introduced me to your friend," he said, looking down at me affectionately, something I hoped Hillary hadn't noticed.

"I'm pretty sure you guys met last night," she said shortly, which made both of us turn our eyes on her. "You were literally galloping around on his back last night. I sure hope you guys met. I'm pretty sure you took 'Ride Wit Me' a bit too literally," she said with a laugh. I didn't remember doing any of that, but from the look of relief on Vander's face, I took it that he did.

"I think the highlight of the night was when you knew every word of that Eminem song. Who knew that a pretty blonde girl like you would listen to rap?" Vander said.

"Oh, I—"

"Vander, stop flirting, give us the food, and then get goin'. You have like six hours to clean everything up before Mom and Dad get home," Hillary said as she reached overtop of me and grabbed the bags from him.

"You can be a real bitch sometimes, you know that?"

"Keely, I'd like you to meet my real brother, Vander. He has finally decided to show up," she said as she shoved a handful of fries into her mouth. I noticed Vander's jaw tighten. But instead of saying anything back, he simply left. He made sure to slam the door on his way out.

"I gotta say, though, that was actually pretty amazing about the Eminem song. You had the whole room cheering," she said to me, the fight with her brother instantly forgotten. "I guess I took you for a Leann Rimes or Celine Dion kind of girl."

"Yeah, Max got me into it. It's kind of our thing."

"Oh really. So what other kinds of *things* do you have?"

"I would throw this pillow at you if I didn't feel like every part of my body was going to fall off."

"Here, have some water. It'll save your life." I did as she said, but the only thing it really helped with was washing down the terrible taste in my mouth.

"Hillary, I can't remember doing those things last night."

"I think it's okay. That happens sometimes. Fry?"

"Thanks. But did you forget stuff, too?"

"Not that I know of, which is good because guess who didn't forget kissing Lucas Trellis? That's right—this girl!" she shrieked, throwing her arms up in victory.

"I swear I'm happy for you even though I don't look like I am," I said with a weak smile, covering my eyes with my hand and still trying my best not to move.

"It was amazing. He wasn't a wet kisser at all, and he did this amazing thing where he licked the inside of my ear. I thought I was going to pass out."

"The inside of your ear? That's so weird."

"It sounds weird, but I promise it's not. Once you start kissing boys, you will know what I'm talking about. Did you and Maxy have a little smoochy smooch?" she asked in a girly voice. I felt my face instantly turn red before I could turn my head away from her. "Oh my God, you did! Tell me everything! What did it feel like? Was he an open-mouth kisser? I bet he's an open mouth kisser."

"No, no, nothing happened."

"Something happened. Your face is as red as a freaking stop sign!"

"I guess talking about kissing just makes me a little embarrassed," I said, trying to pass it off as nothing.

"Well, we need to get you to snap out of that real fast!" she said as she stared dreamily up at the canopy above us, most likely thinking about Lucas and his dry kisses.

"Hey, Hill, do you know if Lucas was drinking last night?"

"No, he said he didn't want to hurt his vocal chords, because he has a big audition coming up."

"Don't you find that a little strange—that he wanted you to drink so much when he wasn't having any?"

"I don't really care what he does with his life, just as long as he does that ear thing to me again," she said, still smiling happily to herself. It was like she had transformed back into the Hillary who played with dolls and cared too much about what other people thought.

We sat there in silence for a long time afterwards, both thinking about the night before and what our kisses meant. I didn't know what to think of my kiss with Vander, wondering if he really was as bad as Hillary let on. The one thing I did know was that alcohol made me bolder, braver.

"How long do you think my parents are going to ground me? Ten years? Fourteen? Until I'm old and riding around in one of those Hoverounds?"

"Do you think they will even find out?"

"It would honestly take like four hundred fairy godmothers to get the smell out of our living room carpet. We are definitely going to get busted."

Except that she was wrong. When we finally pulled ourselves out of bed and went downstairs, there wasn't any sign that three hundred people had ever been there. The couch held a patterned pillow instead of a girl covered in vomit; all the bottles had vanished from the kitchen counters; each vase and picture was back in its rightful place; and the living room carpet smelled like something fresh out of the laundry.

"Like magic, huh?" Vander said as he sauntered through the front door, laughing at our dropped jaws.

"I have to say, you don't do too many things that impress me, but...I'm impressed," Hillary said.

"I want to hear you say it again."

"Not going to happen," she added shortly. "So, how did you pull this one off?"

"I told you. Magic."

"I know that Harry Potter is cool and all, but even I know that stuff is fake."

"I just called in my reinforcements. What can I say—they listen to me," he said, looking quite smug. Hillary just nodded like she understood and didn't bring it up again.

For the rest of the afternoon, we stayed in Hillary's bed, doing nothing at all. I made sure to take a shower before my parents came to get me, scrubbing off the smell of stale alcohol that lingered on my skin. I didn't see Vander for the rest of the day. But as I walked to my dad's car later that night, I couldn't shake the feeling that I was being watched. All of the windows were dark in the upstairs except for Hillary's, but hers stood empty. I could sense him out there, looking down on me. It gave me that same chill up my spine as when his dark eyes fell on me for the first time. I had yet to figure out if it came from excitement or from fear.

It would have been an understatement to say that people started noticing me after that weekend. It had somehow spread through the entire eighth grade that I not only did a keg stand, but I was also the Viper's newest girlfriend. I didn't even know what a keg stand was. At least half of the rumors that went around didn't seem true, but even I wasn't able to know for sure. Either way, I had gone from the eighth grade zero to the eighth grade hero in less than twenty-four hours.

And Max seemed to be the only one who wasn't happy about it.

I didn't see him until lunchtime that following Monday, but I knew something was off the second I sat down at our table. For the first time, his friends were directing questions at me, asking if "this" was true or if "that" really happened. I tried to quickly answer them, wishing more and more that it was just Max and me. Max concentrated on eating his food in silence, not looking up at me once.

When the next bell finally rang, signaling that lunch period was over, Max rushed out before everyone else. I ran after him, failing to catch up until halfway down the hall.

"Max, hey, is everything okay?" I said in a hurried breath. He refused to look at me and shrugged my hand off his shoulder.

"Yeah, fine."

"No, you are definitely not fine. Come on, why are you mad? Was it something I did?" He turned to me, his eyes seeming more golden than blue that day. His mouth opened as if he was about to answer. Instead, he turned and continued on down the hall. That time, I didn't run after him.

By the time I made it to our next class, he sat with his head resting on his desk. I made sure to knock my desk into his when I sat down. If he was planning on ignoring me all day, I was at least going to remind him that I was still there.

For the rest of the school day, he sat with his head facing forward. He didn't bother turning around, even when he passed the papers back. I walked alone to our next class, and for the first time in a year, he didn't go to my locker when the final bell rang. It didn't matter that I had people high fiving me in the hallway or acknowledging me for the first time in my life. All that I cared about was that Max wasn't speaking to me, and I didn't know why.

I didn't stay after school that day, even though the "it kids" had asked me to hang out. Instead, my dad drove me home, just like any ordinary day. He talked to me about the new jobs he was looking at—about how he was thinking of going back to work again. Ever since the terrorist attacks, he had been staying home, working on a book that I wasn't sure he was even writing. My mother didn't say anything about it, though—she just let him try to do whatever he could to make himself feel okay again.

I said I was happy for him, and I meant it. I didn't say anything about my newfound fame, though. I talked about the Boston Tea Party and how people dumped boxes and boxes of tea into the harbor. Dad said it sounded a lot like my bologna strike five years before, where I tried secretly flushing my unfinished sandwiches down the toilet. I told him that mine was worse because at least the Boston Tea Party didn't clog up the pipes. He laughed at that, and I was thankful he took my mind off of Max for at least a little while.

I went straight to my bed when I got home, pulling the covers over my head to block out the afternoon sunlight. I drifted off without falling completely asleep—caught somewhere in-between. It wasn't until a couple hours later that I heard a knock at my door.

"Hey, Keely," my dad said, poking his head around the door. My head felt groggy, and I squinted through a dark room. "Someone's at the door for you." I looked over at my clock and saw that it was past ten, meaning that I had slept straight through dinner. I pulled on a sweater and some sweatpants before I sleepily made my way to the front door.

I was surprised to see Max standing on the other side. My parents hovered awkwardly near the front entryway, so I stepped out onto our porch, despite the cold October air, and shut the door behind me. It had barely clicked closed when he started talking.

"It was nothing you did. And it isn't because you got drunk and did all of those crazy things. I don't care about that. I'm actually happy that happened—not that you got really drunk but because now people actually *see* you. What it is I do care about…it's just that, you know, there are just some things that I wanted to talk to you about." He had started to pace, and his hair stuck to his forehead, which was damp despite the freezing air.

"Max, you aren't making a lot of sense."

"I don't think you should kiss Vander again," he blurted out, as if pushing a physical barrier between us. At first, I didn't know what to say to him. I was unsure about how much he knew.

"But—"

"I didn't know if I just dreamed it or saw it happen, but then when everyone started calling you his girlfriend, I just…I knew that I didn't imagine it." Max and I never talked about serious things. Ninety percent of the time we talked about silly stuff, like how he had a weird obsession with old keys and how I once got my arm stuck in a pool table pocket. The other ten percent we just enjoyed each other's company, not really saying much of anything.

"Well, I am definitely not his girlfriend. I don't even know the first thing about being a girlfriend."

"Do you want to be his girlfriend?"

"I don't know, probably not. Where is this even coming from? I thought you and Vander are friends. You *are* his faithful or whatever it is he called you."

"It's not what you think. I'm just doing what I have to."

"What are you talking about?" He looked flustered, like he had admitted more than he wanted to.

"Listen, my parents aren't rich. My mom's a social worker, and my dad works as a janitor. They don't have a lot of money, and I know that things like college are gonna cost a lot of money when I have to go." It was typical Max, already planning for things that no other eighth grader would have even considered.

"Okay, so what does that have to do with anything?"

"They say that you get tapped before you become a freshman. If you make it in, everything is pretty much taken care of for you."

"Max, I'm really trying here, but I don't have a clue what you're talking about."

"The Underground," he said, as if that was supposed to explain everything.

"Okay, so it's a secret group."

"It's more than a group. It's like a…program."

"A program for what?"

"I don't know. All I know is that if you make it out as a senior, you can pretty much go to any college you want, and it's all taken care of."

"So, I'm guessing you got tapped."

"Yeah," he said, looking almost embarrassed about it.

"If it's so secret, then why did Vander make such a big deal about it at the party? If it's a secret, aren't people not supposed to know about it?" I said, not meaning for it to sound so snobby.

"People kind of know who's in it, but they don't know what goes on. Like, I heard about the Underground from my cousin, and he was never tapped."

"Why do you think they tapped you?"

"Honestly," he said with shining eyes, "I don't really know. What I do know is that it wasn't something I could easily turn down."

"I'm not going to get in the way if that's what you're worried about."

"No, that's not it," he said, biting at the corner of his mouth. "I didn't mean to tell you all this stuff and make you feel weird about it. I just wanted to tell you that Vander isn't good enough for you. I don't trust him. That's all."

"And you're telling me this because…"

"Because I'm your friend. And friends watch out for each other."

"Okay."

"Okay?"

"Yeah, okay. I will stay away from him." The relief spread across Max's face, reminding me why I liked doing things for him time and time again. He being happy made me happy, and there was a part of me that liked him more than I was willing to admit.

"You're the best, Keely," he said when he wrapped me in a hug. "I have to go because my mom is waiting for me, and I told her I would only be a couple minutes. I'll see ya tomorrow at school!" He jumped down my porch steps two at a time, his normal pep reinstated.

He had almost reached the car that sat at the end of my driveway when he turned back towards me. He said, with the spotlight from my barn illuminating his smile, "And Keely, thanks for the goodnight kiss the other night. You should tuck me in again sometime." And then he was gone.

At first glance, towns like Ridgewood appeared perfectly ordinary. There was a boutique movie theatre downtown that played old films; there was a monument of people no one knew in the middle of Town Square; and there were an unnecessary number of stop signs and speed bumps on every street within a mile of a school.

But just as with most things, not everything was exactly as it seemed. Like an oil painting, there were many strokes underneath that went into creating the illusion.

I guessed I just wasn't looking close enough.

Eighth grade was when I began seeing the deeper layers, but it was also the year that I saw what I wanted to. The girl I looked at in the mirror began wearing makeup and spoke a little differently—saying things like "that's dope" and abbreviating things that probably didn't need to be. My ball of clay had started to take shape, and I tried to convince myself that I was the one doing the sculpting. But that wasn't true.

I allowed others to poke and prod me, molding me into whatever shape they wanted. The more parties I went to meant the more I had to lie to my parents. Each time, I had to drink more to get back that same good feeling. The more friends I made, the fewer friendships I felt like I had.

It changed me into the exact person they wanted.

It happened on a Thursday, exactly four days before my first day of high school. I was lying in the hammock in front of my house, listening to a CD. I didn't hear the car pull in or even notice the two girls who got out. It was one of those luxury cars, the type that only rich daddies could get for their daughters.

I didn't realize they were standing over me until I felt the heat of the sun disappear in their shadows.

"Keely Millen?" one of them said, her face silhouetted by the sun.

"Yeah?"

"You have until the date written inside to decide. We only ask once, and this is to be burned when you have made your decision." The other one handed me a thick, rolled-up paper, sealed with red wax.

They then turned and walked back to their car, leaving me staring at a long matchstick embedded in the wax. I recognized one of them from some of the summer parties—she was an upperclassman and probably one of the most popular girls in the high school.

I didn't open it right away. I already knew what was inside—an invitation to the Underground. The girls had a different group than Max's, but it was all a part of the same secret society. People said the girls' one was harder to get invited into, but it was also the hardest to get out of.

Scrawled in neat, hand-written calligraphy, it said I had until Homecoming night to decide. If I accepted, I was to go to the old ice skating rink behind the elementary school that midnight in September. Near the bottom, almost out of sight, there were two words written in red: **Burn Me.**

I didn't tell anyone about my visit that day, not even Max. Hillary noticed something was different about me—distant, she said—but then again, she had been saying that for months. I could tell that she didn't understand how much I needed it—to be a part of something. She wanted it to be just her and me against the world. But the problem was, I had already done that. I tried the whole two makes three against it all. And in the end, it only left me as a lonely "one." A part of me wanted to do something so un-Keely. It brewed inside, making me want to be someone who didn't care so damn much.

And yet, there I was, on the day of Dani's third anniversary, kneeling before her stone in our backyard. At first, I didn't know what had brought me out there. All I knew was that she was the one person I needed to talk to.

I held the invitation in my hand, as if trying to pass it over to her. I felt the weight of her there with me, as if she was waiting for me to explain why I was kneeling there, trying to find my words. My eyes roved over the flowers surrounding her stone, all as beautiful as the day I had put them there—just like Debbie promised they would be.

I started talking to her then, telling her things that I would say if she was still there. I talked about Hillary and that she was like her—always caring for other people. But I didn't know if I wanted to be taken care of anymore. I told her about the teeter-totter and the ball of clay—about how I was trying my best to be a person she would be proud of. And I talked about how it sometimes felt too hard.

Max came up a few times, making his way into my mind as I told my dead sister about my new life. He helped me forget about the bad things, I told her, and made me feel special. I talked about how it probably wasn't good that I preferred to forget things more than remember them. But it made life easier that way.

I talked about Vander and how she would be proud that I kept my promise about staying away from him. I shared how it was turning out to be harder than I had thought. He had somehow snuck his way into my life. There would be times he would show up where I went, like the grocery store one town over. Sometimes, it seemed a bit too convenient to be just by coincidence. I told her not to worry about it, though, because everything was under control. He never did anything, especially when Hillary went to the parties with me.

I saved the Underground for the end, mainly because it was the one thing I was afraid to talk about. Even without her being there to say it, I had a feeling that she would have never let me do it. She would have protected me from it, and I would have listened to her. And that was when I realized—I hadn't gone there for her permission. I had gone there to tell her, for the first time in my life, I was going to do something she would have been against.

I took the match out of my pocket, striking it against Dani's rock. The metallic smell filled my nose. I touched the match to the paper, its corner catching the light almost instantly. The fire burned all the edges first, leaving me staring at the writing that eventually shriveled in on itself. When it became too hot for me to hold any longer, I placed it on the top of her rock, watching it blacken into nothing.

I failed to notice the single spark that landed on one of Dani's perfect flowers. Its petal melted into a shriveled ball, sending the stem drooping forward—the ground forever stealing it away from the sun.

Chapter Eight
September 12, 2003

We were like bananas. Stuck together, we were ripe and yellow. But the moment one was torn apart, all the rest turned black and rotten.

That was how I felt, thinking about the months leading up to Brook's sixteenth birthday. He stole her away, little by little, taking pieces of the rest of us with her. And in the end, we expected that Brook and Kai's story would soon be over.

Brook's cage filled up all around her—a new dresser, tall bed frame, and thick throw rug appeared in the once empty cell. He had created a kingdom for her, as he had for Clara before her. Kai's cell remained bare and untouched, only a stained mattress proving his presence.

She didn't like to admit it, but I knew that it was constantly on her mind. Brook mostly talked about her dad—old trips to see the sand castle competition at the New York State Fair and him spinning her around on the Coney Island boardwalk. Living in the past was her way of escaping the present, and I wondered if I would be that way as well. I hoped that I too would be able to remember the good times as I waited for my turn to come.

I felt selfish for wanting to keep her with me in the present, far away from her thoughts of how life used to be. Things were starting to change for me, and I knew that my real acting would soon begin. I needed to learn what to do, even though I knew it would force her to return to the place where good memories couldn't exist.

"Soon, he's going to bring you into a new place, the dressing room. He only takes the girls in there," she said when it was just the two of us alone in the cells.

"And what will happen when I go there?" I asked shakily.

"You have to play dress up."

"What if I've never really played before?"

"You will have to teach yourself. Don't worry, at least he doesn't stay in the room with you as you get ready."

"Do you wear costumes?"

"No, it's not that kind of dress up. But there are a whole lot of different clothes in there, and they aren't like any of these," she said, pinching her white uniform. "Most are dresses but some are pants and sweaters. I usually try to wear the jeans. Sometimes he forces me to wear a dress, but that doesn't happen too often. The clothes are all super girly, just so you know. Like, there's a lot of pink and too many frills," she said, looking as if she had a bad taste in her mouth.

"And when do I have to do this?"

"From now on, every time he takes you out. You will have to put your white clothes on again when you come back to your cell. But you're going to play dress up whenever you go out there," she said, pointing to the metal door at the far end of the room.

"Okay, I guess that isn't too bad."

"Well, that's not all," she said, her voice fading out at the end.

"What do you mean?"

"There's more to it. Like, makeup…and a wig."

"Why do you think he makes us do it?"

"That I don't know. My only guess is he wants us to look like some sort of princess."

"It doesn't make any sense, Brook," I said, starting to feel panicky.

"I know. I felt the same way. I *do* feel the same way."

"I don't want to do it. I won't do it."

"Trust me, it will be better for you if you do. I know it's weird and makes you feel like you're just giving in to what he wants," she said, stopping mid-sentence. She looked down at her gloved hand that sat in her lap, brushing it softly with her other hand. There were tears in her eyes when she looked at me again. "I never planned on showing you. Before, it wasn't important for you to see it. But I don't want it to happen to you."

I had noticed the gloved hand countless times before. But I knew, just by the way she held it close and covered it with her bare one, not to ask about it. I held my breath as she slid off the white, satin fabric. Three of the fingers appeared to stay with the glove as she removed it. Underneath, her thumb and pointer were normal, but small stumps took the place of the remaining fingers. Each disfigured end appeared a different length—all looked thin and shriveled. They were red at the tips, as if they still caused her pain.

"I thought if I showed him that he couldn't control me, it would make it better for me. When he took me into the dressing room for the first time, I just sort of snapped. I put on the makeup like he asked, but I made myself into a clown instead of the pretty girl from the picture he gave me. The worst part was the wig, though. I ripped all of the hair out except for a tiny clump. When he came back and found me…" she said, her voice trailing off.

"He cut off your fingers?" I asking, choking on the words.

"He was so angry, Dani. Angrier than anybody I have ever seen. At first I thought he was just going to get mad and throw a couple things, but he just turned crazy. He hit me in the face a couple times and then used my own blood to wash the makeup off my face." She paused, as if she went away for a little while, falling back into those awful memories. "I'll never forget how he took the knife out of his pocket, popping up the sharp blade."

I couldn't find my voice to ask her the questions that ran through my mind. *Did it hurt? Does it ever stop hurting? How did you ever get it to stop bleeding? Were you afraid he was going to keep going?*

"I thought he wasn't going to stop," she said, as if I had silently asked the question. "There was a part of me that thought it would be the end, but something stopped him. After he cut into them, he dropped the knife, almost like he couldn't believe he was the one who did it. And you know what I did? I just sat there. The knife was right at my feet, and all I could do was sit there looking at the spaces where my fingers should have been."

"Brook, you had just gone through something terrible. That's how anyone would have acted."

"I think about it sometimes, though—that maybe I wouldn't still be trapped in this basement if I had picked up that knife. Maybe, none of us would be." I wanted to tell her she was wrong—that it wouldn't have changed anything. But I wondered if she was right.

"Did he feel bad for doing it?" I said instead.

"No," she replied with a firm voice. "He blamed me for making him do it. I think he was just annoyed he had to go on making a pretty princess out of a girl with a hand like this."

"What did you do after it happened?"

"I don't remember much else about that time. I couldn't look at it. There was so much blood, and a part of me hoped it wouldn't stop."

"Don't say that," I said, reaching through the bars and taking her ruined hand in my small one. She stiffened for a moment, but I didn't let it go.

"I had to wear bandages on it for a while. Once it started to heal up, though, he said he never wanted to see it again. That's why he makes me wear the stuffed glove."

"You don't have to wear it around me. I don't mind."

"Thanks, Dani. That's nice of you to say. But I don't like to see it, either. I can't help but think of my mother when I see it. She used to say I had such beautiful hands, just like my grandmother had said about hers.

We were a family of beautiful hands, and now…" she said, crying as she looked at her jagged hand inside mine. I moved my fingers so they covered the three stumps, showing only the perfect two left behind.

"I think your mother would still think they are beautiful." She looked down at her hand in mine. For a moment, I thought she believed me. But then she slowly pulled away and delicately slipped her hand back into the stiff, spotless glove with its fake fingers.

"You know what? Maybe you will be the one to figure it out. I was hoping it could be me, but I think it was you all along."

"Don't say that, Brook. We can find out together," I pleaded. But she looked like she had already made up her mind.

"I will never forget that first time he made me go back to the dressing room. A new blonde wig, identical to the one I had ripped up, was sitting there waiting for me. That was the moment I started to let go. I started giving up. No matter what you do, it's never going to stop."

"Do you think we shouldn't play pretend anymore?"

"No, because it's the one thing that we can control. The hard part is that you can't start believing the lie too. Like, for me, I feel as if I lose a little bit of myself every time I put on that wig. That is the only time I am a tiny bit grateful for my ruined hand. My fingers burn—reminding me I am Brook and not his made-up princess. You have to make sure that you don't lose the little bits of Dani, too."

"I won't. I swear I won't."

"I believe you, and I hope you find a way to stop him."

"But why can't we stop him together? Why can't I help you in the same way you have helped me."

"The sun doesn't light up the world expecting it to owe her," she said with a small smile.

"What?"

"It was a saying of my dad's. It means that people shouldn't do things just because they are expecting something back."

"But I'm not doing it because I owe you. I'm doing it because I want to."

"Wanting is just a poor man's version of owing."

"Is that one of your dad's sayings too?" I joked halfheartedly.

"No, but I guess it's mine now," she said with a small smile.

"Well, you can keep your sayings, and I'm going to keep my poor man wanting to owe you, or however the heck it went."

"Okay," she said, wearing a shade of relief.

It was Brook's turn to lose hope, and I intended to get it back for her.

The dressing room reminded me of Nana's attic. Narrow racks of clothes lined the small room, hanging in clear, plastic bags atop metal, rolling stands. The room was dim, graying the white walls and carpet closest to me. It smelled slightly of must and mothballs. The clothes appeared like bright Post-it notes, mostly in shades of pink, scattered throughout the perfect rows. Large, black numbers on white tags sprang from the long clothing rods, their garment bags growing in size as they counted upwards along each line. Down the center of the room, there was a long, red carpet that split the largest row, leading towards a bright light.

At the other end of the scarlet path sat a wide vanity. It was pretty— the solid wood painted a clean white with flower carvings that extended into its thick legs. There was something childish about it, like the kind I imagined little beauty queens using to change themselves into life-sized Barbies. In the middle of the table was a closed, black box, lit up by circular spotlights that hung above the large wall mirror.

It wasn't until I approached that I noticed the wigs. There were shelves of them, neighboring the wide vanity. They were long, flowing waves of thick, blonde curls sitting atop faceless white heads. One stood empty, its bald top shining under the light.

Slipped into the mirror's metal frame, there was a photograph of a beautiful, blonde girl whose hair matched the wigs. She leaned against a tree, smiling back at me with her long hair spilling down her shoulders. A dress hung over the tall, rose-patterned armchair that rested in front of the vanity. A note clung to the hanger—thick, black lines cut through the white page. "You have 30 minutes. Wear this," it read. An identical note appeared on top of the black container.

I took a seat at the vanity, releasing the box's silver clasp. Its top popped open, revealing the perfect rows of colored powders and capped cylinders, black pencils and tiny tubes. It reminded me of the watercolor paints I used as a kid, but these powders were all in shades of white and pink. Even a paintbrush sat beside them. I glanced up at the picture taped to the mirror, looking again at the girl. She looked like a teenager, reminding me of the girls in the *Seventeen* magazines that Hannah used to steal out of her big sister's bedroom. But there was also something innocent about her, something childlike. Maybe it was her light blue eyes or the tiny dimple that sat beside her warm smile. Or possibly it was the bright pink dress with its puffy lace sleeves. She was the princess I had to pretend to be.

The person looking back at me through the mirror appeared strange and alien. Only my aquamarine eyes appeared familiar. My blonde hair had darkened, appearing a dirty, mousy brown. I could no longer see the tiny freckles that had once sprinkled my nose, and my skin appeared pale. It made me feel better knowing that my plain appearance took me further away from the pretty girl. But I also looked older, less like the young girl from my memory and more like the photograph beside me.

After I had quickly slipped on the puffy dress, I tried my best to make my face look like the girl's from the picture. However, I came out looking more like a Halloween version of her. I looked for the closest shade of pink powder to match my eyelids to hers, but the one I used was a bit too red. Using the black pencil, I colored in my eyelashes but couldn't quite get them as thick and dark as the girl's. I couldn't tell if the colored stick or powder had been used for her rosy cheeks, so I tried a little of each on mine. I used the same method when I moved on to my lips, but I had a hard time staying inside the lines.

He came through the door the exact moment my thirty minutes was up. I immediately froze, staring back at him as he appeared through the door in the mirror. He slowly walked towards me, down the blood-colored carpet. I feared he would think I painted my face all wrong on purpose, like Brook had. My nails dug into the edge of the white table.

"Let's take a look at you, my lovely Pandora," he said in a singsong voice. I rose and turned towards him slowly, hoping at least my matching cheeks would be enough to satisfy him. He looked at me suspiciously, and I felt myself cower when he moved closer. "Well, I am sure you will do better next time." I held my breath as he paused, closing my eyes as I waited for him to finish. "But this time, it will do." When he continued past me, I released the air stuck inside my throat in a slow, silent stream.

He moved towards the shelf of wigs, stopping as his hand slowly rubbed his chin. He pulled one from a blank head, ever so gently fluffing the curls with one hand while resting it on his fist in the other.

"This one will match perfectly," he stated, as if he had selected it from a wide range of choices. When he reached me, his icy hands touched the back of my neck as he stuffed my dead hair into the cap of the wig. The elastic band fell tightly around my skull. His hands petted through the curls, combing them slowly and gently through his large hands. I couldn't help but flinch each time the chill of his fingers grazed past my skin.

"There, there. I'd say it's fitting on you," he said in a voice I hadn't heard before. It sounded higher, like he was speaking through his nose. Something changed in his stare, as if he was noticing me for the first time.

He took me to meet Mika in the greenhouse. As usual, there was a textbook on my desk with the regular "homework assignments" alongside it. I had become used to the routine of being "dropped off" and getting through the "school day" as quickly as I could. However, that time, he followed me into the room and commanded that Mika join us.

Mika wore different clothes, too, but his weren't as fancy as mine. His were simple blue jeans and a plain T-shirt, making him look like just an ordinary kid. He studied me carefully, trying to identify who lived underneath all the hair and makeup. It made me feel embarrassed, as if I had chosen to look that way.

"Prometheus, aren't you going to tell her how pretty she looks?" he scolded.

"You look pretty," Mika said, his eyes not meeting mine.

"And aren't you going to comment on how nice her dress looks?"

"Your dress looks nice," he mumbled.

"Thanks," I said, unsure how I was expected to act. Dias ran his hand once more through my fake hair before he turned to leave. Mika and I stood rooted in our spots, knowing we had only moments before he was back behind his shielded glass.

"Is that really you under all that?"

"He made me put it on. I didn't have a choice," I said defensively.

"Are you going to have to wear that from now on?"

"I think so. But I won't have to wear a dress every time."

"Will you still have to wear the wig and all that…stuff on your face?"

"I guess," I said, self-consciously readjusting the wig on my head. I lowered my voice so that only Mika could hear. "There was a picture of a girl. She had blonde hair, just like this, and he wanted me to do my makeup like she had."

"Who do you think she is?"

"I don't know, but I get the feeling that she means something to him. He treated me differently when I put all this on."

"What do you think that means about me? Do you think he's trying to turn me into someone, too?"

"Maybe," I said, thinking of Kai and Chet's grown out hair. I looked more closely at the clothes he had on, but none of it looked suspicious or out of place. There weren't any designs on his T-shirt. He had on an ordinary pair of jeans.

"Do you think I'm supposed to be a specific person, like you? There wasn't any picture for me to look at. He just gave me the clothes in the bathroom and told me to put them on."

"I'm not sure. But I'm guessing that we're probably going to find out."

From then on, that was how it was. We wore our costumes each time we left our cells, even when we did our sessions alone with him in the attitude room. My costumes stayed the same. Each time, I chose from the long lines of clothes, creating the same mask underneath the golden crown. But Mika's started changing. He began wearing shirts with unfamiliar names on the front. They looked worn down, their colors faded. There were holes in the sleeves and rips up the back, as if Dias had collected them all from a second-hand store.

Even though we played dress up outside our cages, we always returned to our cells in white jumpsuits. He made sure I wiped away all of the makeup, which, over time, made my skin red and raw. I returned my fancy clothes to their hangers, and Mika left his rags in a heap on the bathroom floor. Dias put us away, like dollies returned to their boxes. We were just another set of toys in his messed-up playhouse.

Other than the different clothes and caked-on makeup, not much else changed. Mika and I continued to do our "lessons" on useless topics. We learned about a shooting at McDonald's, popularity of the Rubik's cube, a fiber opitc cable that crossed the ocean, the murder of some guy named John Lennon, a volcano eruption in Columbia, the fall of some wall in Germany, a Super Bowl win by San Francisco, and the creation of a computer named after a type of apple. The lady in white continued to repeat her lessons over the large wall screen. We continued to go to the playroom, thankfully just the two of us. I didn't take off my wig, even when we were in there. I didn't want to chance him catching me. Eventually, Mika and I got used to the costumes. We still knew that, underneath all of it, we were just Dani and Mika.

But Brook and Kai seemed to have lost each other somewhere in the pretending. We barely saw Kai anymore, and I didn't have the heart to keep asking Brook about him. More and more things were getting to her. She started changing, too, but not in the way that Kai had. Whatever was happening to Kai was Dias's doing. It felt planned and purposeful. Brook's cracking, on the other hand, wasn't because those things were happening to her. It was because they weren't, and that terrified her.

It was frightening, watching Brook slowly leave us in pieces. I wanted to believe that we could handle anything. I was my own person, and in the end, he couldn't affect me. But that was a lie. We were all connected, us to each other, as well as to him.

In the end, Brook had given up. She no longer talked about getting out or tricking him at his own game. I tried to make her not lose hope. Mika kept reminding her about his baseball trick. But none of it worked. She had already left us.

So, when the day came that I could do something about it, all I thought about was bringing Brook back to me—the girl who held my hand in the dark and promised me we would find a way out. I had been waiting for my opportunity, not knowing when it would come.

Whenever he took me anywhere, I made sure to watch him, to see what he did and how he did it. I saw how he used a single white keycard, the one he kept in his back pocket. He would swipe in and out of each room, turning the button to green before the handle would click and release. There were four metal doors left that we hadn't seen behind. I found myself studying one door more than the others. It was the one in the middle of the hallway, next to the bathroom. It looked older than the others, its metal stained and tarnished. I knew, behind that door hid our freedom.

When that day came, it was late afternoon. I knew because the lights had already begun to fade. I was lying on my mattress, my hair still wet from my shower. Mika was scraping something into a rock embedded in the wall, and Brook sat in the dirt, her back leaning against the bars that split our cells. Once again, Kai was missing.

Dias came in right on time to take Brook for her shower. But when he opened her cell door and called her, she wouldn't budge. She just continued sitting there, running her finger through the dirt and whispering faint words under her breath.

"Athena. I said let's go." He looked annoyed, especially when his commands only made her finger draw more frantically along the ground. I stood up from my mattress, nervous what would happen next.

He walked over to her, his keys still dangling from the lock in her open cell door. His hands remained clenched at his sides as he neared her spot in the dirt. He stood over her, looking at the drawings that she didn't try to hide.

"What have we got here?" he said curiously, clipping his metal rod back into its spot at his side. He had his back to me as he peered at the meaningless lines on the floor. As he leaned over, I noticed the white peaking out of his back pocket.

I moved slowly so he wouldn't hear me come up behind him, my toes curling inside my shoes as I walked. My hands gripped the sides of my pants as I stared at the long, motionless stick attached to his belt. There was a slider next to the black handle, numbered one through five. A collection of lightning bolts bordered the five.

And then I reacted. Leaping forward, I grabbed ahold of the handle and rapidly flipped the slider from one to five. The rod came to life in my hand, buzzing like a firecracker as I drove its tip deep into his right leg. I didn't release the black button, even after he dropped to his knees. My other hand grabbed the exposed keycard.

"Brook! Get up, Brook! You gotta run!" She continued to sit there, drawing the little lines around Dias's screaming heap next to her. I kept yelling her name over and over as I returned my other hand to the rod, trying to keep it steady against his writhing body.

It wasn't until she looked up at me that she returned. Brook scooted backwards away from the bad man. "The keys, Brook, the door!" I shouted, her gaze switching to the open escape. Dias had settled to an occasional twitch under the continuous electricity. She bolted to her cell door, pulling the ring of keys from it.

Her hands shook as she shuffled through the various metal flags, looking for the one to my cell. "It's the purple one! Look for the one with the purple tape!" I yelled frantically as I looked from Brook to Dias.

"I'm trying, I'm trying!" she yelled back, the keys fumbling in her hands. "I got it! I got it!" she said as she drove the key into the slot, turning it with a heavy click. My large door groaned open, and I released Dias's rod and ran towards my escape. When I burst through the opening, I saw Mika. His mouth moved, but the words couldn't register. He extended his arms out through the bars, tears covering his cheeks.

"Grab the keys!" I yelled to Brook as I ran towards him. When my outstretched hands reached his, I felt Brook pull me back, yanking me towards the main door.

"No! No, I can't leave him!" I yelled, but she just kept dragging me farther away.

"Dani, we have to go! Slide the card! Slide the card, Dani! He's coming!" I looked back at Brook's cell and saw Dias sliding his limp body through the door opening.

It was our one and only shot.

I jammed the keycard into the slot over and over, the light repeatedly showing red. I felt him behind us, drawing closer. Brook ripped the card from my hand and slid it slowly downwards, the handle magically clicking beneath the green light.

The bright hallway echoed as we slammed the heavy door behind us.

"I think he's keeping Kai over here!" Brook yelled, immediately running to a mystery door directly to our right. She kept inserting the card into the reader, at first slowly and then more rapidly as it kept showing red.

"Why isn't it working?" I asked in a terrified voice.

"I don't know! It's not turning green!" We started banging on the door, screaming Kai's name. But we were only met with the hallway's dead stillness.

"We have to get out of here, Brook. We don't have a choice," I cried, repeating her words. "When we get out, we'll bring back help. We have the keys and the keycard. He won't get them. They'll be safe." She had tears streaming down her face as she continued to stare at the empty cardholder. She nodded slightly, causing two tears to roll off her chin and onto the tiled floor.

"We have to do it for them. If we don't get out, then they never will, either," she said. I didn't know if it was more to convince her or me.

"For them," I repeated back. We moved quickly to the older-looking door. It towered over us as we stood there. We held the keycard in the ready. The stillness was all around us, bringing me back to that awful day in the forest, trapped inside the deafening quiet. The swipe of the keycard scraped within our ears.

Red.

Red. Red. Red.

"No. No. No, no, no, no," Brook repeated over and over. I felt my fingers flutter against my leg, trying to keep up with my racing mind. She slid the card slowly and then faster and faster.

I took the card out of Brook's hand and went to each of the doors. The bathroom. The attitude room. The playroom. The greenhouse. The activity room. The dressing room. They were the only ones that turned a precious green. The other four flashed red.

"It only goes to the rooms he takes us to, Brook! It's completely useless!" I yelled, the panic growing inside my chest. It was just another one of his tricks. Even right up to the end, he had us fooled.

The red door hovered at the end of the hallway. Our eyes drifted to it, as if pulling us towards it. Our footsteps were slow and resonant as we neared it in the unsettling calm.

We went to the keypad on the heavy door. The black numbers were listed one through nine in rows of three, the zero sitting at the bottom. It was an old lock, matching the ancient wooden door with its peeling, red paint. Four of the numbers appeared faded: 1, 7, 8, and 0.

I hit the four numbers, trying one sequence after another. The numbers teased my mind, as if the answer hung right in front of me. I racked my brain, praying the combination would come to me. But the door continued to hold its secrets.

The terrible wail pulled us away from the black numbers. It shot down the hallway—sounding over and over—coming from one of the metal doors. "It's Kai!" Brook shouted, the terrifying noise growing louder as we rushed towards it.

We made our way down the line, the words within his cries growing clearer. "Stop! Please stop! Someone! Help!" the voice called. We placed our heads up to each of the silvery doors. Their metal surface felt cool against my ears, but all I heard from the inside was quiet. It wasn't until a single door remained that we knew. The screams were coming from the room that held our cells.

"It's Mika," I cried out, the tears instantly burning my eyes. "Brook, where are the keys?" I asked, frantically scanning her hands.

"I don't have them! I thought you took them!" she yelled, rubbing her white glove anxiously with her bare hand. Then, it hit us both that the ring of keys had been left hanging from my cell door. Mika was supposed to be safe, but his sobs told us we were wrong. Our eyes shifted to that final door. "Do we wait for him to come out?" she asked weakly.

"No. We have to help him! We have to make it stop!" We listened to the horrific soundtrack around us, replaying over and over. The screams started to sound more desperate, and I knew we didn't have much time left. My fingers began to quiver against my leg as I looked at the doors around me. My racing thoughts slowly came together. "Follow me." I told Brook as I headed back down the hall.

I took the blank keycard from her outstretched hand, leading the way to the greenhouse. The lights buzzed and flickered to life when we walked into the room, my eyes searching for the best spot. I looked from desk to desk, heading deep into the "classroom." It wasn't until I reached the large table holding the ancient TV that I climbed up. I steadied myself on the wide surface, reaching up towards the ceiling. My hands gripped the plastic cover and tore it down from above. It thumped to the floor beneath me.

I felt along the six-foot tubes, which were still slightly cool to the touch. The bright warmth had not yet reached them. Using my fingertips, I carefully rolled one of the bulbs the way Bumpy had shown me in his workshop. It easily came loose within my hands.

"What are you going to do with that," Brook asked as I jumped down and placed the fluorescent light on the table.

"I'm gonna get us out of here." I reached for one of the textbooks on the shelf and returned to the large table, raising the heavy book above my head. The glass shattered as I brought it down on the fragile tube. The bulb split into two pieces, just as I had planned—one for each of us. I raised each section into the air, grabbing their smooth end pieces and inspecting the opposing jagged ends. "A sword for you, and one for me. Let's go," I said, handing Brook her piece while holding on to mine.

We made our way back down the hallway, Mika then silent. "I don't know if we want to go back in there, Dani," Brook said, her voice shaking. The quiet was almost more frightening than the screams.

"Dias is our only way out," I answered. "He's gotta know how to get out of here, and we're gonna make him tell us."

"How?" she said in a small voice.

"With these," I said, holding up my spiky bulb. "If he doesn't tell us, then we're gonna stick him where it counts!" I hoped I sounded brave. The thought of seeing blood made my stomach instantly turn. But I shoved the image out of my mind as I grabbed ahold of Brook's gloved hand.

"He's so big, Dani, much bigger than us."

"I hurt him pretty bad with his spark stick so he shouldn't be as strong. There's only one of him and two of us. It's going to work because together, we equal more." In that moment, she pulled me in for a hug. It was the first time we didn't have bars between us. She cried into my shoulder, her tears quickly soaking my shirt's thin fabric. Neither of us spoke. All the words had been used up. When I eventually drove the keycard into the slot, the green appeared with a single swipe.

The room was dark. The lights had completely faded out, and nothing stirred inside. The glow from the hallway created a tiny slit down the black, caged room. As we widened the door, the brightness trickled further down the narrow path between the cells. When it reached the far end of the room, he stood directly in its way—his shadowed eye sockets staring back at us. A crumpled body lay at his feet.

"Now, now girls," he said, straightening his spine. I tried not to stare at Mika's unmoving body. "I see that you have had your fun, but now it is time to go back to your rooms." He brought his massive hands together in front of him. My heart raced deeper into my chest.

All of his strength had returned.

"Pandora. You will put down your little toy now," he said, reminding me of the tube I had forgotten at my side. Somehow, it looked smaller than I had thought.

"We want to go home," I said, my voice feeling childlike. I tried to force the courage back into my bones, but it had already slipped away without me even realizing.

"Don't be foolish. You are home."

"Stop saying that! This isn't my room! This isn't my home!" I yelled, my voice wavering.

"You ungrateful child. You are well fed and have fresh water. You have books to learn from, a bed to sleep on, clothes on your back…you will learn to be more appreciative."

"We promise not to hurt you. Just let us out," Brook piped up beside me, her sword looking unsteady.

"You mean, give you this?" he said calmly, holding up a red keycard. He instantly noticed the surprise that filled my face. "You didn't think I'd actually use my master in front of you, now did you?"

"Give it," I said forcefully, taking a step forward. Suddenly, he threw his head back, giving out a deep, booming laugh.

"You are a curious one, Pandora, just like I thought. I see the way you watch me. I had a feeling you would try something, but I do applaud you for taking it as far as you did. Light bulb," he said, motioning to our swords. "I would have never thought of that one." If I didn't know any better, I would have said he almost sounded proud.

I felt foolish standing there, him laughing in our faces. I couldn't help but think it was just another one of his games.

"I could have gone out there and dragged you back here, but I didn't have to. I knew you would come back," he said smugly. "So many people use force when they don't have to. All they have to do is figure out what people care about the most."

"Is that what you call hurting Mika? Not using force?" I asked, sounding more scared than I had wanted.

"But I didn't do that to him. You did," he said in a childlike voice.

"No! You did this! You did everything to us!" I screamed.

"I'll tell you what. If you girls go to your rooms, I will forget this little tantrum ever happened. How does that sound?"

"And if we don't?" I challenged.

"But you will. And I know this because of him," he said, looking down at Mika's still body. "You can't even bring yourself to look at him. You didn't just come back for this card, now did you, Pandora? You came back to save him, too."

I'd hoped it wasn't so obvious. I didn't want him to know just how much I cared.

"So, what's it going to be?" When neither of us moved, Dias grabbed Mika by his neck, dragging his body up the sides of his cage. His limp legs tightened and squirmed as he pulled him up the bars. Dias's grip continued to tighten. "Do you see what you are doing, Pandora? You will kill him, you impetuous child!" Mika's throat gurgled, the life leaving his body.

I felt my desperate pleas lodged in my throat, scraping to get out. But I knew they wouldn't stop Dias. I was the only person who could do that. Brook's gloved hand settled on my arm, silently asking me to stay. I thought of Brook's story and how she never grabbed the knife at her feet when her fingers went missing. It made me realize that I was just like her. I had always been someone who thought of herself as a fighter. But I was wrong. I was just another silly kid, scared of the monsters in her closet.

"Don't be a fool, Pandora. It would only end badly for everyone. And it would be all your fault," he said, his eyes wide and crazy.

"Don't listen to him—he's lying!" Brook said frantically, trying to break through to me.

"Can you be so sure, Pandora? Can you open that box and know exactly what's going to come out?" he yelled out over Mika's suffocated gulps.

I heard my fake sword smash against the ground. My legs betrayed me by walking to the small cell, giving way as soon as my body entered. Dias instantly released Mika, who fell facedown into the dirt, unable to fix his broken breaths. Blood dripped from his face, causing the ground around him to turn black. I watched as Dias marched over to Brook, slapping the broken bulb out of her limp hand. Her body had turned lifeless without me by her side, like a forgotten puppet with no one to hold her strings. I tried not to listen when his metal rod buzzed to life, jerking her floppy body back to her cage. Or, when Mika's body hit the ground as he was thrown back into his cell. Dias went from cage to cage, slamming the three doors one after another.

It wasn't until we were safely returned to our boxes that he began to limp. Dias's every breath quickened as he slithered up and down the narrow pathway, his right leg dragging behind him. His electric rod sat at his side. He tapped the red card against his good leg.

He stopped at my cell, shoving his hand through the bars. "Give it to me."

I scooted my bottom forward and placed the small, white card in his hand. He returned it to his back pocket and placed the red one inside the front flap of his shirt, positioned directly over his empty heart.

He began to smile, the holes in his face catching the shadows of light along with his sharp teeth. "When will you ever learn, Pandora? You just can't help but open up those boxes." He turned to leave, saying before he left us in blackness, "Now be my good girls, and go to sleep." The door closed with a roaring slam.

I crawled to my mattress. Brook quietly whimpered, and Mika's corner remained silent. As I sat, trembling in my damp cell, his words kept replaying in my head. *You just can't help but open up those boxes.*

They came in the middle of the night—first the girl and then the boy. He put them in Chet and Clara's empty cages. They both started out with a single mattress and a plastic dresser, like all the rest of us before them.

The girl's name was Macy. Her face was small and delicate, with dark, doll-like eyes set against cocoa-colored skin. She cried for three days straight, even after the lights dimmed into darkness.

Damien was different. He asked lots of questions and had a habit of talking faster than his tongue could move. There was a slight accent to his voice, but it only came out when he said words like "out" and "dangerous." He reminded me of Chet—too skinny with large, curly hair. There was a knick in one of his eyebrows that caused the hair to curl up, making me think he was always plotting something. *It was a good thing*, I thought.

They were also given names from the ancient stories told by the Greeks. He gave Macy the name "Aphrodite," whom I discovered was the goddess of love. Dias told her she was known for her beauty but also that she was a meddler and stuck her nose in places it didn't belong. Damien was named Dionysus, whom supposedly drank too much and was filled with violence and rage. Dias said it was inevitable that the god would lose control, that he would eventually give way to madness.

It made me think about how the pattern started and continued. That coming year would mark the beginning of Mika's change—the endless and terrible cycle. *Was that the madness he was talking about?*

For me, only the questions seemed to remain. But for Brook, they had run dry. She didn't ask what made me go back to my cell or wonder why I didn't try to fight. She didn't want to find out why Dias had trapped us in his twisted version of the Underworld. Instead, she talked about picking cherries in the spring, roasting marshmallows with her mother, and learning how to swim at the rec center down the street. Her thoughts would pour from every pocket of her, and I soaked all of them in, trying to keep those little parts left of her with me.

It made me think about what Brook had said to me. *The sun doesn't light up the world expecting it to owe her.*

I couldn't shake the thought that kept popping into my head. *What would happen if the sun went away?* It was the only question I could answer.

Everything would go black.

Chapter Nine
September 12, 2004

The Underground wasn't about making people like you. It wasn't about making friends and certainly wasn't about keeping the old ones. It was all about power—who could give you the most and discovering how quickly it all could be taken away.

I learned that we each had a part to play in the struggle for control.

With over sixteen hundred students in my high school, I thought it would be easy to blend in. I wasn't on a sports team or a part of any school clubs, so people weren't supposed to know my name. I should have been treated like any other ordinary freshman, nervously tiptoeing up and down the halls and keeping out of the upperclassmen's way. But I was wrong. By the end of my first day of high school, everyone knew my name. They didn't treat me like the other freshmen. And it all had to do with one single moment.

It was in the middle of lunch. Fletch, Buzz, Tommy, and I all happened to share that period, and we sat at our own table near the middle of the cafeteria. Even though I had barely seen them the previous year, it felt like we had picked up where seventh grade had left off. The three bragged about their "wicked" skateboard moves, trying to one-up each other with their stories of recent falls at the local park. However, it seemed to be more for my enjoyment than for theirs, as each already knew the other's story. Buzz seemed a little off at first, probably because he, more than the others, didn't like that I went to high school parties. Hillary had said that they were "straight edge punks" and didn't like the drinking scene.

Just before the bell rang, he strolled into the cafeteria. Vander kept his eyes locked on mine as he walked towards me, his hands held behind his back. When he arrived at my side, he placed a single, white flower on the table in front of me. A hush fell over the entire room, everyone focused on me.

"See ya later, Keely," was all he said, turning to leave without a backward glance. I looked down at the calla lily in front of me. It was my nana's favorite flower, and Bumpy always made sure to get them for her birthday. Except for the yellow rod blooming from its middle, it appeared a perfect white.

"Who the F does he think he is, Zorro?" Tommy joked.

"Do not even touch that thing, Keel," Buzz said, his face noticeably irritated.

"That guy seriously needs to get a new move, I tell ya," Fletch said.

"He usually does this?" I asked.

"Yeah. He loves giving girls stupid ass flowers," Buzz said.

"He always gives them this flower?" I said.

"Gross, put that down. It probably has herpes on it or something," Tommy said as he knocked it from my open palm, shielding his hand with a napkin.

"Do you know why he gave you it?" Buzz asked, his irritation visibly growing.

"I honestly have no idea," I said, hoping that my eyes didn't give me away. I may not have known all the specifics, but I knew it was to send people a message. He was letting them know that I was with him, whether I wanted to be or not.

Word spread quickly, as it only took Hillary one period to come find me. She pulled me into the girls' upstairs bathroom, refusing to say a word until she made sure we were alone.

"They asked you, didn't they?" she said after checking the final stall.

"What are you talking about?"

"Don't play dumb, Keely. My brother doesn't do that shit unless he has a reason to. When did they ask you?" I hesitated, looking for an easy way out of telling her the truth.

"A week and a half ago," I said quietly.

"And are you going to do it?" We stood there in silence as I tried to avoid making eye contact with her. "Keely, listen to me. Don't do this. They're all crazy and just brainwash people into thinking what they want."

"And how do you know that? You aren't even in it," I shot back, my voice sounding harsher than I had intended.

"You think I have to be in with them to know who these people are? Well, spoiler alert, I don't."

"Max is in it, and he isn't like that."

"Yeah, but Max is a fool and has no idea what he has gotten into," she said, sounding bitter.

"You know, for once in my life, people are treating me like I'm somebody. Don't you get that?"

"Keely, you have always been somebody! You are funny and kind, and the best part is that you don't even know it. It's what makes you so good."

"Well, then maybe I'm sick of being just good." She sighed heavily, as if the weight of her breath had become too much to carry.

"They don't care about you, and they won't ever care about you. The only reason they asked you was because my brother told them to." Her voice fell flat.

"Think whatever you want, Hillary," I said angrily.

"It's not me thinking anything! I'm telling you what I already know!"

"Look, I know you're mad that I got asked and you didn't, but that doesn't mean you get to tell me what to do."

"You're joking, right?" she said sarcastically. "You actually think I'm mad that I didn't get tapped? Ha! That's honestly *hilarious* because you know what I would have done if they asked me? I would have lit that thing on fire right then and there and shoved it straight up their asses."

"You know what, you really can be such a bitch sometimes." It came out before I could stop myself, and the worst part was that it sounded like I meant it. She looked as if my words came with a physical blow. I thought that maybe she was going to spit them back at me, and I almost hoped she would. Instead, she swooped up her backpack in one quick motion and left. I simply stood there, staring regretfully at her retreating back.

Hillary and I didn't say a word to each other for three weeks. We only crossed paths once during the day, each keeping our eyes facing forward as we passed the other in the hall. I could tell the rift was taking its toll on the three boys, who awkwardly shifted in their seats whenever Hillary's name came up. They pretended like everything was all right between us, but I knew their loyalty was with her.

A large part of me wanted to tell her I was sorry. I knew she was only looking out for me, just like Dani would have. But I also didn't want her to try to talk me out of it. I was going to do it, whether she liked it or not.

The one person I felt like I could confide in was Max, but even he was against me joining. He didn't say all the things Hillary had, but he too thought Vander had bigger plans.

"I just don't trust him. There's something off about it," he said.

"Off about it?"

"Off about Vander, off about the whole thing, I guess. It doesn't make sense."

"So, you're basically saying that there's no way I could have been tapped on my own. That's pretty much what you're saying."

"No, I'm not saying that. All I'm telling you is that he is super weird about you. He asks me things, like if we have ever kissed or 'done it,' and it gives me a real bad feeling."

"He hasn't even done anything! All he did was give me a flower and now everyone is freaking out about it. Maybe he isn't as bad as everyone thinks."

"I'm sorry, that flower thing was flat-up weird, and everyone thought it too. He's treating you like you're his possession, Keely."

"I can handle myself, okay? I'm sick of everyone trying to take care of me. I'm fine."

"Well, I guess we will find out tomorrow then, won't we?"

Homecoming was the single day that everyone wore maroon, even the kids who normally dressed in black. As expected, the senior class dominated everyone in the pep rally. Amy Taber was selected as the Homecoming Princess for the freshmen, and the cheerleaders led the classic chants. The sophomore class surprisingly beat out the seniors for the first time in thirteen years in the hallway decorating contest. People claimed it was because a tenth-grader, Ben Reedy, was an artistic prodigy, but we all knew they only won because Principal Linglee's daughter was in that class. The day unfolded exactly as I had imagined—face paint, pep rallies with packed bleachers, and maroon jerseys. However, my mind kept drifting away from the school spirit excitement. Homecoming meant a lot more to me than who won the tug-of-war competition or if I got to wear a football player's away jersey during the big game. I knew everything was about to change.

The celebrations ended in the annual Homecoming School Dance. That night, I found myself dancing inside the very circle I stood outside of three years before. The popular kids stared at me, but it was different from when I was "that kidnapped girl's sister." Trish Booker kept admiring my curled updo, and Gaby Davis copied my dance moves. I tried to push aside the thought that the people I was joking and singing along to Ashanti with knew absolutely nothing about me. Instead, I convinced myself it was all I ever wanted—to be a part of something.

Four boys asked me to dance, but the only invitation I accepted was Max's. He wore a maroon tie and gelled back his hair, making him look like a fancy gentleman straight off the Titanic. He sang along to the songs as we swayed back and forth, making my cheeks warm against his. I didn't know whether it was the sound of his deep voice in my ear or the way he held me a little bit closer during the chorus. But before I could figure it out, someone's hand slipped between ours and pulled me away.

"Sorry I'm late to this thing. Thanks for taking care of her for me, Maxy." I suddenly found myself in Vander's arms, his fingers traveling down my back. I could smell his strong cologne, doing little to cover up the strong smell of alcohol on his hot breath.

"You ready for tonight?" he asked, leading my body to the slow beat of the song.

"I think so," I croaked out.

"You don't sound too sure."

"I'm just a little nervous, I guess."

"There's no reason to be nervous. We all go through it."

"What's going to happen?"

"You don't want me to ruin the surprise, now do you?" I pretended to focus on moving with the song instead of replying. Over Vander's shoulder, I scanned the crowd and looked for Max, finding him sitting at a faraway table. He was leaning over in his chair, his elbows resting on his knees and his fists clenched. His hair was no longer crisply set, giving away that he had been raking his hands repeatedly through it. Even through the dimness, I could tell he was staring hard at us.

Thankfully, the lights came on after the song ended. However, Vander lingered, his fingers remaining over my hip even after our bodies had stopped moving. I uneasily tried to slip past his wandering hands.

"I'll see you later, Keely. Good luck tonight," he said with his classic wink. Before I could stop him, he leaned down and kissed me briefly on my lips. It was just long enough to leave behind the taste of stale beer on my mouth.

I was slow to turn and walk back towards Max.

"I don't like this, Keely. I don't like him. I don't like the way he looks at you. I don't like any of it," he said when I reached him. His jaw was tightly clenched, causing a muscle to tick near his temple.

"Why did you let him dance with me then?"

"Why did *you* let him dance with you?" he challenged back, leaving us at a stalemate.

"Honestly, Max, I don't know what to do," I said, my head bowed.

"Keely, do you really want to do this tonight—to become a part of this?" He took my hands inside his, pulling me close to him. Max had been a part of the Underground for a couple months by then, but he had told me little about it.

"Why is it okay for you to do it but not for me?"

"I don't know. It's just different for the girls. I don't want it to change you," he answered.

"It's not going to. I promise you that it won't," I said, trying to appear confident. But the truth was, I didn't know if I could keep that promise.

Already, I had felt myself changing since I had turned thirteen. I liked to think that I had a say in it all—that I knew what I was doing. However, most of the time, I didn't even know who I wanted to be.

I left the dance alone that night. Max's mom picked him up early, leaving me waiting alone outside the school gym. I rubbed my bare arms to try to keep the warmth inside and away from the cold September air. Surrounding me, there were long lines of parents, all searching eagerly for their kids from within their warm cars. I stood off to the side as the other students went down the rows looking for their parents. I knew it would be difficult for my dad to miss my poufy, pink princess dress. It was the one Nana had given me for my last birthday, and at the time, I hadn't intended on ever wearing it. Mom took about three dozen pictures of me in it before I left for the dance. I imagined them hanging alongside the photos from school picture days in Nana and Bumpy's house.

"Keely!" someone shouted, pulling me from my thoughts. I turned to see Hillary walking towards me, wearing sweatpants and her favorite wizard shirt. "I was hoping I would find you here. I bribed my mom to drive me. You know how much she hates missing her Friday primetime programming," she said with a slight smile.

"*Law and Order*, I'm guessing?" I said as I smiled back at her.

"Yeah, some crime show like that."

"What did you say to convince her?"

"I agreed to go antiquing with her next weekend," she said, rolling her eyes and putting on a long face. I tried my best not to laugh, especially since Hillary always saw "antiquing" as cruel and unusual punishment.

"You must have really wanted to come here then," I said quietly.

The three weeks of silence settled between us. I could tell she wanted it to end just as much as I did. "Listen, I didn't come here to talk about the other stuff…from before. I came to tell you that I'm not going to stop being your friend. No matter what you do, I'm not going to make you choose between being my friend and joining that *thing*. I know I'm supposed to be mad and pretend not to care what you do, but I think that's dumb. I do care, and I'm going to keep caring. I just want you to know that I'm going to be there, whether you want me to be or not."

I walked towards her and threw my arms around her neck, my princess dress shoved between us. "I'm so happy you're here," was all I managed to say. And it was enough.

Just like the invitation read, I went to the ice skating rink at midnight.

When I arrived, there were already five other girls from my grade gathered under the high parking lot lights. One I recognized as Amy Taber. She stood there casually, as if it was just any day that someone told her to meet at a dried-up ice skating rink in the middle of the night.

None of us spoke. Instead, we stood there and nervously shifted side-to-side, listening to Amy pop her gum. I shoved my hands deeper inside my sweatshirt and watched my breath fog up the cold air. Fifteen minutes passed before the trucks arrived. They kept their lights off as they approached. It wasn't until they were all parked in front of us that their lights popped on. The brightness momentarily blinded me, making it difficult to see the figures coming toward us.

More than twenty people piled out of the line of trucks, each person dressed entirely in black. I couldn't make out their faces behind the dark ski masks, instantly making me want to run.

"Put this on," a male voice ordered before my feet could take me away. A black-gloved hand held out what appeared to be a thick potato sack. I did as he said, even though I already felt faint and short of breath. The heavy bag smelled stale and musty inside, and it didn't take long for a suffocating feeling to surround me. I reached up frantically to try and rip it off my head, but someone grabbed ahold of my hands, pulling them to my sides.

"It's okay, it's okay. You're going to be okay, Keely." I recognized the voice; it was Max's. As if by magic, I felt the air come back to me. I gripped his hand, refusing to let go as I heard footsteps around me. The bright lights seeped into the bag as my feet fell into step with the others. Someone pulled me into the truck bed from above, forcing me to let go of Max's hand.

I instantly pulled my legs into my body when my jeans hit the grooved tailgate. Someone took the spot next to me, pushing up against my side and blocking the wind's chill. I knew it was Max when I felt his rough hand slip into mine and give me his familiar, light squeeze.

We drove for about ten minutes before the road changed to crunchy gravel. The bounce of the truck gave away the rough dirt road. The edge of the truck bed struck me each time we hit a divot, sending pain shooting into my side.

"We're almost there. Not much longer now," Max whispered into my ear, his voice the only thing I had to keep me calm.

Five minutes later, we came to a stop. That was when I began to smell the smoke. It leaked into the sack covering my face, the smell of burning wood covering the last hint of my remaining hairspray. Max pulled me to my feet, guiding me to the edge as I heard the metal tailgate groan. I felt someone grab my hips, lifting me to the ground. The hands stayed on my waist longer than necessary.

Feeling the ground underneath my feet, the overwhelming desire to run returned. I wanted to feel my legs moving beneath me, promising my escape. I could feel the bad man return from the furthest recesses of my brain, his needle finger drawing closer. I didn't need to see to know where we were going. They were taking us into the woods.

I wanted to scream.

Instead, I buried the sound inside of my throat and continued to let the hands push me forward. The smoke became thicker with each step. I tried focusing on the crunch of leaves and the snap of sticks underneath my shoes. After all, I had promised Dani to be the person who stayed.

It wasn't until the footsteps all grew silent that they pulled the sacks off our heads. We found ourselves standing in the middle of a massive circle, surrounded by the thick forest and people all in black. Each dark figure held a burning torch. The six of us girls huddled together, like helpless antelope right before the lions went in for the kill.

At first, none of us moved. I wildly searched for Max's firewater eyes behind the inky masks. All the eyes looked wide and unfamiliar in the nighttime, except for one pair that didn't need the light to give it away. The brief wink quickly told me all I needed to know.

"You are the chosen. You are the worthy. You are the faithful." The female voice pierced through the silence. It seemed to echo long after the words stopped, as if the trees became her loudspeaker. She and another small, cloaked body took two steps into the circle before removing their masks. I didn't recognize either of the girls, particularly beneath the red paint covering their faces. They both held long, black rods; they were the kind used to poke burning logs within fireplaces.

"Who are we?" the girl yelled again, this time turning her eyes to those standing around us.

"We are the chosen. We are the worthy. We are the faithful." They said it in unison, growing louder with each word. The girl to my left gripped my hand. I knew that her name was Chelsea. We had shared almost every class since first grade, but never once had she said hello to me. Her eyes appeared large and scared when I turned to look at her. I could tell that she was on the verge of tears.

"You are here because of a decision, one that we all made before you. To be great. To be better than the others. To take what you want. The Underground represents the things that people can't see, those that the others will never understand," the girl boomed. "You, with the childish haircut. Come here." She pointed at Chelsea, who was slow to release my hand.

Chelsea walked towards the head girl, her legs noticeably shaking. Another girl in black entered the circle, that one lugging a white bucket alongside her. The scarlet insides dripped over the clean surface. She placed it in front of the two unmasked girls. The pair motioned with their pokers for Chelsea to kneel, her back still to us.

"Red is the color of blood, of fire, of love, of hate. It is the strength, power, and wrath of the Underground, and we never wash it from our skin." As the two girls recited the words together, the masked one dipped her bare hands into the bucket and spread her fingers over Chelsea's face.

One by one, we were removed from the smaller circle and each transformed. I was the final one to march forward. I tried my best to avoid looking towards the other five girls, their faces dripping red. When I took my spot in front of the bucket, a metallic smell filled my nose. The liquid felt surprisingly warm when it met my skin. It ran trails down my face, trickling off my forehead and gliding over my lips. It seeped into the corner of my mouth, confirming what I already knew.

It wasn't paint. It was blood.

I wanted to scrub it from my face until there was no more left. I wanted to erase the smell of iron that filled my nose. I wanted to spit out each drop to take away the terrible taste. But I also wanted to be a person who stayed.

So I continued to kneel there as it dried and hardened. I let it become my new face.

The circle began to close in around us, the people in black positioning their torches straight out in front of them. The heat from their fire grew hotter, making me feel that we would slowly be melted into a pool of blood and poured into a fresh bucket. Suddenly, the girl with the booming voice raised her hand, causing them all to stop in their tracks.

She slowly walked towards us, slipping between a crack in the tight circle. Her eyes shone from the fire, unblinking. I was the first one she went to, her hand lifting my chin upwards.

"In pain there is always pleasure," she whispered, just loud enough for me to hear. She pulled down on my chin, forcing my mouth to open as she dropped a white pill inside. It was small enough to slide easily down my throat, leaving me little time to think as it disappeared into the depths of my stomach. I watched as she went down the line, dropping a tiny pill into each black hole that opened within the new bloody faces.

At first, nothing happened. But slowly the current began to build within me, spawning a creature inside. It traveled to the tucked away crevices, casting its frozen breath onto each one and numbing the pain. My head started to feel light, dizzy. My feet tingled beneath me, as if preparing to lift into the air at any moment.

A commotion started around us, but my attention continued to fade. The two lead girls made their way slowly around the circle, placing the tips of their pokers through each of the torches. But I was already gone, floating above the black circle. The cold, wriggling feeling had overtaken my body.

I let them lay me down and turn me onto my stomach. They removed my shoes and socks. My tongue snuck its way out of my mouth, blending with the dead leaves and moist dirt covering the ground.

"Together, we will find our meaning," I heard them all chant at once. It was then that I felt the heat break through my frozen walls, its fire licking my feet. Screams erupted all around me, and I tried to find their source through my foggy brain. But then I realized. They were coming from me.

The room was not my own. It was small, almost half the size of mine. A single desk filled the corner near the small window. The long shelf lined the wall at the opposite side, filled to the brim with books. The other walls sat bare, with the exception of the scattered framed certificates—the kind that teachers gave out to kids in elementary school for even the smallest of accomplishments.

The blankets were pulled up to my chin, and my arms rested snuggly at my side, telling me someone must have tucked me in. I turned my head to find water and ibuprofen on the bedside table next to me. The white medicine bottle triggered my vague memories of the previous night, and the burn returned to my feet beneath the covers.

I gasped at the pain, causing a stir nearby. After carefully rolling myself to the side, I found Max sprawled out, still asleep. He appeared tired, and his normally flat hair stuck up at odd angles.

"Hey," I croaked, weakly dropping a pillow on top of him. He awoke with a start, hitting his head against the edge of the bed as he rapidly sat up.

"You're up. How do you feel?" he said as he rubbed his temple.

"I could ask you the same thing," I tried to joke.

"You should take that," he said, pointing to the ibuprofen. "You're going to need it."

"What did they do to me, Max?"

"What they do to everyone. Trust me, I know how you feel." He brief-ly grabbed his feet as he said it, proving the pain wasn't just in my imagina-tion.

"Can I see?" I asked softly. He removed one sock and lifted the bot-tom of his foot for me to see. Sunken into its heel sat a dark, red "U."

"It's going to hurt like hell for about a month, but it'll eventually get to be like mine. I put ice packs on yours last night and some of this burn cream so it wouldn't hurt too bad when you woke up."

"How did I get here?"

"I had them drop us off at my place because we couldn't take you back to your house looking like that. And I didn't think you'd want Hillary to see you that way, either."

"Max, why would they do this?"

"I don't know, maybe to remind us—that we are one of them now?" He didn't look at me when he said it and focused on putting his sock back on.

"Did anything else happen...you know, after?"

"The drug they gave you kicked in quick, so you and the rest were pretty out of it. But the one girl—Chelsea, I think her name is—had a pret-ty bad reaction to it. I think she's okay now."

"Did she have to go to the hospital?"

"No...we aren't allowed to do that. It's against the rules," he said sourly.

"So what does this mean? Do they basically own us now?"

"I don't know, Keely. When I had to go through it, I thought it wasn't so bad...but to see it happen to you..." His voice trailed off, and for a second, I thought he was about to cry. Instead, he lifted his eyes back up to mine, a fury taking shelter inside. "All I know is that we have to watch out for each other. I promise to be there for you, no matter what happens, okay? Do you trust me?"

He looked at me desperately, as if he needed to hear me say the words—that I believed he would take care of me.

"I trust you. I always have, and I always will," I said.

And I meant it.

Max was right—it hurt like hell. Regardless of the amount of gauze I lay-ered over the bottoms of my feet or the amount of cooling cream I lath-ered on, the burns just kept on burning. For the first three weeks, I took cold showers. But even that did little to take the pain away.

I kept the pain hidden from my parents and Hillary, but the boys knew something was wrong. Buzz asked me what was up every day at lunch, and each time I told him I was fine. The questioning eventually stopped, but I knew it wasn't because he started believing me. Even though he returned to tapping his pen against the table and appeared distracted, I got the feeling that Buzz picked up on a lot more than he let on.

At first, life wasn't much different from before my initiation. I still sat with the boys at lunch and hung around with Max and Hillary after school, until they each went off to sports practice. Basketball preseason started early for Max, and Hillary decided to go out for the cross country team since Lucas and she had broken up over the summer. Their relationship didn't make it very far; Hillary had realized all he wanted was to get into her pants. It turned out that breakups made people into pretty fast runners.

I didn't hear anything from the Underground for several weeks following Homecoming night, but I noticed people started watching me more closely. It wasn't obvious at first, but I began to see the same faces, regardless of where I went in the large school. It made the pit return to my stomach, taking me back to that fiery night. They kept their distance, but I had a feeling that they weren't going to stay away forever.

It was a week before Thanksgiving break—almost a month and a half after I had become one of them—when they came to me. I was home alone on an especially cold Saturday, my parents visiting a sick friend at the hospital. They didn't knock or wait at the door like normal people did. Instead, they walked right in.

There were four of them, one much shorter than the rest. The other three were freakishly tall and noticeably attractive girls. I recognized them from the varsity volleyball team. All of them were starters.

"Keely Millen," the short one said as they entered my room. I leapt off my bed, sending my *Seventeen* magazine spilling onto the floor. Immediately, I reached for my slipper for protection. "Woah, chill, girlfriend. That isn't a way to treat your sisters now, is it?" She tilted her head in a puppy dog kind of way, which reminded me of the girl from that night—the one with the booming voice.

"You are with…the Underground?"

"We prefer not to speak that aloud in public, and you should learn to do the same," she said harshly. I looked around my room, contemplating pointing out the fact that there was no one around to hear. I decided to keep my mouth shut. "I'm Rachel, and these three are Frieda, Luna, and Tressa." The other three made no move to introduce themselves and remained like mannequins posed behind her. Their names reminded me of the celebrity parents who gave their kids ridiculous names, as if that would automatically guarantee their superiority in life.

"You're a peculiar one, Keely Millen," the one named Luna said. She didn't mean it as a compliment, which made me instantly self-conscious as she looked around my room with judging eyes. "People act like you are something special, but we have noticed you have a tendency of hanging around the Ridgewood riffraff. This is a real concern."

"You are now in Transition Phase, where we help you become a true Underground sister," Frieda said with an obvious fake accent. I didn't know if she was aware that she wasn't exotic or foreign but rather just a typical, white Jersey girl. As before, I kept my thoughts to myself.

"If you want to be considered a sister, there are rules that you must follow," Rachel said. It was the third time I had heard them use the word "sister" in the five minutes they had been there, making me increasingly more annoyed each time they said it. "First, if you want to be a sister, you're going to have to start dressing like one."

One by one, they each went to my poor excuse for a closet and grabbed handfuls of clothes, removing everything from the shelves and drawers. They dumped them into a pile on my floor, barely looking at each piece before swiftly flinging most of them into the "dispose of" pile. Approximately three shirts were left for me to wear, along with a lonely pair of jeans. Even my ankle socks didn't make the cut.

I stood there silently as they went through my room, marking most of my belongings as garbage. When they finished, I had fewer possessions than a homeless person.

"Tressa, bag this and dispose of it. Then bring in the stuff from the car," Rachel ordered. Tressa did as told without complaint, and it struck me that she hadn't said one word since she walked into the room. She was a wallflower, like me, except she had learned how to bloom a little better based off her Barbie good looks and perfect complexion.

The other three waited as Tressa did Rachel's bidding, none of them paying me any attention. I stood there awkwardly in my own room, feeling very aware of my pitiful two posters and holey pajama pants.

"Did you actually listen to her full voicemail though?" Luna asked the other two.

"Honestly, I couldn't even get through it. Her voice made my ears bleed—I mean, like, literally gush blood. She sounds like she sucked down an entire tank of helium and then was punched in the throat," Frieda said, as if she had any room to talk.

"She is clearly not worth any of our time. We all know that anyone still using Victoria Secret body spray clearly has issues," Rachel said in a snobby voice. I looked over at my desk and saw the Love Spell perfume sitting on top, almost hoping that they would notice mine, too. For the entire time that Tressa was away, they managed to dissect each part of the mystery girl's voicemail—finding five minutes of conversation from the brief thirty-second message.

When Tressa returned, she had at least five stuffed shopping bags in each hand. I didn't recognize any of the names on the outsides, most in gold and black print against expensive-looking textured paper.

The bags held at least five thousand dollars worth of clothes; I knew only because the tags were still attached. There were skinny jeans, tight skirts, patterned dresses, high heels, tank tops, crop tops, string thongs, shorter than short shorts, fancy boots, padded bras, and four-piece headbands. I felt my eyes glaze over as they revealed the items, describing each one, as if I was supposed to know what they were talking about.

"What ones would you like to try on first?" Luna asked excitedly. I was nervous to even touch the delicate clothes, let alone put them on.

"I don't know what to say—this is all so nice of you. I have like a hundred dollars saved up, but I'll try to save more so I can pay you guys back for this," I said uncomfortably.

"Don't be silly. This is a gift from us. We *are* sisters after all, aren't we?" Frieda said. Maybe it was the way she said it or how she ran her hand through my hair, but it made my skin crawl.

For the next hour, they made me try on everything they had bought me, making sure I changed into each outfit right there in front of them. I had never been naked in front of anybody except Dani before, and it wasn't something I wanted to get used to.

"What's that on your leg?" Luna asked, pointing to the long scar on my upper thigh.

"A dog bit me when I was little," I said timidly, trying to shove my legs into a pair of jeans as fast as I could.

"Wow, we can't have that now, can we?" Luna asked seriously to Rachel.

"We could probably just have someone fix it for her. My daddy knows some people in plastics, and they do that kind of stuff all the time," Rachel responded, as if I couldn't overhear their "private" conversation. Thankfully, it was the last pair of jeans before I could move on to the accessories.

Frieda fussed with my hair while Tressa silently did my makeup, getting so close to my face that I could smell her peppermint gum.

"You know, Keely, you really are quite pretty. Your hair is a bit of a mess, and you need to stop slouching so much, but I think you have a lot of potential," Frieda said.

"Thanks..." I said, unsure whether or not I was supposed to take it as a compliment.

"And that thing with your right eye," Rachel said as she leaned in close to my face. "I thought we were going to have to get you a color contact for that, but I actually kind of like it."

"Thanks," I said again, not knowing what else to say.

"You aren't much of a talker, are you? Is it because your sister was killed?" Frieda said casually, as if she had just asked me what I had for breakfast.

"She was kidnapped, stupid," Luna spit back.

"Same difference. So, is it?" I sat very still and made sure that I didn't look up at her. If I did, she would have seen how much I hated her.

"I've always been quiet," was all I managed to say.

"I guess that's okay. Tressa doesn't say much, either, and look at how pretty she turned out." Frieda held out Tressa's arm and presented her to me, as if offering a look into my future self.

"Girls, we have been here long enough. We have to get going or we're going to miss *True Life*," Rachel said with a clap of her hands. It physically hurt me not to clap my hands along with her, except my reason would have been very different.

I figured that since they had found their way in, they would also find their way out. I stayed in my chair with the four layers of tan icing that Tressa had plastered on my face. Just as they were all almost out of my room, Rachel popped back in, likely missing the look of annoyance that flared up on my face.

"Oh, and Keely? From now on, you're to sit with Frieda and her friends at lunch. You're no longer to see those three Goth boys or that weird girl with those alien shirts."

"They're wizards," I said a little too quickly.

"Whatever. I don't really care what they are. I don't want you to be seen with them. Oh, and one more thing. You aren't allowed to hang out with Max Lerman anymore."

"But why not? He is one of...*us*," I said frantically. I made sure to emphasize the "us" so she would think that I was taking the whole sisterhood crap seriously.

"Listen, we make the rules, and you follow them. If we tell you to stay away from them, you better damn do it." It wasn't until she slammed the door behind her that I fell to the floor, and for the first time, I cried tears for myself.

I didn't know how I was supposed to do it. However, the sting that permanently stuck to the bottom of my feet reminded me I had no choice. For the first time in my life, I felt like I had friends who cared about me. They stayed by my side because they wanted to, not because they had to.

And I had to give them up.

I didn't realize how deeply I had dove until I found myself at the bottom, and I couldn't find my way back up.

The boys didn't say anything when I passed by them that following Monday during lunch. I took my seat at Frieda's table—the "Cake Shop," as Hillary called it. Hillary said that if girls put on that much makeup, they were just asking to be picked on for it. I only allowed myself to look back at the boys' table one time, and I instantly regretted it. Just Tommy looked back at me, the hurt written in his face. Buzz and Fletch kept their heads lowered, refusing to even acknowledge they had seen me turn.

I dreaded the moment when Hillary and Max would meet me at my locker. I had planned out what I would say to them—that I would just have to stay away for a little while and soon things would go back to normal. However, neither of them showed up at our usual time. I tried to take it as a small miracle, hoping it meant that we could still go one more day as friends.

After school, I went straight home. Thankfully, my parents didn't say anything about my new wardrobe or the fact that I hadn't said a word to them that entire day. I went directly to my room and crawled into bed, wrinkling my three-hundred-dollar outfit. A dreamless sleep came over me, all except for the end when the darkness began to crumble.

I awoke with a start, realizing that the shaking came from outside my mind. Hillary stood over me, her hands on my shoulders, looking down at me with an almost crazed expression.

"Wake up! Wake up, would you! Come on, you freaking zombie! Keely! It happened again! I found them!"

"What are you talking about? What happened again?" I said, trying to rub away the grogginess. Instead of answering me, she pulled out a folded map from her backpack and whipped it open across my bed. I looked down at the familiar colored dots, their positions mirroring my map from three years before.

"I know you didn't want me looking anymore, and I really did plan on leaving it alone. But I just had to know. I started about two months ago, pretty much the day we had our fight. It's been three years since Dani was taken, which means that this is the year it would happen again. I started by looking for any kidnappings that I may have missed from the beginning of the year. When I kept coming up empty, I started to think that maybe we got it wrong—maybe we just saw something that we wanted to see. That was, until I found them."

She pulled out two folded newspapers from her bag, dropping them onto the bed. I had a hard time focusing on the printed words, realizing that I was crying.

"I know, I know, Agnes is going to kill me if she finds out I took her stupid newspapers, but I just couldn't help myself. Macy," she said, pointing to the newspaper on the left, "ten years old, taken from right outside her home in Ballston, New York, on August thirtieth. And this one, Damien, another ten-year-old, kidnapped from Brandon, Vermont, on September second…just three days later. I added them to the map, and it backs up everything. He has to be taking them somewhere in the circle. My guess is that it's closer to the coast than we thought."

I looked down at the two new purple-colored dots, and the tears only came faster.

"Hillary…" I choked out. She must have mistaken my emotion to mean something else because she wrapped me in a hug and bounced us both excitedly on the bed.

"I know! I couldn't believe it either when I found it! I couldn't wait to show you all day!"

"Hillary…I can't," I said through my choked-up tears. She pulled back from me, confusion filling her face.

"What do you mean you can't?"

"I mean I can't—all of it." I didn't look up at her as I spoke. "She's gone. I said goodbye to her, and I promised myself that I wouldn't go back to that place. I can't lose her all over again. I won't be able to take it."

"But don't you see? This is your chance to get her back!"

"I'm not going to get her back, okay! It's over. It's so fucking over." I cried into my hands as Hillary sat motionless beside me. It was the first time she had ever seen me cry, and I could sense that she already knew it wasn't just about Dani.

"Keely, is everything okay? I thought you would be happy about this." Her voice sounded strange and small.

"No. Everything is a mess. It's just such a mess," I said, shaking my head back and forth. I glanced up and saw her looking around my room, her eyes drifting to the collection of empty shopping bags piled in the corner.

"They got to you, didn't they?" She said it in a way that was more knowing than judgmental. She found her answer when I looked up at her. Suddenly, she slid off the bed and began pacing the room. Hillary ran her hands through her hair, exposing the natural auburn roots that hid underneath the freshly dyed blue.

"Everything just happened so quickly…"

"Did they tell you to stay away from me?"

"The boys too…and even Max," I said with my head down. She took a seat on the floor, her back leaning against the end of my bed. I silently stared at the back of her motionless head.

Slowly, Hillary stood up and began collecting her things off of my bed. She folded the map with great care and made sure to collapse the newspapers along their previous creases. Even though I realized what it meant, I didn't try to fix it. I just let her pack up her things and didn't say a word.

She paused before she made her way to the door. When she turned to face me, her eyes were misty. "I meant it when I said I wasn't going to stop being your friend. I'm not going to stop caring, but this I can't do for you. I can't make you choose me over them. I can't be the one to tell them to fuck off for you. That is something you have to do for yourself. I'll stay away if that's what you want, but just know that I'll be there when you need me to be. But there is one thing you need to do for me. I don't care what they said—don't get rid of Max. Even though he is in this stupid thing with you, he's good. He's the only one of us who can help you right now. And with these people, you're going to need it."

She turned back towards the door, and her hand rested on the knob. Her words that followed would live inside of me for the rest of my life. They burned their way into me, so much deeper than any hot poker ever could.

"Maybe this is what Dani was talking about when she said for you to be bigger. Maybe the biggest thing any of us can do is find the strength to run away."

"Max, when we were in seventh grade, what made you want to be my friend?" I asked. We were at his house again, working on yet another "school project." It was the only way we could get our parents to let us hang out past ten; we even did fake projects, just to make it believable. It was the only time I was able to see Max and actually talk freely with him, without having to worry about someone watching. Those were the few nights—us tucked away in his pillbox-sized room—when the worries briefly disappeared. I needed those times when I didn't have to hide behind my makeup or pretend to be someone I wasn't. I could just be Keely.

It was snowing outside—a little strange for early April—but I hoped it would delay my parents from picking me up for at least a little while longer.

"That's an easy one," he said. "I knew you were the type of person who gives up her chocolate pudding easily."

"Come on, I mean it."

"I don't know, I just liked you. You were different."

"Like a weird different?"

"I mean, you did say you liked the taste of envelopes and that you thought skunks kind of smelled good, so obviously I thought you were a *little* weird," he joked. "But it was a good weird. You weren't like the other girls." Those were the words I used to never want to hear. I remembered hoping that people wouldn't notice I was different from the other girls, the ones who cared about boy bands and wrote all over their hands with gel pens.

"Do you still think that—that I'm different than the other girls?" He hesitated a moment before he answered.

"Yeah...I still think that you are special, even with everything that has happened this year."

"Do you think that I've changed?"

"Do you?" he challenged back.

"Not fair, I asked first."

"Well, I guess you have. You dress different, you talk different, you don't smile as much as you should. You have done things that I didn't think you would do. But I think that, underneath all of it, you're still you."

I wanted to say he was wrong, that I hadn't changed as much as he thought, but I knew that would have been a lie.

We quickly fell back into our comfortable silence, me reading my magazines and Max finding ways to distract me. It was a game for him—to see how easily he could get my attention while I tried to concentrate on something else. It reminded me of dogs that went around their owners' homes, grabbing various clothing and possessions to see which one they cared about most. They quickly figured out the best ways to capture the attention.

"You want to know the real answer—why I actually wanted to be your friend?" Max asked.

"Not unless it has something to do with stealing an extra carton of milk," I tried to joke. "And I saw that, mister. You can put it back now," I said as I saw Max slowly pull my composition notebook out of my bag.

"I swear you have the best peripheral of anyone I know. And no, wise guy, it's not because of that. It's because of this," he said, leaning over to open the top drawer in his bedside table. He pulled out a folded piece of notebook paper and held it carefully in his hands, as if it was a valuable possession. The paper looked crinkled, with gray smudges hinting it had been kept in a backpack for too long. The corners appeared worn down and slightly curved along its edges.

He slowly unfolded the paper. It was a drawing—mine to be exact. I remembered making it that first month after Dani was taken, back in sixth grade. It had taken me three periods to finish. That day, I had especially missed her. I had wanted to see us together again but not just in my memory. Even with my shabby lines and poorly proportioned spacing, you could still tell that it was a picture of Dani and me. Our faces were pressed together, as if we were a rare pair of Siamese twins featured on a TV medical show. We were both smiling, and I recalled drawing a matching, happy sun in the top corner. I had thrown the picture into the garbage after English class, unable to get the cheerful feeling to stick.

"I saw you drawing it. You spent all day on it, and I don't think you looked up from your notebook once. I shouldn't have taken it, but I figured something that took so much time didn't belong in the garbage." I couldn't decide if I was more mad or thankful that he had kept it.

"What did you do, take it out of the trash?"

"Yeah," he said, looking almost ashamed. "I didn't mean to get all up in your business."

"It's whatever," I said and handed it back, trying to act like I didn't care. His face dropped as he took the paper.

"You don't even want to know why this made me become your friend?"

"Because you think I'm broken since my twin sister was kidnapped," I said as if I already knew the answer.

"You really think that's the reason why?" He acted hurt, but I simply shrugged. "Well, that's not why I did it, okay? It's because that is when I realized you are like me."

"That makes no sense at all."

"You don't see it, and I knew you wouldn't," he said, handing the picture back to me. "I want you to look at it. Really look at it—what do you see?"

"Two happy, blonde girls with really flat hair," I said sarcastically.

"You know what I see? I see two people who, at first glance, look very much the same. But if you look closer, you can see all the differences. This one," he said, pointing to the figure that was supposed to represent Dani, "is drawn with all the smooth lines. She has a straighter smile, her eyes are bigger, and she's taller. You can tell you spent the most time on her, trying to get all of the best parts in there. Then I look at the other girl, almost a copy of the first. But she doesn't stand quite as tall, her hair is a bit messier, her eyes are too close together, and her mouth doesn't quite make a smile. You know what else I see?"

"What, Max? Please tell me what else you could've possibly seen," I said, the annoyance reaching my voice. Max acted like he didn't notice.

"There are eraser marks all around the second girl, like you needed to point out every place where she wasn't as good."

"I'm not really sure what you want me to say. Are you asking me to agree with you—to congratulate you on something?"

"Keely, I'm trying to say that I don't see it. I don't see this girl that you think you see. The girl I see looks like this." He slowly pulled out a second paper, carefully passing it towards me. The sheet appeared new and fresh, without a single wrinkle. Even though it was folded like the other one, the creases were crisp, more exact. I opened it, trying to ignore the pounding inside my chest.

Inside appeared a single figure. She was slender but not too skinny. Her hair was pulled back into a ponytail that fell in perfect waves over her right shoulder. Big, bright eyes were set against an oval face with pink lips. The right one wasn't quite as blue as the left; a brilliant, golden yellow cut through the one half, as if someone had stolen a slice of the sun and placed it in her eye. Each feature looked designed for the girl. She was beautiful.

"I've held on to your drawing for the past three years because I wanted the chance to tell you that you were wrong. Those parts that you think are so bad...they are my favorite things about you."

"You became my friend because you wanted to tell me that I'm not as ugly as I think I am?" I tried to joke.

"No, I became your friend because I thought we could help each other. I'd show you that you're beautiful, and you'd be more likely to protect me from Jenna Milmer's boogers," he said with a smile.

"You're annoying, and you totally ruined the moment," I said as I chucked a pillow at him.

"Oh, we were having a moment, were we? You want to kiss me right now, don't you?" The yellow in his eyes burned further into the blue, leaving just a cobalt rim along the edges. My eyes drifted to his mouth, and I imagined what his lips would feel like against mine.

"You wish, Max Lerman," I said, throwing another pillow at him instead. The silence fell over us again, but that time my focus wouldn't return to the mindless magazines.

"What did you mean before—when you said I was just like you?"

"I don't know," was all he said at first. "Maybe because you are constantly searching for what's wrong with you. You also know that feeling—that you aren't good enough."

"And how is that anything like you?" Max suddenly went quiet, pretending to read the meaningless certificates that lined his wall. I knew better than to pry the words out of him. Instead, I simply sat there with him.

"I haven't ever told anyone this," he said after a long while. "I know I joke a lot about how I can do things because I'm a Lerman, but the truth is, it isn't really true."

"What isn't true?"

"My parents don't know that I found out." He hesitated, taking a deep breath in before going on. "I'm not really their son. They adopted me when I was two." I sat there, rooted in my spot, unsure how to respond.

"Wait, how do you know? Does your little brother know?"

"No, I don't think he does. The only reason I know is because I found the papers. I was looking for my dad's old baseball glove, which he said was in one of the old cardboard boxes in the garage. The first box I found was filled with stacks of papers and old pictures. I don't know why I kept looking through it. I mean, it wasn't like I thought the glove was in there. A part of me always kind of knew, even before I saw the certificates and the legal documents. I'd always wondered why there weren't pictures of me as a baby, even though my little brother has a full album of his own. I have jet-black hair, but everyone in my family is blonde."

"Do you know who your biological parents are?"

"No, it was a closed adoption. But we all know why people give up babies—either they have a crappy life or something terrible happened to them. Whichever one I was, the fact is, I wasn't supposed to have this life." I crawled up onto the bed and lay down next to him, my head propped up with my arm.

"Max, whether you were supposed to or not, you *deserve* this life. You deserve good parents and a good family."

"You asked me one time...why I went to all those support groups," he said, ignoring my statement and keeping his eyes facing forward. "I went because I wanted to know how bad life could have been. I went because I wanted to remind myself that I'm only a Lerman because I was lucky, not because I was supposed to be one. I probably would have had a pretty bad life, and I felt like I owed the world something, like I needed to prove that I didn't underestimate it."

"And how do you feel about it now?"

"You want to know? I mean, do you *really* want to know?" he said, his face showing no hint of a smile.

"Yeah. I want to *really* know," I said.

"I don't care. That's how I feel. Like, who cares about what could have happened to me? Who cares the reasons my parents had for giving me up? Now is what matters, the things I have right here. I've heard the stories. I remember the girl whose sister had been gunned down in front of her. I remember the mother whose son ran off just before he turned eighteen. And I remember the eleven-year-old stuck on heroin because his brother shot him up with some when he was nine." The look on his face made me think that he'd been carrying those stories around for a while.

"When I first moved here, I sometimes went to a support group that met in the city. There was this one homeless guy who came every now and then. At first, he didn't say much. He would just sit there, listening to everyone else talk. But one day, he started talking and couldn't stop. I'll never forget what he said. He talked about how he used to own all kinds of businesses; he had this beautiful wife, and she got pregnant with their first kid. They had this great life, but he didn't appreciate what he had. He said that he started drinking a lot, most of the time for no reason at all. He would fill plastic bottles up with vodka and drink it like water, and it got to the point where he couldn't do any of the things he once could. His stores went out of business, his wife left him, and he wasn't allowed to see his daughter anymore. He'd been homeless for almost eighteen years. And no matter how hard he tried, he couldn't get back to the place he once was.

"At the time, it was just another story. But I've been thinking about that guy a lot lately. Maybe it's because I have been doing the very thing I said I wouldn't—underestimate this chance. I already have this great life, but then here I am, a part of this stupid group who just gets me wasted and high. They tell me what I have isn't good enough and that I can have even more. The greed started to get to me. It almost made me forget that I am already so damn lucky."

"So, what are you going to do?" I asked.

"I think I'm going to leave the Underground."

"But they said that we can't...they said that if we ever left, they would make sure our lives were ruined," I said, fumbling over my words.

"Who says—a kid three years older than me with a rich daddy? Keely, don't you see, they are already ruining us! They branded us like we're livestock, for Chrissake! I mean, just look at what they've done to you. They told you to get rid of all your real friends, they forced you to wear these ridiculous clothes, and they've even started telling you what you can and can't eat. Really, where does it end?"

"They do not tell me what to eat," I said defensively.

"Really, Keely? So you're telling me those weird seaweed snacks you were eating the other day had nothing to do with that Rachel girl?"

"They really aren't that bad. And they are full of vitamins and minerals that help with breakouts."

"My point exactly. Just listen to yourself. You don't even sound like Keely anymore, at least not the one I know. You sound like some stuck-up girl who stares at herself in every reflective surface she passes." I sat up and scooted away from him. His words felt like a slap across my face. "Look, I didn't mean it like that. All I'm trying to say is that they're changing you, and I don't like it."

"Well, maybe it isn't about you, Max! Did you ever think that maybe I like fitting in for once? That maybe, just maybe, I have people looking at me like I'm not some weirdo. For the first time, they look at me like I'm worth something."

"Why does it even matter what those people think?"

"You just don't get it. It's easy for you to judge me because you don't know what it feels like to be the last one picked for things—to be someone who is constantly getting left out. You don't know what that feels like, because everyone likes you. They've always liked Max Lerman. Everyone wants to be your friend. Well, newsflash, it isn't that easy for everybody else."

"Keely, please," he said, taking my hands in his. "Please, just trust me on this. You don't need them. We don't need them. Please." He looked at me with pleading eyes, and it was almost enough to make me give in. But somewhere along the way, my clay had hardened. That was the new Keely. For once, I felt like I could do something big. I could be a Dani.

"I'm sorry, Max. I just really think I need to do this. I know you don't understand. You think I'm making a mistake, but this is something I need to figure out on my own." His head fell, and his disappointment hurt me more than I thought it would.

"This is just so much bigger than you, Keel. Trust me, I've felt it too. This kind of thing swallows people up, and it doesn't care about how it spits them back out. This is how people get lost."

"So that's what you're so worried about—that I'm going to get lost?" I replied.

"No," he sighed, "I'm afraid you aren't ever going to find your way back."

That year, I learned about the roles we play. I discovered that to get the things I wanted, I had to become something else—someone greater.

At least that was what I told myself.

The thing was, the longer I put on my layered makeup, dressed in the fancy European clothes, and made my voice sound like Rachel, the less it felt like pretending. The line grew thinner between make-believe and reality.

Chapter Ten
September 2004

There was a memory that returned to me in the blackness. It was the beginning of January, and we were heading into the city to catch a flight.
Even though Mom had told us to pack a week in advance, we still ended
up leaving the house late. My favorite Goofy hat had gone missing that
morning. It was the kind with one ear longer than the other, and I insisted
that we couldn't go to Disney World without it.

By the time we left the house, only a little over an hour remained before our flight took off. Dirty slush covered the streets in lines that looked
like a freshly tilled field. There weren't many cars on the road in those early
morning hours. I remembered the quiet and the darkness.

It happened so quickly that I almost didn't see it coming. We were
crossing through an intersection, the light still shining a bright green. She
was small and hunched over. A long, plaid blanket hung from her shoulders and dragged through the slush behind her. Mom screamed, causing
Dad to slam on the brakes. The car skidded sideways through the greasy
snow. I sat there, holding on to the thin ears that hung down from my hat,
and watched as our car drew closer and closer to the little, cloaked lady.
Our car struck her, my back window hitting her first. She turned her face
towards me, seconds before it happened. But I couldn't see her face
through the shadows.

The part that haunted me the most wasn't the heavy thud or the slight
raise of the car as we ran over her tiny body. It wasn't the screams coming
from everyone but the little, old lady. It was the reddish tint that seeped
deep into my window's spider web crack, continuing to snake its way
through long after the car came to a stop.

The cops kept calling it an accident—a devastating and unfortunate
accident. They said the woman had cataracts in her eyes so she couldn't see
too well. They said she must have "died on impact," likely saving her from
any pain. I watched as they carried her body away in a black bag, her tattered blanket left behind in the muddy snow. We eventually got back into
our car and returned home, none of us wanting to go to Disney World
anymore.

I often replayed the events in my mind, trying to picture how it could
have ended differently. There were times when I imagined myself packing

my Goofy hat first so that I wouldn't have needed to look for it in the first place. Other times, I pictured myself giving up on the search earlier. I tried to see our car crossing the intersection before the old lady even put on her green and red shawl. But each time, it always ended the same. Her body collided with the side of the car, and the crack kept spreading over my window, leaving behind her deafening silence.

Everyone said I wasn't to blame—that sometimes, bad things just happened. That was the part I hated the most.

No matter how much I wished that it didn't have to happen or that the next time would be different, it didn't change the fact that Brook and Kai were gone, just like the others before them. We were all stuck in that cycle, unable to change the outcome. All we could do was wait for it to replay over and over.

I never got over the woman and her dragging blanket, so I knew that Brook would stay with me in much the same way. The morning of October 1, 2003, felt a lot like that early winter day. Everything felt cold and damp, with too little time.

The night before, Brook and I had slept with our mattresses side by side, our bodies pressed tightly up against the bars. "Are you scared?" I asked her.

"A little bit but not as much as I once was."

"What's changed?"

She hesitated before she answered. "My mother."

"Oh," I said, unsure what she meant by it. "Do you think you will see her again?"

"I don't know. I think there is a heaven but not the kind that people normally talk about."

"What do you think it's like?"

"My mom said it's probably easier than it is on Earth. She expected that up there, we wouldn't have bodies to keep alive. And she didn't think there would be houses or cars or money like we have down here. She said that no matter what heaven holds, it has to be beautiful."

"How did your mom die?" It was a question I had avoided asking Brook over the three years we had known each other.

"She had breast cancer. My grandma died of it, too." It made me think of Nana—how she too might not have been alive anymore and how I wouldn't have known either way. "She was pretty sick at the end. After she died, I got angry a lot, so that's why my dad got me the necklace."

"Why were you angry?"

"Because she acted happy that she was leaving us. She kept talking about it being better that way and that she was okay with it. It was supposed to make me feel better, but all I heard was that my mother didn't care she was dying. I see now that I was wrong, though. It was better that she didn't have to live like that anymore. It's the same way I know this isn't how I want to live."

I rested quietly next to her, waiting for her to continue and knowing nothing I could say would have made it better.

"Mom didn't like goodbye. She liked 'see you later.' Maybe that means I will get to see her again. What do you think?"

"Yeah, I think so," I said, knowing it was what she wanted to hear. But in reality, I didn't know what to think. Hearing her words made dying sound easy, like taking a quick trip to the grocery store. But I knew that even short trips, like a week's vacation to Disney World, don't always end up the way I expected.

"Can you do something for me?" she asked abruptly, like the question had been hanging over us for a while.

"Of course."

"I need you to give a letter to someone. He probably still lives in Bronxville, first apartment on the sixth floor. The address is written on the back." I heard the paper shuffle in the darkness before she slipped it through the bars. "I found the envelope inside one of the books in the greenhouse. It took me a couple weeks to rip out enough blank pages from the different textbooks, but he shouldn't notice they are missing."

My fingers skimmed over the pointed corners. Even though I couldn't see the thin package, I was sure it said "Dad" on the front, written in her big, loopy handwriting.

"Can you promise me that you'll make sure he gets it?"

"Okay."

"You need to say it. I want to hear you promise me."

"I promise," I said, hoping she couldn't hear me crying weakly beside her. She didn't ask me anything else, as if she had read my thoughts. Instead, she began to sing softly to herself. The words were faint, but I knew the song right away. My hand automatically moved to the pendant still hanging from my neck, the tips of my fingers following the grooved words that matched the song.

For the final time, I fell asleep to Ricky Jenks in my ear. However, in that moment, it only reminded me of broken promises.

Brooklyn Parker didn't cry or scream when the bad man came for her. Instead, she flashed me her warped, metallic smile and followed him out the cell door. It wasn't because she was happy or excited for it to be over—her shaking knees and trembling hands told me otherwise. It was her final gift to me. She wanted something good to be left behind, similar to what her mother had done for her. She wanted my last memory of her to be a good one.

That smile remained in my mind. It was the most beautiful thing I had ever seen.

There weren't goodbyes or heartfelt hugs through our bars. It was just a simple, "See you later." Then, she was gone. They both were. He cleaned out their cells as he had with Chet and Clara's before them. Dias removed Brook's calendar from the stone wall, taking away my last connection to time outside of the cold basement. He stuffed it into a black garbage bag, along with her drawings and small stuffed elephant. Finally, he raked the dirt inside Kai and Brook's cells into long, straight lines. The last visible traces of their existence were erased. Yet, I still saw them all around me. Brook was in the cinnamon-scented shampoo that I used each night before bed. I heard Kai's throaty laugh as I drank my milk with the cereal still in my mouth. Their absence seemed almost larger than their presence, especially at night. I no longer moved my mattress over to the bars, but I could still feel Brook's clammy hand in mine as I fell asleep.

Even though it felt almost unbearable without her, I had one thing that stopped me from falling completely apart. It was that letter to her father. Each time I looked at the crisp, yellowed envelope, it was just enough to keep me from giving up. The last piece of Brook was in that letter. Even though I wanted to have it all for myself, I didn't open it. Instead, I tucked it away in the shallow ground next to my unwritten letter to Keely. I told myself that someday, I would be able to give it to him.

I tried to tell myself that at least I still had Mika. However, the guilt inside never completely went away after the escape. It reminded me that I had given up Brook to save him. Mika kept promising me that he would never change—that I shouldn't worry, because he wasn't like the others. But it was his year. I had seen Kai change, and I couldn't help but imagine the Mika that Dias would create—his own twisted version of Prometheus. I hoped I would be wrong.

He started taking Mika away only a few weeks after Brook and Kai disappeared. At first, it was just for a few scattered days here and there. But even in those short intervals, I couldn't sleep. Although Macy and Damien rested only a couple cells down from me, I still felt alone. I didn't know how Brook had done it—kept on fighting and scheming after Clara and Chet went away for good. Part of me wanted to help them, but another side thought, *what's the point?* It would only remind me that Brook was gone and that I had taken her place.

When Mika would return, I tried to ask him about where Dias took him. Initially, he would put it off. "I don't wanna talk about it," he would say, or, "Maybe later." But after the dust had settled again, he would open up in fragments.

"Just little things," he told me when we were alone in our cells. "He keeps me in this place. It's dark, and it gets cold at night. Sometimes, he doesn't give me any food, and I don't really get any water. I don't get let out like I do in here. He doesn't even let me leave to go to the bathroom, so I have to go in the corner. There isn't a drain or anything like that, so it just sits there the whole time. It's bad when I'm in there, but I can handle it. I think I can get through it."

"Mika, that sounds terrible," I responded. I was happy the lights were dimmed so that he couldn't see my horrified expression. "Does he…hurt you?"

"Not really…at least not too bad. He zaps me with his stick sometimes, but it doesn't hurt that much."

"Do you think it's going to get worse?" He went quiet for a short while, before continuing on.

"In the springtime, we got a lot of ants in the house. My dad told me once that ants are easy to figure out. They are workers, so they like to go out and collect things to bring back to the nest. He said that in order to get rid of them, we had to use that against them." He fell silent again, as if part of him regretted starting the story in the first place.

"So, my parents would put out these traps…these little circular discs. They had something sweet inside that would get all the ants to go to them. They would just flock to those things, and in the beginning, I thought it was just food to get them all in one place. I thought that we would just capture them all and put them back outside. But that wasn't it. Dad said that wouldn't stop them from coming back."

"What was inside of them?"

"Poison," he said. "The ants would take the poison back to their nests, thinking that it was food. They didn't even know that they were about to kill all the rest."

"What made you think about this?"

"I can't get rid of this feeling that I'm one of those ants—like he is feeding me this poison, and I don't even know I have it. I'm worried that I'm bringing it back with me, and it's going to hurt all of you."

It wasn't necessarily what he said that scared me; it was how he sounded when he spoke the words. There wasn't hesitation in his voice or room for debate. He sounded like someone who knew he was speaking the truth.

It happened the way Brook had said it would. We did fewer and fewer things together. The tasks in the activity room changed, and they became mostly independent assignments, like puzzles and handheld games. Occasionally, Dias would have us play board games against one another but not in the playroom. Instead, he made us go to the activity room where he could watch us.

It felt like I had an advantage in every activity he made us do together. When we played Monopoly, I would start out with more money and already have several properties. Sometimes, I tried to cheat to give Mika an advantage, but Dias would just give me an even greater lead the next time. Since the games usually lasted only forty-five minutes, Mika didn't have much of a chance to catch up. He was destined to lose. As for the puzzles he gave us, I knew that mine were easier, even though I never got to see Mika's. He would place us on different sides of a divider and would loudly announce each time I won. Regardless of how slowly I went, I always finished first.

There was only one "game" where I didn't win every time. Dias didn't bring it out until several months after he began taking Mika away for longer periods. It was different than the others, and I didn't like how it made me want to win. For the first time, it felt like it was me against Mika—every man for himself. Brook never mentioned it to me, but it was the kind of game that she wouldn't have forgotten.

Dias called it "Shockwave." We sat across from each other on the far ends of a long wooden board. There was a large, red button placed on each end. Before the game would begin, Dias would place a metal clip on the end of my left index finger and another on Mika's. It clamped on like a clothespin, but I soon learned that its tight pinch was the least of my worries.

The object of the game was to be the first person to hit the red button when it lit up. If you were the slower one, you would get a zap from the clip. There were three different settings: low, medium, and high. Each side of the board had a slider to pick the intensity, and we were in charge of deciding how bad the shock would be for the other person. Both sliders were hidden from the other person's view. You had to pick it before the round started, and I always made sure to have mine set to the lowest level.

Mika said he kept his on low, also, but there were times that made me question if he was telling me the truth. Instead of a small pinprick, sometimes the shocks would shoot down my entire hand and send a vibration that hurt long into the next round.

It seemed to happen the most after a string of my wins. He would look up at me through his overgrown hair, his dark, ragged clothes making him look more sinister than the Mika I knew. There would be anger in his eyes, something I hadn't seen before. Those would be the times that Dias let him win.

I kept telling myself it was just another one of Dias's tricks. But over time, it became harder to see where Dias's role ended and Mika's began. I would ask Mika about why he did it, why he changed the shock to a higher setting. He would deny it every time, saying it was all in my head. That scared me more than anything. I feared Mika couldn't see that Dias had already gotten to him.

Regardless of what Mika was turning into, my part stayed exactly the same. I still had to wear my costume, even when Mika wasn't there. Dias treated me differently when I was dressed as the girl, even when it was just the two of us. His voice took on a different tone, becoming gentler and almost tender. He would speak to me in simpler phrases and words, as if I was a small child. Even though he still carried his metal pole, he rarely threatened me with it. It was different from the way Brook had described him, as he had only been that way when she was around Kai. There were days I found myself spending more time on my makeup, as if a small part of me wanted to please him. I felt like I was no longer his Pandora. Somewhere along the way, I had become the girl from the picture.

On the days that I was alone in the activity room, he didn't have me watch the videos of the woman in the white room. Instead, he put on Disney movies, the animated kind that Keely and I used to watch together. In the beginning, I enjoyed it. They took me away briefly from the suffocating basement for a couple hours, and I lost myself in the stories with their happy endings. But as time went on, I grew to hate them. Each story repeated over and over. The characters—those pretty, pretty princesses—reminded me of how he saw me. They were how he expected me to be, and I hated them for it.

The playroom became a place to get away from the tricks and games. Sometimes, I spent my afternoons there, although Mika no longer went with me. They were the few times when I could still feel like Dani. I didn't draw pictures or play with the makeshift board games. Instead, my eyes often wandered to the shelves filled with the lost toys. They reminded me of old portraits; the eyes seemed to follow me in every direction. Their beaded faces watched me from their ledge, as if challenging me to play with them.

One day, I felt a new pair of eyes staring at me. I walked to the long shelves and stood in front of them, scanning the rows. My eyes flickered to the turned-up parts of the fake fur and the yellowed stains from past use. The action figures had the same discolored nicks in them.

Then I saw it. If I hadn't been standing so closely, I would have missed it. Tipped over on its side was a blue elephant—Brook's blue elephant. My arm reached out to take it down and away from the other abandoned toys. But my hand stopped mid-air; I couldn't bring myself to do it. Instead, I picked up the stuffed monkey sitting beside it—the one with only a single ear left. Its body was shaped like a cylinder, the top half folded over. It was one of those circus monkeys with cymbals in its hands, the type that clapped along to music playing from its insides. However, it wasn't filled with a mechanical box. Instead, there was a crinkling in its place.

I turned the monkey over to find the Velcro flap on the bottom. The two tabs were firmly attached, disguising the narrow slit. I pulled the sides apart and slipped my hand through, unsure what I would find. I expected it would be nothing—just some cheap replacement filling to make up for what was gone.

Instead, I found a balled up piece of paper. The edges were jagged on one side, as if it had been ripped out of a journal. It was a letter.

C—

It was supposed to be you and me in this together. I thought you were enough, that we were enough. But then somewhere along the way you turned into a little bitch and had to go fuck it all up. Why the fuck would you choose her over me?

So, I'll tell you what I am going to do. I am going to take her to the shed. You will have a simple choice. Her or me.

Ren

I froze, holding the stuffed animal and its ugly insides. The paper shook in my hand. I wasn't sure exactly what it all meant—what it had to do with me, with any of us. I read it over and over, trying to find the parts that sounded familiar.

The shed. Brook had mentioned a shed once—it was something Kai had told her about. He didn't say what happened there, only that he hated going.

I went from one stuffed animal to the next, trying to find other letters stashed away. But it was the only one. I made sure to return the crumpled letter to its hiding place, ensuring Dias wouldn't find it. For some reason, I didn't think he knew what hid right in front of him.

In our next "session," I made sure to ask him where the toys had come from. His eyes lit up when I mentioned the stuffed animals.

"They are very nice toys, aren't they, Pandora? I am very pleased you like them."

"Yes, they are very nice. They have been played with a lot. Do you know who they used to belong to?"

"Toys are only good if they are loved by children," he said, avoiding my question.

"Did any children love them before me?"

"Yes, some more than others."

"Who loved them the most?"

"So many questions today, Pandora. If I didn't know any better, I would say you were up to something." I automatically dropped the subject, making it the last time I mentioned anything about the stuffed animals. I didn't tell anyone about what I had found, especially Mika.

He was changing right before my eyes, and there wasn't anything I could do about it. Mika's disappearances became longer, even more extended than Kai's. *Maybe that's a good thing,* I tried to tell myself. I hoped it meant that Dias was having a harder time cracking through Mika than the other boys.

But just as with every other feeling of hope, Dias squashed it.

"Would you like to see him?" Dias asked me one day in the attitude room. He knew I was worried about Mika. For many days, I had sent most of my food back up the tube without touching it. It had felt like a couple weeks since I had seen him. However, I couldn't be sure without Brook there to tick away the days from her calendar. "I can show you if that would satisfy you. However, you may not like what you see. Are you willing to take that chance?"

"Where is he?" I asked.

"He is just down the hall."

"Take me to him," I said desperately. I readjusted the wig on my head, hoping he didn't notice how quickly I fell out of the character I had worked so hard to play.

"As you wish, dear Pandora. But just remember, each box you open comes at a price."

"I would like to see him, please," I answered, trying to recapture my pretend princess. He took me to a new door that neighbored the one that led to our cells. He removed the red keycard from his front pocket, turning slightly to look at me before sliding it into the reader. I held my breath as he pushed open the door. Dias stood off to the side, holding it open and waiting for me to enter. I hesitated, as his wide and stiff smile stopped me.

A bright light spilled from the doorway, briefly blinding me as I stepped into the room. At first, my eyes only saw white as they slowly adjusted.

The room had padded cushions on all sides, reminding me of cream-colored leather couches. The room was empty, all except for the small, curled-up figure in its corner. It was Mika. His clothes appeared a crisp white, but his hands and face were covered in red. It dripped down, staining his clothes. I couldn't tear my eyes away—it was blood.

I ran to him, collapsing on the ground at his side. My mouth hung open, but no words came out. I reached out to lightly touch him. The moment my hand met his arm, he jerked up into a crouched position. His dark eyes popped out against his red, painted face. It was as if a wild animal lived inside of them. I looked for the source of the blood, but I couldn't find a single cut or opening.

"What are you doing here?" he snarled, his voice deep and raspy.

"But you're not hurt. There is so much blood. Why is there so much blood?" It was all I managed to get out. The words cut into me, each feeling like glass inside my mouth. I already knew the answer.

It wasn't his blood.

"You shouldn't be here. You don't *belong* here," he hissed.

"What happened, Mika? What did he make you do?" I whispered so that only he could hear me.

"Get out." His hot breath slapped my face. I rose slowly, backing away from the monster that had taken over my Mika. He never looked away from me. He didn't even blink as I retreated out the door.

I tried to run away from the room, but Dias caught me in the sterile hallway. His arms reached around my back. For a moment, I didn't realize that I was against his chest, wrapped in a hug. I ripped myself away, pushing hard against him.

"Take me back to my room," I demanded, hating the way it sounded on my tongue. Since the incident with the keycard, I tried sticking to the script. I needed him to believe that I could still be his pretty, little princess.

"As you wish," he said with a twisted smile. He took me to the dressing room, allowing me my ten minutes to change out of my costume. I didn't look at myself in the mirror, avoiding the horror that remained on my face.

I put my scratchy, white uniform back on and let Dias return me to my cell. Without asking, he knew I didn't want my shower that night. I just wanted to be returned to my bed. More furniture had been added to my cell, my stained mattress resting on a spotless wooden bedframe high above the floor. They were all there—the woven rug, the wooden desk, and the matching dresser—each positioned as they had been for the others. They were all reminders that my time was drawing closer.

It wasn't until the final door clanged shut that I finally let myself cry. It wasn't just for my lost Mika; it was also for myself. I couldn't push the words from the letter out of my mind. Mika's voice recited them over and over in my head. *I am going to take her to the shed. You will have a simple choice. Her or me.*

They became the new words of my nightmares.

Chapter Eleven
September 12, 2005

They said that it would make me feel good. "Even if it tastes bad at first, it won't last very long," they told me. It was what a sister would do.

I first tried them at a high school party in the beginning of my sophomore year. The girls pulled me into a bathroom and brought out the capsules. Some were blue and white; others were decorated in cartoons. I tried telling myself that they were just like the Flintstones vitamins I took as a kid.

"What is it?" I asked that first time.

"Just something to make you feel good. It's harmless—everybody does it," Remy said. She was a friend of Frieda's and likely the only nice one out of the group I sat with at lunch. Rachel stood in the corner and inspected her manicured nails, giving me the feeling she was only there to ensure I took it.

Remy broke open one of the capsules, spilling its pile of white crystals onto the sheet of toilet paper she had placed over the vanity. She methodically rolled it into a tight ball, locking the tiny pieces inside. Then she handed it to me, looking at me expectantly.

"I'm supposed to swallow this?" I asked nervously.

"Yeah. Just drop your head back and throw it in. It goes down better when it's wet, so here, take it with this," she said, handing me her beer.

I stared at the tight, white wad, telling myself that it was only a cotton swab and that I would be fine.

"We haven't got all night," Rachel said impatiently.

Without allowing myself to think about it, I tossed the ball into my mouth and downed the beer as quickly as I could. The clump stuck to the back of my throat, releasing some of the contents into my mouth. It tasted like unsweetened chocolate, bitter and sharp. I began coughing and gagging. Remy continued to hold the beer against my lips, making the wet lump drift further down my throat.

"It's only going to get worse if you stop now. Just keep washing it down until it's gone," she said in a soothing voice. Rachel left soon afterwards, only making me feel worse about the entire situation.

"What's it going to do to me?" I asked once the nasty taste subsided.

"It's gonna make you feel *real* good. You'll thank me later," Remy said with a wink as she made her way out the door. Afterwards, I was alone in the bathroom, unable to look at myself in the mirror.

I remembered locking the door and lying in the tub, nervously waiting for the change to come. After what felt like an hour, it arrived. The sensation came over me like the flip of a switch, immediately relaxing my tense muscles. Like they had said, it was a pleasant feeling. I felt happy and loose, like a puppet freed from her strings.

By the time I returned to the party, the adrenaline rush had fully spread through me. My heart beat faster, even though my body felt like it moved in slow motion. My voice sounded like my own, but the words came out rapidly, like they were propelled by something else.

"There you are. I have been looking all over for you. Where have you been?" Max said as he grabbed ahold of my arm. His touch left behind a seemingly permanent trail of goose bumps. Even though the sisters had told me to stay away from him, he didn't care about following their rules. He stuck with me just like he said he would, in school and at the parties. And he didn't hide the fact that he liked defying them.

"I was just upstairs you worrywart," I joked, leaning my body into his. It felt like an electric shock when my leg rubbed against his. A surprised look shot across his face, which only made me feel bolder. I wrapped my arms around his neck and pushed my body up against his. He instantly became still, his arms stiffly hanging at his sides. Then, ever so gently, he rested his hands over my lower back and pulled me in closer. I felt his lips brush my ear and his warm breath tickle my neck. My stomach pleasurably tightened.

"You doing okay, Keel?" he asked tenderly.

"It feels so amazing," I said breathlessly.

"This feels amazing?"

"Everything," was all I managed to say. I should have felt strange standing in the middle of a packed room with my body intertwined with Max's. But that didn't seem to matter. I pushed my chest against his, imagining our racing heartbeats dueling against each other to set the pace. I could feel the effect spreading through Max the longer we stood there, my hips pressed snugly against his.

"Have you felt like this for a while?" he said, his voice breathy. His fingers had slipped underneath my shirt, drawing light circles into my lower back. It was an almost painful kind of pleasure.

"For like twenty minutes. It is indescribable." He became instantly still, his hand pausing against my skin. Suddenly, he pulled back and glared down at me.

"Did they give you something?" he asked, his hands digging into my shoulders. "Keely, I need you to tell me if they gave you something." His fingers burned holes into my shoulder blades.

"It was just a little piece of toilet paper," I said flippantly. Suddenly, he grabbed my hand and yanked me up the stairs, dragging me to the bathroom.

"Open your mouth," he said as he locked the door behind us and pulled me over to the open toilet. I did as he said. He put his finger straight down my throat, causing me to vomit all over the seat.

"What the hell was that for?" I said pathetically, puke still dripping from my mouth.

"You need to get that stuff out of you." He dumped out a plastic beer cup and filled it with water from the sink, handing it to me. I took it angrily, the exhilaration already starting to lessen. He had me drink the whole cup before he refilled it, making me down the second one, as well.

The nausea spread over me in waves, so I sat down on the floor and put my head against my knees. Max sat down next to me, wrapping his arm around my shoulders. I felt his head rest on top of mine.

"They tried to make me take it, too," he said softly. "They had us all take it, but I puked it up before anything really happened to me. I know they said it is fine, but it's not fine. Brad got these really bad seizures the night we took it, and then Kenneth—the kid in our grade—wasn't able to sleep for a week straight after that first time. I know it makes you feel good, but it's not real." An aching cramp replaced the pleasurable tightness in my stomach, pulling it in every direction.

"I'm sorry," I replied pitifully.

"Don't be sorry. It's not your fault." His ran his hand up and down my arm, erasing the goose bumps that he had created. "Keely, I don't want to do this anymore. I'm done. Let's end it, together." It was the first time he had talked to me about leaving the Underground since that night in April. I knew the only reason he had stayed so long was because of what he promised me. He had stayed for me. But that time, I knew he meant it. It was the first promise he was going to break.

All I said was, "Okay."

I told him we would end it before Homecoming night. He wanted to just write them a letter and be done with it, but I knew that wouldn't be enough. It had to be with the entire group, in front of everyone. I figured the only way they would let us go was if they all heard it from us. That way, they could see we didn't mean any trouble by it—that we just wanted to be left alone.

"They are going to make an example out of us, that's what they're going to do," Max told me one night. We were tucked away in my room, which had come a long way since its two-poster beginning. Artsy paintings filled my walls, the kind with senseless squiggles that people somehow found greater meaning in. Jewelry stands containing thick necklaces and dangly earrings had replaced the action figurines on my shelves. My ceiling appeared empty; only discolored and faded outlines remained, reminding me of the stars that had once been there.

"I think we need to tell all of them at once that we want out," I said.

"You're wrong. If we say it in front of everyone, it's going to start something. It's about power, and if they think other people are planning on leaving too, they are going to do whatever they can to squash us."

"But no one else is planning on leaving. They won't even have to worry about that."

"You think we are the only ones? Brad told me two weeks ago that he is waiting for my lead and then he's out, too. Two of the junior guys were talking in the locker room the other day about how they've had enough, but they don't want to be the first ones to leave. We are going to be the start of something, and it's going to happen whether we like it or not. But we need to do it as quietly as we can so that the attention is off us. If they think we are leading this thing, it's only going to make it worse."

"Okay, so how are we supposed to do this?"

"We just stop showing up. You stop talking to those girls, we don't go to those parties anymore—especially the ones out at the lake. We just lay low." The lake parties started the summer after freshman year. They were the private Underground gatherings that happened on the first Saturday of every month. The parties were always at Jeff Tillman's summer home; he was one of the senior boys. It was just a thirty-minute drive from his main home in Ridgewood. His parents owned a massive house that sat on the edge of Lake Tappan, with the River Vale Country Club right up the road. They weren't like the other parties, though. There was something off about them, like we were all there for a much bigger reason than to get drunk and smoke pot.

"It's not that easy, Max. It's not like they're just going to leave me alone."

"It is that easy. You stick with Hillary and the guys. She's always been a good friend." I bowed my head, ashamed whenever I thought about what I had done to them.

"How are you so sure that they are going to take me back? After I just ditched them like that...they probably hate my guts." But I knew that wasn't true. None of them were cold or mean to me—only distant. They stayed away as if they thought I wanted it that way. But I got the feeling that they were waiting for something. They kept track of me from afar, and it made me hate myself even more because I didn't deserve it.

"Just trust me on this. Give it a chance. It's all going to be okay," he said as he patted my hand. I hoped that he was right—that everything would just go back to the way it had been.

But it didn't. It only got worse. The more the girls thought that I was pulling away from them, the tighter they held on. I felt imprisoned. Maybe it had been that way the whole time, and I just hadn't realized it. In the beginning, I had kind of liked being told what to do. I thought it meant I could turn into the Keely I had always imagined—the masterpiece instead of an unfinished project.

In reality, the Underground had turned me into something ugly. I had become someone else's piece of work, but it was nothing I would want to call my own. Only one thing made me forget about everything. It was that pile of crystals wrapped in crinkled toilet paper. I would parachute it down my throat when they brought out the cartoon capsules, even though I had promised Max I wouldn't. During those few short hours, I let the good feelings replace the bad ones. It never felt quite like that first time again, but it offered me enough of an escape, even if it was for only a little while.

At first, Max believed that I was trying. He thought that I was pulling away like he had. But then a month went by, and little had truly changed. I would make excuses, finding reasons to show up at the parties on the lake. I continued to sit with the Cake Shop at lunch. It wasn't until October's lake house party that everything changed.

Remy picked me up from my house that night, and I was thankful it was just the two of us in the car. She had become the closest thing to a friend in the "sisterhood." As usual, she came dolled up, glitter covering her straightened hair and shiny eye shadow compensating for her bland eyes. That was her thing—wearing something sparkly and bright to make up for her dull personality. No one was home up there, as my mom would say.

"Hey, Remy. Can I ask you something?" I said, sitting nervously beside her. She didn't bother turning down the new Usher song when she answered.

"You're my sister. You know you can ask me anything," she said with a pop of her gum. I tried to ignore the cringe that spread through me when she said that word.

"Has there ever been, you know, someone in the Underground…who left?" I asked. I didn't want her to see how deep my question went, so I focused on the car lights in front of us.

"I wasn't in it yet when it happened, but there was one girl that tried to leave. She didn't say why, just that she didn't want to be a part of it anymore. But she eventually came back."

"What made her come back?" I tried to keep my voice even, but it didn't completely mask its shakiness.

"I guess she just changed her mind," she said, bopping her head along to the song.

"That's interesting. I was just curious, is all," I quickly added.

"Does this have anything to do with your friend, Max?" She said it so casually that I didn't realize she had turned to look at me.

"No, why do you ask?" I responded, hoping my voice somewhat resembled indifference.

"Because he has been acting strange. He hasn't been showing up to things. Frieda told me he even blew off Jeff last week. No one blows him off." I tried to stifle a sudden chuckle. "I also heard Rachel talking about it. She was saying that if he's doing what they think he's doing…he's going to be punished." When I looked over at her, she quickly caught the fear in my eyes. "Keely, you have to stop him. Tell him not to do it."

I wanted to tell her that it wasn't just him—that I wanted to leave too. But I didn't know if I could trust her.

"What do you mean by punished?" I asked softly.

"I don't know, but it sounded bad. And I get the feeling that something is going down tonight, and it might have to do with Max." We didn't talk for the rest of the drive, leaving me with the sinking pit in my stomach.

Remy was right. That night, everything felt different. When we arrived, the house lights appeared dim, and I couldn't hear the loud beat of the bass coming from inside. When Remy and I walked in, most people hovered near the front door, like they were waiting for something. They all whispered quietly amongst themselves. Normally, we all went to the basement to smoke weed and listen to Frieda talk shit about half the girls from school. But that night, no one made any movement towards the basement. The girls stood silently near the others, all holding their drinks, as if more for appearance than anything else.

I snuck out onto the back deck, desperate to get away from the tension. It was barely fifty degrees out, but the cold air felt better than the stuffy fog inside. No one joined me, giving me a chance to prepare myself for what I knew was coming.

It wasn't long before the commotion began at the front of the house. Yelling erupted, but I was too far away to recognize the voices. I rushed down the deck steps and ran to the front, my fears confirmed when I reached the driveway. Five guys stood over Max, all holding baseball bats. He was kneeling on the ground, a small trickle of blood coming from his nose. Jeff—the biggest one—towered directly over him, shoving him to the ground with his boot each time he made an attempt to get up.

The crowd filled the front lawn, only adding to Jeff's excitement. He always loved an audience.

"Take a good look," Jeff shouted out, "at what a traitor's face looks like." He yanked Max's head up by pulling on the front of his hair. Max's eyes immediately fell on mine. "We accepted him as one of us. We let him feel the power of the Underground. We made him our brother, and what does he do to us? He turns his back on us! He spits in our face! He is unfaithful to those who have given him everything!" Jeff screamed, spit flying from his mouth. I felt the vomit rise up from my stomach as he threw Max's head into the blacktop. Jeff's hands tightened around the bat, swinging it above him as if preparing to step up to the plate.

Max raised a hand above his head, as if signaling a truce.

"Jeffy, it looks like our little traitor has something he wants to say," said one of the other five. The boy pounded his bat against the pavement excitedly.

"Get him up," Jeff said to the other four. They pulled him to his feet. Max flinched when he tried to put weight on his left foot. For as long as I had known Max, I had never seen him look scared. Even though he tried to appear brave, he looked terrified.

"What have you got to say for yourself, traitor?" Jeff taunted.

"I don't want to cause any trouble. I promise I won't say anything—I just want out. That's all."

"Oh, that's all, is it? So, you're trying to tell me that the mark on your foot means nothing to you—that you were lying when you said you were worthy enough to be one of us?"

"It's nothing against you. It's just not for me. I don't mean any offense by it," he said, his voice childlike.

"Do you hear that, people? He doesn't mean us any offense. He spits in our faces day in and day out, but he tells us he doesn't mean any offense. What do you have to say about that?" The horde around me started yelling, their voices sounding like a united roar. I looked around me at the pleased faces, horrified to see their excitement grow the faster Jeff swung his bat overtop his head.

"You know, every good basketball player needs a shooting hand, am I right?" Jeff asked, again addressing the screaming crowd. Before I could see it coming, Jeff slammed his bat against Max's outstretched hand. The ugly crack sounded out into the night air. Max wailed and drew his hand to his stomach, hunching over as if preparing himself for more blows. But I had a feeling they weren't going to come so quickly. With Jeff taking the lead, they would be drawn out.

When Max finally lifted his head, I expected there to be tears. I expected the fear to still be there. Instead, all I found was hate—deep-seated and unwavering hate.

"Is that all you got? Is that all you people got? Come on, tough guy! Is that the best you got?" Max started yelling, limping over and pushing his face into Jeff's. An immediate hush fell over the group—even Jeff was stunned into silence. Even though Max was two years younger, he was still slightly taller than Jeff.

"You all sit there drinking your booze and smoking your crack, and you think that makes you better than everyone?" He started laughing in a crazed way, his beautiful teeth stained red with blood. "Oh it *kills* me just how funny that is. Well, I got news for you—it makes you fucking losers! Yeah, that's right. You guys are fucking l-o-s-e-r-s, and I'd rather be brothers with a steaming pile of horseshit than call you people my family."

All of a sudden, someone started to clap. It was slow and drawn out, echoing through the night air. Vander walked out from the crowd as it parted around him. A smirk was planted firmly on his face. His clapping continued until he stood directly in front of him—Vander's body relaxed and Max's tensed.

"That was a nice little speech you had there, Lerman. Really moving, I have to say. It's really refreshing to hear you finally say what you think instead of skulking around like a little pussy. You think you're pretty special, huh, standing here and shouting all these things you know nothing about. You think it makes you tough? You feel like a big, strong man now? Well, I got news for you, too. You're nothin'. You're a nobody. You're a piece of trash that I'd rather burn than keep around because the stench is so bad."

"You can say what you want, and you can even bring your boyfriends with their puny little bats to hit me a couple times. But you will never break me."

"Oh, is that right? See, from where I'm standing, that's exactly what I'm going to do." Vander leaned in close and whispered into his ear, something only Max could hear. Whatever he said caused rage to spew out of Max. He threw himself onto Vander, trying to hit him with his good hand before Jeff and the boys quickly pulled him off.

"I swear to God, if you lay a finger on her I will fucking kill you, you hear me!" He yelled just before the bats started coming down on top of him. Vander looked down at Max, his half-moon dimple smiling over the curled ball getting blasted below him.

A burning scream erupted from within me as I saw them beat him, the cracks and thuds ringing out all around me. My feet kicked in before my brain could. I rushed towards him, throwing my tiny body on top of him. I looked into one of the terrible, shadowed faces before the blow crashed into my forehead. Two things crossed my mind before everything went black. The first was that Max's body felt motionless under mine. And the second, I hoped that I could be enough to shield him from the pain.

They said I probably had a concussion but that I would live. Probably. I woke up to Remy standing over me, and concern filled her face. My head felt like it was split in two separate pieces. I reached up and felt the massive welt on my forehead, shooting pains vibrating my skull each time I touched it.

"You probably shouldn't move too much," she said, pushing my shoulder back down into the bed. We were in a bedroom. I could hear the party underneath us—Underground life back to normal.

"How long have I been asleep?" I asked groggily.

"About a half an hour. You really should try to rest."

"What happened? Where is Max?"

"That was pretty damn stupid if you ask me," I heard Rachel say, ignoring my question. She sat in a large sofa chair in the corner, her face full of disdain.

"He's her friend, Rach. What was she supposed to do?"

"If she stayed away from him, like I told her to, this wouldn't have happened."

I managed to push myself up into a sitting position, unable to listen to her annoying voice even a moment longer.

"Where do you think you're going?" Rachel stated sharply as I scooted off the bed.

"I'm going home, if that's okay with you," I replied, moving slowly towards the door without waiting for her answer.

"Well, that's *not* okay with me." She jumped up from her perch and stood in front of the door, blocking me in.

"Either you move, or I will make sure you do." She stood over me, drawing her face in close to mine. It was the first time I had ever really looked at her. Underneath all of the makeup and expensive clothing, she looked plain. Up close, she didn't look so intimidating or scary. She looked like a weak girl just pretending to be something she wasn't.

"Fine. You can go if you want." Rachel acted like it was her decision instead of mine.

"Remy, can you drive me home?" She quickly nodded back at me.

We slipped out through the back door so that no one would see us leave. Remy had parked her car away from the house, about five minutes up the road. I walked quickly, despite the banging each step created inside my head. Remy did her best to keep up with me.

"Keely, you really should slow down. You got hit pretty hard."

"What happened to Max, Remy? You need to tell me what happened to Max," I said frantically, once we were far enough away from the house.

"I—I don't know. I think they took him home."

"You think or you know? Remy, he could be dead somewhere!"

"I don't know. I've been with you the whole time. I know that they took him away, but I don't know where," she said pathetically. I felt the panic building inside, and the paralyzing uneasiness swept over me.

When we finally reached Remy's car, I yanked the door open and reached for my purse, which still lay on the floor from earlier. I grabbed my phone and punched in Max's speed dial, but no one answered. After I hung up, I dialed his home phone. His mother picked up on the third ring.

"Lerman's, this is Carol speaking."

"Mrs. Lerman, is Max home?" I shot back, my voice sounding frightened.

"Keely? Sweetie, I thought he was with you."

"No, he's not. I'm wondering if you can check to see if he is home."

"Okay, sweetie. Hold on one sec." I heard the phone rustle as she placed it down and imagined her walking from the living room to the bottom of the stairs. "Hey, Pete, is Max up there?" I overheard. His dad answered, but the muffled reply was too distant for me to make out the words.

"Is he there?" Remy asked. She sounded on the verge of tears.

"I don't know, they're checking now." Her footsteps grew louder, as she walked back to the phone.

"Keely, he's not home as far as we can see. Is everything okay? You sound like something's wrong."

"Mrs. Lerman, can you please check one more time, like on the porch or in the backyard?"

"Keely, I need you to tell me what's going on. You're starting to scare me."

"I think Max is hurt," I said, tears streaming down my face. "Please, I need you to tell me if he is there." I heard her move quickly towards the front door, the phone still in her hand. I listened as she pulled the door open, its knocker banging against the wood as she swung it to the side. There were five seconds of absolute silence before I heard her scream. She dropped the phone, and I could hear her yelling her husband's name, telling him to call 911.

Then the line went dead.

"They found him. We need to go to the hospital," I said, fastening my seat belt.

"But I don't know if we are supp—"

"Remy!"

"Okay, okay," she said as she put the car in drive and sped off into the night. I kept my eyes closed the entire drive back to Ridgewood, mainly because the lights from the oncoming cars sliced through my skull. It left me alone with the thoughts inside my broken head. *Please, God, not Max. Don't take Max, too.* I wasn't the praying kind, but in those desperate moments, I did my best to become one.

We arrived at Valley Hospital in less than thirty minutes. She dropped me off at the front, her hand catching me before I left the car.

"I can't come in there with you. It doesn't mean that I don't care, I just don't think it would be good if I did." I nodded my head to tell her I understood. "I know you don't want to hear this now, but they are going to ask questions. They are going to want to know what happened."

"And I'm going to tell them."

"I don't think you should," she said tearfully. She looked scared. "I think it would be bad for you. It would be bad for Max."

I grabbed my purse and got out of the car, pausing before I closed the door. "Thanks for driving me, Remy. It means a lot."

The hospital lights blinded me as I walked through the main entrance. Only a handful of people were scattered about the waiting room. They stared oddly back at me. I ran to the front desk, ringing the bell several times, even though the receptionist sat right in front of me.

"May I help you?" she asked blankly.

"Yes, do you know if a boy named Max Lerman was brought in?"

"I'm not authorized to give out that information."

"But it's an emergency!"

"Rules are rules, sweetheart. Can't break 'em. Can't change 'em." She returned to the crossword in front of her. I felt disoriented as I looked about the waiting room, nearly missing Mrs. Lerman hunched against Max's dad in the far corner. Her shoulders were visibly shaking. I hesitated before walking to them. Max's brother sat a few seats away, his head buried in his hands. I quickly took down my hair from its bun, hoping it fell fully over the growing lump on my forehead.

I approached them cautiously, unsure of what I would say. Remy's words rang in my head. Before I had a chance to talk with Max, I had to be careful. It had all become more serious than I had ever imagined, and I didn't know how far they were willing to take it.

"Mr. and Mrs. Lerman?" I asked nervously when I reached their chairs. Mrs. Lerman jumped up and immediately pulled me into her chest, holding me tenderly. She didn't question me or demand that I tell her what happened. She just held me close to her, rocking me slightly back and forth. Mr. Lerman came up behind her and wrapped us both in a hug, reminding me of my parents. Lewie, Max's younger brother, then put his arms around his mother. We stood that way for a while, intertwined together.

"Thank you," Mr. Lerman said gruffly into my back. "Thank you for saving our son." I didn't say anything back but simply cried along with them, hoping that four people's wishes to God would be enough.

The doctors came out two long hours later. They said that he was stable, but he had suffered a pretty terrible beating. They said he was lucky to be alive.

Max had a broken wrist, several cracked ribs, a sprained ankle, and a concussion, but he was going to be okay. I collapsed back in my chair after the news, the relief giving way to light-headedness.

They let us in to see him shortly afterwards. When I saw him lying in the hospital bed, the dim light cast over his swollen face, I felt the shame and guilt wash over me. It was my fault. I could have prevented it. If only I hadn't been so scared and selfish.

The four of us sat around his bed, waiting for him to wake up. I tried to fight off sleep in the uncomfortable hospital chair, but my head kept lolling to the side, regardless of how hard I tried to keep it up.

"Sweetie, what is that on your head?" Mrs. Lerman asked as she pulled my hair back, revealing my welt. "Oh my goodness, Keely, how did you get this? Were you with Max when it happened? Did they attack you, too?"

"I—no, it's nothing. It happened yesterday—falling out of bed," I said, self-consciously pulling away from her and replacing my hair overtop the lump. I knew she didn't believe me. But Max started to wake up, allowing me to escape her questions for at least a little while.

I watched from my corner as his parents hovered over him, his father smoothing his hair and his mother continuously stroking the arm that was without a cast. They kept asking him what happened, demanding to know who had hurt him. But he refused to answer. They told him that the police would be coming by to speak with him, and he said that he would tell them the same thing. His mother cried as she begged him to reconsider.

Max seemed especially focused on Lewie, who stood next to the bed with his head down.

"You okay over there, champ?" Lewie didn't say anything. He just nodded and shook his head to the different questions that Max asked. "I'll be okay in no time. We can work on that jump shot of yours, okay? I'll even let you beat me a couple times." Lewie smiled at that one, the crinkles at the corners of his eyes reminding me of Max, even though I knew they weren't blood brothers.

"Is Keely here? Did she come with you?" I heard Max ask. I sat off to the side where he couldn't see me. I stayed very still, so as not to draw attention to myself.

"Yes, sweetheart, she's here. She was the one who called us. That's how we found you," his mother said, starting to tear up again. I got up from my chair and walked over to his bed, preparing myself for the full image I had avoided. My bottom lip quivered as I stood beside the bed, his eyes watering as he looked up at me. I kept my hands on the edge of his bed sheet, nervous that my touch would hurt him. His eyes roved over my body, searching for the places that I might be injured, too. Before, I didn't know if he remembered me jumping on top of him. But it was then that I knew.

"You okay?" he asked softly, his eyes glancing up at the patch of hair that covered my forehead.

"Are you?" I said with a small smile, challenging him the way that he had taught me. He reached his good arm across the bed to take my hand in his.

"I am now."

It was our little secret. He made me promise not to tell anyone, but it wasn't because he was afraid they would come back for him. No, it wasn't for him. It was for Lewie. They said that if he was to tell anyone what had happened, they would do something even worse to his younger brother.

I told him I could be the one to speak, to tell the police what really happened. But Max wouldn't allow it. He said he would never forgive himself if something bad happened to me, too. So we kept our mouths shut.

It wasn't like people didn't ask—almost everyone did. There wasn't anything in the paper about it or any coverage on the news. But we knew people would ask why the Maroon's starting guard couldn't play that season.

Car accident. Fell off a roof while helping his father. Just plain dumb luck. Those were the things that we told people, and after a while, they just began to accept it. His parents went with the lies. They either somehow knew what was really going on, or they trusted Max that blindly. My parents were harder to convince, especially after my mother discovered my welt the following morning. She grounded me for two weeks when I stuck to my story—that I had just fallen out of bed. She knew a bed couldn't leave a mark that size.

"I know what happened to Max, Keely. You aren't fooling anybody," she said, hoping her psychiatrist voice would intimidate me. But I had become a good liar over those past two years. She was starting to question if I was the same Keely from before—the one who couldn't tell a lie without her chin shaking or look someone in the eye without spilling her guts.

"I told you. He fell off his roof. I mean, yes, it *is* weird that we both got hurt around the same time for dumb things, but that doesn't mean it's not possible."

"No one ends up looking like that just from falling off a roof," my dad chimed in, moving to stand next to my mother in their united front.

"Well, it was a tall roof," I shot back, unnerved. They stood their ground, and I stood mine, willing them to give in. My dad eventually took a deep breath in and sighed heavily out. I knew I was off the hook, at least for a little bit.

"Keely, your mother and I are just very worried about you. You aren't home a lot. You say you're sleeping over at friends' houses but then end up coming back at all hours of the night. And you've been wearing all these ridiculous clothes. We have no idea what is really going on here."

"My grades have been good, just like you asked," I said flatly.

"We know, and we are very proud of you for that," Dad said.

"I—we want you to be able to do things with your friends, but this is starting to get ridiculous," Mom piped up.

"Okay." They paused and looked at one another, clearly waiting for me to say something more.

"That's it? You aren't going to fight us on this?" my mom asked skeptically.

"Nope," I said, popping my lips on the "p." It wasn't until then that I noticed just how tired my parents looked. My dad had thick bags under his eyes, and a section of my mom's hair had turned completely gray.

I moved forward, placing my head in the space between them and wrapping my arms around their sides. They both stood still, as if that reaction had become unfamiliar to them.

"I'm sorry. I didn't mean to hurt you guys."

"It's okay, doll," my mother said as she began to stroke my hair. "You do know that this isn't getting you out of your grounding, right?" she said, her voice still skeptical.

"Yup," I answered as I smiled into her shoulder. I figured being grounded would give me at least two weeks to find a way out of the Underground.

However, Hillary didn't let my made-up story pass as easily. Almost a year had gone by since we had last talked. She dropped by my house right after school on the Monday that followed Max's attack.

"They did that to him, didn't they?" she said as she bounded into my room. I was in bed with the covers pulled tightly over my head. I heard her stomp towards me before she threw back the blankets, a horrified look crossing her face when she saw my forehead.

"Jesus, Keely! It's like a whole other head growing out of there!"

"It's really not as bad as it looks," I said, pulling away as she reached out to touch it. It was strange having Hillary in my room again. It felt like I didn't deserve her friendship after ditching her the way I had. I pulled my knees to my chest to ward off the instant chill from my missing covers. She climbed onto the bed and sat down directly in front of me, as if waiting for me to build up the courage to look at her.

"He's been coming to me, you know. Max—he talks to me, tells me how you're doing, if you're okay. He also told me that you guys were trying to get out, that you didn't want to be in it anymore." I simply nodded my head. "I thought that by staying away you could figure it out on your own, ya know? But after what happened to Max…"

"It was terrible, Hill. They just kept hitting him, and everyone was just standing there…cheering. They were *cheering*."

"Keely, you have to go to the police."

"No, you have to promise me that you're not going to say anything.

Max doesn't want anyone to know. Hillary, they said they would go after his brother next if he says anything. What they did was—it was horrible, but he's out. It literally almost killed him, but at least he got away from it."

"So, where does that leave you? If they did that to Max, I don't even want to imagine what they're going to do to you."

"I don't know yet. I think there is only one way I can do it without being beaten to death." I paused, mostly because I knew she wasn't going to like my idea.

"What? Come on, spit it out!"

"I have to talk to Vander. They listen to him."

"No. Trust me on this, Keely. I have lived with him my whole life, and I know he is my brother and all, but there is something seriously wrong with him."

"I know he can be a jerk sometimes—"

"This is different. He was the kid who burned ants under the sun with a magnifying glass. He was the one who put firecrackers in bird nests just because he liked to see the eggs crack and the baby birds shrivel up inside. You don't get it. *He likes hurting things.*"

"Well, he hasn't done anything to hurt me so far, and honestly, this really is my only shot."

"There is still one other way. You could go to the police."

"And tell them what? That there's this group of girls who make me wear too much makeup? Hell, I don't even know if I can trust the police! Cooper Townsend—you know, the junior football player with super red hair—he was talking about how he got pulled over for drunk driving two weekends ago, and all he had to say was that he was in the Underground. They let him go. He didn't even get a ticket."

"There just has to be someone who can help you."

"There is. Vander. The only way I can leave is if they let me, and Vander is the one who can make that happen."

"But Keely, why would he let you leave if he was the one who wanted you there in the first place?"

"What do you mean?"

"Max thinks that the whole reason you were tapped was because of Vander and that he wanted to keep you close to him."

"Now, that's just ridiculous. The guy literally never talks to me!"

"Think about it. In the past, there have always been five girls and five boys tapped each year, right? Well, then why were there six girls your year? You were the last one, an extra one, Keel."

"Okay, let's say you are right. Then that still means he has to care about me. If he cares about me, even a little, then I can use that to help me."

"I'm going to tell you a story, and after I tell it, you can decide for yourself what you want to do." She waited for me to nod my head, giving her the go-ahead. "It happened when we were younger—I was eight, I think, so that would have made Vander ten. Anyways, there's this stone barn in our backyard that we used to play in together. It was kind of like our secret hang out. We were playing back there one day, and out of no-where, this one area of the floor completely fell through. We found this whole basement underneath us. In it, we found a foxes' den. There were two babies, just these tiny, little things, and they were pretty much dead. Maybe the mother got killed or just wasn't able to come back. Either way, no one was going to take care of them. We gave them food and water, and for a couple days, we kept going back there. One of them ended up dying, so I stopped going because it made me too sad. But Vander kept going back. He fed that fox up until it was full-grown. I would see it walking around our backyard sometimes, like it was some damn stray cat or some-thing.

"Anyway, one day, I decided to go back there. Sure enough, there was Vander, sitting by the barn with his pet fox. I watched them for a long time, just sitting there together. It was strange to me—how something that was supposed to be wild and mean could be like that fox was with Vander.

"I was so busy watching the fox and how he looked up at Vander that I didn't notice when he picked up the rock. It wasn't until Vander smashed it down right on that little fox's head that I realized what had happened. He just kept picking it up and smashing it down, over and over and over, for no reason at all. I was so shocked that I couldn't even scream. It wasn't until later that night, when I was in bed, that I finally let myself cry. I just kept thinking, 'How could someone spend so much time keeping some-thing alive just to end up killing it?'"

"I don't know," I said, my voice sounding suffocated.

"Do you know the part I will never forget?" I shook my head, unable to find my voice again. "The part I will never forget is the look on his face after he did it. He just looked so...happy."

We sat there in absolute silence, Hillary's story hanging in the air. I felt chills all over, but that time, it wasn't from the cold.

"So, let me ask you again. Do you still think you can trust him?"

I told him to meet me in the history section of the public library. It was private enough that no one would overhear us, but it was still in the range of the security cameras. I would be safe.

At first, I didn't think he would show. Ten minutes turned into twenty, and by the time half an hour had passed, I was sure he wasn't going to come. I had slipped him a note in the hallway that specifically said three o'clock, but I questioned if my threes had dipped too low and instead looked like eights.

"Hello, Keely," he said deeply, causing me to suck in a quick breath. "I didn't mean to startle you. Were you expecting someone else?" I turned to find Vander standing there, leaning casually against one of the bookcases.

"No, I wasn't. I'm just a little jumpy, is all."

"I didn't think you handed out handwritten notes to just anyone these days," he said, his flirty crescent smile growing.

"I wanted you to meet me here because I thought you would be the best person to talk to," I stated matter-of-factly, hoping to take control of the conversation before he did.

"And you picked the history section of the public library?" he asked lightly, taking a few slow steps towards me. It made my heart immediately quicken inside my chest, but I had come to learn that it wasn't a good thing.

"Yeah, because I knew we could talk in private."

"But not too private, right?" he said, his eyes shifting briefly to the security camera behind me.

"Vander, I need you to let me leave the Underground." I let the words spill out, hoping to release them before I lost my nerve. He stopped walking towards me, his face emotionless. I thought I saw a flicker of something flash across his eyes, but it was gone before I could give it another thought. He sighed heavily and put his hands on his hips, as if thinking deeply to himself.

"Could this have something to do with Max?"

"No, I've felt like this for a while. I just don't think I...fit." I had thought carefully about what I wanted to say to him before we met. Leaving Max out of it was my priority.

"Sure you fit. Just look at you. Look at how beautiful the girls made you."

"But that's the thing. I don't care about that. I just want to be me...the real me." I thought he was going to make it difficult—that he would call me ungrateful and tell me how foolish I was. But he didn't. Instead, he did what I had hoped he would do. He acted like he understood.

"Alright. Okay, I'll let you off the hook. But don't you tell anyone that

I'm being all soft on you, because I have a reputation to keep up. You got me?" he said with a smile.

"I won't say a word, I promise!" I replied, almost with a clap of my hands. I gave him a hug as he opened his arms to me, as if sealing our agreement. His shirt carried the familiar scent, so strong that it slightly stung my nose. As usual, I was the first to pull away as his hands lingered on my hips.

"There is one thing that I'm going to need you to do, though. Come to the lake party next weekend. It can be your...send-off, in a way." It made me uncomfortable even thinking about going back there. "I can announce it to the group, just so everyone knows that it's okay you're leaving. That way, no one will give you any problems, if you get what I'm saying."

"Yeah," I said hesitantly. A small part of me wanted to trust him. I wanted to believe that it would be the kind of farewell party where everyone talked about the good times and wished each other well at the end. I had a feeling, though, that it wasn't going to be that type of send-off. But as I stood there, gradually sliding my body out of Vander's persistent fingertips, I came to realize that it really wasn't a question. It was a demand. "Okay, I'll be there."

Vander smiled down at me, but there wasn't happiness behind it. Instead, there was something sinister—like he had me right where he wanted.

I told people different things about where I would be that night. My parents thought I would be at Hillary's. Max thought I was still grounded at home, and I told Hillary I would be going over to Rachel's house to tell her I was leaving for good. No one knew about my secret meeting with Vander or the agreement we had made, hidden behind the dusty books of Ridgewood's public library.

I didn't have a good reason to lie to them, other than it would be easier for all of us if they didn't know the truth. That way, they wouldn't have to worry. I could just get it over with.

Tressa picked me up that night. Remy had been keeping her distance ever since she left me at the hospital. Whether that was her decision or the Underground's, I wasn't sure. Tressa and I didn't talk much on the ride over there, which wasn't out of the ordinary for us. She had one of the "Now" CDs in her stereo, which had a whole bunch of songs that were popular the year before. I was thankful that at least it had one song by JoJo on there.

She parked her car down the road from the lake house, just like she normally did. But that time, I noticed she was farther away than usual. After she turned the car off, she stayed in her cheetah-patterned seat, her hands still firmly placed on the steering wheel. I sat there with her, unsure what to say, especially after riding together mostly in silence.

"Your friend, Max, how is he doing?" she asked, her eyes still facing forward. The question seemed forced, as if she didn't quite know how to ask it.

"Um, I guess he is doing better. He has to have surgery on his wrist, but the doctors said he will be okay." I didn't know how much she wanted to hear, especially since her face remained blank.

"And does he hate us for what we did?" she passively questioned.

"Probably. I think he hates why it happened more than what happened, though." She turned to look at me then. For the first time, I felt like an actual person stared back at me. It was like looking into a house that always had its shades drawn. I finally got a chance to see who lived inside.

"I think I hate us for what we did." Her eyes grew larger, almost as if she surprised herself by saying it. Just when I thought, maybe, I would have an ally there that night, the shades pulled down over her eyes again. Just like that, she went back to being the cool, aloof Tressa. She got out of the car first and started walking down the road without me. I sat there, before getting out myself, and watched as she left me without a backwards glance.

I planned to go in and get out as soon as I could. As I got closer to the house, I realized it wouldn't be that easy. *Who would drive me home? How long did I have to stay before Vander had my "send-off?"* Even though I felt like I was making a mistake, I quieted the feeling by reassuring myself that it would all be over soon.

I just had to get through that night.

Walking into the house felt a lot like that first day of sixth grade. All eyes were on me, but none of them were welcoming. Amy and Rachel talked in hushed whispers near the entryway, the hum immediately stopping when I walked through the doorway. Most of the others ignored me completely, all except for Brad, who was one of the few who had stayed friends with Max. We both fell into nervous chatter with one another, neither of us saying much of anything.

"Do you want a sip of my drink?" Brad asked, extending his cup to me. "You look pretty nervous. It may make you feel a little better." I took a small sip, thankful that it was more cranberry than vodka.

"Thanks," I said with a small smile.

"You can stick by me tonight, if you want. I told Max that I would watch out for you." He leaned in as he said it, quiet enough so no one would hear.

"Does Max know that I'm here?" I asked quickly.

"I'm not sure," he said, his voice trailing off. "Did you not tell him?"

"I didn't want him to worry. I've got it all under control," I said, trying to sound convincing.

As if on cue, Vander came strolling into the room, his cup held high.

"Why the hell are you fools hanging out around here? The real party is downstairs!" he yelled out, the crowd obligingly making its way to the basement door. I stuck myself to Brad, who thankfully made no attempt to follow the group.

Before I knew it, the room had cleared, leaving only the three of us in the empty entryway. Brad looked uncomfortable as he stood there, with Vander looking at us curiously. Vander wore a different kind of smirk on his face.

"You going down too, buddy?" he said to Brad.

"That depends on if Keely is," he answered, his voice slightly wavering. He had a hard time looking Vander in the eye, which didn't go unnoticed by the Viper. Vander then slapped his hand down on Brad's shoulder, signaling to him that his presence was no longer needed.

"Why don't you go on down ahead of us. We will be right behind you. There are just some quick things I need to discuss with our Keely here." Brad looked like he was about to throw up, but he continued to stand his ground, even with Vander's fingers digging deeper into his shoulder blade.

"It's okay, I'll be right down," I said, hoping I sounded encouraging.

"That's a good boy," Vander said as Brad reluctantly made his way to the basement door. He looked back at me one last time before he disappeared down the stairs, leaving me with an uneasy feeling. "New watch dog?" Vander said with a deep laugh.

I didn't reply as I stood next to him, reminding myself that everything would be okay.

"You seem all uptight tonight. This is your going away party. You should relax!" His chipper tone made me uncomfortable.

"When are you going to tell everyone?"

"Someone really knows how to ruin her own party, huh?"

"I'm just anxious, is all. I want to get it over with."

"Now, that isn't the kind of attitude you should have at a party. You should be enjoying yourself. Here, come with me." He grabbed ahold of my hand and pulled me into the kitchen. Liquor bottles littered the countertops. "I'll mix you up something extra special. You won't even be able to taste the alcohol."

I stood there awkwardly while he began creating his concoction. His hands rapidly poured several mixers into the plastic cup. He kept his back to me, but I made sure to watch how much of the alcohol he poured in. When he finished, he walked over to one of the drawers and pulled out a butter knife, stirring it all up before handing it to me.

"This is your goodbye drink, so we have to make sure it's good and mixed." My eyes immediately fell on the shiny, blunt knife still in his hand, and I couldn't help but think about Hillary's story of the fox. "Go on, give it a taste."

"I don't really want to drink tonight."

"One drink isn't going to kill you. Besides, there's barely a shot in it."

"Okay, one drink. And then we tell them. Deal?"

"Deal. Just one drink." He held up his own beer as a cheers, so I clicked my plastic to his glass and quickly downed the drink. I figured the sooner it was gone, the quicker I could be out of there. Vander slowly sipped his beer as he looked over at me, his back set against the counter behind him. His face appeared like he was sharing a private joke with himself.

"What?"

"Nothing," he said with a chuckle. "I was just wondering if you ever think about that kiss we had." I could feel my face getting hot, the mixture of emotions making me angry with myself. "You must think about it." He pushed off from the counter and moved gradually towards me.

"I don't really. But I'm not saying it wasn't nice," I added, trying to avoid making him upset.

"You don't? I have a hard time believing that."

"I guess I don't feel like...*that* towards you. We are friends. Or, at least I hope we are." He stood close to me, holding his bottle tightly by the neck. It reminded me of how farmers on TV held dead chickens just after they rang their necks.

"I think you must not be remembering very clearly." He let his words hang in the air before he fully closed the gap between us. I dropped my drink in surprise as he backed me up against the wall, his body pinning mine in place.

"Vander, please get off me," I said, trying to remain calm. I craned my neck to the side to escape the beer smell on his breath. He dropped his lips to my neck, sucking on my skin until it began to hurt. I tried pushing against his chest, but he only pressed tighter against me until my lungs felt pinched in his vice. He grabbed ahold of my face and stuffed his lips into mine, digging into my mouth with his tongue.

Suddenly, I felt myself growing weaker. My body began to fall slack against his. Lead weights seemed to attach to my eyelids, threatening to seal them shut. It was as if my body had turned against me when I needed it the most. Once again, I was trapped inside, a spectator to another terrible moment.

He pulled his face away from mine, a smile creeping across his lips. I couldn't scream or move my dead legs. I just stared back at him drowsily, feeling my mind drift away from my body.

"What's happening?" I heard myself say, my voice slurred.

"What can I say? I have quite the effect on the ladies." His horrible laugh cut a slice through my mind, allowing me a brief moment of realization. But it was all too late.

I woke up with Vander on top of me. My mind felt dazed, as if I was a second behind reality. I heard banging in the background—something hard against a thick door. Someone yelled from the other side, but I couldn't make out the muffled words. My eyes felt glazed over as I looked around, trying to snap my memory back together. It was a little girl's room. Stuffed animals lined the walls along the floor. A tea party was set up in the corner for a gathering of two: a stuffed bear and a plastic elephant.

Then I remembered. Jeff had a sister who was seven. Her room was the only one in the house that nobody was allowed into.

"I know, baby. I know how bad you want this. You've been so patient. Don't worry, I'll give it to you." My neck felt weighed down. It wouldn't move when I tried to lift it from the pillow that it rested on. I felt a shiver brush over my body, making me realize that my shirt was missing. I turned my head and looked back to the line of animals, noticing my bra at their feet. It made me feel sick seeing it among the children's toys, like a snake slithering through a field of flowers.

My arms were above me, my face cradled between them. I attempted to reach my hands down to cover my bare chest, but something held them in place. My wrists felt itchy, and a slow burn spread underneath my palms. I strained my eyes to see what prevented them from moving. A thick piece of rope went in and out of my blurry vision. It took me a moment to realize that I was tied down to the bed, the four ends of the thick rope wrapped around each bedpost.

I lifted my head again and saw Vander down near my ankles, freeing my pants from my feet.

"Please," I managed to say, my throat feeling layered with cactus needles, pressing into me each time I tried to swallow.

"Don't worry, baby, I'm hurrying." I tried to turn my body on its side when he climbed on top of me, but he pushed my shoulders back down into the mattress. It was a tiny bed, the kind only made for one person. There was some kind of Looney Tunes character on the covers, but I couldn't make out exactly which one it was.

"Please," I said again. I tried to push him away with my legs. They felt weak and tingly. He straddled me, weighing my legs down with his own.

"You're going to find out why they call me the Viper, baby." He looked down at me with a devilish face. It reminded me of stone gargoyles found in cemeteries.

"Please...stop." I began squirming underneath him, which only made his weight feel heavier. He brought his face down to mine, his half-moon dimple shining back at me.

"Oh, don't be like that. You're gonna like it, I promise." His mouth pressed into mine, his tongue sliding over my closed lips, trying to pry them apart. I went to turn my face, but he held it in place with a single hand. His teeth bit down into my bottom lip. I cried out in response, which allowed him to force his way inside my mouth. He tasted like cigarettes and booze, the bitterness soon mixing with blood from my gushing lip.

When he lifted his mouth from mine and moved on to my neck, I started to scream. He reached his hand up to cover my mouth, stifling my cries.

"You're ruining the moment, Keely. You wouldn't want to do that now, would you?" he said, his eyes just inches from mine. I stared horrified back, seeing nothing but their thick, black circles.

He lifted his hand from my mouth very slowly, testing me. I took a deep breath and screamed with everything I had left, causing him to violently shove a lump of fabric into my mouth. I bit down on it, trying to force it out with my tongue. However, he only pushed it deeper into the back of my throat, making me gag.

"That's my good girl," he said soothingly as he made his way down my body, his lips leaving behind a wet trail that felt like oil on my skin.

His head was then at the most private part of me, his hands trying to force my legs open. He grabbed on to my underwear, which ripped apart in a single swipe of his hands. He held them in his palm, as if it was a prize he had won.

My eyes darted around the room, thankful for the many nightlights that lit up the walls with a yellowish glow. When Vander moved off of me to remove the rest of his clothes, I was able to see the chair leaning against the door, the top of it shoved up underneath the doorknob. The door shook every other second, quaking against the force on the other side. I was so focused on that *thump, thump, thump* against the door that I wasn't prepared when Vander came back on top of me, his flesh touching mine.

I closed my eyes, preparing for the pain to come. In that moment, I had given up—thinking that maybe if I just lay still, the faster it would be over. But the pain never came. One second, he was on top of me. The next, the door was in splinters on the floor.

Vander was suddenly thrown off of me, leaving me exposed, naked and bare. I looked over to see Max on top of him, driving his fist into Vander's face, each blow turning his head. It wasn't long before Vander lay motionless on the floor, blood seeping into the perfect, white carpet.

I felt several hands on me then as they wrapped me in a blanket and reached for the ropes that held me to the bed. It wasn't until they pulled the fabric from my mouth that I heard my screaming. I fought against them, unable to focus on any of the faces around me.

"It's okay, Keely. You're safe now. No one is going to hurt you." It was Buzz, and I felt his hands drumming against my arm as he spoke, just like Dani used to. I looked over and saw Tommy on the other side of me, tears falling down his face as he quietly untied the rope from my wrist. They held on to my hands once they were freed, standing on either side of me.

"'s okay, Keely," I heard Tommy say through his tears, doing his best to make me feel comforted. I curled myself into a ball, dropping my hands from their grasp so I could pull the blanket tighter around me.

Their voices started to sound like one big noise as I tried to shut them out. The only one I could hear through the commotion was Max's. He was then at my side, his cheek against mine. It felt wet, but I wasn't sure if it was more from my tears or his.

He wrapped me in his arms, telling me that he was sorry, that it was all his fault. He told me that he loved me.

I tried to speak, but nothing came out. My mind felt as if it was closing up, like a potato bug rolling into a tight ball. I felt myself fold into him as he lifted me onto his lap, my cocooned body against his warm one. His breathing had become heavy and broken.

"Fletch, get the car warmed up. Tommy, go call an ambulance!" I heard Buzz yell.

"No, we are taking her ourselves. I'm not letting go of her," Max said against me. He shifted me off his cast and onto his good arm, lifting me from the bed. I didn't know why I cared so much, but I made sure to look back towards the sheets. They weren't Mac and Tosh like I had thought.

They were the Tasmanian Devil.

I held on to Max as he carried me out of that house, away from the darkness, away from all the devils.

My mother and father were the only people allowed in the hospital room with me. Mom came in first to hold my hand as the doctor performed the exam, the one where I had to spread my legs all over again. She didn't cry like I thought she would. Instead, she stood strong next to me, holding my hand and not letting go.

All of my clothes were handed over to one of the nurses, and she took a sample of my blood. They asked me a lot of questions, especially after finding the burns on the bottoms of my feet.

"This isn't the first time I have seen those," the doctor said to me, a certain knowing in her voice. My mother's mood ring eyes were the color of pain, the light blue telling me she somehow blamed herself for not knowing what had been happening.

When it was finally just my parents and I alone in the room, I simply lay there with my eyes closed. I didn't want to look at the agony on their faces any longer. They sat on either side of me, holding my hands the same way Buzz and Tommy had. At first, neither of them asked any questions or made me talk about it. Instead, they just held on to me.

Before the doctor came back, my dad said softly, "Keely, I know you don't want to talk about it, but there are officers waiting outside to speak with you. I need you to be strong, baby girl. They're going to need to know who did this to you." His voice broke on the last part, nearly unable to get the words out.

"Okay, Daddy. I'll do it."

That time, I wasn't going to keep my mouth shut. People were going to know what was living within their town, and I was going to be the one who broke it to them. I told the police everything I knew, even down to the stupid code word system people used in the Underground. The only questions I wouldn't answer were the ones pertaining to Max. It wasn't my story to tell.

They took my statement about what Vander had done to me, about how he tied me down and ripped the clothes from my body. I could tell, just from their disgusted faces, they weren't connected to the Underground. They weren't going to let this one go.

"He's going to go to jail for this, I can promise you that," one of the officers said, the one with brown hair but a red mustache. The other officers called him Rusty, something that made me instantly like him.

But what I expected to come from my statements was nowhere near what happened once it got out. Someone from the department sold my story to the local television station, and all it took to light a thousand candles was that one simple match. It wasn't long before it spread. News of the Underground—a secret cult in the very depths of suburban society—soon ran rampant across the country. And for the second time, our picture was put in front of the world. News reporters showed up at my doorstep, asking me about the charges against Vander Atwood and if they could see my branded feet. Apparently, people were sick of hearing about crappy gas prices and how no one could believe Bush got reelected. They wanted to hear the gory details of how teenage kids ruin each other.

Old stories of Dani started to resurface, and I relived it all over again. Talk shows did double features on child kidnappings and how today's teens were facing more peer pressure than before. They talked about "digging up the Underground," and I was put front and center, without me having any say in it. They talked about my past, about how I was the shy one and suffered from depression when Dani was taken. Some of their sources were people I knew—those I had known my entire life. Others were psychologists I had never met. They talked about us on daytime talk shows, saying that I had accepted the former role of my sister and succumbed to the pressures so that I could be more like her. One said it was a trend we were seeing more and more of, that it was all a part of this social identity theory.

I hated to admit that the psychologist might have been right, mainly because I despised how he acted like he knew everything about us. But it still made me think, *maybe that was what I had been doing. Maybe that whole time I had been trying to give the world back its Dani Millen.*

The national spotlight on Ridgewood had a strange effect on the town. Most residents wished it would all just pass on by. I couldn't go anywhere without getting stares, except, that time, it wasn't out of pity. It was out of anger and resentment, for tainting the lovely and perfect town of ours. Many thought I was a snitch, a meddler for turning on my "friends" like that. Some people who I didn't even know approached me in public and said horrible things about me under their breath.

One day, it happened when I was out at the grocery store with my mother. We were standing in the produce section when a woman came up to me, looked me right in the eyes, and called me a dirty whore. My mother stood there, stunned. But once she registered what had happened, she screamed her head off, following the woman down the aisles. Everyone around us just stared, spectators on the sidelines.

We were never allowed back there again.

Amidst all of the fallout, there was one thing that told me it was worth it. Three girls came forward to the police, giving their statements about being raped by Vander Atwood. Two of them were in the Underground, both a grade above me. The other lived in the next town over. I recognized her from the newspaper—the girl who was always pictured in the sports section for being the star on her basketball team.

Investigations opened up for all three girls, but little was found to pin against Vander "Viper" Atwood. There wasn't any clear evidence nor witnesses to what had happened. It was just his word against theirs. People started writing them off as girls just looking for a little attention—as if that was something a girl would actually want to get noticed for. Despite the fact that they didn't get their justice, I still felt like something good had come from it. Even in that small way, they had discovered that they weren't alone.

It wasn't long before I couldn't go to school anymore, because it became so volatile. Vander was out on bail after his dad easily paid it off, publicly stating that he stood by his son and didn't believe any of the allegations made against him. Even after everything they knew about him, after everything they had heard, the people at Ridgewood High still adored him. It was clear that even though the Underground had gone into hiding and had passed into myth, it would eventually be back.

It made me think of what my mother had told me: people only get as much power as others give them. We all were the very people who created them, and we didn't even know it.

There were a select few who thought what I had done was heroic—that I was trying to change things for the better. Unfortunately, the ones who disagreed were the louder ones. All of the "friends" I had made over those past couple years rapidly vanished. It was as if I had quickly become tainted, a dirty piece of trash needing to be disposed of. The only people who stuck with me through it all were Max and the boys, and even though I was the very thing that broke apart her family, Hillary was there for me, too.

She and her mother moved out of the house after Vander was arrested. They stayed with Mrs. Atwood's sister while they looked for a place of their own. Hillary's mother officially filed for divorce the day Mr. Atwood bailed Vander out of jail. It took Hillary a couple days to come see me after that awful night, but I was wrong about why she stayed away. I had thought it was because even after everything, Vander was still her brother.

When she showed up on my doorstep three days after it happened, I knew it wasn't because she was worried about Vander. Mom told me later that she didn't want to come inside at first—that she didn't feel right about it. I imagined my dad pulling her in from the winter cold, telling her that she would always be welcome in our home. Mom and he went out to run errands so that Hillary and I could have a chance to talk, just us.

She burst into tears the moment I joined her in the living room, where she had been waiting for me. She didn't get up to hug me like she normally did. Instead, I went to her.

I told her what had happened, but I didn't go into detail; she had probably heard enough from the TV. She glanced at the redness around my wrists from time to time, but I told her that it didn't hurt anymore.

"You can say it, you know," she said after we both fell silent.

"Say what?"

"That you hate him. You can say it if you want to. I hate him, too." She knew I felt uncomfortable, so instead of waiting for my response, she just kept going. "I have been thinking about that story of the fox ever since I told you. I've been going back to it, trying to understand why he did it. But when I heard what he did to you, I figured it out. He didn't need to have a reason. Maybe people do things just because they have hate inside of them."

"I think," I said with a pause, "that it isn't just about the hate inside of him. I think it's also about the joy. He likes finding things that are vulnerable—that he can take advantage of. He gets them to trust him, to believe that he is good. Just like he did to me. And just like he did to that fox, he used that against me. I think he gets pleasure out of knowing he can do that."

She thought to herself before slowly nodding.

"Keely, I just want you to know, no matter what happens, I'm on your side. Even though he is my brother, I hope he pays for what he did to you. I hope he pays for what he did to those girls."

We all hoped he would pay. It never occurred to me that he would walk—Rusty had promised me he wouldn't. But once again, life didn't turn out the way it was supposed to. Since he was only seventeen, the case was handled quietly in a private court, where it was just us and the judge. He was charged with "sexual abuse" instead of "sexual assault," all because he didn't finish what he planned to do. It meant that, in the eyes of everyone else, it wasn't as bad—that nothing really happened.

Even though there were witnesses and there was evidence that he had tied me down, Vander claimed that it was consensual and that I wanted it to happen. The one piece of proof that confirmed he was a liar was thrown out; the blood sample showing flunitrazepam in my bloodstream somehow got "botched," making it unable to stand up in court.

He ended up taking the plea bargain: six months of therapy and two hundred hours of community service. And just like that, it was over.

I told everyone that I was going to be fine—that I would get over it. He wasn't allowed to contact me, and I was finishing my sophomore year with a home tutor. But deep down, I didn't know if that would make it okay in the end. I didn't know how I could ever go back.

But I kept those thoughts to myself. I had a feeling that Hillary and the boys would try and convince me I was wrong. They would tell me that everything would go back to normal, continuing on like nothing had ever happened. We all got pretty good at pretending that I was somehow repairing. However, it was only an illusion. It was like a colored wall—just because someone painted a new, fresh shade over its surface didn't mean the ugly, faded, puke-green underneath ever went away. It was always going to be there, no matter how much I tried to cover it up.

I had heard my mother talk about victims of trauma and how she saw people who had a hard time finding happiness again. I used to think that if someone was depressed or angry or scared, they could just snap out of it and decide to make it all go away. But I soon saw it didn't work like that. It wasn't something I could just shut on and off. Rather, it was a living, breathing thing inside of me. The creature came out whenever someone unexpectedly touched me—a brush of an arm or a palm on the back. My skin would rise, and I would feel his hands on me again. I would see them all over my body.

Max was the only one who noticed when I pulled away, probably because he was the one who most often set it off. He would take ahold of my hand or run his fingers against my cheek as he put my hair behind my ear. And each time, I would feel Vander's body on me, holding me down again.

The counselors and advocates I spoke to told me that it would get easier. It was the body's memory. "You won't react that way forever," they said. "With time and therapy, you will eventually be able to enjoy someone else's touch again." I wanted to believe them, but for some reason, I didn't think that my unforgiving body was the only cause of my dark place.

It wasn't until the fifth anniversary of Dani's death that I realized what was wrong.

My inability to be repaired had nothing to do with my traitorous skin. It had nothing to do with not having enough time or even that Vander would never pay for what he had done to me. It was that Dani was the only person who had ever been able to put me back together. I had never been strong enough to do it myself.

That screaming baby my dad talked about never really went away. She just found a new way to scream so that no one could hear her, not even herself. Whatever had been left of me after Dani went missing had been given away to the Underground. It was all to the idea of a girl that I would never become, for people like Vander Atwood.

I thought of all the mistakes I had made because Dani hadn't been there to stop me. It hit me hard to realize that I blamed her for leaving me, for allowing me to become a messed up version of my former self.

On the night of the twelfth, I snuck into my parents' bathroom and took out the little orange container, the one that held the small white pills inside. They were my dad's—the ones he had gotten after his shoulder surgery. They looked similar to the pills they gave us that night out in the woods, when they branded their mark into my skin.

I poured them out onto my bed, staring at each of their perfect, circular shapes. There were fourteen in all—the number my mother had said would make everything better when I reached it. One by one, I dropped them on my tongue and swallowed them down, waiting for that feeling to take over. I wasn't thinking about what was going to happen; the only thing I thought about was escaping it all for a little while.

I just wanted the pain to go away.

Chapter Twelve
Fall 2005

There were two things I knew to be true. One, he was trying to turn me into someone else, and I wasn't sure how close he was getting. Two, there was a part of me, and I didn't know how large a part, that knew I was going to die down there.

I didn't know exactly how long, but I knew there was about one year left of waiting. That was what I did. I waited. I didn't plan any more grand escapes or hold out hope of being rescued. When it came down to it, the only thing that mattered was what would happen in that red room. One way or another, that was where it would all end.

I would continue putting on his costumes, watching his films, completing his silly tasks, and making him believe that I was the pretty girl from the picture. Even when I wiped away the makeup from my face and returned to the white clothes, I still pretended to be her. I had become a girl held together by a zipper, my two sides fastened into one.

Mika only fell deeper into Dias's spell, which meant that it was up to me to make the game plan. I was his catcher, after all. The letter filling the monkey's insides would be our changeup, our trick play. I didn't know how, I didn't know when, but I couldn't shake the feeling that it held our last chance to save the game.

Chapter Thirteen
September 12, 2006

The wings she had made for me must have been strong enough. I never hit the ground. They said I was lucky to be alive, that there was a point when they thought they might not have been able to bring me back. I felt it too, where I was slipping past this world and into another.

But Dani wasn't the one who greeted me when I reached that place in-between.

Instead, it was a girl with dark hair and freckles scattered across her face. She looked at me as if she had known me for a long time, but I only had a vague memory of her. I couldn't remember her name, but I recognized her by the dress she was wearing—the one her mother had gotten her. She didn't say anything to me, as if glue had sealed her lips together.

We weren't standing in a white room like the ones from the movies. Instead, we were beneath a giant cherry tree in a wide-open parking lot. It felt as real as if we were alive. She stood at the bottom of the tree and simply pointed up, high into the overhanging branches. I asked her what she was trying to tell me, but she simply continued looking upwards. I followed her eyes to the writing etched into one of the distant branches, too far away for me to decipher the words.

So I began to climb. I pulled my clumsy body up the drooping branches, trying to reach the scrawled words. The higher I climbed, the farther out of reach the branch became. I looked down at the girl, appearing small below me. Her bright, blue eyes looked into mine. Even though I could feel the bark beneath my bare feet and smell the cherry blossoms, space and time passed strangely in that unfamiliar place.

The moment I stopped climbing, the tree vanished underneath me, and I fell back down onto the concrete pavement. But I didn't splatter like a rotten cherry against it. Rather, it pulled me in, the solid ground softly catching my fall. The girl then came gracefully to my side and crouched down next to me. Her crystal eyes shone in the bright light that seemed to come from everywhere. She appeared to be my age, maybe a year older. I watched as she raised a single gloved hand, the shimmering silk covering her delicate fingers. She carefully removed the fabric from each one, revealing the porcelain skin beneath. When she had finished, she reached the ungloved hand towards me. Her fingers were long and delicate, and her shapely nails glistened in the gentle light. I stretched my hand for hers.

Then I woke up.

It was instant. One second I was there with her and the next I was alone in a hospital bed, nurses and doctors standing over me. I was screaming and thrashing, my body no longer my own as they tried to hold me down. I was in a hospital gown, a flawless white.

Then I remembered the pills and how I had lost count as I placed them in my mouth. They slid so easily down my throat.

People, especially doctors, kept wanting me to tell them why I did "it," unable to say the dirty words out loud. But they had it wrong. I didn't try to kill myself. I wasn't supposed to die so young—I was supposed to live to be a hundred and six, just like my mother had told me.

No, I wanted to be able to live again but without all the pain. I needed to get away from it all, even if only for a little while. I didn't realize how selfish that was until I saw my parents there in my hospital room, clinging to me on either side of the gurney.

The doctors said that they gave me a drug to reverse whatever it was that I took. "Naloxone," they called it. It made me wish there could be a drug like that for everything in life—that when things got bad, I could just take something to reverse it all and send me back to the way things used to be.

One thing I was sure of: for me, nothing would ever be the same again. When they released me from the hospital, I went home to find my things packed up and loaded into my dad's car.

"You and Dad are leaving for Reading today," Mom told me. "I need to finish up some things here, but I am going to be up there too in a couple days." She said it in the same voice she used when asking me to clean the dishes or tidy up my room. It made me think she had been planning it for a while. We hadn't returned to Reading in almost five years. The thought of going back there made my head swell.

"But what about school? What about my classes? How long are we going to be gone for?" I asked as I looked dejectedly at the packed car. It didn't look like we were preparing for an average weekend trip. I had just started my junior year at a high school in Oradell, the next town over. Even though I had gotten much of the same treatment as I had at Ridgewood, at least it was easier to get lost in the crowd. I didn't have Max or Hillary there with me, but at least I got to see them after school and on the weekends. I thought it was enough.

"I don't know how long we are going to be gone. It's going to be for as long as it takes."

"As long as *what* takes?" I still felt drowsy, and tears welled up behind my eyes.

"Honey," she said as she leaned down to hold my face in her hands. "We can't stay here anymore. This place is taking you away from us, and we need to get out of here."

"But Mom, I can't go back there," I cried.

"I know. I know you can't. It's going to be hard for all of us. But maybe it will bring us closer to her. Maybe it will make us a family again." I could see in her face that she believed it, and I had always thought that Mom had a better understanding of things than anybody else I knew. Well, maybe other than Dani.

So I believed her.

Mom had already called my friends, and they showed up a few minutes before my dad and I were supposed to leave. I said goodbye to Buzz and the boys first, making sure to tell Tommy that he should never change his hair—that I liked it exactly the way it was. I told Fletch he was the coolest kid I knew, and I thanked Buzz for always looking out for me. I also gave him my favorite pen—the one Bumpy had made for me with my initials carved into the handle.

Hillary was next, and I hoped I could tell her everything that she needed to hear to know that none of it was her fault. I told her I loved her, and that even though I didn't know if I believed in God, I still thanked him for giving me her. She cried, like always, and I loved it all the same.

Max was the one who stayed in his car and made me go to him. He kept a single hand on the driver's wheel and didn't turn to look at me, even after I had reached the passenger's side window. He had recovered and returned to his familiar, handsome self. A small, purple scar sliced through his eyebrow, the only sign of the things that had come before. It reminded me of a comet cutting through the night sky.

"I'm not saying goodbye to you," he said, refusing to look at me.

"Well, then what are you doing here?" I joked, hanging on the car door as I opened it. He didn't laugh, just like I knew he wouldn't. I moved into the seat next to him, placing my hand on his arm. That time, he was the one who flinched. "Max, I'm sorry."

"For what? For almost killing yourself or for leaving?" He looked through me, his eyes fiery with anger. My mom told me that he had showed up at the hospital, demanding to see me. They didn't allow anyone other than my parents through, something I didn't have a say in.

"I wasn't trying to do that," I said softly.

"Well, you could have fooled me," he shot back angrily before his voice instantly became gentler. "You're not allowed to do that again, okay?" he whispered.

"Okay."

"And from now on, you aren't allowed to even think about that scumbag again."

"Okay."

"And every time you think of what it feels like, you're going to remember this." And that was when Max Lerman kissed me. His lips instantly softened when they met mine, begging me to kiss him back. He cupped my head in his hands, my mouth opening as his thumbs gently brushed my cheeks. I kissed him back as my hands automatically moved to meet his. The hum spread through me, awakening parts inside that I didn't even know were there.

When he finally pulled away, I fell slightly forward, as if our mouths were magnets resisting the separation. I could still taste his cinnamon gum on my lips. He rested his warm forehead against mine, his hands still splayed across my cheeks as we each tried to catch our breath.

"Okay," I said again, feeling his forehead scrunch against mine as he smiled.

"Good," he said back, the confidence once again in his voice. "Did I ever tell you that I love you?"

"Yes," I whispered.

"Well, I think that you need to hear it again. I love you, and I'm not going to stop. I should have said it sooner…I should have said a lot of things sooner. But I'm saying it now, not because you need to hear it, but because *I* need you to hear it."

The purr continued to flow through me, overpowering me in a way that a white pill never could.

"I love you, too."

"And you're not going to what?"

"And I'm not going to stop," I said, repeating his words back to him. I kissed him one last time before I left, letting the feelings wash over me again and rewriting my body's memories.

As Dad and I drove away that day, I remembered looking back in my rearview mirror, seeing the five of them standing there, all facing me. I didn't need to see their faces to know there was love in them. I already felt it deep inside of me, there to stay.

Nana and Bumpy cried when we pulled into the driveway. Both of them stood on the front step, holding each other as if they had been waiting there forever. Even though I hadn't seen them that often over those past five years, Bumpy still smelled like his workshop and Nana's hug held the same warmth. It made me feel good knowing that some things never changed, in spite of the passing time.

Their house was as I remembered it. The clay sculpture still sat on the small table in the front room, and Nana's liquor remained stored away in the top cabinet of the kitchen. The chair was still conveniently placed nearby, permanently separated from the rest of the set in the breakfast nook. Nothing had changed since I last visited those many years ago—all except for the line of photos of me in my pink homecoming dress that hung in the living room and our room upstairs. The rickety bunk bed had been disassembled, Dani's bed removed from mine. Gaping holes were left behind in each of the four posts of the bottom bunk, making it painfully obvious that it was missing its other half. A large picture of a pink rose had replaced our wall of pinned-up drawings and finger paintings, probably something that Nana had picked up at a garage sale. I knew they had done it to try to make it easier for me. Somehow, it only made it more difficult to return to our special room.

Nana and Bumpy didn't ask any questions about us being there. They didn't try to make me talk about what had happened down in Ridgewood. All they said was that they were happy we were there, that their "beautiful Keely" was back under their roof. Those first two weeks we just hid away together, finding excuses to avoid eating Bumpy's soup and laughing at Nana try to sweet-talk Dad and me into making her a second gin and tonic. She joked how she had two extra victims to work with. Even though all the doctors had said Nana wouldn't survive long with her cancer, some-how she was still alive and strong, the same sassy woman my bumpy married fifty-five years before.

Mom came to stay with us halfway through the third week, her car just as full as Dad's had been. They told me we were staying there indefinitely, which made me doubt if we would ever go back home. Mom told me she was taking time off from work, that she had more important things to fix than other people's problems. And Dad's book, the one we all questioned if he was even writing, ended up getting published by a big company in New York City. We could cut all the ties, and he could take us anywhere we wanted to go.

At first I didn't know how Reading was supposed to fix me. I didn't know why my parents thought it was going to be the cure for the dark thing that lived inside of me. It was just another town that had left its ugly mark behind.

I found my answer in the last place I thought I would. When I returned to our tree house, it was different from how I had remembered it. It looked smaller, and the branches surrounding it had grown denser, shielding it almost completely from view. The leaves had started to fall off the trees, covering the forest floor in a blanket of orange and brown.

Only two rungs of the makeshift ladder remained nailed to the trunk. However, I was tall enough then to reach the slabs of wood and pull myself up. I crawled inside, soon finding myself in a graveyard of what once was. Sometime over the years, the squirrels and chipmunks had found our treasures, ripping the insides from Dani's stuffed animals and scavenging through my different knickknack boxes.

I looked down at our destroyed belongings, once our most prized possessions. Somehow, I wasn't angry. Even though time had touched everything—even weathered the wooden floor—part of us still existed there. Timothy the Tiger began to look like his former self as I pushed the white filling back into his belly. Despite the acorns and dried leaves that filled one of my boxes, I could still smell the raspberry scent from the wax candles once kept inside.

It made me think about how life had affected me. It had ripped at my insides and spilled me onto the floor for all to see. I was ravaged in more ways than one. But I started to see that underneath it all, I was still there. Just like Timothy the Tiger, there were ways to make me feel full again. We may not have looked the same as before, a little lumpier and a bit more tattered. But we could be fixed. It was just about finding a way to make sense of the fragments—about rediscovering the parts I thought were lost forever.

Standing there, in the place I promised myself I would never return to, I saw that I had been wrong. It wasn't about giving the world another Dani—a girl that everyone liked and wanted to resemble. What I needed to give it was someone who didn't get it right the first time around. The world needed someone who found strength in places she didn't know existed. It needed a Keely.

That year, I found myself. Not again, because I wasn't even sure that I had ever found myself in the first place. The very place that ended up breaking me, finally pieced me back together. Despite it putting me behind, I took the year off from school. I used the time to find the right stuffing—the things to make me feel full again.

Mom and I drove to different support groups around the area, both of us listening to other people's stories to help us make more sense of our own. We heard the tragedies they survived and how they found life again. They talked about the deaths of loved ones, missing limbs they thought they needed, and losing the faith they promised themselves to always keep. It made me realize that none of us were ever alone in our pain. I had always been surrounded by others fighting the same battle, even if it had been for different reasons.

I found myself speaking up more, sharing secrets with people I didn't even really know. But it didn't change the fact that I moved them—that we moved each other. It made me think about when Dani had told me I needed to speak up more because she said I had so much to say. Until then, I didn't realize she had been right.

Max and Hillary saw the difference in me when they came up to visit. Sometimes they came together, but other times I asked that they come alone. I told Hillary it was because I wanted to have our "girl time," but the real reason was because I wanted time alone with Max.

We didn't have sex. Even if Mom and Dad hadn't forced him to sleep in the guest bedroom down the hall—the one with the wooden door that Dad could hear creak in the middle of the night—we wouldn't have done it. I wasn't ready for that yet, and I knew I wouldn't be for a while. But that was okay. He took his time with me, erasing little by little the bad memories that Vander had left behind on my body.

Max officially became my "boyfriend" the day I turned sixteen, my dad likely cursing that he hadn't changed the rule to eighteen for when I could start dating. My birthday came at the beginning of August, exactly one month before school was supposed to start back up. I had already made my decision of what I was going to do, but I figured I owed it to Max to tell him first.

"I've decided that I'm going to stay up here. I'm going to Reading Memorial next year, and I hope you know it has nothing to do with you. I just think this is what I need to do." We were lying out back in Nana and Bumpy's hammock, Max with his arms at his sides like my father had instructed. Max bowed his head as I told him, almost as if he expected me to say it. I nudged him in his side, hoping to make him turn towards me.

"There's nothing I can say to get you to change your mind, huh?" he said, his chin still against his chest.

"I need to do this, Max."

"I know. I get it. I wouldn't want to go back into that mess either," he said, giving me a small smile.

"How has it been for you?" I asked, wrapping myself around his arm—my dad never saying anything about where my arms could go.

"Oh, you know. Just the same old stuff."

"Come on. I mean it."

"Well, it's not the greatest. I'm pretty sure the Underground's back, but it seems like they are being more careful this time."

"Did Brad ever end up leaving?"

"No. With him being a senior this year and everything, he figured he would just stick it out. He still thinks it will help him get into college."

"Wait, that wasn't all a lie?"

"I think it isn't for some people. It helps the country club boys, if you know what I'm saying, but they would get help making it in anyways."

"Brad was the one who called you that night, wasn't he."

"He knew something was wrong when Vander asked to be alone with you. I'll never forget the feeling I got when he called me and said that Vander was carrying your limp body up the stairs."

"But you stopped it. That's what matters." We tried to avoid talking about what had happened that year. I told myself it was mainly because it upset Max to think about it. A silence fell over us, both of us lost in our own thoughts as we slowly rocked in the rope netting.

"You said once that you and your sister had this thing," he began to say. "You said that you and Dani gave yourself a number for when you were together."

"Yeah. Three," I said, my voice trailing off.

"Three," he repeated, as if somewhat confused by it. "You know, I was surprised when you said it was only three. It just seems like that would be too low." I laughed unexpectedly, causing Max to turn and face me. "What?"

"It's just that, it's exactly what Dani used to say. She would bribe me all the time to make the number bigger, but I never gave in."

"Why not?" he asked, catching my smile.

"I don't know. I guess I just felt like the part I played was too small for a higher number."

"Well, I think that's just crazy. You want to know why?"

"Why's that?" I said, bringing my face close to his.

"Because you alone equal more than three. You're ten, twenty, a million. And you know what else? What you give me can't even be counted. I honestly couldn't even put a number on it." I leaned in and kissed him—I didn't even care that my parents were probably standing like busybodies at the living room window. I knew Nana would eventually shush them away.

"We'll settle on infinity then," I whispered quietly to him.

"Infinity it is."

Reading Memorial High School was about the same size as Ridgewood, but I soon found out it functioned entirely different. There weren't really cliques—in fact, I had a hard time even knowing who was labeled "popular" and who wasn't. And it was all because of the school's star senior quarterback, Topher Vern.

I hadn't seen him in over six years, and even after living across the street from each other over that past year, we somehow never crossed paths. Sure, I heard about how great he was from the local news and saw his picture in the newspaper more than a couple times. But I really didn't know much else about him.

The boy I remembered from my childhood was little like the person he had grown into. He was taller than before—if that was even possible—and he no longer wore the smug look on his face. Instead, he was barely seen without a smile, and there was not one person he didn't say hello back to when he walked down the hall.

I had forgotten all about him and how he gave Dani and me that poison ivy all those summers ago. I had also forgotten about the pet feeder and the crickets, something I soon remembered when he approached me that first day of school.

"Keely Millen. I thought I would never get the chance to see you again," he said from behind me. I immediately stiffened against my locker, the loud voice taking me by surprise. However, I slightly relaxed as I turned to find his wide, friendly smile.

"Topher Vern. Someone I hoped I would never see again," I answered with a sideways smirk as I gripped my books.

"I guess I deserve that," he said, still wearing his smile. "I never apologized for what I did, you know, back at camp."

"Which part?"

"Well, all of it. I wish I never did it." I was stunned, not only by his words, but also by how sincerely he said them.

"Then I guess I'm sorry for what I did, too," I replied, looking nervously up at him. He laughed, letting me know that there were no hard feelings still held against me.

"You guys really got me, you know. I never told anyone this," he said as he leaned down closer to me, "but I peed the bed that night. When I woke up with them crawling all over me, I just let it all go." I put my hand over my mouth, smothering my laugh. "Go ahead, I know you want to. It is funny, and I did sort of deserve it."

At ten years old, I wouldn't have believed that one day I would be standing in the middle of a high school hallway, laughing uncontrollably with Topher Vern. But there I was, with tears running down my face and Topher laughing right along with me.

"What happened to you? Why are you so nice now?" I said, once I caught my breath. That was the only time his smile went away. He became serious, as if it was a question he truly cared about answering right.

"I've thought a lot about what I would say to you, if I got the chance to see you again."

"You do know that I've been living across the street for the past year, right?"

"I know, and I thought about coming over a couple times, but I kept chickening out." He paused, making me feel nervous as I waited for him to continue. "I know I wasn't a nice guy before. I wasn't nice to you, and I wasn't nice to a lot of people. When I heard about what happened to your sister, how it was the same day that you guys put that thing in my room, I thought it had to mean something. It made me feel like if I hadn't done that terrible thing to you, then you guys would have never gone to my house, and you would have never been in those woods that night. It woke me up. I guess I wanted to say I am sorry. But I also wanted to tell you, thank you."

Whatever I thought was going to come out of his mouth, it wasn't that. I had thought about that very thing before, how Topher was the one to blame for Dani getting kidnapped. However, as time went on, I realized I was wrong. The man was going to take Dani whether we were in those woods or not.

"I never thought I would say this, but you aren't a bad guy, Topher." My words had a noticeable effect on him, like they lifted a physical weight off his shoulders.

"I appreciate that. I've really tried to be better."

"I believe you. And I hope you know, it wasn't your fault what happened to Dani." Before I knew what I was doing, I reached up and wrapped my arms around his waist, mainly because it was the highest place I could grab on to. I felt his heavy arms drop to my shoulders, his way of hugging me back.

When we walked away from each other, he going his way and I going mine, it hit me—maybe the power we give to others isn't always so bad.

There was an assignment that every student at Reading Memorial had to complete in the beginning of junior year. Eleventh grade marked the time when teachers began talking about our futures. We were supposed to start figuring out what we wanted to do with our lives, and part of that was learning about college. Prior to then, I hadn't thought much about anything past the next week, let alone after I graduated. So for me, it was a first step.

They scheduled the annual college tour shortly after school had begun. Every fall, the juniors spent a day visiting two of the local colleges. My year, it happened to land on Tuesday, September 12, Dani's six-year anniversary. I didn't like how September 12 had become a yearly event—an entire day spent feeling sorry for myself and the life that couldn't exist. So, for the first time since she had left my side, I decided I wasn't going to spend it trying to remember what she smelled like or all of her stories behind each of her stuffed animals. Instead, I joined the others on the crowded bus as we made the mass exodus.

First, we visited a small community college known for its cosmetology and nursing programs. Given that I barely knew how to style my own hair and had come to hate hospitals, I spent most of my time in the Student Center watching a group of people play Hacky Sack. The second one we went to was a small private college in Beverly, a city along the Massachusetts coastline. I remembered going there as a kid, Bumpy taking us to watch the Navy ships come into shore.

When we arrived, they took us on a tour of the campus. That basically consisted of seeing a bunch of old buildings and getting to walk on the football field. A couple of college students walked around with us, each using dramatic arm gestures to act out their rehearsed speeches. They kept using lingo like "legit" and "for real," which made me think that they were trying too hard to act older than us.

The only part that I looked forward to was the lecture scheduled for the end of the day. They said the professor was somewhat of a campus legend. He only taught on Tuesdays, and there was a waiting list for the one class he taught each semester. They told us that we were lucky to have come on a day that he would be there.

"Professor Ogden is pretty much famous in the psychology community. He's written a bunch of books and has won several awards for his research on fratricide. He's pretty legit," said the college boy who walked backwards while leading us to the lecture hall.

We arrived early and were put in the front row to prevent the football players, who sat in the back, from checking out the high school chicks. Or, at least that was what our tour guide said—the same one who had been hitting on almost every girl in my class.

It was a large lecture hall, and I was surprised to see how quickly the seats filled. People spilled over into the aisles, the latecomers having to find spots on the floor. There was little chatter in the room, especially as the starting time drew closer.

At exactly three o'clock, the lights dimmed, and an immediate hush settled over the room. A large projector screen slowly lowered in front of us, its mechanical clicking the only sound in the quiet room. The platform at the front of the class remained empty, as did the large aisles on either side.

"He starts every class this way. It's all about the dramatic effect," the pervert tour guide said as he leaned over into my row. He popped his head through the space next to me, looking back and forth between my female neighbor and me. His breath smelled like beef jerky, and his smile revealed a large piece stuck between his front teeth. It wasn't until the screen lit up and the audio came on that he finally leaned back into his chair.

It was a scene from a movie I didn't recognize. A boy with bleach-white skin appeared on the screen, his body an almost translucent color. He was in a school gym, surrounded by a group of guys. They taunted him, telling him in not-so-nice ways that he was different. There was a moment in the scene when the leader of group, the one they called Johnny, challenged him to a fight. The boy didn't fight back like Johnny wanted him to. Instead, he leaned in close and told Johnny the reason why he was so mad all the time. The bleached boy somehow knew that Johnny's stepfather beat him at home, making him feel the need to do it to someone else. This only seemed to make Johnny angrier, leading him to take the poor boy outside, strip him of his clothes, and throw him in a pool of mud. The scene ended with Johnny looking down at the boy who lay facedown in the dirt and saying, "Now you got some color."

"The movie *Powder* is an American drama that features an albino teenager's struggle with his unique gift—the ability to sense the thoughts of those around him. His telepathic powers come from an electromagnetic charge that flows through his body. He sees what others cannot." The deep voice resounded over the loudspeaker, its source unknown. "Now, this is a work of fiction, but there are three psychological truths I would like to pull from the narrative. The first is the illusion of the truly independent mind. We each would like to think that our thoughts and actions are ours alone. However, that is a fallacy. Your decision of what to eat for breakfast, whom to befriend, even your choice to come to this class is really not your own. It is a product of the millions of experiences that have come before it. They all lead to this one single moment."

Suddenly, a tall, lanky man stepped out from behind the screen, his wide eyes focused on the center of the room. "The second is the fear of lost autonomy. Paralyzation, imprisonment, claustrophobia, immobilization—they are some of the physical ways that our independence can be snatched from us. However, the loss of mental autonomy—as in this clip, eliminating the barrier that keeps our thoughts truly our own—I would pose *that* is quite possibly even more terrifying."

I didn't realize how tightly my hands clenched my seat until my palms began to burn. My stiff back pressed against the cushion behind me. He walked slowly across the stage as he spoke, into and out of the shadows that revealed the deep pockmarks in his cheeks. The hairs stood up on the back of my neck each time his eyes widened at the end of a sentence.

"Bradford Tatum's character, Johnny, said, 'Now you got some color,' as he looked down at Powder in the mud. My question for the class today is why. Why did Johnny feel the need to paint Powder brown after he said those things about his step daddy?" There was a widespread rustle as everyone got out a notebook to write it down. However, I stayed completely still, never taking my eyes from him. He was older, probably in his fifties, but he still looked familiar. He had a habit of pushing his large fingers into his palms as he spoke, as if trying to dig out the words.

"I'm going to give you all one more truth before we head into our lesson today. The third truth is that—" All of a sudden, he stopped speaking, his words hanging above the packed lecture hall. It wasn't because he had forgotten what to say, and it wasn't because he was trying to leave the room in suspense. It was because he was looking right at me. In that moment, I realized why my hands couldn't let go of my chair and why my breath felt trapped at the bottom of my throat.

He was the man from the woods. I knew, not because I recognized his face or the sound of his voice. It was the feeling of when his eyes settled on mine. He was staring at me, not because he had seen my picture on TV or on some missing person's poster taped to a pole all those years ago. He looked at me because he knew my face, like he had seen it for the past six years.

Before I knew what I was doing, I felt myself rise from my chair and hover above the seated class. I clenched my fists at my sides as I willed the words from my brain into my voice. They were the words I had told myself to forget long ago.

"I apologize for doing this, but something has just come up, and I'm going to have to end class early today," he said quickly as he took off his microphone, soon disappearing into the same darkness he had come from.

The room went into a confused uproar around me as I pushed my way through the crowded row. I ran out of the auditorium, hoping that I could stop him. I burst through the main entrance and into the bright quad. Except for the lonely, scattered trees, it was empty. As students from the class began to spill out from behind me, I knew that he was already gone.

It only made sense that on the same day Dani had left me, she would somehow come barreling back.

I knew two things for certain after I had left that auditorium. One, even though I had no proof or evidence, I knew without a shadow of a doubt that Carl Ogden had taken my sister. And two, his eyes answered the question that had been tormenting me for six long years.

Dani was alive.

My sister had been alive the entire time. It explained why I had never felt her with me at her stone with the green flowers. It was why she didn't meet me when I brushed past death. And it was why I couldn't ever really let her go.

Dani was alive, and I was going to be the one to find her.

My parents took me down to the police station after they had picked me up, where I was again met with only nonbelievers. I could tell that my parents didn't exactly know how to react to my claims either, but they still believed in me. My dad demanded that the police search his house, but I had a terrible feeling that she wouldn't be there. His house was only ten minutes outside of Beverly—nowhere near where Hillary and I had originally thought he would have come from.

They told us to go home, that they would try and bring him down to the station for questioning. They said that if he had nothing to hide, he would come willingly. For some reason, I had a feeling he would do just that. There was nothing we could use against him, and I didn't want to take a chance on waiting for him to bring us to her. I didn't want him getting to her first.

When I arrived back at the house, the first thing I did was call Hillary. I didn't have any of my notebooks or maps, but I knew she would have saved them. She was a little under two hours away at Amherst College with Fletch and Buzz, just a few weeks into their freshman year. She picked up her cell phone after the second ring, and I immediately began spewing the moment she answered.

"Keely, Keely, I need you to slow down. I'm with Fletch right now, and we're having a hard time understanding you."

"I saw him. The man who took Dani. He was right in front of me. He looked at me. He looked at me like I was her, Hill!"

"Breathe, Keely. You need to breathe. You need to tell us his name."

"Carl Ogden," I said breathlessly.

"Okay, Fletch is pulling up WhitePages right now. You said he lived in Massachusetts?"

"Yes, but I don't think that's where she is! You need to look at the map—at where I put the circle. Do you have it with you?" I asked frantically.

"Yes, yes. I'm in my room. I have it here somewhere." I heard ruffling on the other end of the phone, the sound scratching through my ear. She came back a few drawn-out minutes later. "Alright, I'm looking at it now, and it doesn't go into Massachusetts. But it does run through New Hampshire, Vermont, and Maine."

"Is there any way that we can see if he owns any houses in those places?"

"Fletch can look that up right now. Here, I'm going to pass the phone over to him so he can talk to you."

"Hey, Keely babe. You doing okay over there?"

"I don't know. I'm freaking out," I said, my hands shaking.

"I know. It's all going to be okay, you hear me? We got you," he said, his voice coming in smooth and soothing over the phone. "Alright, so I ran searches on all those four states, and the only Carl Ogden that's coming up is the one in Massachusetts. I found a Carline Ogden who lives in Alfred Maine and a Carla Ogden who is in Old Orchard Beach. Both of those places are inside the circle."

"But how are we supposed to know which one is right? How can we know if they are even related to him?"

"Let me run a search to see if he has any family in the Northeast. You said that he's some famous author, right? He has to have some kind of information online." The line became quiet on their end, except for the sound of typing. They were only gone for all of five minutes, but with each second that passed, I felt more and more like she was slipping away from us.

"Guys!" I screamed into the phone, unable to wait any longer.

"Okay," Hillary said, taking the phone back. "In here, it doesn't say anything about him having any extended family in the area, but there is this one article we're looking at now that mentions his brother, Paul, who has been living overseas for the past eighteen years. It says here that it was only the two of them growing up, but it doesn't sound like they were all that close."

"Is there anything more about the brother? Does he also have a place in the States?"

"Fletch is looking at his bio now. Here, I'm going to put you on speakerphone."

"Hey, it's me again," Fletch stated, his voice echoing. "Alright, it says here that his parents lived somewhere outside New York City but that his grandparents lived up North. So I just looked up who his grandparents were, and it turns out that his grandfather is Hugh Ogden, you know, that famous painter? Okay, fine, maybe I was the only one who actually paid attention in art class."

"Fletch!" I screamed.

"Sorry, sorry. So, I want you to take one guess where Hugh lived."

"Fletch, I'm seriously going to kill you! Just tell me!"

"New Hampshire, Keel," he said, making all of the blood rush out of my head. "I just checked WhitePages to see if there are any Paul Ogdens living in New Hampshire."

"And?" I said, anxiously.

"You better sit down for this. One Paul Ogden came up. Dover, New Hampshire, which is right in your circle. But that's not all. We just mapped the address, and it said it couldn't find the exact location. It dropped the end point in the middle of a side road."

"What does that mean?" I said in a voice I barely recognized.

"It means that it's there. It's just in a place that no one can see it."

It took a little over three hours for all of them to get to Reading. Hillary, Fletch, and Buzz came in from Amherst, while Tommy and Max made the trip up together from Ridgewood. We rode in Fletch's minivan, marking one of the few times he was thankful that his parents made him bring it to college. I told them to park down the street, that way no one would see them. My parents had me on lockdown while they waited to hear back from the police. They were notified that Carl Ogden had gone down to the station without a fight. He claimed that it all must have been a big misunderstanding. Dad said they were going to keep an eye on him overnight— that they would have a squad car parked outside his house just in case.

We knew, if we were going to have any chance at it, that would be the night.

I got the signal right around eight o'clock. Fletch flashed the head-lights twice, just far enough away that I had to look in order to see it. I went downstairs and told my parents that I was going to take a shower, meaning I only had about fifteen minutes to make it out of there. The bathroom had the only window that was right next to the gutter pipe, the one that went down the side of the house. It had been Dani's escape plan for as long as I could remember.

I made sure to turn on the shower as well as the sink faucet so that they wouldn't hear me open the creaky window. It was higher up than I had remembered, but I made my way safely to the ground before running off into the night.

All five of them were there. It was almost comical seeing them crammed into the back seats. Crusty, old French fries covered the floor, and Fletch's unpacked junk from college took up half the space.

"Sorry about that, Keely. Didn't have much time to clean out the van," Fletch joked, turning around to look at me from the driver's seat.

"I wouldn't care if you pulled me in a little, red wagon as long as you got us there," I said, surprised that I even had the ability to joke in a mo-ment like that.

Our nervous energy filled the van as we made the hour-long drive to Dover. None of us really spoke as we listened to the radio stations fade in and then out. I sat in the far back with Max, focusing on the feel of his arms around me. We drove until the map directions ended, leaving us on a deserted side road.

"Okay, it basically says that we are here. Everybody keep your eyes open. I don't really know what exactly we're supposed to be looking for, but it has to be somewhere around here," Hillary said from the front seat. We all peered out into the night, looking for anything that seemed out of place.

"There! Right there!" I heard Tommy yell from the seat in front of me. We all turned to where he pointed, noticing the small opening in the forest wall. Crooked tree branches hung down over it, hiding the rough path. Fresh tire marks appeared in the uneven grass that led into the blackness below the bowed trees. Fletch reversed the van, turning off the road be-fore nosing through the covered opening.

The long stretch of dirt road cut through the woods. Trees hovered in the narrow space around us, making it look like we were heading into a tunnel. Fletch turned the music off, and we sat in silence as we made our way towards whatever awaited us at the other end. I felt Max grip my hand. I held him back, pulling our linked hands towards my chest. Overhanging twigs scraped the sides of the van, seeming to swallow us whole as we traveled deeper into the dark space. If it weren't for the headlights, everything would have been pitch black—even the moon couldn't find its way through.

The road seemed to go on forever, twisting and turning through the dense forest. It made me feel like we were rats in a scientist's maze, one dead end away from becoming lost forever.

"What is that?" Hillary said as she leaned forward over the dash, pointing into the distance. It was hard to see much of anything as Fletch crawled slowly forward. We squinted down the unlit path. As we drew closer, we realized it was a concrete barrier—the kind normally found on construction sites. A large "Private Property" sign was nailed into the cement, its words scrawled in bold, red letters. The van came to a stop right in front of the blockade. Fletch and Buzz jumped out to see if they could move it. However, by the looks of it, it wasn't going to budge.

"Well, this is as far as we can go. What's the plan, Keel?" Fletch said as he hopped back behind the wheel.

"Are you sure you want to do this?" Hillary asked, giving me an out if I wanted it.

"Guys, it's him. I know it's him. It just has to be," I said with force.

"Well, I guess this means we are gonna have to walk the rest of the way."

We agreed that Fletch would take the van back to the main road and let us know if anyone else came down the path. Before he left, he pulled out a flashlight that he had stuffed into an old McDonald's bag under his seat. None of our phones had any service, so I was thankful when Buzz distributed walkie-talkies that he had brought along. It made me think back to how they had helped Dani and I escape the Vern House of Animal Horrors. It made me feel that life, as I knew it, was about to change again.

I couldn't explain it, but the moment I stepped out of that van and into those woods, I felt closer to her. I could feel her there, as if she was standing right next to me.

The five of us continued silently on past the blockade. Hillary stood in the middle, holding the flashlight as the rest of us trailed closely behind her. The weak stream of light raked over thick debris. We stepped carefully over the downed branches scattered sporadically around us. Max still held my hand, trapping my clammy pool of sweat inside. The road continued on for about a mile before we reached the dead end. A car stood at the edge of the woods, but its rusted shell and sunken tires told us it had been forgotten there long ago. Hillary shined the light past the spider web crack that covered the side window, revealing its hollow insides.

"So, I guess we just little-red-riding-hood into the woods now?" Hillary joked, trying to lighten the situation. For the first time since I had met Buzz, he was completely still. His hands weren't banging against his leg, and his feet weren't tapping to the beat playing inside his head. Instead, he stood motionless and stared at me, his eyes shiny and eerie in the dark shadow of the light.

"Whatever happens here tonight, I want you to know that we wouldn't want to be anywhere but here. We love you, and that means we love Dani, too." Buzz said intensely, as if focusing all of his energy on the steady flow of his words. In that moment, I could tell that nothing else was on his mind. I took his hand in my empty one, flanking myself with him and Max.

We moved into the dense woods, carefully making sure that no one was left behind. Decaying tree trunks littered the carpet of dead leaves. We eventually noticed the thin path that cut through the woods. It looked worn from use, the dirt exposed and indented below the rest of the forest floor. We trekked down the slim pathway in single file, Hillary heading up the front with Buzz taking up the back.

I couldn't see anything except for Max's shoulders in front of me. From time to time, I felt Tommy's sneakers scrape the backs of my heels. Even though he didn't admit it, I knew he was the most scared out of everyone. He murmured, "Sorry," each time he grazed me, even though I told him not to worry about it. The dig of his shoed toe felt almost reassuring after a while, reminding me that I wasn't alone.

"I think there's something up ahead," Hillary said as she picked up the pace. We walked about twenty feet until the line came to a dead stop, each of us running into the next like a set of dominos. "Keely." It was all Hillary got out.

"What! Hillary, what is it?" I shouted back. She turned around, her flashlight's bright glare making me squint.

"Keely, I see a house." I felt all the blood turn cold inside my body. She was in there; I just knew it. But I had no idea what I was going to find. I had no idea if the person in there was the Dani I remembered. The doubt crept in, and I worried she wouldn't be alive.

"You okay?" Max asked as he wrapped his arm around my waist. I pressed my face into his chest and counted to fourteen. "Do you remember that first group session we had with Ms. Tabitha?" Max continued, without waiting for my answer.

I nodded my head. "Yeah, how could I forget? Carrie thought the whole session was really about her stupid BB gun scar," I tried to joke. In reality, the memory that filled my mind was the image of Max, leaning forward in his chair and looking up at me through his fire and water eyes.

"You asked about the scabs that kept getting ripped off." He bent down and kissed me, his lips thawing my cold ones. "Keely, there is a reason that this one never healed. You have been waiting six years for the answers. The only thing left to do is get out there and find them." Hillary was still standing there with the flashlight, waiting for my go-ahead.

"Alright, let's go," I said, holding Max's hand a bit tighter.

The trees parted, and we stepped out into the open yard. Crickets sounded around us, the chirping the only thing that separated us from the strange silence. The neatly manicured lawn opposed the surrounding wilderness. It felt like a figment of my imagination.

"You know what, I'm really starting to regret ever seeing *Silence of the Lambs* right about now," Tommy tried to joke, but none of us really felt like laughing.

I pulled away from Max and made the first step forward, instantly causing the entire yard to be lit up by spotlights. The unsettling brightness showered us from the top of the building.

Everyone froze.

The lights made the night sky glow. I couldn't shake the feeling that he was somewhere out there and would be able to find us. I had to remind myself that Fletch hadn't contacted us yet.

At first the lights were blinding, but slowly my eyes adjusted. The yard was much larger than I had originally thought. A massive structure loomed in front of us, reminding me of an olden day castle. Its walls were made entirely of stone, and the small window slits had metal bars overlying the glass. A thick pole stood in the middle of the yard, the kind that I had seen on elementary school playgrounds. Except, this one didn't have a ball and string. Instead, there was a chain—the kind that secured vicious dogs to the sides of trailers. There was some grass kicked up around the pole, and I hoped, more than anything, that it was an animal's foot that had made those divots.

"We should start to move if we want any chance of getting the hell out of here," Tommy said shakily.

"Yeah, I agree. The sooner we get in, the sooner we can get out," Hillary said. We made our way towards the heavy slab of wood that covered the entrance. The doorknob was a large lever that made no hint of moving when we pushed against it. Three separate locks lined one edge, appearing to belong to deadbolts locked from the inside. Max started making his way to each window, yanking on the bars, which were firmly embedded in the stone.

"Ugh, there just has to be a way for us to get in," I said as I pulled on the door's metal lever one more time. I walked around the side of the building, keeping my eyes pointed up as I scanned across the dark windows. I noticed the thick bars covered all of the ones closest to the ground. Rows of flowers and bushes surrounded the sides of the building, sharply contrasting with its ashy walls. The flowers were real, many still in bloom, their beds freshly weeded.

The crickets had stopped chirping. As Max and I kept walking towards the back of the fortress, another light shot on. I felt like we were stage actors, our presence announced by the spotlight from above. The lights behind us shut off, as if trailing our movement around the large complex.

"It's gotta be motion censored," he said under his breath.

"So you don't think someone is up there doing it?" I asked nervously, moving closer to him.

"Say it with me: he's back in Beverly. He is not here."

"He's back in Beverly. He isn't here," I repeated, feeling him take my hand again.

I expected to find a door in the back, but we were only met by an empty stone wall. Large trash bins lined the backyard, the kind designed for garbage trucks to lift with levers. They felt out of place, as no garbage truck would have been able to make it out there. All of the lids were closed, but I had no desire to look inside.

"Guys! Guys! Over here!" I heard Tommy yell from the far side of the building. We rushed towards the sound of his voice; the lights popped on and off like flashing cameras as we started to run. He stood with Hillary and Buzz, all three of them looking towards the sky. About fifteen feet up, there was a small window halfway between the first and second floor. It was tiny, but it didn't have any bars on it. It was just big enough for a small person to slide through.

"Okay, but how are we going to get in there?" Buzz said, the pen I had given him drumming rapidly against his leg. Max's sullen look told me that I would be the one going in.

"You ready for this?" I must have looked scared because he leaned down to bring his face close to mine. "Keely, you can do this. If you get scared in there, just remember that we are right outside. We aren't going anywhere."

"You are so strong, Keely. Stronger than you know," Hillary said, placing a hand against my back.

"You can talk to us the whole way through," Tommy said as he strapped a walkie-talkie to the back of my pants. His hand lightly rubbed my back. I stepped away from Max and looked out at the four standing in front of me. My eyes felt wet, and it wasn't until I reached up to touch my face that I realized tears covered my cheeks. The emotions hit me all at once; the biggest one was love. I saw it carved into their faces, in the creases around their mouths and the inkiness of their eyes. They had become my sculptors in their own ways, pushing my stuffing back inside, making me whole again.

One by one, they each stepped forward to give me a hug, likely taking my tears for fear instead of thankfulness. I couldn't find the words to tell them how I felt, so instead, I simply hugged them back. I hoped it would be enough to let them know.

At first they tried to lift me up like a cheerleader, but it was clear that none of us had that kind of experience. It would have taken at least three more people to build a high enough mount. Instead, we built a human ladder. Max was the tallest and formed our base. He stood at the bottom and braced his hands against the wall. Buzz climbed up onto his back, eventually pushing himself into a standing position atop Max's shoulders. With Tommy and Hillary's help at the bottom, I clawed my way up Buzz's back, digging my knee into his shoulder to push myself up. I heard him stifle a groan underneath me.

"Sorry, Bumblebee. I wish I wasn't so bony."

"Oh it's okay, Steel-knees. Feels like a massage down here, just lovin' it!" I swallowed my laugh, trying to keep myself from tumbling backwards. I focused on hanging on to the jagged stones that jutted out of the wall. By the time I pushed myself into a crouching position, I was eye level with the window. I tried to lift it from the bottom, but just as I had feared, it was locked.

"Is it opening, Keely?" Max groaned, his voice sounding strained.

"No. It isn't budging at all!" I said, quickly losing my calm.

"Keels, you're going to have to break it. Use your walkie, but make sure that you keep your head down when you do it," Hillary shouted up to me.

My legs felt wobbly as I stood up from my squatting position, lifting my head slightly above the window. I raised the walkie-talkie with my right hand and pressed my body against the wall, turning my face away from the glass. I aimed for the bottom part of the window, hoping that the inner latch would be nearby. On the third attempt, the glass shattered, sending the shards spilling inwards. I carefully felt for the low latch, the lever turning easily like the new windows Mom and Dad had put in the kitchen before we moved to Reading.

The window slid smoothly upwards, and my face met a wall of stale air. It was pitch black inside, something I tried to ignore as I pulled myself through the opening. I crashed into the room, the broken glass cutting my palms as I caught my fall.

"You okay, Keel? Is everything alright?" I heard Max shout anxiously from below. I held on to my shirt to try to stop the bleeding and stuck my head back outside.

"I cut my hands, but I'll be fine. I'm going to try and open the front door so wait for me there." I turned back around and tried to let my eyes adjust to the darkness. I wished I had brought the flashlight with me. The surrounding blackness was suffocating. I had to consciously remind myself to breathe, desperately trying to keep the paranoia away. I pulled out my walkie-talkie and used the dim glow from its screen to light my way.

I walked forward with my hands out in front of me, my body hitting bulky objects as I tried to feel my way through. I held the small receiver close to the looming shapes, revealing white, wooden furniture stacked at all angles. They were everywhere, all kinds pushed towards the center of the room. Some were small tables and chairs, but most were tall dressers.

"What do you got up there, Keel?" Max said through the walkie.

"There's a whole lot of furniture up here," I said back.

"Well, try and make your way to a wall. Try to see if you can find some way out."

"Okay." I ran my fingers across the smooth wood, supporting myself as I tripped over and collided into the scattered furnishings. Eventually, my toe struck the wall. I slid myself through the thin space along the wall, hoping it led to a way out. I kept one hand in front of me while the other continued trailing along the wooden furniture. The blood continued to dampen my hands, dripping down my fingers and no doubt leaving a trail behind me.

As I felt along, I noticed some of the pieces had thin grooves carved into the wood. At first, I thought they were meant to be there. However, as I moved my hand down one of the dresser's sides, I realized they were put there. I held the walkie's lit screen up close to the wood, uncovering the mystery.

They weren't decorations or drawings. The entire side was covered in little tallies, every four lines containing a slash through them. There were hundreds of marks, all clumped together in neat, little rows. Those at the top were bigger, but towards the bottom, they appeared small and more dot-like than anything else. It was clear. Someone had been keeping track of something and clearly didn't know how long it was going to take.

I bolted down along the wall, pushing my body frantically through the thin pathway and away from the haunting scratches. Within seconds, I found the door and burst through the opening. Dimmed lights lined the long and narrow hallway, casting shadows over the jagged stones. The cold air felt thick and heavy. I took a sharp left and began running down the thin hall, the jutting stones nicking my shoulders as I reached full speed. I didn't stop until I reached the stairs at the end. They were stone steps that steeply spiraled down to the first floor.

The light from the large spotlights revealed the open living room. The bright glow poured through the tall, barred windows, casting long shadows across the dark floors. It was barely furnished. Only a large, white sectional and a metallic coffee table filled the space. The floors were made of polished wood, the kind that reminded me of old courtrooms. It smelled of cleaning supplies. Even in the dim light, I could tell the room was spotless.

"Keely, what's going on?"

"Keely, are you there?"

"Talk to us!" Their shouts mixed into one as they called through my walkie. I could hear their voices coming from outside as well, blasting through my receiver after a short delay. I followed the sound, which led me into a front hallway. It didn't take me long to find the colossal front door.

"Keely, are you there?" I heard Tommy yell frantically.

"Come on, girl. You have to give us something!" Hillary said.

"I'm here! I made it down!" I yelled back, banging my fists on the door to reassure them. I immediately flicked on the light switch near the door, turning on the chandelier above me. Instead of finding deadbolt handles, there were three keyholes that mirrored the locks from the other side. It hit me—they were not simply to lock people out; they were also to lock them in.

"Guys! I can't open the door! It needs some sort of key! I—what am I supposed to do?" I felt the panic begin to rise inside of me.

"It's okay, Keely," I heard Max utter from the other side. "Try to look around and see if there is some sort of key nearby. There has to be something in there to get it open."

I looked around me, seeing no hook or shelf that could have held a key. I continued searching along the walls of the tall entryway. A distant hum began as I walked farther away from the sealed entrance. I followed it to a swinging door, the muted light reflecting off its wavy, metallic surface.

Lights immediately shot on when I entered the room, briefly blinding me. As my eyes adjusted, I saw that the room was massive, almost spanning the entire length of the building. There was a line of stoves and wide sinks, industrial dishwashers and towering refrigerators. A long stainless steel table sat in the center of the room, its counters covered by plastic containers and trays. But the only thing I found myself focusing on was the row of large tubes coming out of the floor. There were eight in all, two groups of four. Each thick cylinder had two buttons on its front. A single light shone for each one. They all glowed bright green.

"Um, guys," I said into the walkie, my voice trembling.

"What? Shit, what is it?" Hillary said. She kept asking, growing louder each time I didn't answer her. Instead of responding back, I walked slowly towards the tubes, my eyes falling on the pieces of masking tape attached to the plastic. There was writing on each, and it wasn't until I stood in front of them that I realized they were Greek names. "Aphrodite." "Dionysus." "Prometheus." "Pandora."

"He labeled them..." I said aloud, the sound of my own voice making me quiver. I turned to run, desperate to get away from the ominous, plastic channels. It wasn't until I turned to exit that I saw the metal ring hanging from a thick, black nail beside the swinging door.

I pulled the circle from the wall, examining the collection of aged keys. They looked identical, all except for the colored tags that lacked any other identification. Their thick ends didn't match the locks on the front door. They reminded me of keys designed for antique steamer trunks and olden day jewelry boxes.

And jail cells.

I didn't run back to the door but instead prepared for what I had to say.

"Guys, I found something," I said into the walkie, cutting off Hillary mid-sentence.

"Seriously, what the hell, Keely? You can't just scare us like that and take a million years to respond!"

"I'm sorry, I didn't mean to scare you guys. I found something." I didn't hear any noise from their end, so I went on. "I found keys, but they're not for the front door. They're for something else."

"Keely, don't go anywhere until we get inside. You shouldn't do this alone." It was Max then.

I searched back through each of the large rooms, unable to find any trace of another set of keys. The wide-open space gave few places to look. There weren't any cabinets or drawers, nor shelves or hooks where he could have stored them. Hillary and the boys continued to give me encouragement, but as the time drew on, I knew what I had to do. The only thing I found was a black, metal grate in the floor behind the spiral staircase. A thick hinge bordered one side.

"Guys, there's a hole in the floor. It looks like the only way left to go is down," I cried, blinking back tears.

"We can find a way in. There just has to be another way," Max shot back.

"Max, we don't have time, okay! This is the only way. I am gonna have to do this alone." It went silent on the other end, telling me they knew I was right.

"Are you sure you want to do this? We will be here the whole time, right on the other end, but…are you sure this is what you want? No matter what's down there?"

"Max, I have to. I'm the only one who can do this." It scared me to have to say it out loud, but then I heard Dani's voice faintly in my head. *If you can live through the Tower of Terror, then you can do anything.*

She was asking me again to do something even if I wasn't ready, even if I was scared.

I turned my focus to the cavity covered by metal. The cold air drafted upwards from the depths of the darkness and through the spaces between the crisscrossed iron. I lifted and swung the heavy cover away from me, opening the black hole. I lowered my walkie into it, the screen casting a dim light through the space. It revealed a single concrete step. I ran my hands along the chamber's wall until I felt the switch embedded in its side. The light flickered on, revealing a steep and narrow stairway down.

"It's here. This is it."

"Hey, Keely?" Max said.

"Yeah?"

"Go get your sister back." I could hear his smile on the other end, making me feel like I could laugh or cry at any moment.

"K," was all I got out before the line went quiet.

I hooked the walkie onto my pant's pocket and scooted towards the opening. The stairway was wider than I had originally thought but just as steep. I stretched my arms the width of the passage, making me think that it would be a tight squeeze for a tall man. The frigid cement stung at my palms, the dried blood clinging to the scattered cuts that I had briefly forgotten. By the time I reached the last step, my radio channel had turned entirely to static, so I dialed the volume button back to zero. *So much for the walkie's tunnel coverage guarantee,* I thought.

I was on my own.

There was another silver door at the bottom of the steps, its edges browned and tarnished. My reflection looked strange in its skewed reflection, making me feel like I was a distorted figure out of a Picasso painting. A card reader was situated above the handle, reminding me of those designed for hotel rooms. Attached to the wall to the left of the door, there was a row of six black hooks. Only three were filled. Two of the hooks held keycards. One was white, the other red. The third hook contained a long rod that hung from a looped cord. I didn't dare touch it. I didn't even want to imagine what it was used for.

I should have known that the red card would be the one that worked. There was a loud mechanical click before the levered handle gave way. The door was heavy as I pushed it forward. It surprisingly didn't make a sound.

I stepped out into the middle of a hallway that looked nothing like the rest of the dusky house. It was a long corridor, covered from floor to ceiling in only white. It reminded me of the alien spaceship horror film Hillary and I had watched together one summer. Two doors stood at either end of the hallway—one in silver, the other bleeding red. The long line of bright ceiling lights faintly buzzed.

I went to the door directly across from me, holding my breath as I slid the red keycard into the slot. The lights flickered on when I stepped inside, revealing a storage room, its white walls covered in metal shelves and cabinets.

The room was large—almost as big as the janitors' room in Ridgewood High—and it was filled with all sorts of cleaning supplies. There were shelves upon shelves only of bleach. Beneath them were rows of white fabric that first appeared as cleaning rags. But on closer inspection, I realized they were clothes. There were shirts, pants, underwear, socks, and trainer bras, all folded in neat piles.

Everything appeared clean and sterile except for the far corner. Clumps of dirt clung to the rusted blade of a tall shovel. The soil looked fresh, probably only a couple of days old.

I quickly left the room, scanning the hallway. All the doors, except for the scarlet one, appeared the same grayed metal. I counted eleven identical ones in total. Strange sliding locks appeared outside some of the doors, telling me they too were used more for keeping people in than out. *To keep Dani in.* My heart began to thump faster inside my chest as I found one with the deadbolt firmly fastened. I slowly inserted the red card into the reader.

When I opened the door, there weren't any lights that blinked on.

Light spilled into it from the hall, revealing a grainy dirt floor. The air smelled like rotten food and vomit. As I opened the door wider, the light traveled deeper inside and shone against a long row of steel bars. It took my eyes a few moments to adjust. There was a shadowed silhouette behind them.

"Hello?" I didn't get any response back, not even a stir. "Is anyone there?"

I moved closer towards the bars, stepping out of the light and into the darkness. I could sense the figure rustling in front of me.

"I'm here to help you. You don't have to be scared." My hands reached out to find the bars. Suddenly, a hand reached out and grabbed ahold of me, pulling my arm into the depths of the cage.

"I told you never to come here!" the voice growled from behind the barrier. I felt his spit against my face with each word, his heavy breathing close to my ear. His grip tightened around my wrist as he pulled me further in.

"Stop! You're hurting me!" I yelled, but he didn't stop. The pain spread into my shoulder, my arm feeling on the verge of being pulled off.

"You were supposed to stay away. But you just never listen, do you, Pandora."

Pandora—one of the names from the kitchen tubes.

"I'm not Pandora! Who is Pandora? I am looking for a girl named Dani. Is she here?"

"Tricks, tricks, tricks. All your tricks."

"This isn't a trick! I'm telling you the truth! My name is Keely. Keely!"

"Keely…" he said, slow and concentrated. All of a sudden he released my arm, sending me tumbling across the dirt. I scooted away from the bars, wrapping my arms tightly around my knees so that he wouldn't be able to grab me again.

"Yes, Keely. Do you recognize that name?" I said, holding my shoulder.

"Keely…" he repeated, as if he was trying to remember something long forgotten. My eyes focused on the darkened silhouette that had seized me. His head was wedged between the bars, the shadows covering his face. I could make out the rough outline of his wild hair.

"What's your name?"

"My name?"

"Do you know Dani? Is she here?" I said, my frustration building.

"Dani…" He repeated her name over and over, more to himself than to me.

"I need to know where she is! Please, tell me where she is!"

"If you say you are not Pandora, then why do you have her voice?" he said suspiciously, breaking out of his trance. I stayed very still, hugging my knees tighter.

"What did you just say?" I whispered.

"Your voice. It's just like hers."

The thoughts flew rapidly through my brain—Pandora was Dani. She was alive.

Without hesitation, I bolted from the room, slamming the door behind me. I continued to hear the prisoner scream, "Pandora!" as I made my way up and down the narrow hall. I opened each door that lined the path, hoping to find Dani inside. However, they were all eerily empty—presentation rooms, a child's playroom, a padded chamber, a cramped bathroom.

By the end, only two rooms remained—those at either end of the hallway. I kept my back to the red door as I made my way towards its opposing one.

My hands went numb as I slid the keycard into the reader and watched the light turn green. The door creaked open, causing the sound to echo deep into the black space. Like the other room, the lights didn't come on. It was only lit by the brightness that trickled in through the doorway.

Again, I saw a room with metal bars. However, the bars were on both sides, lining the sides of the room and stretching wider and deeper. The hallway's light tracked down the middle, as if pointing the way through the path between the cells.

"Is anyone here?" I said into the silence. I heard movement to my right before a dark shape darted across the cage. "I'm not going to hurt you! Please, I'm looking for my sister. Her name is Dani. Do you know if she is here?"

"Keely?" I heard through the quiet. It came from deep within the murky jail, a tiny and distant voice. I held my breath, swearing at my mind for playing tricks on me.

I waited quietly, the air inside of me feeling like drying concrete. I watched as a single arm appeared out of the darkness. It poked out through the bars and into the slice of light. It came from the very last cell.

I moved slowly towards it, my heartbeat thumping against the sides of my skull. It wasn't until I drew closer that I saw it.

It was a peace sign.

I immediately fell to the floor and started crying, my emotions overtaking me. I crawled through the dirt towards her hand, desperate to get to it. When I reached the front of her cell, I pushed my arms between the bars and felt hers wrap around me. Neither of us spoke. In that moment, I felt all the empty spaces inside of me fill again.

"You came for me," she cried into my neck.

"I thought I would never find you," I managed to get out. I had thought about that moment for those last six years and what I would say to her. Each time, I imagined myself saying the same thing. I would tell her how much I missed her and how life wasn't good anymore without her in it. And then I would tell her I was sorry—for running away and leaving her and not trying to stop him.

As we stood there and I felt her hands on my back, all those words were forgotten. We were ten years old again, and Dani was about to tell me her biggest trick yet. In that moment, I wanted to tell her about Topher and how we changed him. I wanted her to know about Max and all the people who came with me to look for her. I even wanted to tell her the bad parts, like my scorched feet and how I almost went to hell. But then I remembered that we were already there, deep underneath Satan's garden.

"Is he here, Keely?" she asked, panic filling her voice. "Did you follow him here?"

"No, he's back in Beverly. We figured out where you were."

"We? Are other people here with you?"

"Yeah, they're waiting outside. All the doors are locked so I had to climb through a window."

"We need to go. We can't stay here." All of a sudden she became frantic, not like the Dani I used to know.

"I have a set of keys right here. Do you know if one opens your door?"

"The purple one. It's the purple one." I quickly found the flagged key and popped open her door, watching as my twin sister stepped out into the light. She had deadened, brown hair, which looked damp and stuck to the sides of her face. Her skin was pale, an almost deathly white. The clothes hung loosely from her frail body. But despite all that had changed, there were still those same stretch-of-the-ocean eyes that looked back at me— the perfect version of mine.

There was so much left to be said, but we both knew we didn't have the time. Dani took the keys from my hand and ran to the cells closest to the door. She fumbled with the clunky collection of keys, and eventually, two other kids stepped into the light. They were smaller than us and appeared younger. The girl immediately went to the boy, her wild hair mixing with his as they clung to one another.

"It's okay. We're going to take you home," I said to them, but my words didn't seem to fully register.

"We can leave as soon as we find Mika," Dani said.

"Who is Mika?"

"He's my friend. I can't leave him." I then remembered the angry boy in the other room. He called me Pandora, but he didn't seem friendly.

"I know where he is. I can take you to him, but I don't know if he's going to come with us." She didn't seem surprised by what I said but still looked determined about her choice. It was the same look she used to give me before convincing me to break the rules.

The four of us slipped into the hallway, and I took Dani to the bolted door. When it clicked open, the other two kept their distance, trembling and clinging to each other in the hallway. Dani ran to the front of Mika's cage, stopping a couple feet from the bars.

"Mika, it's Dani. I need you to try and listen to me," she said, as if speaking to a child.

"Get away from me," he hollered as he flung himself to the edge of his cage. "I told you not to come here!"

"Mika, you are confused. I know he told you that you shouldn't trust me, but he's a liar. You can trust me. I'm your catcher, remember?"

"Pandora goes places she doesn't belong. She can't be trusted to keep her mouth shut," he spat.

"Mika, I am not Pandora. My name is Dani, and you are Mika. You can pitch a sixty-two mile per hour fastball, remember? You told me once that if you could be anyone in the world, you would be Simba from *The Lion King*. I mean, who wouldn't want to be Simba, right?" She kept saying his name, trying to break through to him. The longer we stayed there, the more nervous I became.

"Can't you see I don't want you here? Why won't you just leave me alone?" he shouted, but it seemed to have little effect on Dani.

"Mika, did I tell you Keely is here? Remember when I told you about Keely? About how we drove that lawn mower into town so we could get candy? Do you remember how much you loved that story?"

"Leave me alone!" he shouted as he shook the bars like a caged animal.

"Mika, I can't open this door until you calm down."

"Dani, we have to go. I don't think he's going to come with us," I said pleadingly.

"I can get through to him. I can't leave him like this."

"We'll go get the police. They'll come back for him."

"But what if he comes back? He will kill him," she said as she looked over her shoulder at me. Her eyes were swollen with tears. "I just need a little more time. Why don't you take the others up, and get them away from here? It would be better anyways if we split up, just in case he comes back."

"Are you crazy? I'm not leaving you down here!" I said hysterically. She moved away from Mika and came to me, putting her pale face close to mine. "I just got you back, Dani. I'm not going to do it," I whispered as I pressed my forehead against hers.

"You come back then. Get them out of here, and then come back to get us," she said insistently.

"I don't know if I can do that."

"You can. I know you can. Even without Mom's saltwater spray," she added with a smile. I couldn't believe she remembered that after all those years. I didn't know how it was possible, but somehow, she was still my Dani.

"Okay, I'll do it. I'll bring them up, but I'm coming right back."

"I know you are."

The pair grabbed on to the back of my shirt as they followed closely behind. I took them up the steep stairs and through the floor grate, immediately turning on my walkie as we burst through the opening.

"Guys! Go to the window! We are coming out!" I yelled. The channel became alive with their questions, but all I focused on was getting the two kids to that window and returning to Dani. We made our way up the tight staircase and down the long, gloomy hallway. When we reached the room of furniture, I held the girl's hand.

"It's okay. This is the way out. I'm going to take you to my friends who will get you out of here."

"Are we really going home?" she asked, pulling on my arm so that I would look at her. Her face was terrified.

"But won't he find us?" the boy asked.

"We won't let that man hurt you anymore," I replied. They followed behind me as I wove us through the crowded room and towards the slit of light at the far end.

"Be careful of the broken glass," I said when we reached the window, noticing neither of them had shoes on.

"Are we jumping from the window?" the boy asked uneasily.

"It's not that high. I'm going to help you down, and my friends at the bottom will catch you."

"But I'm afraid of heights. I get real sick when I get up high," he said.

"What's your name?" I asked, crouching down so my eyes were level with his. Even though he must have been around thirteen, he appeared small, like a child.

"Damien," he said into his chest.

"Okay, Damien. I need you to count to fourteen for me. Close your eyes and say each number in your head. By the time you get to fourteen, you will be brave enough to do it."

I went to the window, counting in my head as well. When I stuck my head out, I saw they were all down there.

"Keely, thank God! What the hell happened?" Max shouted up to me.

"I'll tell you later. I have two kids coming down to you."

"Did you find Dani? Is she with you?" Hillary yelled.

"I have to go back and get her, but she's here. She's alive," I said, my voice cracking when I reached the end. I turned back to the two kids. "Who wants to go first?"

Neither of them said anything, both appearing like they were about to throw up.

"Okay, Damien, I'm sending you first." I held out my hand, and he surprisingly placed his in mine. Carefully, I helped him through the window and held his hands tightly as his legs dangled from the opening. The others caught him at the bottom, Tommy taking the biggest hit by the sound of it.

When I turned back to the girl, she stood close to me, staring up at me with her chestnut-colored eyes.

"Are you an angel?" she asked softly.

"No, I'm just a girl who wanted her sister back."

"Dani's your sister?"

"Yeah, we're twin sisters actually."

"She does kind of look like you. It's a good thing you came because it's her year."

"What do you mean?" I asked.

"Her and Mika. Dani said this is the year he will take them to the red room." My body went cold when she said it, the image of the crimson door burning in my eyes.

"Well, I'm not going to let that happen. You're going to stay with my friends. They're going to take you away from here." I helped her through the window and held on to her wrists as I lowered her down the stone wall. They caught her as she fell the rest of the way and then looked up at me, as if expecting me to follow.

"I have to go back for Dani. I'll be back soon," I shouted down to them.

"Keely, why didn't she come with you?" Max yelled back as he anxiously looked up at me.

"She had to help someone. I will be right back with the two of them." Before anyone could reply, I slipped back into the stale fortress and made my way back to the door. My walkie erupted with their broken responses, and I turned the volume knob back to zero. I already knew, just from the growing pit in my stomach, that I shouldn't have let her convince me to leave again.

I moved quickly through the house. When I reached the opening in the floor, the light no longer came from the hole in the ground. I couldn't remember whether or not I had flipped the switch. I tried to bury the uncomfortable tingle that crept up the back of my neck. When I snapped the lights on again, the tight and narrow pathway was still empty.

As I rushed down into the depths below, the little girl's voice played repeatedly in my head. The volume grew as it rang through my mind, and I automatically brought my hands to my ears to will it to stop.

This is the year he will take them to the red room.

When I reached the bottom, I fumbled for the red card, unable to remember where I had placed it. I patted at my clothes, finding it buried in my back pocket. When I slid it into the reader once, and then twice, the green light didn't appear. My eyes wandered to the hooks along the wall. All were empty. My hands began to shake as I reached for the handle. The door slightly gave way against my grasp. It wasn't until then that my gaze moved to the widening crack in the door. An eye stared back at me—its black pupil slowly widening. At that moment, I saw the long, dark stick snake through the door, biting me deep in my side. It was only then that the voice in my head went completely silent.

The ground was hard and cold. It felt like cement beneath my cheek. My eyes flickered open, unable to register where I was. Everything in my mind felt foggy. My hands were positioned behind my back, something binding them at my wrists. I tried moving my legs, but they were stuck together in the same way. As I squirmed, I felt the burn of rope grazing over my skin, stirring up the memories I had locked away.

I tried opening my mouth to scream, but something covered my lips, keeping in the sound. It was then that I saw the boots at my head. Hands abruptly clamped around my shoulders and pulled me into a sitting position. My clothes were wet, soaked completely through with a dark red liquid. I looked down at my ankles bound in front of me. My eyes slowly drifted to the set of bare feet several yards to my right, dirty toenails peeking out from beneath shiny fabric. It was a pink dress—the kind that little girls wore to weddings. I turned to look at her and found myself staring at a painted face beneath big, blonde curls. She reminded me of those sad faced dolls that Bumpy had told me about so long ago. I watched her tears make trails through her bright makeup.

It wasn't until then that I saw her lips saying my name. It was Dani. She was tied up like I was but without tape covering her made-up mouth.

"I'm so sorry. I should have gone with you," she said, causing more tears to pour from her eyes. I couldn't say anything back, but she knew I was scared. "Everything's going to be okay."

As I looked around me, I knew that she was lying. We were in some kind of bunker. There was a big, boarded-up window in front of me, and the walls were covered with crimson liquid. Carcasses of dead animals littered the floor, and I knew from their stench that they were real. Various kinds of farm equipment hung against the far wall, and my mind couldn't even imagine the terrible things they were used for.

To my left, there was a bulkhead door. A long bar was shoved between its two handles. The hatch was massive—the splattered fluid covered it as well.

Even though he stood out of view, I knew he was there. I heard him shuffling, just out of the range of my peripheral vision.

When he stepped further into the room, I saw he wore all black, just as I had remembered. There was something different—more sinister—about him in that room compared to the lecture hall. I stared hard at the face I could never picture before. It somehow looked exactly how I had imagined it. There was no kindness there, especially when he looked at me. The only time his eyes softened was when he looked at Dani.

"Welcome," he said as he stared through me. "It is nice of you to join us. I've never had the pleasure of having a real spectator before. It looks like I won't need *her* this time." He pointed to the space beside me, and I turned my head in the direction of his finger. To my left, there was a blow-up doll, bound and tied in the same fashion as I. A blonde wig sat atop its head, which had partially fallen off its slouched figure. Duct tape covered the mouth, pulling its air-filled face inwards at the cheeks. The same red liquid that covered my clothes was scattered across its plastic skin.

"We're a few weeks early, my little Pandora, but now will just have to do," he said as he turned his focus to Dani, forgetting me in the corner. He gazed intensely down at her. "We can get started as soon as we fix you up." He walked towards her, a kit in his hand. Although he held it like a palette of paints, I soon realized it was makeup. He picked up a brush and squatted in front of her, dipping it into one of the red squares before reapplying the circles to her cheeks. Little by little, he filled in the areas that her tears had washed away. He did it in a way that didn't seem like a kidnapper of kids, taking his time and gently attending to each feature. Dani stayed perfectly still with each stroke, doing exactly as he instructed.

I told myself that she was just playing a part. The Dani I knew didn't do anything without having a plan, and I assured myself that she knew what she was doing. However, a small part of me worried that I was wrong.

After he finished, he stood up and disappeared through the door at our right. He moved in a controlled fashion, as if even his steps were part of the performance. The door was painted red. It was only then that I knew for sure where he had taken us.

I muffled muted sounds against my tape to get her attention, but she remained facing forward. She looked at me from the corner of her eye but didn't say a word. Her expression was hidden behind the layers of makeup.

It wasn't long before he returned, but that time he wasn't alone. Beside him trudged a tall boy. The boy had his head lowered, and he stared with crazed eyes that darted back and forth between the two of us. His hands weren't bound but instead set in fists at his side. Blonde hair spilled wildly over his face, all except for a small patch at the front that curled off to the side. It wasn't until he turned to fully face me, the shadows outlining his figure, that I recognized him as the boy from the dark cage—Dani's friend named Mika.

"Look at what you've done," the man shot at Mika as his cold eyes briefly glanced at me. He swiftly grabbed the back of Mika's neck and forced his head in Dani's direction. "*She* knows what you did." Mika's expression was almost painful, as if he took the man's words to be true.

"She was supposed to stay away. I-I told her to stay away."

"But she didn't stay away. She followed you here. She knows what you are," he said, looking at the carcasses that surrounded us.

"Maybe I could tell her that I didn't mean it. What if I just tell her that I didn't mean it?" His voice had become small and desperate, and his features appeared childlike. It was then that I recognized him from the newspaper—the little boy with the baseball bat, trying to pose like a future star. His voice broke as he started to cry, which caused the man to slap him firmly across the face.

"You did mean it! Monsters don't do anything by accident," the man in black bellowed.

"Then what do I do now?" he whimpered.

"You already know. You tied her up so she couldn't get away. You've already made your decision, haven't you?" Confusion filled Mika's face as he tried to figure out what the man meant. He looked down at his balled fists, as if they would tell him what to do.

It wasn't until Mika opened his hands that the man gave him the handgun. He took it awkwardly in his hands, staring down at its inky surface. I looked over at Dani. Her eyes were focused on Mika. She remained completely still, except for the slight trembling of her lower lip.

"Monsters can't change. The evil lives inside of them. It is alive inside of you right now," the man shouted violently. Mika continued to look down at the gun, turning it over in his hands.

"Monsters can't change. The evil lives inside of them," he repeated back. Mika appeared in a trance, only sinking deeper under the man's spell as the words replayed over and over. When Mika finally returned his eyes to Dani, I knew that the man had won. A muscle in Mika's jaw steadily pulsated. His lifeless eyes stared through her, as if they only carried death inside of them.

The seconds slowed to minutes, and Mika steadily raised the gun and pointed it at Dani.

"Mika, you don't want to do this. You aren't a monster. You are good. *There is only good inside of you.*" Dani's words came out as a whisper, but they somehow echoed through the room. She said it with the ferocity of someone who knew it to be true. I wanted to believe her, that deep down, he was good. "Fight it. Don't give in to him," Dani pleaded.

"Monsters can't change. The evil lives inside of them," Mika said blankly, the slight quivering of his gun the only change from Dani's words.

"Mika, don't you remember what you told me—about how you dropped your shoulder so it looked like you were a slow swinger? You told me that you did it to trick the pitchers, so that when they gave you a fastball, you would be ready for it." There was a brief flicker of recollection that crossed his face, and Dani began to talk faster. "You told me that I would be swinging and that I needed to be ready. You told me that you were going to be my fastball."

"She is a liar. She is only trying to trick you into letting her go," Dias had moved to the far end of the room, like a coach at the sideline.

"Mika, listen to me. What if we were wrong? What if you're the one who was supposed to swing all along? It's the last pitch, and he's just given you your fastball," she said, looking down the barrel of the gun. "Swing, Mika. Swing it at him."

There was a moment when I thought he might just do it, that Dani had broken through to him. But then, as if each word was a bullet sent straight through my chest, he said, "Monsters can't change. The evil lives inside of them."

The gun went off. For the second time in my life, I wished it had been me.

Chapter Fourteen
September 12, 2006

I could feel the bullet burrow deep inside of me. It was sharp and piercing, a splinter that broke apart the zipper that had been holding me together for so long. I looked over at my sister, who was screaming against the tape that covered her mouth. Her face crumpled in the same way it had six years before, something I had prayed I would never see again.

It was the end. My end.

Except, the last thing I expected to hear when that time came was clapping. It was slow and drawn out applause without much enthusiasm. It wasn't until he stood in front of me that I realized it was coming from Dias.

"Bravo. Bravo," he said, a smug look plastered across his face. "I can't say that I didn't see it coming, but that was quite a performance." He walked over to Mika and ripped the gun out of his hand, which was still outstretched in front of him. Mika looked dazed, as if he didn't quite believe he was the one who pulled the trigger.

Although my body felt the bullet lodged inside, I couldn't find the hole when I looked down at my chest. There wasn't any red bleeding through my pink dress.

"I thought that finding the right ingredients would be difficult," Dias went on. "I figured I would have to adapt, try new things. But I didn't. It turned out that people are very predictable. In the end, it always comes out the same." He slowly emptied the gun, dumping the old bullets onto the cement floor and exchanging them with new ones. The new bullets were pointy, while the ones that rolled across the floor had green, flat tops.

"It doesn't matter where you come from or who your parents are. It doesn't even matter if you're a good person or not. Everyone is breakable one way or another." He returned the ammo clip to the gun, its deafening slam making me flinch. Mika stood rooted in his spot, tears spilling down his face. Dias walked over to him, dragging the gun's barrel up Mika's chest and into the base of his neck.

"You envied her, so much that it drove you to despise her. You with your long hair and dark music, your sick rituals in your disgusting shack. *You make me sick*," he said, his face inches away from Mika's. "She cared about you. She wanted to believe you were better than that, so she followed you that day. She found you and your little girlfriend." Dias pointed his long finger into Keely's corner before continuing to slowly circle around Mika. "She saw all of the things that you had done to her. Tell me, which did you do first? Did you slit Catherine's throat or did you shoot her in the head and then do it? I think you wanted to see her suffer. You wanted to watch her squirm before you finally pulled the trigger. Didn't you, Curt?"

Catherine. I recognized that name. I had seen it somewhere, a place that I had looked several times.

The children's book—the one from Poppy.

Mika opened his mouth to respond, but no words came out. He wanted to give Dias the answers he wanted, but they would never come. He didn't have the answers, because it wasn't his story to tell. It was somebody else's. I thought the whole thing was about us—me and Mika; Brook and Kai; Clara and Chet. But I was wrong. It wasn't our story at all.

"I want you to take a good look at her," he said, grasping Mika's chin and pointing it towards mine. "Take a look at her beautiful face, at how her hair falls perfectly over her shoulders and her eyes sparkle in the light. You were about to take that all away. You would have shot it clean off if I had let you."

"I'm so sorry," he cried, more to me than to Dias.

"Oh, you're sorry, are you? Is that what you felt when you looked down at her body and saw what you did? Were you sorry when you raised that gun...and blew off her pretty, little face?" Dias raised the gun at me while looking at Mika as he talked. "I want you to tell me, you son of a bitch! What. Did. You. Feel. When. You. Ruined. The. Face. Of. My. Beautiful. Ren?"

The gun was back on Mika, digging into his skull. But I could no longer focus on where the gun was aimed or the fake bullets that littered the floor. All I could think about was that name.

Ren.

My beautiful Ren. My beautiful Ren. My beautiful Ren.

Catherine.

My beautiful Catherine. Catherine was the one who wrote the letter. She was the one who dragged her to the shed. *Her,* I thought, my mind trying to keep up. I looked over at Keely, tied up nearby. Dias's words rang in my head. *She found you and your little girlfriend, seeing all the things that you had done to her. Girlfriend. His girlfriend. Curt's girlfriend.*

Curt.

C. The letter was written to Curt, the one Dias thought was responsible for all of it. But he had it all wrong. It had been buried with us the entire time, and I was the only one who knew the truth. The girl from the picture, that pretty, pretty princess he made me be, was nothing like he thought she was.

But I was her and she was me. I couldn't tell him the truth, because being his beautiful Ren was my only way out.

"Poppy?" I heard myself say. Dias turned around, the gun lowering limply to his side.

"What did you just say?" he said, barely above a whisper.

"Poppy, please don't hurt me anymore," I said, allowing the tears to fall from my eyes. He looked at me as if he could see through me, seeing someone else on the other side. "Please don't hurt me, Poppy."

"I would never hurt you," he whispered, his eyes glazed over. His mouth hung slightly open, but I wasn't sure any air was going in or coming out.

"But you are hurting me. You are the one who has the gun." He looked down at his hands, seeing the gun, as if it hadn't been there that entire time. His face looked confused. "You brought me into this shed, tied me up, and pointed a gun at me. Why would you do that, Poppy? Why would you do that to your Ren?"

"But I...I didn't do this. Curt did this. He did this to you." He didn't have to look at Mika for me to know what he meant. Mika stood like a statue behind him, hardened in place.

"No, it was you who did this. Curt was never there," I said, trying to move his attention away from Mika.

"No. *I* wasn't there. *He* was. He was there in the woods. He dragged you to the shed and killed you just like he did to her," he said, pointing at Keely. His words came quicker, and he began to pace in front of me.

"You brought me here. You brought me to this shed, and you plan on killing me," I said, repeating the words I needed him to hear.

"He's the one! He's the one that took everything. I was the one who always protected you!" My eyes never left the gun, which he waved wildly in the air and kept returning to Mika's chest.

"Just like with all of the children's stories—all those goddesses and what they had to watch out for."

"So you do see. It was all supposed to keep you safe."

"But it didn't keep me safe, Poppy? Because I am here, even though you warned me to stay away."

"Yes, Catherine. If only you listened to me."

"What if you can still protect me? What if you still had the chance?"

"I would give anything for that chance," he said, dropping to the ground and kneeling in front of me.

"You can stop yourself from hurting me," I said, looking down at the gun. He followed my eyes that led to his hands. "You can end this. You can save me. You can be my hero, Poppy." His face collapsed as he began to cry, dropping his mouth to my bare feet. I felt his lips against them, his wet saliva slipping between the slits of my toes. A single word escaped his mouth, but I couldn't understand it through his cries.

It wasn't until he pulled his lanky body up and towered above me that I realized what he had said.

Goodbye.

He turned, lifted the gun, pointed it straight at Mika, and pulled the trigger. I had barely registered it when I heard a second click, watching as the back of Dias's head was there one moment, and then it was gone. It was blown open, leaving behind a gaping hole of black.

A scream erupted from my chest as I threw myself to the ground, worming my way through Dias's blood to get to Mika. My chin dug into the floor, the warm liquid quickly covering my painted face. The blonde wig fell off my head, its perfect curls sucked into the growing pool of red. I yanked my hands hard against the binds that held them together. My skin tore as I pulled them through the knotted ropes. When they were finally freed, I had nearly reached Mika's body. He was completely still, blood streaming from beneath him.

"Oh God. Oh God. What have I done? What did I do?" I screamed over and over. I pulled at the ropes holding my feet in place, freeing myself from the last binds Dias would ever have on me. My hands shook as I put them on Mika's bleeding chest, trying to find where all of it was coming from. Even through the black of his clothes, I could see the red seeping through it, directly over his heart. My mouth hung open as I cried overtop him, bunching his bloody shirt in my hands. I couldn't bring myself to look at his unveiled eyes, knowing that no one would be staring back.

I then felt hands on me, pulling me away. I heard Keely in my ear, but none of her words registered. She tried freeing Mika from my hands, but I kept telling her no. I kept telling her that I wanted to stay.

She wrapped her arms around me, but that time I let her take me away. I felt her lift me into the air, folding me into her chest. Her body felt strong underneath me, mine weak and small. I buried my face into her shirt and breathed in her familiar scent. After all that time, all those years that my memories had slowly slipped away from me, I had never forgotten the smell of my sister's skin. It was faint but lingering, like the smell that hung on flower petals. I knew because it was the exact opposite of mine.

I continued to sob as she carried me to the far end of the room, away from the red-colored door. She went to the hatch with the barred handles, pulling it free and pushing up on it with her back. Dirt fell down along the cracks as she shoved open the door, bursting through uprooted blossoms. Keely flung the sheet of metal to the side, crushing a patch of tall flowers into the ground. The night air struck my body, the chill seeping deep into my bones.

It was the most beautiful cold I had ever felt.

I heard voices all around me, and I didn't struggle as I was handed over to new arms. He held me close to him, tucking my head underneath his chin. Keely grabbed ahold of my foot, her clammy hands touching the very place Dias had left his saliva behind. Her touch was warm, heating my frozen skin. We were together again, but this time I wasn't going to leave her.

As we ran away from that place—the Underworld that held all the dead bodies—I couldn't help but think.

Hope had found her way out.

People heard versions of the story, taken from the pieces left behind. The newspapers and TV stations spoke of the cages, the food tubes, the white walls and dirt floors, the playroom of left-behind toys, and the six dead kids buried in Satan's Garden. The reports focused on his methods, the notebooks filled with details about his victims from years before he took them and the three different pairs of boots that matched the sizes in the police reports. But Keely and I were the only ones who truly knew what happened in that room twenty feet under. No one else knew the whole story of the Ogden Kidnappings.

His name was Carl Ogden. He was a psychologist, a man who thought he had all the answers. However, there was one that he would never have—the answer to the question he thought he never needed to ask— *why?*

I looked for it online—in the newspaper archive that Keely had shown me. It wasn't hard to find the article from 1987, the one that spoke of "The Waring School Tragedy." The story was passed off as the result of a deranged boy, Curt Wix, who gruesomely murdered two girls in a shed tucked away in the woods behind his home. Reports said that he then turned the gun on himself after brutally stabbing his girlfriend and executing his stepsister. Curt was labeled a "loner" and "emotionally unattached," most blaming it on his mother's death when he was thirteen. She had married Carl Ogden three years before her passing, bringing two ten-year-olds together under the same roof. Catherine Ogden was Carl's daughter from his previous marriage, which had also tragically ended in death—a drug overdose. Reporters spoke of Catherine and Curt's relationship, sources calling it "incredibly close" but "at times volatile." The media painted it as a "sibling rivalry" case, claiming that it had to do with a "confused and jealous boy who watched violent movies and listened to angry music." Catherine was the main focus in many of the reports, described as a girl adored by all with a bright future. Newspapers used the same photo I had seen for those past three years, her hair appearing a glowing blonde despite the black and white print.

They called it an open-and-shut case. The one thing that no one cared to know was what happened to Carl Ogden after their deaths. His part was lost in all the devastation.

I tracked the few news stories of him from the years immediately following the tragedy, particularly the time leading up to when he started his "work." The old articles only talked of the great things he had done, the awards and accolades for his brilliant research on fratricide and sibling rivalry. But it was only a small snapshot of the story. More recent news reports revealed his many research proposals that had been turned down for approval due to being "inhumane" and "unethical." His twisted theories were what started it all.

People saw him as a man who took his work too far. He came to be known as the "Grim Reaper," a man who left death in his wake. But they didn't see the other parts. I may not have known exactly what drove him to kidnap kids or make them relive the same dreadful past. Maybe it was guilt or grief or an obsession to prove it wasn't his fault. But I knew the answer he would never have. None of us would know exactly what happened in that shed on October 1, 1987. But I knew that Curt wasn't entirely evil, in the same way that Catherine wasn't solely good. They each stood somewhere in-between.

I didn't tell anyone Catherine's secret. It was a burden that only I could carry. At times, I worried about it becoming too much—that I wouldn't be able to keep it locked inside and return to the life I started with. But then I would think of Keely. She was different—bolder and less timid; yet she was still the same. Despite everything, she was the one part that I didn't have to try to make fit again.

It took us a while before we shared the things that had happened over those six years that had separated us. She talked of the maps and her hunt for me. She told me about the terrorist attacks and how they had brought her and Max together. I tried not to cry when she read me my eulogy and showed me the perfect flowers surrounding my grave. There were times when it hurt to listen, like when she told me about the Underground and what Vander had done to her. But then I would think about all the good that she had found, despite it all. Her friend, Hillary, and the four boys. They were there when I couldn't be, and for that, I would always owe them.

When I told her what it was like for me, down there in the basement of boxes, I made sure to talk about the good things. I told her about Kai and his theory on Twenty Questions. I spoke of Mika and his tendency to talk in baseball riddles and how he would have been the greatest pitcher to ever live. I made sure she knew what he was really like, not the version that she saw that horrible night. And then I talked about Brook. I told Keely about her beautiful hands and how she had kept me alive down there in the dark.

Keely didn't tell me right away about how Brook had come to her. Where exactly that happened, I didn't know. What I did know was that in spite of all of the badness—all the evil cast out into the world—there was still more of the good. I learned there was something larger than all of us. The things that had separated us had also brought Keely back to me.

That was the part Keely refused to agree with. She felt responsible because she had run away all those years ago. But I told her that she just wasn't looking close enough.

"But Keely, if you never left me, if you came with me and didn't run away, I wouldn't have made it out of there. I'm here because you stayed. You saved my life," I said as we wrapped ourselves together under the covers one night. We lay on our sides with our foreheads touching. Even in the dark, I could see the expressions flutter across her face. She fell silent, thinking to herself in her Keely sort of way.

I then felt her hand on mine, holding out two fingers to me instead of her typical one. And then she said, ever so softly, "I think we saved each other."

Epilogue

My cab pulled up outside the long string of apartments. All of them were painted different colors, yet they still looked like one never-ending building. I stood on the sidewalk long after my cab had pulled away, staring at the brown one with the bright red door. I double-checked the number on the building a dozen times, but it always ended up being the same "1414" written on the envelope. The letter was dirty and frayed around the corners but had remained unopened. It was the third time I had come to stand in front of the red door, telling myself each time that nothing bad waited for me behind it.

I questioned how he could've still lived there, but I guessed some people had a harder time leaving things behind than others. He lived in apartment 6A, the one that had a tiny balcony off the window that faced the street. I looked up and saw he had a couple of potted plants sitting on the grated ledge, their stems drooping over the railing to look down at the people who strolled by.

Instead of turning around and walking away as I had before, I found myself climbing the stairs and heading towards the line of buttons. I ran my finger down the list, stopping on his name and pushing the buzzer next to it. There was a quick beeping sound, and then all I heard was quiet. I waited, but nothing happened. After some time had passed, I reached for the button a second time, almost hoping that I could back out once again.

"Hello?" The voice came as a loud crack over the speaker, making me jump back from the door. I froze, unsure whether to walk away or stay. "Anyone there?" he asked again. I walked slowly back to the keypad and pushed the black button beside the speaker.

"Hi, Mr. Parker? I am a friend…I knew your daughter. I was wondering if I could come up and speak with you." There was a long silence afterwards, and for a second, I thought he was no longer there. My hands began to sweat as I waited, the writing on the front of the envelope slightly smearing beneath the dampness. Right when I started to think he wasn't going to respond, a buzzing sound went off, and the red door cracked just enough to let my fingers slip through and pull it open.

I grabbed on to the cool wood and walked in, meeting a wall of hot air. It was hotter than usual for the beginning of September—an uncommon heat wave, as they called it—and I guessed that people likely didn't want to bring their AC units back out.

I took the stairs, even though I had already begun to sweat from the heat. I wasn't quite ready to face him, but I hoped I would be by the time I reached the sixth floor. The sweltering warmth seemed to only get worse as I kept going up. By the time I reached the top of the building, the moisture had spread through the back of my shirt.

His apartment door was closed when I reached it, but I somehow knew he was standing on the other side, looking at me through the peephole. I stood directly in front of the door, allowing him to get a full look before deciding whether to open it or not. The necklace started to feel hot against my chest, almost like he knew I was wearing it, even though it hid underneath my shirt.

The man who opened the door was not what I had expected. He was short, only a little taller than me. I'd imagined him having all black hair, but instead, it was a Santa Claus white. Half of it was missing, leaving behind a horseshoe outline on the top of his head. His face looked young, despite the toll taken on his hair. The man didn't have the same blue eyes or the rosy red lips, but he had freckles just like she did. They were dispersed across his face, the same painter leaving behind that familiar splatter.

"Hi, Mr. Parker. My name is Dani." I didn't quite know what else to say.

"I know. I saw you on the TV." I could tell he was reluctant to speak with me. I didn't think it was because he blamed me in some way. No, he had a hard time looking me in the eye without tearing up because I reminded him of everything that he didn't have anymore. Me standing there told him that she really wasn't coming back.

"I meant to come see you sooner, but…"

"It's okay. I understand. You don't have to explain yourself."

"I have something that Brook wanted me to give you," I blurted out, unable to hold the words in any longer. His eyes immediately locked on the envelope in my hand. He covered his mouth with his palm, suppressing the cries that began to overflow past his fingers. I held out the letter to him, but he didn't take it right away, letting it hang in the space between us. He looked at it the way people did to urns, wondering how it could be all that remained of his loved one.

He eventually reached out to take it, cradling the envelope inside his hands. His fingers traced and retraced the smudged "Dad" on the front, not quite able to recreate her exact loopy letters. I waited patiently for when he broke open the letter that I had kept sealed and protected for the past four years. His hands shook as he held the pages, her words filling the front and back of the seven sheets of paper.

I tried to imagine what she wrote—how she could fit in everything she wanted to say. She probably left out all of the bad parts and told him that the happy years with him were enough to make her life worth it. It probably talked about *Jeopardy!* and how she knew he would win it some day. I bet it spoke of what life would be like if none of it had changed, what they would have been doing right then. I imagined it talked about cherry trees and how Ricky Jenks was the best singer of all time, no matter what anyone said. And then it probably talked about her mother, how they would be together again. Brook would somehow make it seem okay, but I could tell, just by looking at him read the letter, things like that would never be alright.

"Your daughter is the reason I am standing here. She kept me safe, and if it wasn't for her..." I said, my voice drifting away. He looked up from the pages and listened to me with an intensity that wasn't there before. "She made me promise that I would give it to you. I'm sorry I held on to it for so long. I think the reason I didn't come sooner was because this was the only thing I had left. My promise to her kept me alive, and I guess I was just afraid of not knowing what to do when I didn't have that anymore."

He simply nodded his head, telling me he understood.

"I also want you to know that Brook never stopped being Brook. The man who took us, he wanted to make us into something—someone different. But she never gave in. She was very brave, and I want you to know that she was that way until the end."

"Thank you," he managed to say. His voice was filled with pain, but his face told me that his heart held more than that. We both stood there together in the hallway, our sweat and tears mixed into one. After the words were all used up and spent, I felt the physical weight of my promise lift off of me. I already missed its heaviness.

"Oh, I almost forgot," I said, right before I turned back towards the stairs. "I think this belongs to you now." I pulled the necklace from my neck, but before I could get it over my head, he stopped me.

"She would want you to have it. I already have her with me," he said as he gently guided my hands to return the necklace to its place over my heart. He then reached up to pull out a worn chain from under his shirt, revealing the same cherry tree as Brook's. I knew where to look for the writing and noticed his said something different. "We'll Carry On" was carved into three of the branches. *There will come a day when things get lost and taken away. But we'll stand together, and we'll carry on.*

It should have made me feel odd having matching necklaces with a man I barely knew, but somehow, it made me feel more connected to the world than ever before.

I left the building that day feeling the weight of the past seven years on me. The memories were etched into my being the same way those words were carved into the cherry branches. I remembered those who had been lost, broken, and taken away, knowing they each would live on in some way through me. I would continue to carry them the rest of the way.

After all, one plus one will always equal something larger. Together, we create something greater than we ever can alone.

AUTHOR'S NOTE

Stories are nothing without the people who read them. As a way of giving back to those who have welcomed Dani and Keely into their lives, I've put together a collection of "special features" for you to enjoy. I believe that a story shouldn't end here, in the back recesses of a book or in its final sentences. It should be continued and carried on.

You will find your additional content on my website, www.kitlyman.com. This section can be found underneath the "Satan's Garden" tab, and it is intended specifically for readers. The password to access these pages is:

WeEqualMore

For those who would be kind enough to take the time to review *Satan's Garden* on either Amazon or Goodreads, I will also give you access to an exclusive extended feature of this book as a special thank you. After you have reviewed the book, send an email to kit@kitlyman.com with the subject line, "Book Review." I will be going off the honor system, so you do not need to submit your review to me personally. I will provide the feature, regardless of the content of your review.

It is my hope that *Satan's Garden* can spark a greater conversation. If Dani and Keely's story means something to you, I encourage you to share it with your friends and family. Thank you once again for being my reader, and I hope this is only the start to the stories we can share together.

BOOK CLUB QUESTIONS[1]

1. What are the notable parallels between Keely and Dani's chapters throughout the book?

2. What is the significance of the girls' handshake, and how did it change over the course of the story? *

3. Various religious references exist throughout the novel. What are some of the ways they are incorporated into the narrative?

4. What do you think are Keely and Dani's respective religious beliefs?

5. Debbie tried to explain to Keely what "faith" is. How would you define it?

6. Discuss the similarities and differences between the girls and their respective relationships with the other characters.

7. What do you think happened in the shed on October 1, 1987?

8. In your opinion, what were Carl Ogden's main motives for kidnapping children? *

9. What are the multiple meanings and perspectives of the prologue? What are the signs that give away the prologue's narrator? *

10. In chapter six, Dani buries an unwritten letter to Keely. If she had written it, what do you think it would have said?

11. What are the multiple meanings of the title, "Satan's Garden?" *

12. What is Carl Ogden's third truth?

---

[1] All questions marked with an asterisk will be included in the special features' section of her website, containing the author's personal thoughts.

13. In what ways does Carl Ogden's lecture in chapter thirteen overlap with the themes throughout the book? *

14. What are the similarities between the first and thirteenth chapters?

15. Why do you think Vander killed the fox? How is it similar to what he did to Keely? How is it similar to Dias?

16. How would life be different if Dani was never kidnapped? *

17. What are some recurring images/colors throughout the story? *

18. Throughout the book, there are juxtaposed references of "darkness" and "lightness," "warmth" and "coldness." How are these images used thematically in *Satan's Garden*?

19. In general, do you believe that people are "all good"/"all bad" or somewhere in-between?

20. Describe the multiple levels of Dani's relationship with her kidnapper.

21. What is the intention/meaning/purpose behind each of the rooms down in Dias's Underworld?

22. Discuss the connections between Keely's "Underground" and Dani's "Underworld."

23. What is the meaning behind the Greek stories Dias tells the children? What does it say about his feelings towards them?

24. Why did Carl Ogden call himself Dias, and how does that relate to the story? *

25. Max carries around stories with him from the support group members. What are the stories that have stuck with you over the years?

26. There are many things that the mother taught the girls. What are some lessons that your parents taught you as a young child?

27. What does Bumpy's story about Gus teach us about grief? How does it differ from "Keely's Stages of Grief?"

28. The story alluded to Pandora having multiple intentions behind opening her box. What do you think was her real reason?

29. Discuss your thoughts about the scene between Brook and Keely at the beginning of chapter thirteen. *

30. In what ways are Dani and Keely together and apart throughout the story?

31. What was Dias's purpose of first using blanks in the gun? *

32. What is the symbolism of the stuffed animals used in the book?

33. What was Mika in the end: the catcher, the pitcher, or the batter?

34. Talk about Ricky's song and its greater meaning for the book.

35. What is your story behind the seven circular burns on Dias's hand?

36. What is the symbolism of Dani and Keely's glow-in-the-dark stars? *

37. Ms. Tabitha and Debbie both assume roles associating to therapy. How are they different?

38. In what way do you think support groups hurt and/or help people coping with grief?

39. What is the meaning behind Debbie's silk flowers?

40. In the book, the mother talked about people only getting as much power as others give them. How is this message carried throughout the book? Are there times when good can come from evil? *

41. Discuss how Dias treats the kids. How did he strip them of their

identities? How does this relate to kidnappings in general?

42. What are the roles of the various letters found in the story? *

43. What role did furniture play in the story? *

44. Going through the book, what analogies stuck with you?

45. Who is your favorite side character and why?

ACKNOWLEDGEMENTS

I believe that no piece of work is solely one person's. It is a body created by many, each individual giving a part to make it become a living, breathing thing. *Satan's Garden*, my very first novel, exists because of all the people who have loved, moved, changed, and supported me along the way. You all are my sculptors, and I wouldn't trade your sets of hands for anything.

Gail and Nathan Lyman: the two people who made me believe I could set the world on fire, even if it was in the smallest of ways. You turned an abomination of a child into an actively dreaming woman, who stands taller than she ever thought she could and no longer wears sweatpants underneath her dresses. You never gave up on me or ever doubted the person I could become. For that, I owe you everything. Dad, you not only gave me the "toolbox," but you also taught me how to use it the right way. Whether it be driving me across the country (three times) or always lending an ear to my next crazy idea, you have played a massive part in bringing this book to life. Even though you weep more than men are "supposed to" and almost always get the last glass of red wine, to me, you are absolutely perfect. Mom, you have dedicated your life to your girls, and I want you to know that it all mattered. All of the museum trips I begrudged, the stories you told us as kids, the teachings of obscure marine animals, the adventures at parks, the very long vacations spent inside a pop-up camper, and the constant reminders of never to give up, they got me to this point.

Laura and Tony Sidari: my partners in crime, my "production company," my roundtable, my inspiration. There isn't exactly one place I could begin and one place I could end when I think of how to thank you. Not only have you two allowed me the opportunity to really give myself to this book, but also, you both have been such an integral part in making *Satan's*

Garden what it is. Laura, you are the true Midas of this world. It has been said that no writer can exist without an editor, and you have proved that to be true. I couldn't have asked for a better person to share this book with, who understood Keely and Dani the way I had hoped and who made this story into what it was supposed to be. You were the girl who taught me how to kick a soccer ball the right way and the narrator to all of our child-hood fantasies. It only made sense that a story about sisters would become as beautiful as it did with you being such a huge part in telling it. Tony, you are everything I imagined a brother would be. Protective, caring, funny, ball-buster, and most of all, loving. I will never forget all the terrible mov-ies we have watched together or all the days we spent shoved in a closet recording, "One moment she was there, and the next...*she was gone.*" I am always reminded of everything you have done. It is all around me. It lives in the logo that sits at the top of my website and in the music narrating Keely and Dani's trailers. You care about them because you care about me, and the beauty that we have created together is because of that love. I will never forget that.

Liz Peterson: a sister who never has anything but an encouraging word to speak and an easy smile to give. You have Grandma Lucy's heart, and I feel like a part of her will forever live on inside you. Thank you for always being there for me.

Robert Boehm: my grandfather, the greatest storyteller who ever lived. Even though you are no longer here to read this, I need it to be known that you exist at the heart of me. I wish you could be alive to see that I followed your advice. I gave my stories a place to live, and I hope you know that you changed my life.

Morgan Eastlack: the Hobbes I searched for far and wide. Your ability to capture an entire story in a picture is a grace that only few are given, and I couldn't have picked a better artist to tell mine. You add so much to my life, Mojo, and I want to thank you for understanding me in a way no one else could.

Jamie Chappius and Jordan Tetro: my fearless beta readers. You two were there since the very beginning and made me believe that this story could move people. Being a writer is more vulnerable than I had ever thought, but you both gave me the confidence in opening myself up like that. I couldn't have asked for anything more.

Megan Kaminska: my truly biggest fan. I have never met anyone so encouraging and supportive as you, and I want to thank you for being such a monster part of my life. Your friendship means everything to me, and it gives me the strength to write stories like this one.

Carolyn Barry and Ken Schiefer: the crucial parts of the KCK. The two of you light up my world. Carol, thank you for being as thick as a thief, and Ken, I will forever be your work spouse.

Anish Malpani: my newest friend but also one of my greatest advocates. Your passion and creativity connects me to you, and I am so thankful to have met you during my greatest adventure yet.

I would also like to thank three people who have helped me find my voice as a writer. Seph McKenna, you taught me the art of storytelling and gave me an appreciation for learning my craft. You set me on a ceaseless search to broaden my study of story, and I cannot express just how much I have learned from working with you. Joel Gotler and Leslie Conliffe, you took a chance on me when I had everything to prove. Your belief in my writing fueled my fire in more ways than you know.

And lastly, to all of the friendships I have made over the years. Thank you for showing me what it is supposed to feel like.

29637631R00192

Made in the USA
Charleston, SC
18 May 2014